Into the GigaVerse

Book 1

M. L. Tilford

Hardcover ISBN 978-1-968876-06-7

Paperback ISBN 978-1-968876-04-3

eBook ISBN 978-1-968876-05-0

Cover Art by Aria Tilford

First edition 2025

For my dad, who sparked my interest in both Sci-Fi and reading

Contents

1

Welcome to StellarGigs

"The universe spins, the war rages, the coffee runs out. But somehow... I'm still standing."

— Commander Axton Starforge,
Steel Hearts: Echoes of Andromeda, S4E13

Good jobs these days are about as real as unicorns, whispered about in hushed tones, rumored to exist somewhere else, but never actually seen. Instead, younger generations were left chasing gigs that promised 'flexibility', a magical word that somehow translated to working three part-time jobs, being on-call 24/7, and still having to decide which bill got ignored each month.

Linda knew the pattern well.

Every job she had had since college ended the same way: underpaid, overworked, under-appreciated. It wasn't her fault nobody could see her potential. A bigger paycheck would fix that—she was sure of it. Maybe then she wouldn't feel like such a screw-up.

Which was how Linda Greyson found herself perched on a painfully ergonomic plastic chair in the Los Angeles office of StellarGigs. A tech startup that promised steady, high-paying gig work with benefits. Not to mention, a signing bonus large enough to wipe out her student loans, or at least leave a polite scratch.

Her bank account was already circling the drain, rent was due the following week and bill collectors were haunting her phone like angry ghosts, leaving passive-aggressive voicemails that always ended with, *"We look forward to your prompt payment"*. On top of it all, her ex-boyfriend had walked out a month ago, whining about her "lack of direction." Easy for him to say, he had a cushy nine-to-five. Now she was stuck with the full rent and a fridge full of condiments. If she could just land steady money, she'd prove him wrong. She'd be fine.

Desperation had a way of making even the most suspicious offers seem reasonable, and StellarGigs' pitch had been just suspicious enough to feel like hope.

Their tagline was plastered on billboards, bus stops, and online ads: *"Your next gig is just a galaxy away"*. Clever marketing, probably dreamed up by some over-caffeinated nerd who thought watching sci-fi counted as a side hustle. But it had worked. Here she was, one of dozens of hopefuls, sitting awkwardly in the waiting room, clutching the last scraps of her optimism.

Linda glanced around. The room was packed with the usual suspects. Fresh college grads sat in mismatched business attire, nervously clutching portfolios as if they contained anything besides recycled cover letters. A couple of exhausted freelancers scrolled aimlessly on their phones, no doubt applying for more gigs in real time. In one corner sat a man with the haunted look of someone who hadn't slept since the Great Recession. He stared at the wall as if he could see the specter of affordable housing on the other side, whispering that he'd never actually own a home.

Linda thought of old friends—doctors, researchers, software developers—people who always looked so smug on social media. Of course they were happy; anyone would be, making that kind of money. It had to be nice, solving life's problems with a paycheck instead of a panic attack.

The air was thick with exhausted hope, the kind that comes from having tried everything else and still ending up there. Gig work might be soul-sucking, but *steady* was a rare commodity these days, and people were willing to sell what remained of their dignity for it.

This wasn't just a job hunt. This was survival.

"Linda Greyson?"

A petite woman emerged from the recruiter's office, clipboard in hand, her crisp white button-down tucked into a pencil skirt so sharp it could have sliced bread (*without* leaving those annoying finger imprints). Her hair was pulled back into a severe bun with the kind of tension typically reserved for suspension bridges. The professional smile plastered across her face had the kind of energy you only see on infomercials, just before the words, *"But wait, there's more!"*

"That's me!" Linda blurted, springing to her feet as her heart did a nervous tap dance against her ribs. She picked up her knock-off designer handbag from the chair next to her and smoothed her blouse with trembling hands. Linda prayed that her outfit still gave off 'competent and employable', despite being hastily ironed on her bed an hour earlier.

"This way, please." The recruiter turned on her heels with military precision, her shoes clicking like a metronome of anxiety.

Linda fell in behind her, and on impulse, snapped off a jaunty four-fingered salute.

"Reporting for duty, ma'am" she said with a half-smirk.

The recruiter stopped. Turned.

Her face was a perfect void. Not offended. Not amused. Just blank, like a wall that she had just tried to impress.

Linda cleared her throat before following, palms suddenly clammy. Humor always helped break the ice, right? People liked personality. The recruiter was probably just too uptight to get it.

Wow, I bet she's fun at parties, Linda thought.

The office was... disappointing. Linda had expected sleek desks, futuristic lighting, maybe even a ping-pong table for that casual tech startup vibe. Instead, it looked like a waiting room ripped straight out of a dentist's office from 1985, complete with faded motivational posters. *"Flexibility is Freedom!"* proclaimed one, over an image of an astronaut doing yoga. *"Not just a job, a purpose in life!"* invited another, featuring a poorly photoshopped planet Saturn holding a briefcase.

If only, Linda thought.

In the corner, a water cooler gurgled ominously, daring someone to try their luck with it.

"Please, have a seat," the recruiter said, gesturing to a chair across from her desk. A relic so overloaded with forms and papers that it looked like it might collapse under the sheer weight of bureaucracy.

Linda sat, gripping her hands tightly in her lap to stop them from shaking. The recruiter slid a thick stack of forms across the desk. The pages looked like they'd been photocopied so many times the text was beginning to blur into hieroglyphs.

"Just your typical stuff: NDAs, liability waivers, arbitration agreements. Nothing out of the ordinary," the recruiter said, with the same breeziness you'd use to offer someone gum.

"Great," Linda said, her voice a little too high-pitched to sound convincing. "And, uh... what exactly does the gig work involve?"

The recruiter gave her a smile so tight it could have been a grimace dressed up as kindness. "It varies," she said cryptically. "That's the nature of gig work."

Yeah, real helpful.

Linda flipped through the forms, her anxiety growing with every page. Legal jargon danced before her eyes like malevolent spirits; phrases such as 'perpetuity', 'non-compete', and 'mandatory binding arbitration'. She skimmed over one section titled 'Terms of Galactic Employment'. More branding nonsense, she was sure.

With a shrug, she signed at the bottom. What was the worst thing that could happen? A bounced paycheck? Been there, done that.

Just as she was about to hand the papers back, the recruiter leaned forward, her voice dropping into a conspiratorial whisper. "Most people don't read the fine print," she said, eyes gleaming. "But you seem smart. So let me give you a little advice."

Linda leaned in, pulse quickening. Maybe this was some kind of inside scoop, something to help her avoid the worst gigs.

The recruiter tapped the top of the stack. "Whatever happens," she said slowly, "make sure you always finish the gig."

Really? That's it?

Linda blinked. "Uh... okay?"

"Wonderful!" The recruiter's voice returned to its unnaturally chipper tone. "Now, let's talk specifics." She shuffled the papers with practiced efficiency. "It shows here on your application that you have no living family."

"None that I'm aware of." Linda said. *Who knows where dad is. He might as well be dead for all I care.*

"No boyfriends... girlfriends?"

Pretty sure that's illegal to ask. "Nope, single and thriving." *God, why did I say thriving?*

"Wonderful," the recruiter said with a smile. "With that out of the way, we believe you'll be a perfect fit here at our StellarGigs family. Our highly competitive starting salary is fifteen hundred a week, which is nonnegotiable until your second quarterly review. But you will receive that payment every week regardless of whether you're actively on assignment."

Holy crap!

Linda's jaw slackened. Fifteen hundred. A week. Her brain, which had been budgeting in negative numbers for months, short-circuited.

"Fifteen hundred a week? Guaranteed?"

"Guaranteed," the recruiter confirmed. "And, when you complete your contract term, you'll receive a bonus depending on the length of your initial commitment."

"What's the catch?" she asked cautiously.

The recruiter's expression shifted to one of sudden seriousness. "Just one: You'll need to relocate long distance. Transportation provided of course. You won't have to worry about jet lag—our methods are very efficient."

Linda shrugged. "Relocate where?" She could handle moving. It wasn't as if anyone in L.A. would miss her. Honestly, it was kind of perfect. She could reinvent herself somewhere new.

Her mind raced with possibilities: New York, Switzerland, maybe Paris. She could almost smell the croissants. Of course she could just as easily end up in Branson, Missouri, but that wouldn't be the end of the world. Probably.

The recruiter flipped a page and gave a vague wave of her hand. "That will depend on the assignment, but don't worry, housing is provided."

"I'm fine with that," she said, practically vibrating with excitement.

"Excellent," the recruiter beamed. "Now, given the resources we're preparing to invest in you, we do ask for a long-term commitment."

Guaranteed pay, free housing, and travel included? Linda nodded vigorously, her brain already tallying imaginary paychecks. Not the standard minimum wage that most of her previous jobs offered, but something that could put her ahead of her debts for once. "No problem at all."

"Great. Now, how long would you be comfortable with? Do remember that the final bonus will increase depending on the length of your contract. We offer a six-month, one-year, or two-year commitment that can be renegotiated at the end of your term?"

"What's the bonus for the two-year contract?" Linda asked.

"That is..." The recruiter checked her notes, "...one-hundred thousand at the end of the term."

Linda could barely process the numbers. More money than she'd ever seen, let alone earned. She didn't hesitate. "Two-year."

The recruiter slid over the final document. "Sign here, please."

Linda scrawled her name with such enthusiasm she nearly tore through the paper, her heart pounding with a cocktail of excitement, relief, and the faint taste of hope disguised as victory.

She told herself this was it—the job that would finally make her feel like she wasn't wasting her life. Not because it promised purpose, exactly, but because it promised enough money to buy the illusion of it. That was close enough, wasn't it?

"Welcome to StellarGigs," the recruiter said, standing and extending her hand, a hint of satisfaction lingering in her gaze. Like a cat who just watched a bird fly into a window.

Linda shook it, barely containing her grin. For the first time in months, things were finally looking up.

The recruiter's smile stretched just a little too wide. "Now, if you'll proceed through that door for processing." She gestured to a panel that hissed open like it had been waiting for the moment all day.

Linda turned to look at it, and for a split second, the light flickered in a vaguely medical way. She hesitated, just for a heartbeat. Then shrugged it off. Money was money.

2

The Chair Will See You Now

"They tested my limits. Then they tested the results. I passed, but I'm not sure what I lost in the process."

— Commander Axton Starforge,
Steel Hearts: Echoes of Andromeda, S3E1

Linda had always believed that the strangest part of a new job was navigating office politics, but as she stepped into the hallway labeled *"Processing"*, she began to suspect that StellarGigs might redefine her entire concept of 'employee onboarding'.

The moment she strode through the door, it came sliding down, integrating seamlessly into the wall. The hallway was clinical, with white walls, floor, and ceiling, as if the architect had forgotten that color existed. She turned around and saw a blinking yellow line projected on the floor. "Guess I go this way." She muttered to herself. Every time she stepped off the line, whether by accident or intentionally, the glowing path flickered angrily.

Eventually, the line led her to *"Processing Room 1A"*. The door slid open with an unsettling hiss, revealing another plain white room that seemed to hum with clinical indifference. At its center sat a metal chair that looked like it had been specifically designed to communicate "we do not care about your comfort". It was bolted to the floor, a little too cold, and suspiciously utilitarian.

"Please, have a seat," chirped a voice from nowhere.

Linda looked around, but the room was empty; just the chair, harsh fluorescent lighting overhead, and the faint smell of antiseptic.

"Well." She muttered the word with reluctance. "This feels... welcoming."

This isn't right. What is this? You can still walk out. But then you'll lose this job. Come on Linda, it's not like you have a choice. There's like five bucks in your wallet.

"Crap," she said under her breath.

The moment Linda sat down, the cold metal of the chair pressed onto the back of her knees, spreading an icy chill across her skin. For a moment, nothing happened, just the buzz of the fluorescent lights overhead and the faint, sterile scent.

I guess I'm doing this.

With a soft metallic hiss, the armrests sprang to life. Straps slithered out like snakes, wrapping tightly around her wrists and ankles. The sensation was quick, deliberate, and far too precise to feel reassuring.

"Hey! What the hell?" Linda yelped, jerking instinctively, but the straps only coiled tighter, cinching with a final, smug snap. A sharp pinch bit into the underside of her wrist. Needle. Vein. Precision.

No, no, no, no, no.

A cool sensation bloomed beneath her skin, spreading through her limbs like ripples on the surface of a pond. The initial jolt of panic ebbed almost instantly, replaced by a peculiar, detached calm. Her heartbeat slowed, her thoughts softened at the edges, and suddenly, the whole situation seemed... distant.

Oh, this isn't so bad. This actually feels pretty good.

"Do not be alarmed," a disembodied voice cooed with eerie politeness. "This is standard procedure."

"Are you sure you're not a serial killer?" Linda slurred with a little chuckle, trying to wriggle her fingers. The straps responded, tightening just enough to make it clear—the chair was in charge.

The overhead lights dimmed with a sinister flicker, and from the ceiling, a series of mechanical arms descended. Each carried a different tool, gleaming and ready, eagerly waiting for their moment.

Well, I guess this is it. Oh well, I had a good run. Linda thought, in a surprisingly calm manner, that even surprised herself. *If I die, at least I won't have to pay off my debt.*

"Processing is about to begin," the voice announced, chipper and emotionless. "Please remain calm."

"Wait, can I at least ask—"

"Phase One: Visual Scans. Please blink as normal."

Before Linda could argue, a camera on the end of a robotic arm zoomed uncomfortably close to her face, the lens whirring with excitement.

"Could you at least say *cheese?*" Linda grumbled. Bright lights flashed like paparazzi on a bender, and the camera beeped approvingly.

"That wasn't so bad," Linda mumbled, blinking the stars out of her vision. "I better not find these on the cover of some tabloid."

"Phase Two: Blood Extraction. You should probably look away."

Did they say blood? For a job onboarding? No, couldn't be.

Then came the second arm. From the opposite wall, another robotic limb extended, this one holding what looked suspiciously like a pair of industrial staplers, but larger. Much larger.

"Blood extraction commencing."

"Wait, wait... blood? Why do you need... OWW!"

The first device clamped onto her arm with a sharp *thunk*, siphoning blood into a container that resembled a big gulp cup, far too large for anything that wasn't part of a horror film. A thin tube gurgled ominously, draining her blood into it.

That's a lot of blood.

"Amount extracted: 37.5%," the voice chirped, as if announcing a sale at a mattress store.

Linda felt the wooziness set in almost immediately. Her head lolled back against the chair, the edges of her vision fuzzing. "Thirty-seven point five? That's... almost half!"

"Please remain calm. You are not legally dead."

"Not legally?! That's the worst kind of not-dead!" Linda slurred, swaying like a drunk sailor at last call.

Before she could fall face-first into unconsciousness, the second stapler clamped onto her other arm with another metallic *thunk*. This time, a bright blue liquid began to pump into her veins. It crawled through her like a glacier, cold and unsettling, repossessing her bloodstream one artery at a time.

Her body shivered violently as the fluid spread from her arm to her chest, then radiated inward, like someone had injected her with winter. But slowly, the dizziness faded, and her vision sharpened with each icy pulse.

"Hemoglobin substitute administered!" the voice chimed. "Congratulations! You are no longer flirting with death."

Linda flexed her fingers cautiously. "Yay."

As soon as her blood sample was whisked away into some mysterious void, the walls hissed and shifted, revealing an array of new tools, each one more perplexing than the last. One arm extended with a dentist's drill, its ominous buzz echoing like a wasp on caffeine. Another wielded a whisk, spinning so wildly it looked ready to whip up the world's most regrettable soufflé. A third arm presented a vibrating tuning fork, humming with dramatic intent. Next was a tiny laser pointer, darting in erratic patterns. Finally, there was a plastic owl (the kind typically perched on rooftops to scare away birds) tilting its head like it was about to impart sage wisdom.

"Phase Three: Memory Cataloging. Please relax and try not to think any embarrassing thoughts."

Linda let out a dry laugh. "Relax? You just drained half my blood and filled me with blue Kool-Aid."

"Relaxation is recommended but not required," the voice clarified.

Without warning, a beam of light shot directly into her skull, triggering a rapid slideshow of her most humiliating memories. The mental blooper reel she'd hoped to bury forever.

There was an online job interview where she accidentally left the dog filter on and completed the entire thing looking like a golden retriever.

Then there was that one time she meant to drunk text her ex-boyfriend but accidentally sent a string of heart emojis and questionable song lyrics to her old boss instead.

And, of course, that time she told a waiter, "You too," when he said, "Enjoy your meal."

Linda squeezed her eyes shut. "Please stop. Please stop."

"Cataloging complete," the voice declared with far too much enthusiasm. "Embarrassing memories archived separately for internal review."

Linda groaned. "Great. Can't wait to have those come up in my next performance review."

"Phase Four: Quantum Calibration. Please collapse all wave functions."

The next arm floated toward her, this one carrying the tuning fork, still humming like it had personal grievances to settle.

"I'm pretty sure I don't know how to do that." Linda squinted. "What's that for?"

"Quantum calibration," the voice answered. "We must align your quantum frequency to galactic standards."

Linda blinked. "I... have no idea what that means."

The tuning fork jabbed her in the ribs with unnecessary enthusiasm.

"Hey, that tickles," she said between giggles.

Her entire body vibrated like a car radio stuck between stations, each muscle trembling and out of sync.

"Calibration complete. Molecular frequency: 1420MhZ. Slight interference detected."

Linda groaned, her teeth chattering like castanets. "Slight interference? I can hear David Bowie singing in my head."

Linda was still trying to stop vibrating when the next arm floated toward her, carrying what appeared to be a taxidermy owl with glowing, judgmental eyes.

The owl's eyes glowed brighter. "Phase Five: Psychological Evaluation. Please answer the following questions honestly."

Linda stared. "The heck?"

The owl blinked slowly, like a disappointed schoolteacher. "Would you trust a watermelon with your deepest secrets?"

Linda blinked back. "Who?"

"Answer recorded: *Context-Dependent*. And that's *my* line," the owl replied, with the same enthusiasm as a DMV clerk announcing that you've failed the vision test. Its glowing eyes narrowing with predatory intensity.

"Next question: If two trains leave opposite ends of the galaxy at the same time, which one develops abandonment issues first?"

Linda blinked. "What's going on?"

"Answer recorded: *Existential Confusion*."

Before Linda could protest, the owl leaned in closer, its glowing eyes narrowing. "Hypothetical scenario: You're invited to a dinner party hosted by sentient mushrooms. What is your opening line to break the ice?"

Linda stared, deciding to just give in to the absurdity of the questions. "Umm... 'Wow, love what you've done with the humidity in here?'"

The owl beeped, delighted. "Answer recorded: *Socially Adaptable.*"

The owl paused for a moment, gears whirring in its mechanical head. Just as Linda thought the ordeal was over, the owl tilted its head and launched into the next round.

"Next question: You're walking through a forest. Suddenly, a raccoon offers you a business proposal. What do you do?"

Linda frowned. "What kind of business proposal?"

"That is not relevant. Please answer the question."

"Uh... I'd hear him out?" Linda ventured.

The owl beeped approvingly. "Answer recorded: *Entrepreneurial Spirit.* Next question: How many ants would it take to overthrow a small government?"

Linda opened her mouth, closed it, then tried again. "What's the size of the budget?"

"Answer recorded: *Resourceful.*"

Linda shook her head, trying to keep up as the questions grew stranger.

"If you were a kitchen appliance, which one would disappoint your loved ones the most?"

Ha! Loved ones.

Linda groaned. "Hypothetically, probably a bread machine."

The owl beeped approvingly. "Answer recorded: *Accurate Self-Assessment.*"

"Final question," the owl announced, its glowing eyes locking onto Linda's like it was peering directly into her soul. "If you were stranded on a desert planet with nothing but a spoon, how long would it take for you to declare the spoon your best friend?"

Linda exhaled slowly. "I'm honestly not sure if I'd make it through the first day."

The owl's eyes flickered briefly before emitting a pleased beep. "Answer recorded: *Emotionally Realistic.* Evaluation complete. Thank you for your patience."

Before Linda could respond, the owl gave an approving whir and was whisked back into the ceiling, disappearing as if it had just completed a perfectly normal task.

"What were the drill and whisk for?" Linda asked, eyebrows furrowed in confusion.

"Atmosphere," the voice responded matter-of-factly.

The straps around Linda's wrists and ankles uncoiled with a soft hiss, releasing her as casually as if she'd just finished a relaxing spa treatment.

"That concludes processing," the disembodied voice chirped. "Welcome to StellarGigs! Please proceed to Orientation Room 7A for your relocation assignment."

Oh good, I'm not dead after all. Yay? Ugh, I guess I have to pay my bills after all. Crap.

Linda slumped in the chair, her entire body still humming slightly, like a phone vibrating on silent mode.

Blood extraction? Molecular calibration? A glowing owl asking ridiculous questions?

This was either the strangest dream she'd ever had or the weirdest onboarding process in human history.

With a groan, Linda pushed herself up from the chair. The yellow line flickered impatiently beneath her feet, as if saying, "Come on newbie, time to earn that paycheck." She sighed and shuffled along, following the glowing path until it ended at a door labeled *"7A"*.

The door hissed open with mild enthusiasm; the unsettling sound of a snake just barely tolerating your presence. Beyond it was an uninviting cylindrical room.

Linda stepped inside cautiously, scanning her surroundings. The floor was a translucent pane of glowing blue-white glass, and about fifteen feet above her, a tangled mess of wires and strange metal tubes dangled ominously, like a mad scientist's chandelier.

"Yeah, this is definitely the wrong room," she muttered, turning back toward the door. But before she could escape, the door hissed shut behind her with a satisfyingly sinister click, leaving no visible seam.

"Oh, come on," she groaned.

"Prepare for relocation assignment," the disembodied voice chirped cheerfully. "Initiating countdown in five..."

Linda's stomach dropped. "What?" She spun around and pounded on the smooth walls. "Hey! Let me out of here!"

"Four... Please remain calm. Three..." The entire room began to hum, vibrating just enough to make her feel like she was standing inside a giant electric toothbrush.

"Two..." The glowing floor intensified, bathing everything in the kind of eerie blue light that made you worry you were about to get probed.

"One..."

Linda clenched her eyes shut, instinctively bracing herself.

"Relocation commencing. Have a safe trip."

For those who have never experienced teleportation, imagine being yanked through a garden hose one size too small, while the hose itself doesn't know what reality it should exist in. One moment, you're standing perfectly still. The next, your atoms are being unzipped, tossed into a cosmic blender, shaken (not stirred), and sloppily reassembled; all with the finesse of a toddler building a tower out of Jenga blocks.

In short, it is deeply unpleasant.

Linda hit the ground like a wet bag of laundry, the world still spinning around her. For a brief, blissful second, she thought it was over. Then her stomach caught up with her.

She vomited spectacularly all over herself. Apparently, oatmeal had not been the right choice for breakfast after all. It clung to her clothes with a kind of commitment she'd never managed in any of her previous relationships.

"Great," she muttered, half-gagging, half-sulking. "I really hope dry cleaning is one of the perks."

3

Coco, We're Not in Kansas Anymore!

"He spoke in frequencies I couldn't understand, but somehow... I knew he'd ruin my life in the best way."

— Commander Axton Starforge,
Steel Hearts: Echoes of Andromeda, S2E24

It took Linda a few minutes to convince herself she could stand. Her atoms had finally stopped vibrating and seemed more or less back in their assigned seats.

Just as she was testing her legs, the door hissed open.

In the doorway stood a creature, the kind you'd imagine if a velociraptor and a swamp had a baby. It had gray-green skin (or maybe scales) that glistened unpleasantly under the flickering fluorescent lights. Its yellow, slit-pupiled eyes locked onto her with the kind of unwavering precision you'd expect from an apex predator.

Its mouth hung open just enough to show off a jagged collection of teeth, the exact shade of 'Oh no!' They weren't the kind of teeth that politely hinted at gum disease, they screamed neglect, like they'd never been within miles of a toothbrush.

For reasons that only made things worse, it wore a white collared shirt and a blue necktie covered with a whimsical array of planets, trying, and failing spectacularly, to appear office friendly. A pair of black slacks clung awkwardly to its legs, completing the ensemble with all the charm of a six-foot-tall lizard who'd lost a bet.

In one clawed hand, it held the business end of a truly terrifying weapon; the kind of device that looked capable of erasing not just problems, but several nearby layers of reality along with them.

The creature made a low, rumbling sound that sat somewhere between a growl and the noise your stomach makes after eating gas station sushi.

"What!?" Linda yelped, panic hitting her like an electric jolt. She instinctively crab-walked backward across the floor, pressing herself up against the far wall, trying to disappear into it through sheer force of will.

What the hell is that thing?

The creature moved forward with the slow, deliberate certainty of something at the top of the food chain. The rumbling noise shifted into a kind of wet wheezing, as if the creature was either trying to intimidate her or struggling with seasonal allergies.

Before Linda could scream, the creature lunged. It pressed the weapon against her neck with a soft click. She flinched at the quick pinch of metal against skin like a flu shot, but given by someone without a medical degree and zero bedside manner.

Then the creature pulled back, staring at her with a mix of satisfaction and mild curiosity.

"Take me to your leader!"

Did that think just speak to me?

Linda blinked, stunned. It sounded like a man with marbles in his mouth, but the words were perfectly clear, even if they didn't quite match the movements of his scaly lips.

"Umm... what?" she managed.

"Oh good, you can understand me!" The creature exhaled with what might have been relief.

"You want to see my leader?"

"Ha! No, not really. I figured that's what you'd expect me to say. I was worried that the nanoprobe wasn't repaired properly." The creature adjusted the weapon, which, as it turned out, wasn't a weapon after all. "I've injected you with a *ChatterNode* and a mild hallucinogenic to help you adjust to your new reality."

"A mild... hallucinogenic?" Linda repeated, glancing down at her hands, which were now a faint shade of 'iridescent flamingo'. Her fingers shimmered like they'd been dipped in cosmic oil slicks, and as she flexed them, they briefly played a harp chord.

She blinked. "I'm pretty sure my hands shouldn't sound like a string instrument."

"You sure? Maybe you just never noticed."

"Yeah, I'm pretty sure..."

The creature gave a small, nonchalant shrug. "In that case, it should wear off in about six hours. Or twelve. Or... well, eventually, you'll get used to it."

"Used to it..." Her voice trailed off in a daze as she stared at her shimmering hands.

"It's normal for you to feel a bit strange after a cross-sector transport of that distance. I'm actually surprised you're even awake." The creature said to Linda. "My name is Coco by the way," the creature announced proudly, although the name did not fit the visual in any way. "Future StellarGigs employee of the quarter, and your new-hire liaison for habitation facility seven-four-three-delta-one."

Coco extended a clawed hand, either offering to help her up or maybe requesting a high-five... err... four. Linda ignored it, scrambling to her feet on her own, keeping her back firmly against the wall.

"What are you?" she asked, trying to keep her voice steady.

"I told you, I'm your new-hire liaison," Coco said with a casual shrug.

"No, *what* are you?" Linda repeated, motioning vaguely at him with both hands, as if trying to encompass everything about his scaly, confusing existence.

"Oh! Right. I forgot. Humans don't get out much." Coco shook his head, as though this was a personal disappointment. "I'm a Veloran. We're from the Draz'kel system, third planet from the star. You probably don't know it, but we're practically neighbors. If you're ever in the mood for a bowl of fermented swamp eels, we've got the best in the galaxy. They've been banned in three systems! A real delicacy."

"Neighbors?" Linda asked, confused.

"Sure are. You may know the system, although your species calls our star HD-40307. Whatever that's supposed to mean."

Linda just stared, her brain desperately trying to process *fermented swamp eels*. "What... what's going on?" she finally stammered, her voice still shaky.

Coco tilted his head thoughtfully, as if considering the question for the first time. "Well, existentially speaking, no one really knows," he said. "But if you think about it, that's kind of exciting, right? Life's just one big beta test. We're all iterations of a prototype nobody remembers designing."

"No, I mean what's going on here. Right now."

"Oh, that. I've been assigned to help you acclimate to your first week at the facility," Coco said smoothly, as if this all made perfect sense. "You're not in Kentucky anymore, as the old saying goes."

He let out a low chuckle, a sound that resembled rocks tumbling down a garbage chute.

"Kansas," Linda corrected automatically, still trying to process the fact that she was talking to what looked like a dinosaur dressed in business casual.

Coco tilted his head, genuinely puzzled. "What?"

"You're not in Kansas anymore."

Coco blinked slowly, his yellow eyes narrowing in thought. "I've never been to Kansas."

"Yeah, me neither," Linda muttered, suddenly unsure who was making less sense.

"I see you didn't bring a towel," Coco said, shaking his head. "Here you go, thought you might need to clean up." He handed one over with the casual air of someone who's seen far worse.

Linda glanced down at her clothes, still speckled with that morning's oatmeal. "Thanks," she muttered, taking the towel and awkwardly dabbing at herself. Unfortunately, the oatmeal had taken on the consistency of cement, but eventually she managed to make herself look semi-respectable.

"Excellent! Well, if you'll follow me, I'll show you around the place," Coco said, turning on his clawed heel and ambling down the hallway.

Wherever Linda was now, the hallway looked eerily identical to the one she had just left back in Los Angeles. Same bland walls, same corporate lighting that made everything look like a hospital. If it weren't for the weird lizard-man leading the way, she might have thought she'd somehow looped back to the gig agency office.

They passed through a doorway and onto a wide promenade, the kind of space that seemed designed for strolling and pretending to enjoy your day. To the left, the walkway stretched into a cavernous open space, bustling with strange creatures of various shapes and sizes. A pigeon flapped lazily overhead, ignored by everyone but Linda.

To the right, "Whoa!" Linda stumbled to a stop, her jaw dropping.

A vast, seamless clear surface stretched before her, a huge floor-to-ceiling window. Beyond it lay the kind of view that would make astronauts weep: a great, orange and red gas giant, endless stars, and nebulae swirled together in cosmic brilliance, with a nearby moon so close she could almost see the craters like freckles.

"That's... amazing!" Linda breathed, still trying to wrap her head around the view.

"It is, isn't it? I was wondering when you were going to notice." Coco puffed up with pride, unstrapping a small device from his belt. It was roughly the size of a smartphone, but instead of a screen, a flickering hologram projected from the top, spinning slowly like it was trying to show off.

"This is the latest model from Zyzax-Tech," Coco said, holding it up as if it were the Holy Grail. "It's got everything: galactic signal booster, a mood-shifting wallpaper, and even a feature that identifies what's edible. Well, mostly edible." He tapped the hologram proudly. "And the battery? Ha! It'll only die at the worst possible moment. It's perfect!"

Linda stared at him, blinking. "I meant, out there. Is that... space?"

She drifted toward the window, pressing a hand gently against the transparent surface, half-expecting it to shatter under the sheer weight and scale of the cosmos now piling up in her tiny monkey brain.

Coco shuffled up beside her, casting the barest glance at the sprawling, celestial view beyond. "Oh yeah, that. Technically, sure. But to be precise, it's Sector 42 of the StellarGigs Corporation Near-Orbital Employment Habitat." He shrugged, like he was pointing out the food court at the mall. "Nice view, I guess. But what's really impressive is this beauty right here."

With renewed enthusiasm, Coco returned his focus to the device in his claws, swiping through menus like a proud tech bro. "See those edges? Razor-sharp resolution. And check this. Built-in anxiety suppression setting. Not certified by the Intergalactic Health Council, but honestly, neither are most life forms around here." He let out another gravelly laugh, as if that was the punchline to an inside joke only other space bureaucrats would understand.

Linda tore her gaze away from the breathtaking view and glanced back at Coco, who was now engrossed in a feature that projected a holographic version of himself, though inexplicably, ten feet tall and wearing a cowboy hat.

"Okay," Linda said slowly, trying to ground herself. "So, just to clarify, we are... in space?"

"Technically," Coco replied, without looking up from the hologram. "But it's not as glamorous as you humans seem to think. You'll get over the whole 'ooh, stars!' thing pretty quick. Trust me, after the first few orbital rotations, it's just background noise."

Linda squinted at him. "Right. And what exactly am I supposed to be doing here?"

Coco gave a distracted wave. "Oh, you know, gig stuff. Missions. Deliveries. Errands. Whatever the system assigns. Could be courier work, assisting alien nobility, or wrangling plasma storms. We don't pick the gigs. The gigs pick us."

"Right," Linda said, eyeing him warily. "I don't really know how to do any of that."

"That's okay, you'll catch on quick. Or, you know..."

"What happens if I... mess up?" Linda looked alarmed.

Coco finally looked up, his eyes narrowing slightly. "Messing up isn't ideal. But hey, no pressure." He grinned, showing off those jagged yellow teeth. "Just... make sure you always *finish* the gig."

Linda's stomach flipped remembering the recruiter had said the exact same thing. "And what if I don't?"

Coco shrugged. "Well, then you get a strike. Three strikes and you're out, just like human basketball. If that happens, StellarGigs assigns you to a *Permanent Gig*."

She frowned. "*Permanent Gig?*"

"Yeah," he said, with a tone that implied it was something between a punishment and a cosmic joke. "No one knows what the gigs are. All we know is, once you're assigned one, you don't come back. Not even in pieces."

Linda swallowed hard. "Fantastic."

Coco tapped the device one last time and snapped it shut with a satisfied nod. "Welcome to the workforce!" He gestured down the promenade. "Let's go check out your new home for the next two years."

Linda glanced at the vast cosmos outside the window one more time, hoping for a last-minute escape plan, then sighed. "Yeah, sure. Why not?"

4

Now Without a Bucket!

"I've commanded dreadnoughts and slept in broom closets. The size of your quarters matters less than the weight of what you carry inside."

— Commander Axton Starforge,
Steel Hearts: Echoes of Andromeda, S5E24

Historically, space stations had been designed with cramped rooms and narrow corridors because transporting materials beyond Earth's atmosphere was eye-wateringly expensive. Every cubic foot of space required more fuel, more engineering, and more money. Which meant that spacious accommodations were about as realistic as finding a five-star hotel on Mars with a complimentary continental breakfast. In the early days of space travel, astronauts were lucky if they got a bed that folded out from a wall and a bathroom that didn't involve a vacuum tube.

But out there, in the far reaches of the galaxy, the old limitations were obsolete. Materials were mined from asteroids or collected from planetary debris, and faster-than-light shipping ensured that even the weirdest galactic knickknacks could arrive before anyone realized how useless they were. In theory, orbital habitats could feature expansive suites, high ceilings, and windows as wide as space itself; luxuries that were once impossible to imagine.

But theory, much like customer service, rarely exists in practice.

In reality, the Near-Orbital Employment Habitat kept everything compact. Not because it had to, but because it *wanted* to. StellarGigs, in its infinite wisdom, realized that smaller spaces meant more workers per square unit, and more workers meant more profit. Why waste time designing comfortable living quarters when you could stack workers like storage crates and call them 'space-efficient'? Comfort, it seems, was never in the budget. If you could fit all the essentials into a shoebox with a door, then that's efficiency at its finest. And if a worker *needed* more personal space? Well, that's what the airlock was for.

So, when Linda found herself crouched in her assigned *private room*, her first thought was, *prison cells at least had a sink*. The room consisted of a bed wedged firmly into one corner, with a small, wobbly table and a chair pressed against the adjoining wall. The two feet of floor space between the bed and the door could charitably be called a walkway, though a full-grown cat might have trouble making the turn without bumping into something. In one corner, a small toilet seat extended from the wall, attached to a black rubber tube. Above the bed, there were storage compartments eerily reminiscent of airplane overhead bins, presumably to house any personal items she could fit, which at that point meant her knock-off Gucci handbag that contained: a bottle of concealer, a prescription for anti-depressants that she couldn't afford to fill, and an expired California driver's license.

On the bed were two piles of neatly folded outfits, both an uninspiring shade of gray that seemed to suggest, 'Why bother?' The StellarGigs logo was proudly emblazoned on the breast, because apparently even in space, branding was everything. The first was a formal blouse with a crisp collar and a row of buttons down the front. Ideal for those rare moments when one wanted to look serious while pretending to understand what was going on. The second was made of a much thinner, scratchy material, clearly designed for sleeping, napping, or just lying down while contemplating the cosmic absurdity of life.

The standout feature in the room was the entertainment screen embedded at the foot of the bed. It could slide up or down at the touch of a button, which gave the whole setup the feel of watching TV from inside a coffin. As a bonus, the screen came preloaded with StellarGigs-approved programming, including such classics as: *Compliance and Chill: The Motion Picture, How to Win Friends and Influence Aliens,* and *The Art of Passive-Aggressive Leadership.*

Linda let out a sigh, sitting gingerly on the edge of the bed. The mattress gave a sad little creak, like it had already accepted its fate. She looked around her new home—a room so small it could trigger claustrophobia in a sardine—and tried to convince herself that it wasn't so bad. After all, she didn't plan on spending much time there.

"Wow, look at you. You must have really impressed the higher ups during processing." Coco said, a hint of jealousy in his voice as his eyes made the rounds. "I didn't know they were still giving out the deluxe accommodations."

"This is *deluxe*?" Linda asked, her eyebrows climbing toward her hairline.

"Yeah, the regular rooms just get a bucket," Coco replied matter-of-factly, as if that were perfectly reasonable.

"Lucky me," Linda muttered, glancing around her shoebox-sized room.

Coco gave her a knowing nod. "Trust me, you don't want to know what the bucket's for."

Linda sighed. "I think I can imagine—"

"It's for pooping," Coco said, matter-of-factly.

Linda stared at him. "Thanks for clarifying."

"Hey, no problem. Knowing is strength," Coco said with far too much enthusiasm, as if he'd just invented the phrase—which, to be fair, he kind of had.

"Have you seen the latest episode of *Steel Hearts*?" Coco asked, pointing to the entertainment screen attached to the end of the bed. "I really don't know how the 404s are going to get out of this one."

Linda shook her head, "The 404s?"

"Oh yeah, the corporate insect swarm has them trapped on Axio Prime. I can't wait to see what happens next!" Coco appeared more excited than ever.

Just then, a long, drawn-out wail echoed through the ventilation ducts. A sound somewhere between a static feedback loop and a ghost in emotional distress.

"Not agaaaain!" it howled, fading into the hum of the recycler fans.

Linda froze, pulse spiking. "What the hell was that?" The smell of burnt coffee wafted through the air, sharp and bitter.

"Air vents turning on," Coco said flatly. "They do that sometimes."

Linda's skepticism was written all over her face.

"So," Coco said, unbothered, "want to check out the cafeteria?"

"Why not?" she sighed.

The cafeteria was exactly what Linda had feared: a chaotic blend of cheap buffet restaurant and interstellar flea market. The air smelled like burnt toast, engine grease, and something suspiciously sweet, none of which made sense together. Long tables stretched across the room, filled with beings from every corner of the galaxy, hunched over trays of food which in many cases, were still moving.

A massive dispenser in the corner wheezed loudly, struggling to pour out what could only be described as 'brown goo', labeled optimistically as *"Nutrient Slurry – Today's Flavor: Surprise"*. Beneath it was a small sign reading: *"If It Wiggles, Please Alert Maintenance."*

The hot food counter offered a baffling selection of items:

Quantum Lasagna – Each bite exists in multiple states simultaneously, so you're never sure if you've finished eating or just started.

Stellar Stew — A hearty blend of ingredients harvested from the far reaches of space. May contain potatoes, neutron star dust, or traces of time itself. Guaranteed to fill you up *or* alter your molecular structure.

Cryo-Nuggets – This delicious 'meat' based nugget is served at a delicious $5°$ Kelvin. Don't forget your gloves, they're a bit chilly!

Mystery Casserole – No one knows what's in it, including the chef. Could be dinner. Could be a sentient life form trying to escape. Either way, it's *probably* edible.

Above the serving line, a flickering hologram of a cheerful chef offered a looping message:

"Bon appétit! Food is fuel. No refunds!"

Linda hesitated by the salad bar, which contained one wilted lettuce leaf and several rocks. A nearby alien seemed to be enthusiastically nibbling on the gravel.

"Not bad, huh?" Coco said, nudging her with his elbow. "And today's stew isn't even glowing. That's a good sign!"

Linda picked up a tray reluctantly. "Any chance there's coffee?"

Coco chuckled. "Sure. StellarBrew, but I need to warn you, it's pretty strong stuff." He pointed to a caution sign over the coffee dispenser that read:

"Warning: May cause time dilation in small doses. Do not operate heavy machinery."

Linda stared at the swirling black liquid inside the pot. "You know what? I think I'll pass."

Coco grinned. "Smart move. The last guy who had a cup ended up meeting himself on the way back from the bathroom."

"Is there anything here a human can actually eat?" Linda asked, trying to mask the growing unease in her voice.

"Sure thing! The Nutrient Slurry is delicious... sometimes," Coco said with a casual shrug. "Depends on your luck."

Linda grimaced. "Maybe I'll just stick to fruit for now." She wandered over to a table displaying an odd assortment of alien fruits. A particularly suspicious apple kept phasing in and out of existence, as if it wasn't fully committed to being there. Meanwhile, what looked like an orange vibrated violently, humming like someone had accidentally left their electric shaver running.

With relief, Linda spotted a relatively normal-looking bunch of bananas. They were yellow, just ripe, and seemingly non-threatening. She pulled one off the bunch.

"AHHHHHHHH!" the banana shrieked at the top of its... peel?

Linda yelped, tossing the 'banana' back onto the table as if it were a live grenade. It rolled lazily to a stop next to the vibrating orange, muttering something about "overly aggressive handling".

She looked around the cafeteria, wide-eyed and panicked, but no one seemed to notice. Or care.

Coco strolled up beside her, unfazed. "Yeah, they'll do that sometimes." He popped what looked like a glowing blueberry into his mouth, chewed thoughtfully, and added, "Don't take it personally. The bananas are all attention seekers."

Linda stared at the bunch, still half-expecting them to start a conversation. "I think I'll skip breakfast."

"Suit yourself," Coco replied. "Lunch doesn't scream as much." He popped another glowing berry into his mouth before adding. "Come on over here, I'll introduce you to some of your work mates."

Coco led Linda across the chaotic cafeteria, weaving past tables crowded with every imaginable kind of life form, some of which Linda was pretty sure she'd never be able to unsee. A creature with at least six limbs waved cheerfully at Coco, each appendage holding a different type of food that all seemed to be on fire. Coco waved back, as if this were the most normal thing in the galaxy.

"Linda, meet your work mates," Coco said, stopping in front of a table occupied by three very different beings.

The first was a small, round alien covered in iridescent fur, shifting colors depending on how the light hit it. He sat hunched over his tray, nervously nibbling on some kind of tentacle, his three eyes darting between Linda and Coco as if silently apologizing for his own existence.

"Hi," Linda said hesitantly.

He jumped, nearly dropping his food. "Oh! Hello! I mean, uh... sorry! Was I, um... in your way? I can move. I'll move." He fumbled with his tray, clearly prepared to vacate his seat on the spot.

Linda blinked. "No, no, you're fine."

"Oh, okay. Good," he said, visibly relieved. "Unless, uh... you'd rather I not be here?" He shifted awkwardly in his seat. "Because, you know, I could..."

"Glorp, buddy, breathe," Coco cut in with a chuckle. "Linda's not going to evict you from the cafeteria."

"Oh! Right, uh... of course." Glorp gave a nervous little laugh that sounded more like a hiccup. "Sorry. I just... Hi. Again." He burped, soft and apologetic, like a foghorn trying not to make a scene. He immediately cringed. "Oh no! Sorry about that too."

Coco grinned. "Don't mind Glorp. He's friendly, just a little... high-strung."

Glorp gave Linda a sheepish look, his three eyes blinking in rapid succession. "If it's, uh... any consolation, I try not to be."

Linda's gaze shifted to the next person—almost human, if not for the gills fluttering at her neck and the green skin that caught the light like glass. A small circular patch clung beneath one ear, half hidden by her hair, the edge lifting as she moved. She was calmly sipping a beverage through a long straw, releasing a lazy stream of bubbles.

"I'm Lira," the green-skinned woman said, her voice soft and slightly muffled by her drink, as she gave Linda a far-off, whimsical gaze. "You're new, right?

That's lovely. You'll get used to things eventually... or, well, you won't. Some folks lose themselves, drift away, and float out the airlock, like little cosmic dandelion seeds. Beautiful, really."

She smiled dreamily, as if picturing a field of drifting corpses. After a moment her hand rose, almost automatically, to scratch behind her left ear before she returned to her drink, stirring it slowly with the straw. The bubbles surfaced and popped in soft bursts, punctuation to a thought she wasn't ready to share.

Linda stared at her wide-eyed, unsure if Lira was joking or not. She was leaning toward not.

"And this here is Zorb," Coco said, gesturing to the last occupant, a tall alien with spindly limbs, a head shaped like a squashed pineapple, and a pair of spectacles perched precariously on what might have been a nose.

Zorb glanced up from the tablet he was reading, adjusted his spectacles, and gave a curt nod. "If you require assistance, please do not hesitate to seek it elsewhere. Helping newbies is a waste of my superior intellect," he said in a nasally, irritated tone before going back to his tablet.

Linda blinked. "Uh... okay."

Coco patted her on the back, nearly knocking the wind out of her. "See? They're already warming up to you."

"Uh huh," Linda muttered, not convinced. Glorp gave her a quick, nervous nod, as if that might somehow help, then immediately looked down at his tentacle snack to avoid eye contact.

"I was just showing Linda here around before heading down to the gig office to get her first assignment," Coco said cheerily, completely unfazed by the tension in the room.

Lira smiled dreamily, swirling her drink with the straw. "First assignments are always special. Mine was scrubbing a warship's antimatter tanks. So relaxing... if you ignore the smell."

Glorp winced. "Oh, I remember mine. I, uh... didn't do things right and they gave me a warning. Well... several warnings." He shrunk in his seat, as if hoping to disappear.

Zorb glanced up from his tablet, adjusted his spectacles with an air of disapproval, and sniffed. "Let me know how your first gig goes," he said flatly. "Statistically speaking, there's an 85% chance you'll mess things up."

Linda stared at him, eyes wide. "Uh... thanks?"

"Don't worry," Coco cut in with a grin. "I'm sure you'll do great. And if you don't, well..." He shrugged. "At least they give you a heads-up before ejecting you into deep space."

Glorp squeaked. "Not always."

Linda gave a slow nod, trying to process everything. She glanced at Glorp, who was now nervously fidgeting with the remains of his tentacle snack. Lira was lazily blowing bubbles in her drink like existential doom was just another Wednesday. Zorb had already gone back to his tablet, his focus so intense that nothing short of a major catastrophe could possibly hope to regain his attention.

A sharp ding cut through the cafeteria drone. Linda looked up as a massive holo-screen flickered on overhead:

TOP EMPLOYEE: CURRENT RANKINGS!

Neon numbers scrolled beside worker names, a glowing countdown clock ticking ominously beside them. At the top of the list, in bright gold letters, was:

PIGEON — 2,005 POINTS

Beneath it, sulking in second and third places, were:

COCO — 1,980 POINTS

CELVIN — 1,750 POINTS

Linda blinked. "Is the top employee... a pigeon?"

Coco groaned, his tail lashing. "Don't even get me started. He never completes any gigs, but he always beats me in the rankings." The screen shifted to a professional photo of a gray and white pigeon staring expressionless at the camera. "I think he may be related to some executive. And that Celvin guy, I don't even know who he is. Always in third place, but I've never seen him before. I swear the system's rigged. But this quarter, I'm feeling confident. I'm going to be number one, mark my words."

"That's the spirit, Coco. You'll, uh... get him next time," stuttered Glorp. Coco glared at him for a moment before regaining his composure.

The scoreboard chimed again, a cheery corporate voice booming: "Reminder: Falling behind in the rankings reflects poorly on your commitment to synergy. Please only utilize StellarGigs approved facial expressions to earn bonus points!"

"How do you even earn points?" Linda asked.

"Oh, that's easy. Mostly by completing gigs, but the system also assigns points for things it notices you do on station," Coco said.

"The system gave me thirty points for attending a coworker's funeral," Lira said wistfully. "I wasn't invited. I just... showed up." All eyes turned to her. "I love parties."

"Alrighty! Enough of that." Coco clapped his claws together, pulling everyone's focus away from the scoreboard. "Let's get you to the gig office. It's just down the hall. Nice and easy. Gig access is seamless. They want you working, after all." He gave a sly grin. "But if you need anything else, like say, your employee ID reactivated or directions to the bathroom, well... good luck. That's when the real adventure begins."

Linda raised a skeptical brow. "So... you're saying the only easy part of this job is... getting more jobs?"

"Exactly!" Coco beamed, pleased with her understanding. "See? You're already catching on. Efficiency at its finest."

Glorp gave her an apologetic smile. "If, uh... if you ever need anything, just ask. I mean... you don't *have* to, of course. Um... only if you want to..."

Linda forced a smile. "Thanks, Glorp."

Coco gestured toward the exit with a flourish. "Let's move! First gigs are exciting—they're like the first day of school, but with higher stakes. And, you know, the occasional plasma burn."

Linda swallowed hard, following Coco out of the cafeteria. As they left, she heard Lira's dreamy voice drifting behind them. "Good luck, Linda. And remember, if things get overwhelming, just imagine yourself floating away into the peaceful, endless void."

5

Assign of the Times

"Its words were perfect. Too perfect. Like someone had sanded down truth until it gleamed... and no longer fit the world."

— Commander Axton Starforge,
Steel Hearts: Echoes of Andromeda, S1E7

When Linda and Coco stepped into the gig office, the first thing that caught her eye was the massive, glowing assignment board dominating the far wall. It pulsed with shifting text, job postings flickering in and out of existence with the urgency of a stock market ticker. Except instead of companies, it listed gigs that Linda wanted absolutely nothing to do with:

Seeking Void Whisperer: Must be comfortable making small talk with existential horrors.

Temporal Librarian: Knowledge of time paradoxes preferred. Side effects may include mild amnesia.

Quantum Tailor: Must stitch garments that exist in multiple dimensions simultaneously.

"Those are the *specialty gigs*," Coco explained, nodding at the ever-changing board. "Workers can request them for extra pay, but they come with risks. Big money, though, if you complete the gigs. Sometimes, if the system can't find someone to take a job, and StellarGigs is set to make a lot of money from it, it will just assign it to some random worker and hope for the best."

The board's text shifted again, displaying:

Gravitational Therapist: Help celestial bodies work through their attraction issues.

Rabid Bureaucrat Wrangler: Seeking brave soul to wrangle bureaucrats suffering from chronic paperwork rage.

Schrödinger's Cat Walker: Must ensure both existence and non-existence of feline companions. May involve paradoxical litter box cleaning.

"Ah man, I had that Schrödinger gig once. Worst part was, I completed the gig, but I didn't complete the gig," Coco shuddered.

Linda noticed some small, rodent-like creatures running around the office. They had twitchy noses and sharp, beady eyes that never seemed to blink. Their tiny hands, tipped with ink-stained claws, darted from desk to desk, snatching up stacks of paperwork as if each sheet was a prized possession. Despite their diminutive size, they moved with remarkable speed, carrying reams of forms back to what looked like burrows, which they constructed from layers of out-dated job applications, misfiled reports, and rejected requests.

Linda raised an eyebrow. "Who are those little guys scurrying around?"

"Oh, those are the bureaucrats. They handle all the paperwork that flows through here."

"They're... building burrows out of it."

"Of course. What else would they do with it? Everything's backed up digitally these days."

The burrows themselves were a chaotic mess of crumpled documents and half-finished forms, piled into strange, hive-like structures along the corners of the gig office. Some of the more elaborate burrows even had tunnels winding through the walls, where the bureaucrats scurried in and out, hoarding triplicate copies for what seemed like an ever-expanding empire of paper. From time to time, one of them would stop to examine a form, mutter in a high-pitched tone, then stuff it into the walls before hurrying off to collect more.

Linda's eyes were still on the bustling bureaucrats when a low, confident voice interrupted her thoughts.

"Well, well, well... what do we have here? A fresh face in the gig jungle?"

She turned to see a robot roll up with a swagger no machine should have. The bot's sleek, metallic frame gleamed in the flickering light of the office; its broad, angular chestplate seemed unnecessary for any practical function and purely for show. Its digital face displayed a cocky smirk, and his voice was deep with a distinct air of arrogance.

"You must be Linda Greyson," the robot drawled, scanning her from head to toe with robotic smugness. "You probably already know who I am. Gig Control and Haphazard Assignment Distributor, 2000th iteration, but everyone just calls me GigChad-2000 for short." The bot winked, if that was even possible. "Don't worry, sweetheart, I've got just the thing for you. The *perfect* gig. You're gonna crush it."

Linda blinked, unsure how to respond to a robot that exuded more confidence than most people she knew.

"Uh, okay..." she started hesitantly.

"Okay? Just, okay? C'mon babe, you're in the big leagues now." GigChad-2000 rolled closer, his wheels humming like a muscle car. "I'm talking primo gigs. None of that standard gig stuff. Stick with me, and you'll be riding high in no time."

Linda shifted awkwardly, feeling slightly overwhelmed by the bot's larger-than-life presence. "Uh, that sounds... great? So, what's the first gig?"

GigChad-2000 leaned in closer, his voice dropping to a conspiratorial tone. "First, we gotta see if you've got the chops. I don't just hand out top-tier gigs to anyone. But don't worry, babe, I can spot potential a mile away, and you've got it."

Before she could respond, the bot's display flickered, pulling up a list of potential jobs.

"Now let's see... Hmm, how do you feel about untangling entropy fields? No? Didn't think so. Alright, how about *Quantum Plumber*? Got any experience fixing reality leaks? It's... surprisingly common."

Linda frowned, trying to keep up. "Reality leaks?"

GigChad-2000 chuckled, the sound oddly arrogant for a machine. "Don't worry about it, I'll find you something... *simpler*. You're new, after all." His display scrolled rapidly before settling on a job. "Aha! Here we go, *Space Llama Herder!* Just you, a couple dozen space llamas, and the cold void of space. Plus, you get a sweet space suit. You can thank me later."

Linda's heart sank. "Wait, I don't know anything about llamas?"

"*Space* llamas," GigChad-2000 corrected, his tone firm but playful. "This is the *perfect* gig for you! I'm really *seeing* you right now. You've got the soul of an artist, don't you? And let me tell you, space llama herding is *pure* art. You're absolutely made for this. Trust me." He gave her another wink... A wink? How was this robot winking?

"I'm not sure I—"

GigChad-2000 cut her off. "Look, you'll be fine. Besides, it's just temporary. You'll be cleaning up dark matter puddles before you know it. Do this gig, and I'll hook you up with something *way* cooler next time. Deal?"

Before Linda could protest further, the bot's mechanical arm extended, producing a sleek, watch-like device. It clicked open with a soft *whirr* as the screen lit up, displaying the job details. It only had six words: "Herd Llamas.

Avoid Asteroids. Don't Panic!" The gig's start time just showed the word: "NOW!"

"Good luck, champ!" he said, rolling away with a lazy wave of his metallic arm.

Coco clapped his hands together. "Ah, classic! Good one to start with. Those space llamas can be... unpredictable, but nothing you can't handle." He looked down at the device in her hand. "Go ahead, strap that on your wrist. It's the *ChronoShackle-9*, we just call it the *Shak*. You'll get all your gigs through it from now on. Plus, it doubles as a watch, and you can play *Snake* on it."

"Wait... you guys have *Snake*?" She asked quizzically.

Coco gave her a knowing nod. "Oh yeah, every advanced civilization in the galaxy developed their own version of *Snake*. It's basically a universal constant."

Linda stared at Coco, then glanced back at GigChad-2000 as he rolled off to his next unsuspecting victim. "This... this is completely insane."

"Yep!" Coco beamed. "But look on the bright side. You didn't get the rabid bureaucrats gig."

As if on cue, the assignment board flickered, then blanked out. A blaring siren filled the office, and the lights flashed red. The board crackled to life with a new message:

** UPDATE **

Rabid Bureaucrats Wrangler: Seeking brave soul to wrangle bureaucrats suffering from chronic paperwork rage.

Gig Assigned: Congratulations, worker Glorp!

"Oh no," came a whisper from behind them. Linda turned to see Glorp just entering the room, his three eyes wide with terror. "Not again..."

The office seemed to descend into a moment of hushed tension as Glorp slouched, his shoulders sagging as though the weight of the assignment had physically pressed him down. Coco patted Glorp on one of his hunched shoulders, offering a sympathetic smile. "Hang in there, buddy. Maybe they'll only be mildly rabid this time."

Glorp looked at Coco with an expression that Linda could only assume was a mix of sadness and dread, his three eyes blinking out of sync. "Last time, they bit me. Twice." He held up a hand and showed Linda a scar. It looked like a paper cut, only somehow worse—redder, angrier.

Linda shook her head. "Is there any way out of these gigs? Like... a loophole or something?"

"Oh sure!" Coco grinned. "You just have to fill out Form 57-Q, in triplicate, get it stamped by a senior bureaucrat—preferably one that's not rabid—and then submit it to the 'Appeals and Denials Department'."

Linda blinked. "And how long does that take?"

Coco shrugged. "Oh, about six to eight galactic weeks. By then, the gig's usually over."

"Perfect," Linda muttered, rolling her eyes.

GigChad-2000, now at the other end of the office, could be heard assigning another poor soul to a gig involving 'anti-gravity mop duty' and 'reluctant wormholes'. He seemed to relish every defeated sigh as much as he enjoyed admiring his own reflection in the nearest shiny surface.

"C'mon," Coco said, nudging Linda. "We'd better get you prepped. Space llamas aren't going to herd themselves, and trust me, you don't want them getting restless. Last guy who let them wander ended up in an alternate dimension. Let's just say it wasn't one of the *nice* ones."

Linda sighed, glancing down at the holographic display on her wrist. "Right," Linda said, taking a deep breath. "Let's do this."

Coco grinned and gave her a thumbs-up. "That's the spirit! Worst case, you'll be sucked into a blackhole. But honestly, that barely ever happens anymore."

Linda shot him a look, and Coco just chuckled, leading the way out of the gig office.

The gig transport room was cluttered and chaotic, with machinery that looked like it had been salvaged from a dozen different eras. The walls were lined with panels that blinked erratically, as if they couldn't quite decide whether they wanted to work or not. A few screens displayed garbled data, while others just showed what looked like someone's high score on an ancient arcade game. The air smelled faintly of burnt circuitry and something metallic, and the floor was littered with stray cables and what might have been a leftover part of a toaster. Despite the disarray, there was a strange charm to it, like the whole room had personality; a scrappy, makeshift vibe that suggested it had seen its fair share of adventures.

Coco stood in front of Linda, holding up a shiny silver space suit that looked equal parts intimidating and ridiculous. "Alright, Linda, let's get you suited up," he said, giving the suit a little shake for emphasis. "This baby will keep you safe from, well, pretty much everything out there... except the llamas' spit. You're on your own with that."

Linda frowned, her voice wavering slightly. "How am I supposed to use this?"

"Oh, it's easy," Coco replied, entirely unhelpful. He then held up a long, sleek device. "And here's your *Quantum Herding Lance*. This will motivate those space llamas. Just press the *red* button to activate it; but whatever you do, don't press the *crimson* button." His voice dropped with a sense of warning.

Linda glanced at the lance, her eyes narrowing at the two identical buttons on opposite sides. "What? They're the same color!"

Coco let out a light chuckle. "You've got a great sense of humor Linda. Has anyone ever told you that?" He didn't wait for an answer. "Now, come on, get suited up."

Linda sighed and stepped into the suit, feeling its weight settle around her. It was bulky, and the joints squeaked with every slight movement. Coco adjusted the straps and tapped a few buttons on the wrist console, causing the helmet visor to lower with a soft hiss. He strapped the *Quantum Herding Lance* onto her belt.

"Now, listen up," Coco said, pointing to the device strapped around her wrist. It was conveniently visible through a clear panel on her spacesuit sleeve. "The return beacon is synced with your *Shak*. Once the gig's done, and those space llamas are all nice and herded, just tap three times and hit the glowing button in the center." He pointed dramatically. "Bam! You'll be transported right back here. Easy as pizza."

Linda eyed the beacon warily. "And what happens if I lose the *Shak*?"

Coco's expression turned serious. "I don't see how you could, but you really don't want to lose it. Teleporting would be... problematic." He gave her a reassuring pat on the shoulder. The vagueness of his response did nothing to comfort her.

After ensuring that Linda was securely suited up, Coco led her to the gig transporter; a platform that looked like it had been cobbled together from spare parts, with wires hanging loosely and a few lights flickering uncertainly. He gestured for her to step onto it.

"Alright Linda, this is it," Coco said, giving her an encouraging smile. "Just remember: keep calm, don't let the llamas bully you, and for the love of the cosmos, *don't lose your Shak*."

Linda took a deep breath and stepped onto the platform, her heart pounding. Coco pressed a series of buttons on the control panel, and the transporter began to hum loudly, a shimmering light enveloping Linda.

"See you on the other side!" Coco called, giving her a thumbs-up just as the world around her blurred and she was whisked away to the gig.

Linda's last thought before everything went white was that she really hoped space llamas were less terrifying than they sounded.

6

Llama Llama Space-O-Rama

"They floated like celestial whispers... majestic, aloof, and very nearly the death of me."

— Commander Axton Starforge,
Steel Hearts: Echoes of Andromeda, S4E26

Space llamas aren't your average intergalactic livestock. For one, their fluffy, glitter-coated fur sparkles faintly in starlight. An evolutionary quirk that somehow both camouflages them against the blackness of space and makes them look like they've just stumbled out of a cosmic disco. Their eyes are huge, glossy, and perpetually judgmental. They gaze upon all things with the air of a creature that knows it's better than you. Floating elegantly in zero gravity, they bob through the void as if born to mock the very laws of physics that bind mere mortals.

Despite their serene, almost regal appearance, space llamas are notorious for their completely irrational tempers. One moment they're peacefully munching on invisible stardust, and the next they're stampeding in every possible direction because one of them mistook a floating rock for a 'space predator'. Herding them is an absurd blend of patience, agility, and the kind of inner screaming only seasoned space ranchers can maintain while outwardly appearing calm.

And then there's the spit. These aren't your garden-variety excretions. Space llama spit is neon-colored, physics-defying goo that, when launched, seemed to take personal offense to all frictionless surfaces. It clings with malicious persistence, slowly encasing its victim in a glowing, sticky cocoon. Herding them is less about skill and more a sanity test, as you attempt to coax llamas into compliance while your body becomes a human glowstick one gooey glob at a time.

Linda materialized into the heart of chaos. Instantly, the sensation of weightlessness hit her. It was as if her body had forgotten how to exist. Her arms and legs drifted aimlessly, untethered from the familiar pull of gravity. There was no up, no down, just the endless expanse of space enveloping her from every direction. Her stomach gave a slight lurch, a reaction to the sudden disconnect between what her brain expected and what her body was now experiencing.

For a moment, it felt surreal, like being suspended in a dream. The cold vacuum wrapped around her, pressing in on her suit with an eerie silence. There was no wind, no air to move through, only the faint vibrations of her own breath echoing inside her helmet. Even her own movements seemed distant, as if she were watching herself from afar. Every action was slower, softer, like swimming through invisible, weightless water.

Linda looked around, wide-eyed, taking in the bizarre beauty of her surroundings. Sparkling llamas floated lazily in all directions, their glittering fur shimmering under the light of distant stars. One llama, its large, disdainful eyes narrowing, seemed to be silently condemning her presence.

The sensation of drifting aimlessly through space was disorienting yet oddly freeing. She kicked her legs experimentally, trying to push herself forward, but there was no resistance. No friction. Every slight movement sent her spinning one way or another. Her body was its own small satellite. Her limbs moved slower than expected, disconnected from the instinctive responses gravity had trained her for.

She reached for her *Shak*—a small, reassuring weight still wrapped around her wrist—and gave it a quick pat. At least *that* was still in place. Everything else was out of her control. Her stomach did another nervous flip as she twisted in midair, accidentally spinning herself upside down, or was it right-side up? In space, it was impossible to tell.

She closed her eyes for a brief second, letting the odd sensation of floating settle over her, hoping the vertigo would subside. It wasn't exactly terrifying, but it was unlike anything she'd ever experienced. Liberating, sure. But also deeply unsettling, like free-falling into infinity.

"Alright, Linda. You got this," she muttered to herself. The words seemed to disappear as quickly as they were spoken, lost in the vacuum around her. Her breath fogged up the inside of her visor, a small reminder that she was still, at least, tethered to her suit and not completely lost in the void.

Her heads-up display pinged the distant outline of a dome-capped asteroid, a red marker highlighting a potential airlock. To the right of her vision, the number twenty-four blinked in ominous crimson digits.

"Alright llamas... let's do this," Linda muttered under her breath. But before she could figure out how to wrangle the herd, a loud, cosmic bleat sounded. Suddenly, the entire flock erupted in a zero-gravity stampede. Space llamas darted off in every possible direction, floating with all the grace of disgruntled ballet dancers.

She lunged for one, but their glittery fur was deceptively slippery, like trying to grab hold of a greased-up nebula. A particularly smug llama spun mid-air, and with pinpoint precision, spat a glob of neon goo right onto her visor. The goo spread, blurring her vision, and as she attempted to wipe it away, the substance clung more stubbornly than an ex-boyfriend at a class reunion.

Her communicator crackled to life. "Linda, you okay out there?" Coco's voice came through, laced with static.

"One of them spit on me. I can barely see," Linda growled, batting away another llama that drifted by, nonchalantly attempting to nibble on her spacesuit.

"No biggie. Just be sure to... *crackle*... and it'll come right off," Coco's voice trailed off into static.

"What? I didn't catch that!"

"I said... *crackle*... be sure to... *crackle*... ing..."

Silence.

"Fantastic," Linda muttered as a nearby llama seemed to side-eye her, its eyes glinting with the unmistakable satisfaction of an animal that knew its spit was now her problem.

Just as she was contemplating her next move, a tiny, ridiculous wiper blade arced across her visor, smearing the goo further but offering a partial view. In the blur of neon, one llama drifted above her, staring down with the languid grace of a creature indifferent to the idea of gravity, or Linda, for that matter.

"How am I supposed to move around?" Linda grumbled, her gaze locked on the airlock in the distance. She glanced down at her suit, half-expecting it to come with an instruction manual conveniently tucked away somewhere. No such luck. The suit was sleek, high-tech, and utterly baffling.

"Alright, think. How hard can it be to control a fancy space suit?" she muttered.

Linda lifted her right arm experimentally, half expecting the suit to follow her movement. Instead, it did nothing. She kicked her leg out, waved her arms, even tilted her head, all to no effect. "What is this? A full-body space coffin?" she grumbled, feeling like a fly trapped in zero-G amber.

She floated awkwardly for a moment, her limbs drifting in slow motion, as the sparkling llamas lazily swam through space around her. One of them, eyes wide and critical, flicked its ear at her as if to say, "Figure it out already".

"Great. So, random flailing isn't going to get me anywhere," she muttered, trying to remember what Coco had said about the suit: "Oh, it's easy."

"Very useful Coco, thanks for the help."

She closed her eyes and took a deep breath. *How do you go forward?* she thought.

Immediately, the suit responded. With a smooth, effortless motion, it propelled her forward, gliding through space like a fish through water. Linda's eyes shot open. "Oh!" she blinked, momentarily disoriented by the sudden acceleration. "Okay, okay. Think, don't move," she whispered to herself.

Encouraged by this newfound discovery, she experimented further. *Stop.* Instantly, the suit obeyed, halting her movement with surprising precision. "Alright, not bad. Let's try turning."

She thought about rotating to the left, but only slightly. The suit gently spun her in the desired direction. "Yes! Now we're getting somewhere." A grin spread across her face as she finally began to feel in control.

Of course, she wasn't *completely* in control. As she drifted forward, a llama floated into her path. Panicking, she thought, *Dodge!* The suit jerked her sideways, but in her haste, she overcorrected. Suddenly, she was spinning wildly, tumbling end over end, her vision filled with nothing but a blur of stars, llamas, and glitter.

"Not again!" she groaned, trying to calm herself. She closed her eyes and concentrated hard on the word: S*top.* Slowly, the suit complied, bringing her tumbling to an awkward halt. Linda opened her eyes again to see the llama, completely unbothered by her chaotic flailing, floating serenely by.

"Great. Now I'm a cosmic tumbleweed," Linda muttered. She shook her head, frustrated. "Alright. Calm down. Just think... slowly."

She took another deep breath. *Forward. Slowly,* she thought, visualizing herself gliding forward at a measured pace. The suit responded immediately, moving her toward the distant airlock with a controlled grace that made her feel like she finally had the hang of it.

She practiced a few more maneuvers, growing more confident with each mental command. *Turn right.* The suit pivoted. *Stop.* The suit obeyed. A smug smile crept across her face. "Telepathic suit controls? Fancy."

Just as she began to relax into her newfound skill, another llama drifted into view. She tried to steer clear of it, *Gentle dodge,* but the llama had other ideas. It shot her a look of deep llama judgment before drifting even closer, forcing her to think, *Dodge harder.* The suit responded too enthusiastically, sending her careening into a spin once more.

"Ugh, not again!" she yelled, managing to stop herself just before she collided with the stubborn creature. The llama, apathetic, continued floating on its glittery way.

"Note to self: Overthinking is just as bad as overcorrecting," Linda sighed. She floated in place for a moment, staring at the distant airlock. "Okay, third time's the charm."

This time, she thought carefully about her next move. *Forward. Smooth and steady.* The suit propelled her with just the right amount of force, moving her toward the airlock without any sudden or chaotic spins.

Linda smiled as she glided through space, the stars lighting up the blackness around her. *Maybe I won't completely mess this up after all.*

Emboldened, she directed herself toward a pair of llamas floating gracefully; orbiting one another like binary stars in an eternal dance. As she approached, their wide eyes locked onto her with visible indignation. They clearly didn't appreciate a human intruding upon their cosmic ballet.

With a grimace, she unstrapped the *Quantum Herding Lance* from her belt, eyeing its buttons. Both buttons looked alarmingly similar. Allegedly, one was red, the other crimson. She squinted, not seeing any difference at all. *Why would they make them the same color? Who designs this stuff?* she thought before muttering. "Well, here goes nothing." She pressed the button closest to her thumb.

A loud crackle followed as an arc of blue electricity shot out from the tip of the lance, fizzling impressively in the vacuum of space. The llamas' ears perked up, their eyes widening, not in fear, but in what seemed like mild annoyance.

"Alright, let's do this," she murmured, her determination now as electric as the lance itself.

Mentally commanding her suit, she inched closer to the llamas, carefully this time. The suit obeyed, moving her forward at a controlled pace. She positioned herself between them and the distant red beacon, hoping to guide them back toward the airlock.

The llamas exchanged a glance, then looked back at her with expressions that clearly said, "Oh, really?"

She raised the lance with what she hoped was authority. "Let's move along now," she said, trying to sound confident.

One llama yawned.

She activated the lance, sending another crackle of electricity into the void. The llamas' eyes followed the sparks. They turned around slowly, their fluffy tails flicking as they began to drift in the general direction of the airlock.

"Ha! Gotcha," Linda whispered, a satisfied smile creeping onto her face.

Just then, one llama glanced back and, maintaining eye contact, spat a small glob of neon goo that floated lazily toward her. She easily dodged it, feeling triumphant. "Missed me!"

Her celebration was premature. The second llama, taking advantage of her distraction, had sidled up next to her and was nibbling on the edge of her suit. She felt a tug and looked down to see the creature chewing thoughtfully.

"Hey! Quit that!" She gently pushed the llama away, which responded by giving her a look of deep offense before finally drifting off toward the airlock.

The countdown on her HUD ticked down to twenty-two.

"Maybe I'm not so bad at this after all," she told herself, watching as the numbers decreased.

With renewed vigor, Linda zipped around the asteroid like a seasoned space wrangler, or at least someone who had given up entirely on retaining any semblance of dignity. In ones and twos, the sparkling llamas, after some reluctant bleating and a few annoyed glares, drifted back toward the airlock, like fluffy, glittery balloons tethered to cosmic stubbornness.

Eventually, the countdown showed one.

But that last llama? It was a rebel. It hovered stubbornly in place, its wide, devious eyes gleamed with either mischief or malice. Linda wasn't sure which. She tried everything. A gentle nudge with the *Quantum Herding Lance*. A slightly more aggressive zap. Even a firm, disapproving glare, which had the same effect as trying to scold a smug cloud of glitter. The llama just blinked at her, its expression disturbingly self-satisfied, as if it held some secret cosmic knowledge Linda was not privy to.

"Come on, buddy. Just move," Linda grumbled, giving the lance another spark in warning.

The llama blinked once, slowly, and with all the condescending grace of an intergalactic monarch dismissing a peasant, spat a massive glob of neon goo directly into her face. The spit spread like a liquid rainbow across her visor, completely obscuring her vision. And before Linda could even process the mess, the llama lunged forward and chomped down on her arm.

"Ow! What the—" Linda yelped as the bite knocked the lance out of her hand, sending it spinning into space. She barely had time to register the llama's unexpected aggression before alarms blared in her helmet.

WARNING! SUIT BREACH!

Her HUD exploded with red warnings as oxygen levels plummeted. Panic surged through her chest like an incoming tidal wave.

"Coco! I've got a breach, what do I do? Hello? COCO?!" Linda shouted, her voice cracking with fear.

OXYGEN LEVEL 82%

No response. Just the crackle of static in her ears.

Linda's heart pounded hard as her precious oxygen hissed into the void. The stubborn llama floated lazily in front of her, chewing on what remained of her sleeve with a smug, self-satisfied look. Her oxygen levels continued to drop.

OXYGEN LEVEL 45%

Sweat formed under her helmet, despite the cold rush of air escaping her suit. Vision was impossible, thanks to the thick coat of llama spit blurring everything. Without thinking, she raised her arm and swiped at the goo, only to realize her arm was now stuck to her visor like a neon glue trap. She yanked it away, peeling off just enough of the spit to regain a sliver of vision.

BREACH SEALED!

OXYGEN LEVEL 19%

The spit—disgustingly sticky as it was—had sealed the hole in her suit. Linda took a deep breath, her pulse began to steady. She wasn't going to die. Not yet, at least. But her lance was gone. Her eyes darted around in a panic before spotting it, spinning lazily in the distance, just out of reach.

With a grunt of effort, she visualized her movement. With that, her suit's thrusters sent her flying toward the drifting lance. She grabbed it and reoriented herself in the llama's direction.

"Alright," Linda muttered, gritting her teeth. "You wanna play rough? Let's play rough."

This time, she wasn't messing around.

She raised the lance and prepared to deliver a controlled zap. However, fate, ever the prankster, had other plans. She'd grabbed the lance the wrong way around. Without thinking, she pressed the nearest button. Had she been any other sentient species in the galaxy, she would have noticed that the button she pressed was not red, but crimson.

A deafening blast of energy erupted from the lance, and before Linda could blink, the rebellious llama was vaporized into a puff of glittery particles. One moment, it had been there, floating like the world's most glamorous balloon. The next, it was cosmic dust, scattered across the stars.

Linda's jaw dropped as she stared at the empty space where the llama had been.

The countdown hit zero.

GIG FAILED!

"You've got to be kidding me," she groaned, floating aimlessly in the aftermath. But for the first time since her chaotic ordeal had begun, Linda allowed herself a moment to breathe, and to take in the cosmic view around her.

The asteroid field stretched out into infinity, punctuated by swirling clouds of space dust that glimmered like forgotten dreams. Distant stars shone in the vast blackness, their light flickering through the glittering remnants of the vaporized llama, as if the universe was quietly mourning its loss. Behind it all, the Milky Way dominated her vision, a massive, luminous river of stars, nebulae, and cosmic clouds stretching across the sky. It was breathtaking, a reminder of just how small she really was in the grand scope of things.

For a brief moment, suspended in the serenity of the universe, Linda felt the weight of her chaotic gig slip away. If she weren't floating in the middle of nowhere with llama goo plastered across her visor, her suit barely holding together, she might've even found the moment beautiful.

With a sigh, she strapped the lance back onto her belt, tapped her *Shak* three times and pressed the button. The world around her shimmered, the galaxy blurring as the white light consumed her. And just like that, she disappeared into the void.

Linda stumbled off the transporter pad, her suit still dripping with neon-colored goo clinging to her like a bad memory. Her legs wobbled beneath her as the sudden return to gravity hit her like a freight train. With a groan, she yanked off her helmet, her hair springing out in all directions, resembling a cosmic porcupine.

Coco stood nearby, arms crossed. His frown was deep enough to suggest genuine concern. That is, until his dry voice cut through the moment.

"When I told you not to press the crimson button, did you think that was just a *suggestion*?" he asked, voice dripping with mockery.

Linda, still trying to regain her balance, shot him a sharp glare. "I told you both buttons looked *exactly* the same to me. Crimson, red, what kind of sadist designed that?" She swiped a glob of goo from her face and flung it at the floor, where it splattered pathetically.

Coco snickered, unable to hold back the grin. "Oh, I thought you were *joking!*" He paused to catch his breath, and with a dramatic sigh, added, "Well, congratulations, you completed your first gig. I mean, technically you *failed*, but completing in failure is *still* completing! So... good job?"

Linda threw her helmet to the ground, sending a satisfying clang reverberating through the room. "Seriously, Coco. I vaporized the last llama. It was like, *poof*, gone. You couldn't have warned me about that?"

Coco shrugged, the corner of his mouth twitching in a failed attempt to stifle more laughter. "Well, I *did* say not to press the crimson button, but here we are. On the bright side, you've still got all your limbs, and hey, now you know exactly what happens when you hit the wrong button on a *Quantum Herding Lance*. Call it a lesson."

Linda rolled her eyes. "Great."

As she peeled off the top half of her suit, more neon goo dripped onto the floor, leaving colorful puddles in her wake. Coco stared at the mess, making no move to help. Instead, he tapped his communicator and leaned back casually, his usual smirk returning.

"So, what's next?" Linda asked, already dreading the answer. She looked down at her arm where the llama had bit her. The skin was cracked and bright red.

"Well," Coco said, dragging out the word. "Your gig report's going to say you were *very* hands-on with the llamas. And by hands-on, I mean you atomized one, so... probably not a great review. But hey! The good news is that there are always more gigs!"

Before Linda could muster a response, a nearby monitor flickered to life with an obnoxious *beep-beep-beep*. The screen, in all its glitchy, low-resolution glory, displayed the bright logo of StellarGigs alongside a line of text scrolled onto the screen.

WELCOME BACK, WORKER LINDA!

REVIEW TIME

GIG SCORE: ★

"One-star? What does that even mean?" Linda asked, frowning in confusion.

Coco nodded sympathetically. "Each gig gets rated between one and five stars. Five stars is the goal. Anything below four, and StellarGigs hits you with a penalty. They deduct GigCreds from your account."

"You've got to be kidding me," Linda muttered, incredulous.

Coco shook his head. "Nope. So, try to keep your scores at four-stars or above. If you hit five-stars, you even get a bonus. Definitely aim for that!" He smiled as if it were easy.

The screen blipped, now showcasing a glowing, spinning wheel of rewards.

PLEASE WAIT WHILE WE PROCESS YOUR BONUS!

"Bonus?" Linda blinked. "For *failing*?"

Coco grinned, leaning in. "Ah yes, the failure bonus. It's usually something pretty neat. Just spin the wheel."

With an exaggerated sigh, Linda tapped the screen. The reward wheel spun with a flourish, the lights on it flickering so wildly it threatened to give her a headache. After a few suspenseful seconds, it slowed, finally landing on...

Cosmic Llama Stickers: Colorful Space Llama Stickers that you can Stick on Anything!

"What? So, like... regular stickers?" Linda asked, eyebrows raised.

Coco, barely containing his laughter, nudged her playfully. "That's a great reward! You can decorate your room!"

"Wow, amazing," Linda replied, dripping with sarcasm. She grabbed the helmet from the floor and shoved it into Coco's arms. "Here, you hold onto this. Maybe next time *you* can figure out which button is crimson."

She trudged away from the transporter bay. Coco watched her go, a faint chuckle still on his lips. "Hey, Linda," he called after her, "next time, aim for at least two-stars. Maybe you'll win a free dessert!"

Linda didn't bother to respond. She'd had enough of space llamas and failure bonuses for one day. All she wanted at that moment was to get back to her shoebox of a room and sleep forever.

7

Debt and Taxes

"We chart the stars, fight the wars, and love like fire in a vacuum. And in the end, the void doesn't even blink."

— Commander Axton Starforge,
Steel Hearts: Echoes of Andromeda, S5E2

When Linda woke up, she groggily checked the time on her *Shak*. The display showed 31:28, whatever that meant. When she had gone to bed, it had shown 21:50.

Great, this thing's broken, she thought.

She slipped out of bed and stretched until her fingertips grazed the ceiling and her nose hovered millimeters from the wall. "Ah yes, the *deluxe* experience. All the charm of a broom closet," she muttered.

With no real idea of what was going on or when her next gig would appear, she decided to play it safe. Linda swapped out her loungewear for the more formal uniform. She figured it was better to be ready for the unexpected, especially in a place where her future could consist of literally anything.

Without any particular destination in mind, Linda decided it was time to explore the station and get a sense of its layout. She left her room and wandered down quiet, dimly lit corridors, her footsteps echoing softly off the metal walls. The station's labyrinthine design made it easy to get turned around, and she found herself weaving through a maze of hallways that seemed intentionally designed to confuse even the most seasoned workers. Just as she was considering turning back, a flickering sign caught her eye:

"The Archive of Anticipated Needs".

Curiosity piqued, she pressed the button beside the door. It creaked open with a shudder, releasing a small puff of stale air, as if the room itself were exhaling after ages of holding its breath. Inside was a cavernous space lined with towering shelves, overflowing with papers and forms. Some stacks were so high and chaotically arranged that it looked like they might collapse at any moment. Faded labels on the shelves read absurd and convoluted titles: *"Form Z-994: Tentative Requisition for Nebula Repositioning"*, *"Form A-72: Galactic Time Clock Appeal"*, *"Form Q-37: Catastrophe Justification Worksheet"*. None of it made any sense to her.

Linda took a tentative step inside, her eyes drawn to the shelves, which seemed to shift and rustle on their own, as though alive. As she approached one particularly cluttered aisle, a form suddenly lifted itself from a stack, hovered in the air for a moment then drifted down into her hands as if it had chosen her.

"Form W-12B: New Employee Orientation Confirmation," she read aloud, blinking in surprise. The room knew exactly what she needed before she even knew it herself. It felt... alive, almost sentient. She could swear the shelves were watching her, waiting, anticipating her every move.

A soft, rhythmic tapping echoed from somewhere deep within the room, but she couldn't tell if it was distant machinery or the station settling. The forms rustled faintly, like whispers. The archive seemed to react to her presence. A shiver ran down her spine, not from fear, but from the eerie precision of it all. The station felt so cold, indifferent most of the time, but here, it was like the paperwork itself was looking out for her.

Linda hesitated, then returned the form to the shelf. The stacks shifted slightly, opening a narrow path ahead of her, almost as if the room was inviting her to explore further. Her curiosity flared, but so did a sense of unease. The last thing she needed was to get caught up in some convoluted paperwork trap. She had a sense that the room could lead her deeper into StellarGigs' bureaucracy if she wasn't careful.

Out of one of the air vents, she could hear screaming. Like a man being burned alive. The screams rose, cracked into a sob, then suddenly cut off—snuffed out as if someone had flipped a switch. A moment later, the air carried the faint whiff of ozone and day-old coffee.

"Not today," she muttered, backing out of the archive. The door slid shut behind her with a disappointed sigh.

She continued her exploration. A few more turns down the winding hallways led her to a different door, this one marked *"Worker Recreation Room"*.

"Now we're talking," Linda said.

When she stepped inside, she found the place surprisingly empty. Considering how busy the station had been when she first arrived, she had expected the recreation room to be buzzing with activity. Instead, it was eerily quiet. Two insect-like creatures sat at a table in the corner, their antennae twitching occasionally as they chatted quietly. Across from them, a large, overstuffed creature that looked like a cross between a bloated chicken and a reptile with a skin condition, sprawled across a sofa, snoring loudly, its beak open wide.

The room was an odd clash of intergalactic styles, as if the designer had started with minimalism but couldn't resist throwing in touches of galactic chic for flair. The walls were sleek and bare, their matte surfaces almost unsettling in their simplicity, broken only by the occasional holographic poster advertising various gig accomplishments. The posters flickered annoyingly in vibrant, neon colors. Their garish brightness offered a stark contrast to the otherwise restrained aesthetic. One featured an overly enthusiastic worker giving a thumbs-up beneath the slogan, *"Just finished herding nebula oxen? Grab a snack!"*

The vending machine in the corner, a towering monstrosity, hummed softly as it offered an array of snacks, everything from *"Universal Protein Gel"* to something called *"Crispy Star Clusters"*, which glowed faintly in a way that made Linda unsure if they were a snack or a biohazard.

Considering she hadn't eaten in a while, she walked up to the strange machine. The monitor lit up with a prompt:

PLEASE SCAN CHRONOSHACKLE TO BEGIN.

She held her wrist up to the scanner, and after a short pause, there was a cheerful *ding!* The screen flashed:

WELCOME WORKER LINDA.

PLEASE MAKE YOUR SELECTION.

To her surprise, the list of items shifted to items she actually recognized. "Wow," she muttered in amazement. "Now this is more like it."

She quickly ordered a bowl of Ramen Noodles and something called Lunar-Zest Fizz, which looked like an off-brand lemon-lime soda.

THANK YOU FOR YOUR PURCHASE, WORKER LINDA!

THE AMOUNT OF ₲15 CHARGED TO YOUR ACCOUNT.

CURRENT BALANCE: -₲125

Linda scowled. "Wait, what? Where'd the other hundred and ten go?" Before she could fully process her spiraling finances, the screen changed again:

ACCOUNT OVERDRAWN!

PLEASE MAINTAIN A POSITIVE BALANCE OF Ǥ (GIGCREDS) BY NEXT PAYDAY OR ACCOUNT SHALL INCUR AN INTEREST RATE OF 21.7% PER GALACTIC WEEK.

"Great, a glitch," she muttered, letting out a long sigh. She picked up her food from the dispenser and found an open table. After sitting down, she looked closer at the food that she had just ordered. Everything looked okay, she could have sworn that the noodles had a slight bluish tint. *Probably just the light,* she concluded, though she briefly considered whether glowing noodles were a regular feature of intergalactic cuisine.

Linda was not what one would call a connoisseur of food. She was typically so broke that cheaper and larger portions were superior qualities in a meal than taste, or even nutritional value. She had cooked her fair share of ramen dinners in her time. The food sitting before her was ramen in the same way a 3D printed model of a strawberry was the same as an actual strawberry. Sure, they looked similar, and might fool someone at a glance, but no one was going to be deceived by the taste, or the plastic. If she had to describe it, the texture was like chewing on a rubber band, and the flavor... it was like chewing on a *rotten* rubber band.

The soda was slightly better, though it left a strange chemical aftertaste and burned the roof of her mouth with every sip. Still, she was too hungry to care. At this point, she just needed to eat something, so she powered through, taste be damned.

As she ate, she noticed above one wall, a large holo-screen silently playing a scene from the show Coco had mentioned. It was a space drama called *Steel Hearts: Echoes of Andromeda.* A crimson-lit battlefield flickered across the screen. Towering metal mechs clashed against a swarm of skittering insectoids the size of shipping containers. Plasma lances carved glowing arcs through the chaos, and flaming projectiles screamed across the smoke-choked sky. Explosions thundered behind a sleek mech painted with the emblem of a shattered heart.

Inside the cockpit, a woman with tear-streaked cheeks and smudged warpaint screamed over the comms. Her voice was visible only through hastily translated subtitles:

Rhys: *"If this is the end, tell Axton... I forgave him the moment he left the airlock!"*

Her fingers hovered above the self-destruct button, trembling.

The screen went black for a moment, then flared back to life. A second mech dropped from the clouds like a vengeful comet, slamming down beside her, shielding her with its bulk. Even with its plating scorched and patched, the mech's outline was unmistakable.

Echo: *"Death will not find you today. Not when our corporate oppressors still fight."*

Rhys: *"Echo! You shouldn't have come back."*

Echo: *"I never left, Rhys. I was just... delayed by destiny."*

He pivoted his mech toward the advancing wall of insectoid wrath, their glowing eyes like a thousand tiny points of death.

Echo: *"I'll draw their fire. Get out of here, Rhys. Go find Axton. And tell him..."*

A long pause as Echo flipped a series of glowing switches. Mechanical limbs unfolded from the mech's back like wings of war, etched with old battle scars.

Echo: *"...Tell him to stop being such a dramatic little plasma biscuit. You're the one who kept us all alive. You're the one who freed us from GalaxJobs!"*

Rhys: *"Echo, wait—"*

Echo: *"Rhys... I've always loved you... Even when I was suffering from... space amnesia."*

He launched into the heart of the swarm.

Echo: *"Chew on this... with a side of dessert!"*

The mech ignited with an unholy radiance as a massive surge of energy burst outward. Lasers fired in all directions, forming a glowing spiral of destruction. Enemy creatures screamed and scattered, their bodies erupting into incandescent shards as the screen shook under the force of the blast.

The screen went black with white lettering across the center:

"Stay tuned for the thrilling continuation right after this break."

A moment later, the battlefield was gone. It was replaced by a glossy-white set, where a gelatinous creature in a doctor's coat sat behind a desk with a circular mirror strapped to its head.

The creature's mouth moved enthusiastically as it gestured toward a glowing blue tube of something, while floating text beside it read:

"Do you suffer from Space Foot? Try AstroSalve. The only placebo recommended by 2 out of 7 unlicensed doctors!"

Linda blinked, her attention breaking like a glass, dropped onto a neutron star. The silence in the room seemed louder than anything the holo-screen could've played. She gave her head a slight shake, like she'd just woken from a dream that smelled faintly of napalm and canned pudding.

She focused back on reality, noticing Glorp come limping into the room. He went straight to the vending machine and ordered something green and wriggling. When he turned around, he almost dropped his dish as he spotted Linda staring at him from across the room. She offered a small wave of the hand, causing him to look over either shoulder, assuming the signal was for someone else. Again, Linda waved to him, gesturing toward the table. Reluctantly, Glorp limped over and sat down.

"Hey Glorp, how are you doing?" She looked at him with concern. "Did you hurt your leg or something?"

"Oh, uh... hi!" Glorp stammered, glancing everywhere but at Linda. "Umm, yeah, so... the bureaucrats, they, um... bit my leg? I think I might need some stitches. Maybe?"

"Oh wow, that's horrible. Why don't you go get that treated?"

"I don't get paid until, uh... tomorrow," Glorp mumbled, his gaze finally settling on what appeared to be a bloated green grub wriggling slightly on his plate. He stared at it for a moment, as if it might offer a solution to his problem.

"You mean StellarGigs doesn't pay for medical expenses? Even when you get hurt on one of their gigs?" She couldn't believe the audacity.

"Yeah, but that's, uh... okay. I'm not *that* hurt anyway. I'll *probably* live, uh... until tomorrow. No big deal," Glorp added with a shaky laugh. He took a bite out of the grub, and as his teeth tore into it, a thick stream of purple ooze leaked out, dribbling down his chin. He didn't seem to notice or care.

Linda blinked, trying to process both the conversation and the sight of what looked like alien jelly dripping from Glorp's face. "Hold on, Glorp. How long have you worked at StellarGigs?"

"Um... about, uh... three galactic years, I guess," Glorp said, as though that number might change at any moment.

Linda raised an eyebrow. "And you don't have *any* money saved up?"

Glorp gave a sheepish grin, looking anywhere but at her. "No. Everything here is, uh... pretty expensive."

"Expensive?" Linda's voice jumped in pitch. "Shouldn't your contract have run out by now?"

"Yeah, no... I mean... no," Glorp stammered, fiddling with the remains of his grub. "I... I signed up for, uh... one year. Well... that kind of got longer when I needed to, uh... borrow GigCreds."

Linda leaned forward, her brows furrowed. "What are you talking about?"

Glorp swallowed hard. "If your balance, gets too far in the negative... StellarGigs will, uh... wipe your debt, if you extend your contract."

Linda stared at him in disbelief. "So how long until your contract ends?"

"Um..." Glorp's eyes darted to the side, as if the answer might be hiding somewhere behind him. "I think... a little over two years from now?"

Linda's jaw dropped. "Wait. Your contract was for a year, but now you'll end up working five or more?"

"Yeah... I guess so," Glorp said with a nervous chuckle, wiping some of the purple ooze from his mouth with the back of his hand. "But, you know, it's, uh... not that bad."

"Oh my god, that's horrible," Linda blurted out. "That's *slavery*, Glorp!"

Glorp waved it off with a nervous chuckle. "Oh... no... it's okay. I mean, uh... it's not slavery. I get paid... just not very well."

"Are you getting paid, or are they just stringing you along, considering you're always running a negative balance?" she questioned him, a rising anger in her voice.

"No, it's fine, really. I really... I like it here. The vending machine has, uh... so many options." He gestured to his plate, where the rest of the wriggling grub sat, pulsating gently. "And, you know, the atmosphere is nice."

Linda stared at him, utterly baffled. "The atmosphere? Glorp, you can barely walk because a bureaucrat bit you, and you have to wait until tomorrow for medical treatment, because you can't afford it!"

"Oh... yeah. Those bureaucrats, they get, uh... a little cranky sometimes," Glorp said, nonchalantly taking another bite of his grub. More purple ooze dribbled down his chin. "But it's fine."

Linda sighed, rubbing her temples. "I can't believe this is real."

"So... why are you up so late?" Glorp asked, clearly eager to change the subject.

"What do you mean? I went to bed at 20:15 according to my *Shak*, but I think it's broken. It's been showing weird numbers." She glanced at her wrist. "Oh great, now it's showing 00:18. It was showing thirty something a little while ago."

"Yeah... the day here is actually thirty-two hours long. That's, uh... galactic standard," Glorp said, his voice barely above a whisper. "Sorry."

"Seriously?" Linda groaned, covering her face with her hands. "I have *no* idea what's going on here. Why doesn't anyone *tell* me anything?" She could feel her frustration bubbling up, tears of anger and confusion threatening to spill over.

"*I* just told you," Glorp mumbled.

Linda took a deep breath. "Thank you, Glorp. It's just... I didn't sign up for this. Or, at least, I didn't know I was..."

"Didn't you... read the fine print?" Glorp asked, genuinely curious.

"Glorp. Nobody reads the fine print."

"I mean, you really should," he added, looking around nervously.

Linda stared at him for a moment, then narrowed her eyes. "Did *you* read the fine print?"

Glorp looked down at his plate, suddenly very interested in the squirming grub. "No," he admitted meekly.

"So, what else don't I know about this place?" Linda's voice had an edge now, the weight of everything finally catching up to her.

"Well... since you didn't read the fine print..." Glorp glanced nervously at her across the table, "you probably don't know, um... that the timeframes, in all the contracts are in galactic standard."

Linda frowned, her heart sinking as a sense of foreboding crept in. "What do you mean?" she asked slowly, each word laced with caution.

"Well..." Glorp shifted uncomfortably in his seat, "a galactic year is probably longer than, uh... a year on your planet."

Her brow furrowed even deeper. "How much longer?"

Glorp scratched the back of his head, as if hoping to somehow make the answer appear. "Hmm, that's... hard to say. How many, uh... hours are in your days?"

"Twenty-four..."

"Right," Glorp nodded earnestly, like a teacher in over his head. "Well, we've got thirty-two hours in a day out here. Funny how hours are standard throughout the galaxy. There's a theory that an ancient race of, um... hyper-intelligent alarm clocks..."

"Glorp!" Linda snapped. "Focus!"

"Oh, right... So, uh... there are thirteen days in a week... thirteen weeks in a month... and thirteen months in a galactic year. We're, uh... kind of big on the number thirteen out here," he chuckled awkwardly, clearly hoping to lighten the mood. It didn't work.

Linda's stomach began to knot, the dread clawing at her insides. "And how long does that make a galactic year?"

Glorp's eyes wandered upward as if consulting an invisible abacus in the ceiling. "That's... about seventy-thousand hours per galactic year. Divided by your twenty-four..." He trailed off, frowning slightly as if he wished math could just vanish. "So, uh... that's a little more than... twenty-nine hundred Earth days... I think."

Linda's jaw dropped. Math had never been her strong suit, but she could estimate. "That's... that's like eight years." Her voice barely rose above a whisper as she stared at him, horror dawning in her eyes. "Wait... I'm stuck here for *sixteen* years?"

The room seemed to warp and tilt around her as the weight of the revelation hit her like an asteroid to the face. She could feel the blood draining from her cheeks, her hands going numb. "No... no, that's not possible. The recruiter said two years. That must've been Earth years. Why would they put galactic years in an Earth contract?"

Her mind raced, spiraling out of control as she tried to grasp the enormity of being stuck there on a floating tin can in space. Doing nothing but wrangling space llamas and unclogging wormholes for *sixteen* years. *Sixteen* years, far from everything she knew, all for some gig job she barely understood.

"I'm sure it's just a misunderstanding," she whispered, almost pleading with the universe to prove her right. But the rising panic told her otherwise.

Glorp, sensing the shift in her mood, fidgeted uncomfortably, his wide eyes darting from his grub to the table, to the floor, and back again. "Uh... yeah... well, they, um... do use galactic years in all the contracts. But, don't worry! Time flies when you're... doing... whatever this is. Right?" he offered, flashing a weak, nervous smile, as if the casual suggestion that sixteen years would somehow breeze by, might comfort her.

Linda stared blankly at the table, her heart pounding in her chest. The walls felt like they were closing in. "I didn't sign up for *sixteen years*," she whispered again, her voice shaking. She could feel tears burning at the corners of her eyes, but she blinked them back. She would not break down. Not yet.

"Linda?" Glorp's voice was soft, filled with the awkward concern of someone who didn't fully understand human emotions. "Are you okay?"

She swallowed hard, her mind spinning. Her fingers gripped the edge of the table as though holding on could somehow tether her to sanity. "There has to be a way out of this," she muttered, more to herself than to Glorp.

"Well," Glorp fumbled, his hands now nervously clutching his half-eaten grub. "You would need a lot of GigCreds to be able to do that... and, uh... well, most of us end up borrowing more GigCreds just to, you know... survive out here."

Linda blinked, her brain short-circuiting. "So, it's a trap? You can't ever get out?"

"Well..." Glorp hesitated, his eyes darting around the room. "Not unless you take a *lot* of extra gigs, and, uh... maybe win the Galactic Lottery or something... It's technically possible?"

Linda slumped back in her chair, her mind spinning. This wasn't a contract. This was a prison sentence. A sentence she'd signed herself up for without even knowing.

Her voice, when it finally emerged, was barely audible. "I'm trapped."

Glorp tried to offer a reassuring smile. "I like to think of it as an, uh... extended stay. Like one of those all-inclusive resorts, except instead of free drinks, uh... you get extra shifts. And instead of Blarnsball, there's the ever-present threat of wormhole accidents. You, uh... get used to it!"

Linda just stared at him, allowing the enormity of her situation to settle in. Sixteen years. Sixteen years of this madness. Maybe she'd laugh eventually. Right now, though, she was just trying not to scream.

Linda descended onto the promenade. It was quiet at this hour, the kind of quiet that magnified every footstep into an accusation. The wide causeway stretched beneath the higher entry level, its polished flooring reflecting the low glow of dormant shopfronts. Most of the stalls were shuttered, neon signs dimming to half-hearted shadows, when an announcement crackled over the speakers.

"Worker Celvin, please report to Human Resources. Worker Celvin, your presence is mandatory. Worker Celvin... failure to comply may result in additional fines."

The line fizzled into static, as though even the speakers were embarrassed to be repeating it for the thousandth time.

Who the heck is Celvin?

She lowered herself onto a bench in front of the window overlooking space. Above her, balconies and stairwells spiraled upward, climbing back toward the higher levels where she'd entered the previous day. It was like sitting at the bottom of a hollow throat, ringed with silent tiers. No voices, no laughter, no bargaining over glowing trinkets, just her own breathing and the faint buzz of an idle drone drifting by overhead.

The quiet pressed against her like recycled air, clean but used.

Even in the widest, most open part of the station, she felt the walls closing in. The emptiness only reminded her that this place wasn't hers. It may never be.

She rubbed her palms together and tried not to think about how much it resembled an empty office building after hours, the same dead hum, the same fluorescent chill.

"Oh, hey Linda," a voice drawled beside her, lazy as a radio that was slowly running out of power.

She jumped slightly as Lira, the green-skinned alien woman, slouched onto the bench, hair mussed, expression somewhere between half-asleep and barely conscious.

"How are things? Heard about the space llamas. Don't let it get to you. Nothing matters. Existence is meaningless..."

"Yeah, thanks Lira," Linda muttered.

Lira followed Linda's gaze upward, toward the higher levels disappearing into shadow. "I love coming to this place. It reminds me of my sister."

Linda turned to her. "Why?"

"She said open spaces made her feel safe. Said bad things couldn't find you if there was sky overhead." Lira rubbed at the circular patch behind her ear. "Guess she was wrong about that."

She hesitated, eyes flickering as if the thought had slipped. "She's... she's coupled now. Five children. Lives on my homeworld."

"That's nice," Linda said, looking back toward space. "I needed some open space. I feel like the station is crushing me."

"It will do that," she agreed, scratching behind her ear. "Small spaces are bad for the soul." She noticed Linda staring, so she tapped the patch lightly. "Softens those edges that are sharp."

"Sharp?"

"Sometimes the edges are inside." A half-smile ghosted across her face, equal parts confession and joke. "That's why so many of us choose to fly away."

"Fly away?"

"It's only an airlock away."

Linda wasn't sure if Lira was joking. She hoped she was. "Right... I don't think I'm there quite yet."

"Oh, okay then." Lira leaned back, eyes unfocused.

The two of them sat in silence, watching a drone sweep past the empty stalls, its single red eye blinking like a tired heartbeat.

"I'm used to small spaces," Linda said finally.

"Oh?"

"Back home I once had a job where I worked in a cubicle. Little beige boxes stacked under fluorescent lights. Rows and rows of them."

"I'd rather be atomized by a supernova." Lira shuddered, as if the idea physically hurt. "They forced you to work there?"

"What? No, I chose to. It was the only job I could find, and it paid the bills."

"So, you worked there because you had to. Doesn't sound like much of a choice," Lira said.

"I mean... when you put it that way."

"Did you sleep on your desk?"

"No, of course not. We worked during the week and had weekends off." Linda let out a small, humorless laugh. "Funny. I used to think I was a prisoner there. Now I'd give anything to sit in that little box again."

Lira tilted her head, studying her. "A prison's still a prison," she murmured.

Linda's laugh thinned out, collapsing into a breath. "Maybe. But at least I could leave."

"And go where?"

"Home mostly."

"Was your family there?"

"No." She hesitated. "There really wasn't anyone." She didn't mean to sound so small, but the words landed that way anyway

After a pause: "It sounds like you're better off in this reality. At least you have us. It's not much, but at least it's something."

Linda blinked, surprised by the warmth under the words. "That almost sounded optimistic."

"Optimism is against company policy."

Linda smiled before she could stop herself. The station still hummed with artificial silence, but beside her the emptiness felt shared—less a void, more a pause that might one day hold something like friendship.

8

Patch Me If You Can

"From a distance, a space battle looks like a symphony—lights dancing, engines flaring. Up close, it's just a song of screams and fire. The trick is learning to waltz while everything burns."

— Commander Axton Starforge,
Steel Hearts: Echoes of Andromeda, S3E7

Linda wandered the station in a daze, barely aware of how much time had passed. It could've been hours or maybe even minutes. Time felt slippery in a place where thirty-two-hour days were the norm. The station was slowly waking up around her, with people drifting into the common areas, rubbing their eyes and muttering.

"Oh, there you are!" Coco's voice broke through her fog. Linda turned to see him trotting toward her, his expression set to annoyance. "I've been looking all over for you."

"Sorry, I've just been, you know... walking around." She replied dreamily, still half-lost in thought.

Coco eyed her suspiciously. "Uh, did you sleep last night? You're looking a little... off."

"Kind of? Not really used to this whole thirty-two-hour day thing."

"Oh yeah, forgot to mention that," Coco said with a casual shrug, as though a glaring detail like that wasn't worth mentioning.

"Yeah, no worries," Linda sighed. "Glorp told me all about it... among other things." She trailed off, remembering the bizarre conversation with Glorp the night before.

"Oh yeah, Glorp died," Coco said suddenly, as if he were commenting on the weather.

Linda froze mid-step. "What!?"

"Yup. Got bit really bad on the leg. Turned into some kind of infection or whatever." Coco shook his head with the kind of sadness someone might reserve for spilling their coffee.

"Oh my god." Linda covered her face with her hands, struggling to hold back tears. "I was just talking to him."

"Yeah, those bureaucrats—filthy mouths on them," Coco said offhandedly. "Glad I dodged that gig. I mean, can you *imagine*?" He let out a small laugh.

Linda's breath hitched. "I can't believe he's really gone."

"Gone?" Coco glanced at her, noticing her welling eyes. "Oh, no, no! They got him up and running again."

"Wait... what?" Linda blinked, confused.

"Yeah, his *Shak* went off early this morning. Meds patched him up, revived him in medical. Poor guy though, added another three months to his contract for the trouble," Coco added with a sympathetic nod, as if *that* was the real tragedy.

"So... he's alive?" Linda pressed a hand to her chest, willing her racing heart to calm down.

"Yeah, well, last I heard at least." Coco smacked his forehead lightly, as if remembering something he'd almost forgotten. "Oh! I was supposed to take you to the gig office early today. Something about a special assignment. They sent you a message on your *Shak*, but... I'm guessing you don't exactly know how to check your messages?"

Linda looked down at the device on her wrist and noticed a small, blinking red light. She tapped it instinctively, and a hologram sprang to life above it, illuminating the space around her.

"Hey Linda! Got a *primo* gig for ya today!" The hologram showed GigChad-2000, larger than life, his voice dripping with faux enthusiasm. "Do me a solid and get here early, would ya? I need this gig done ASAP. Time's ticking, sweetheart! Don't wanna let the gig gods down, do ya?" The hologram blinked out of existence.

"GigChad-2000 is so cool," Coco murmured dreamily, clearly lost in thought.

"Yeah, he's... great," Linda replied flatly, her sarcasm barely concealed.

They entered the gig office at the exact same time as Lira. She was as out of it as ever, like she'd sleepwalked into the office. "Oh, hi again Linda. I was just thinking about the inevitability of death, and how..."

She trailed off just as GigChad-2000 rolled into view.

"Ladies!" GigChad-2000 boomed, his voice dripping with exaggerated enthusiasm. "Wow, look at you two! Ready to absolutely *crush* this gig or what? Wait, don't answer that. I already know. Of course you are! A couple of all-stars strutting into the office, look out folks!" He glanced around dramatically, as if there was an invisible crowd watching. "Guess what? You two power-houses are working together today. Isn't that *awesome*?!"

"Oh... yay," Lira replied, with all the excitement of a plant waiting for sunlight.

"That's the spirit!" GigChad-2000 chirped. "This one's gonna be *crazy* easy. Like, you'll finish it before you can say, 'Intergalactic bureaucracy is the worst!' You're probably wondering, 'Dude, why send two of us if it's gonna be that easy?' Am I right?" He leaned in, lowering his voice conspiratorially. "What can I say? I'm just looking out for my two *favorite* ladies. Think of this gig as a little mini vacation. You've totally earned it."

Linda blinked. "I've been here one day. And I failed my only other gig."

"I know, right? Total bummer. But hey, no hard feelings. No secret resentment on my part, *I swear!* Even the newbs need a breather every once in a while!" GigChad-2000 gave a wink, or at least, the robotic equivalent of one.

"So... what's the gig?" Linda asked, suspicion creeping across her face.

"Oh, did I not mention it yet? My bad! Here's the deets: You two are headed out to perform a simple, routine operating system upgrade on a Xeltrian Battlecruiser. Totally easy-peasy."

"Why do you need two of us for that?" Linda asked.

GigChad-2000's voice rose to saccharine levels of charm. "Well, you know, the Battlecruiser may—or may not, probably not, but maaaybe—be involved in a *small* space skirmish. And there may or may not be hostile forces onboard. But hey, you two are total pros! One of you updates the system, the other stands guard, *just in case*. Easy, right?"

Lira perked up, her eyes gleaming in a way that was more than mildly unsettling. "I *do* love shooting people in zero-gravity. The way the blood sprays... it's beautiful. Like watching a painting come to life in slow motion."

Linda stared at her, horrified, as she started inching slightly away from Lira.

"That's the spirit!" GigChad-2000 said. "Now, hold out your *Shaks*, you superstar go-giggers, you." He waved a sensor over the devices on Linda and Lira's wrists. They responded with two cheerful beeps. "There you go, ladies. Time is of the essence, so let's not dawdle! Time is money, right?" He beamed at them with a robotic smile, then somehow transformed his metal grippers into little finger guns. "*Pew pew*! Nah, just kidding. Get outta here, you knuckleheads!"

As GigChad-2000 rolled away, finger guns still raised in mock salute, Coco's grin stretched ear to ear. He turned to Linda, his eyes glistening with genuine emotion, maybe even tears. "I *love* him so much," he whispered, as if confessing the deepest truth of his existence.

Using the gig transporter was no less unsettling than it had been the first time. One moment, they were in a room full of ominous electrical hums and machine beeps, then the world went white, and suddenly they were on an alien spaceship, surrounded by strange machines. Fortunately, this time there was oxygen to breathe. A small mercy, considering StellarGigs had *neglected* to provide them with space suits. Small details, apparently.

They materialized in the most unsettling alien server room imaginable. The walls were a tangled mess of organic-looking cables that pulsed faintly, as if the room itself was alive. Servers hummed softly, their surfaces smooth and iridescent, with clusters of alien glyphs glowing dimly along their edges. The entire room had an eerie bioluminescent glow, casting everything in shades of green and blue, like they'd been transported inside a giant space jellyfish.

On the far wall of the room, a large window (or maybe it was a screen, it was hard to tell) displayed the outside of the ship, where a full-blown space battle was unfolding. A second ship hovered next to theirs, its design was sleek and angular. Bright bolts of white plasma arced between the two ships in a fiery exchange, the broadside volleys lighting up the darkness of space.

Though there was no sound (space being the silent void it was) the impacts on the hull reverberated through the ship, sending deep, bone-shaking vibrations up from the floor. Each plasma shot that hit its mark rattled the room like a far-off earthquake, the force rippling through Linda's boots and up into her legs, making the consoles and equipment in the room tremble. It was a stark reminder that even in the eerie quiet of space, the violence outside could still be felt. Each hit turned the ship into a giant tuning fork, humming with impending danger.

"Well, that looks promising," Linda muttered, glancing uneasily at the battle outside, a bead of sweat forming on her brow as she clutched her standard issue plasma rifle—*The PaciFire-10000*—firmly to her chest.

Lira, unfazed, stared out the window with mild interest. "At least it's pretty," she said, as plasma fire lit up the black void.

"Go do your thing, Lira," Linda urged. "I've never shot anyone, and I really don't want to start today. Honestly, I don't even know if I *can*."

"Don't worry, Linda. I set your *PaciFire* to its lowest setting."

"Like... stun?"

"Yeah, something like that," Lira replied casually, glancing back at the screen. "It's just a Vicarion ship. Entities that are controlled remotely from their home world. If they board, it'll just be drones. Nothing with a heartbeat."

Linda exhaled, half-relieved. "Okay, that's... reassuring."

Lira moved over to a terminal, her fingers gliding over the controls. The screen flickered to life, displaying streams of alien computer code scrolling rapidly down the display. "This'll only take a few minutes," Lira said, her tone almost comforting. "In the meantime, why not reflect on the vastness of the cosmos? Think about how small and insignificant you are. You could die right now, and nothing would change. The universe would carry on. Your life, utterly meaningless." She turned and gave Linda a serene smile. "Isn't that relaxing?"

"Not really," Linda muttered, crouching behind a row of humming machines that stood about four feet high. She gripped her rifle nervously, aiming it at the doorway in front of her, hoping against hope that no one would actually come through.

"Look how peaceful those ships are," Lira mused, gazing out the window. "Like seeds drifting on a breeze."

Linda squinted at the ships approaching. "Are those..."

"Boarding ships," Lira confirmed, without a hint of concern.

As if on cue, the ship's klaxons blared to life, the shrill noise reverberating through the room. Lira winced. "That's loud. Bad for my relaxation." A deep shudder rippled through the ship as the boarding crafts latched onto the hull.

Lira, entirely unbothered by the impending invasion, casually turned toward Linda. "Have you ever been to Velura-7?" she asked, as if they weren't moments from being boarded. "I went once. The beaches are... indigo. I never really figured out why. No one seemed to know. Weird, right?"

Linda stared at her, dumbfounded, gripping her rifle a little tighter. "Yeah, that's really weird, Lira."

The terminal emitted a shrill, unsettling noise. "Oh, that's not good," Lira said, almost too casually.

"What!?" Linda asked, her alarm rising.

"The system doesn't like what I'm doing," Lira replied, still fiddling with the controls. "It's trying to hack into our *Shaks* and reprogram our return beacon."

"It can do that?" Linda's voice was full of disbelief.

"Oh yes, quite easily," Lira said with a detached air. She glanced around the room, unfazed by the chaos. "Hey, Linda? You see that glowing blue cube on your right? The really pretty one?"

Linda glanced over and spotted a pulsing cube about five feet away, its soft hum in sync with its glow. "This thing?" she asked, pointing.

"No, the other glowing blue cube..." Lira said dreamily.

Linda looked around. Seeing no other cube, she decided Lira was being annoyingly sarcastic. "Okay, what do you want me to do with it?"

"Just grab it and pull really hard."

Linda sighed, placing her rifle down. She gripped the cube with both hands and tugged, struggling for a moment before it finally came loose with a loud *pop.* The cube, mildly cool to the touch, continued to glow menacingly in her hands.

"Problem solved," Lira said, turning back to her terminal without missing a beat.

Linda stared at the cube for a second before absently slipping it into her pocket and picking up her rifle again. Just then, a loud crash echoed from outside the door.

Just great, Linda thought, aiming her rifle toward the doorway.

Linda had thought the swishing doors back on the station were fast, but compared to the blink-and-you-miss-it speed of the Xeltrian Battlecruiser's doors, they were practically sluggish. The sudden, jarringly quick opening of the doorway caught her off guard. Her already frayed nerves got the best of her. Her finger twitched, and a ball of white-hot plasma shot across the room, striking the intruder squarely in the head.

After years of watching reruns of old sci-fi shows, Linda half-expected the figure to stop and crumble to the floor in dramatic fashion. What she didn't expect was for the head to liquify on impact—melting into a grotesque slurry of metal, bone, blood, and brain matter. It was like watching an overstuffed balloon filled with green slime burst. The wall behind the figure now sported a smoking, blackened hole, glowing red around the edges, completely drenched in the stinking green goo, as if someone had flung a bucket of it at the wall.

"Oh my god!" Linda gasped, staring at the mess. "Why does that drones' insides look so... biological?"

Lira, still working at the terminal, barely glanced up. "Hmm? Oh, that was a Xeltrian."

"A *what?*" Linda stammered, her shock intensifying.

Just then, the terminal gave a cheerful *ding.*

"Oh goodie. All done," Lira said, completely unfazed.

Before Linda could even form a response, the world flashed to white as they were teleported back to the station.

"Welcome back—" Coco began.

"You said the rifle was set to *stun*!" Linda interrupted, her voice trembling with anger.

"I said it was on the lowest setting," Lira corrected calmly.

"*That* was the lowest setting?!"

"Of course. Anything higher would've taken out the whole ship. Pretty neat, huh?"

"I've... never shot anyone before..." Linda's voice wavered, the reality of what had just happened sinking in.

"Don't worry about it. It was more Cephalopod than Mammal," Lira offered nonchalantly.

"That's supposed to make me feel better?"

"Sure. Haven't you ever eaten squid? Same thing, really."

"I'm pretty sure the squid I ate wasn't smart enough to build an intergalactic warship!" Linda shot back, incredulous.

"Maybe it could have. If you hadn't eaten it," Lira said with a shrug.

Linda shot her an angry look, but before she could say anything, the nearby monitor flickered to life with its familiar *beep-beep-beep*. The bright logo of *StellarGigs* appeared, followed by a line of text:

WELCOME BACK, WORKERS LIRA AND LINDA!

REVIEW TIME

GIG SCORE: ★★★★

Linda looked at the display confused. "Better than last time, I guess. How do you even get five-stars?"

"It probably helps to not shoot things in the head." Lira deadpanned.

"Ladies, please," Coco intervened.

The screen went blank, only to be replaced by a glowing, spinning wheel of rewards.

PLEASE WAIT WHILE WE PROCESS YOUR BONUS!

"This is my favorite part." Coco grinned like a child on Christmas morning. "Go ahead, Linda, do the honors."

"This better be less useless than the *failure* bonus." Linda said.

With a resigned sigh, she tapped the screen. The reward wheel whirred to life, lights flashing with all the enthusiasm of the big bang. After what felt like an eternity, it slowed, flickering past various prizes until it finally settled on...

Time-Shift Coupon: Redeem for One Hour in the Future!

"Oh, great. So, like a nap, without all the benefits of rest," Linda muttered, her exasperation reaching new heights. "I need a shower," she declared, storming out of the room.

9

Today's Special: Reality

"I've drifted in the dark long enough to know that sometimes the light at the end of the tunnel is just the glow of another reactor core, moments before it fails."

— Commander Axton Starforge,
Steel Hearts: Echoes of Andromeda, S1E24

Linda trudged into the company cafeteria, her stomach growling as she spotted Coco waving at her from a large, circular table in the center of the room. The air was thick with the smell of alien food. A scent somewhere between burnt toast and rubber, with a hint of something she couldn't quite place but hoped wasn't toxic. She had been walking around the station for what felt like hours, trying to shake off the unease of the last gig. The oddity of shooting someone, or *something* that was sentient, still weighed heavily on her, despite Lira's casual dismissal of the whole affair.

The cafeteria buzzed with workers of all shapes and sizes, many of them clutching bizarre-looking food trays, talking in low murmurs. The vending machines along the walls hummed, displaying their usual array of strange snacks: *"Universal Protein Gel"*, *"Crispy Star Clusters"*, and a suspiciously looking green tinted meat type dish that was simply labeled *"Soylent"*. Out of the corner of her eye, she noticed another vending machine near the back of the room flickering in and out of existence.

It appeared to be a beverage dispenser, proudly displaying a banner that read, *"Enjoy an Ice-Cold Beverage... If You're Lucky!"* One second it was there, solid and functional, the next it shimmered like a mirage, flickering out of existence before snapping back to life. Linda stared at it, squinting to read the drinks on display:

Energizing Moon Juice – Extracted from the most energetic craters on the first moon of Karnathis-9. *Now with Less Gamma Radiation!*

Time Freezing Smoothie – A creamy blend of space-time fractals and temporal berries. *When You Need a Breaktime from Breaktime!*

Quantum Quencher – Hydrates you in both this dimension and at least two others. *Disclaimer: Exact taste may vary depending on the space-time continuum.*

Linda shook her head, deciding the specialty drinks weren't worth the risk. Not today. With a sigh, she scanned her wrist at the regular vending machine and ordered some relatively safe French toast with a side of bacon. ₲20 deducted from her company account, sinking her balance even further into the negative.

As her food dispensed, she glanced back at the beverage dispenser—just in time to see it disappear again, along with a very confused worker who had been standing in front of it, mid-order.

She grabbed her food and headed over to the others. On her way, she spotted an alien creature that looked like a cross between a dragonfly and a cockroach. It was wearing a white t-shirt over its carapace, the words "Save Celvin" printed in bright red letters.

What happened to Celvin? Linda wondered for a moment before quickly losing interest.

As she approached the table, Linda noticed Coco was already digging into a bowl of something unrecognizable. Zorb sat hunched over his tablet, scrolling through what looked like a series of performance reviews, his expression permanently fixed in a scowl. Lira was there too, staring blankly into her cup, as if the universe itself held no meaning.

To Linda's surprise, there were two new faces at the table. One was a grizzled, older worker she hadn't met before. His tired eyes spoke of years (no, decades) of working for StellarGigs. His uniform was faded, the logo peeling away at the edges, like it had given up long before he had. The other was a small, bright-eyed alien, jittering with energy. Its fur—bright and fluffy—stood in stark contrast to the weary atmosphere of the room.

"Hey, Linda!" Coco called out; his mouth half-full of something that resembled noodles but probably wasn't. "How's it going?"

Linda slid into a seat next to Coco and across from Lira, her eyes drifting to the two unfamiliar faces. "Who are these two?"

"Oh, right!" Coco beamed, gesturing to the older worker. "This is Rilo, one of the veterans around here. He's been with StellarGigs for... what is it, eight galactic years?"

Rilo grunted, his voice low and gravelly. "Nine, but who's counting? Doesn't make much of a difference." He took a long sip from his cup, the smell of burnt rubber wafting from it. "StellarGigs is always the same, year after year."

"And this," Coco pointed to the jittering furball, "is Beb! Another new recruit. He's been recovering in medical for the last couple weeks"

Beb's eyes lit up at the mention of his name, his tail wagging enthusiastically. "Hi! It's so nice to meet you! I've only been here for a few weeks, but I can already tell this place is super exciting!"

Linda blinked. "Exciting? That's... one way to describe it."

"Oh, yeah!" Beb chattered, bouncing slightly in his seat. "I mean, sure, it's tough sometimes, but every day is a new adventure! I heard your first gig was with space llamas! That must have been so cool!"

Coco chuckled. "Yeah, Linda's had quite the start."

Linda forced a smile, still feeling the weight of that one-star score hanging over her. "Yeah, cool. Really cool. You know, except for the fact that StellarGigs seems designed to keep us in a constant state of barely surviving."

Her comment earned her a few looks, particularly from Rilo, who let out a low chuckle. "You're already figuring that out, huh? You kid, are a quick study."

Linda glanced at him, her brow furrowing. "What do you mean?"

Rilo leaned back in his chair, his tired eyes locking onto hers. "This whole system... it's rigged. We're all stuck here, no matter how hard we work. The gigs, the bonuses, the scores, it's all designed to keep us tethered."

"That's your opinion Rilo. I quite enjoy my job here at StellarGigs," Coco interjected.

"Well, that's just you Coco. Company man through and through," Rilo replied, shaking his head.

Linda frowned. "But there has to be a way out. What about finishing the contract? That's what they told me. Two galactic years and I'm done."

"Yeah, do your job and stop complaining," Coco said.

Rilo shook his head slowly. "That's what they tell everyone. Then you start racking up GigCred debt, taking more gigs to cover living expenses, or you get hit with penalties for scoring too low on a gig. The years add up, and before you know it, you're stuck here forever."

Beb, who had been jittering with excitement, tilted his head in confusion. "I don't know... I mean, maybe if we all just worked a little harder, we'd see five-stars, right? And if we saved our GigCreds, we could pay off our debts. StellarGigs wants us to succeed. They wouldn't keep us here on purpose."

Zorb, who had been silent up to this point, snorted. "Please, Beb. Save the optimism for the recruitment ads. You're too new to see the bars of your cage. This isn't a job. It's a life sentence."

Linda glanced around the table. Coco was busy eating, his usual sunny demeanor intact, while Zorb continued to scroll through his tablet, grumbling about something incomprehensible. Lira stared into her cup, her expression as detached as ever.

"You guys really think it's all just a trap?" Linda asked, her voice filled with frustration.

Rilo shrugged. "It is what it is. Some of us are just better at accepting it."

As he said this, Linda noticed the beverage dispenser reappearing in the background, its existence seemingly a matter of pure chance. A worker standing in front of it pumped their fist in triumph as a drink finally dispensed, just as the machine flickered out of existence again, leaving the worker holding a fistful of nothing. The worker stood there dumbfounded, staring at their empty hand.

Coco, trying to lighten the mood, chimed in. "We have a place to live, meaningful work, and great food to eat. What more could you want?"

Zorb gave him a withering look. "Food? This?" He gestured to the sludge on his tray. "This isn't food. It's overpriced nutrient slop."

Coco waved him off, still grinning. "Aw, come on! Look on the bright side. We get to go on a lot of cool adventures!"

Linda leaned forward, her frustration bubbling to the surface. "So, that's it? Everyone just accepts it? No one tries to change anything?"

Beb's tail stopped wagging, his face full of earnest confusion.

Rilo sighed, running a hand through his graying hair. "StellarGigs controls everything. The gigs, the pay, the contracts. You could try to push back, but it's like spitting into the wind. Just makes a mess. You start down that road, you'll notice your gigs just keep getting more dangerous. Can't cause a ruckus if you aren't around anymore."

Linda's mind raced. She had felt trapped ever since her first gig, but hearing it laid out like this. Hearing that even the long-timers like Rilo had resigned themselves to this fate, made her stomach twist. She turned to Lira, who had been unusually quiet during the whole conversation.

"What about you?" Linda asked, narrowing her eyes. "You've been here long enough. Don't you think this is all a little... wrong?"

Lira didn't even look up from her cup. "We all make our choices," she muttered, her voice barely audible. "You'll get used to it. There's always the airlock."

Linda felt a chill run down her spine.

Coco, ever the optimist, leaned in with a grin. "Come on, guys! You need a more positive attitude, it's one of the top five most valued worker personality traits. Maybe on our next gigs we'll all earn a five-star and collect on that big bonus!"

Zorb scoffed. "Five-stars? Please. You've got a better chance of getting sucked into a black hole."

Linda stared at her tray, her thoughts spinning. The system was rigged. She knew that now. But what bothered her even more was the fact that everyone around her seemed to know it too, and yet they accepted it. No one fought back. No one tried to change things.

Why is everyone so complacent? It's like they've all just given up.

She couldn't accept that.

"There has to be a way out," she muttered, more to herself than to anyone else.

Rilo chuckled, his voice low and resigned. "Only way I know is what Lira here suggested. If there is another way... well, good luck finding it, kid."

The conversation drifted after that, with Coco telling an absurd story about a gig involving space slugs and malfunctioning gravity generators, while Zorb grumbled about his latest performance review. Beb listened with wide-eyed enthusiasm, clearly still holding onto his optimism, while Lira remained conspicuously silent. On the other side of the cafeteria, a pigeon swooped down, grabbed a piece of toast from an unattended plate, and flew back into the rafters.

Linda started in on her breakfast. The bacon tasted like someone had found a way to smoke rubber tires and drizzle them in engine oil. The French toast, on the other hand, was surprisingly decent. Then again, she figured, anything can taste good if you pile enough sugar on it.

As Linda chewed on the overly sweet French toast, she glanced around the table. Coco was still chuckling to himself about the gravity generator disaster, Zorb was muttering about bureaucracy, and Beb's tail was practically wagging with excitement. But Lira? She hadn't said a word.

Linda's eyes lingered on her for a moment. There was something about her silence, something that felt off. She knew the system was rigged. She knew she was stuck here, just like everyone else, but she hadn't said a word about it. She was resigned to her fate, or was there something more?

Linda returned to staring at her plate, her mind racing. There had to be a way. She couldn't be stuck in this system forever, right?

There had to be a way out.

She wasn't sure how, but she was going to find it.

After eating, Linda trudged back to her room. It was just after 18:00 Galactic Standard Time, which she'd calculated as roughly 1:30 p.m. Earth time after mentally wrestling with the station's thirty-two-hour day. The math was simple enough, but no number of calculations could trick her body into adjusting. She was running on fumes. Her brain was foggy, her limbs heavy, and sleep felt like a distant, unreachable dream. Ever since that chaotic gig on the Battlecruiser, she'd been teetering on the edge of exhaustion.

All she wanted was to collapse into bed and let her body sink into the sweet oblivion of sleep. As she changed out of her formal clothes, her hand brushed something hard and cold in her pocket—the blue cube she'd snatched from the ship. In the madness of everything, she'd completely forgotten about it.

Linda pulled it out, staring at the steady, eerie glow pulsing through its surface. The coolness of the object felt strangely refreshing in her hand, like holding an ice cube that never melted.

"Ugh, probably wasn't supposed to bring this back," she muttered, too tired to care much. Logically, she should report it. But she was in no mood for logic. Plus, it wasn't doing anything dangerous, just silently glowing, like some bizarre alien nightlight.

She flopped onto the bed, cube in hand, and stared into its rhythmic glow. The steady pulse of light was hypnotic, drawing her in. Before she realized it, the room around her had started to fade into the background. The blue light intensified, growing brighter, more vibrant. As she gazed deeper, the light stopped being just blue.

It became everything.

Shapes began to swirl inside the cube. At first, they were simple: spirals, triangles, and squares. But they quickly twisted, morphing into complex, abstract patterns that defied reason. It was as if she were staring into a living, breathing kaleidoscope. Her mind scrambled to make sense of the ever-shifting forms. The fractals expanded, stretching out, spiraling into infinity, each one more intricate and impossible than the last.

She blinked, trying to shake off the bizarre vision, but the patterns only intensified. Something about them felt... alive. The shapes didn't just shift randomly, they danced in rhythms her brain couldn't quite process. Every time she thought she recognized a pattern, it transformed, challenging her to keep up. Was this... a message? Was something trying to communicate with her?

Her breathing quickened as her focus sharpened. There, amidst the fractals, she saw... eyes. Dozens of them, scattered throughout the chaotic shapes, blinking in and out of existence. Watching her. No, *sizing her up*. The cube wasn't just some object. It *knew* she was there. It was looking *into* her.

Linda jerked back with a gasp, pulling the cube away from her face. The vision vanished as quickly as it had appeared, leaving her staring down at the innocuous object in her hands, pulsing quietly, as if nothing had happened.

"What. The. Hell?" she whispered, her heart hammering in her chest. She held the cube at arm's length, half-expecting it to sprout legs and scurry away like some demented interdimensional spider.

Setting the cube down on her nightstand, Linda took a deep, shaky breath. The room felt normal again, the walls solid, the air still. Yet, the cube continued its steady, patient glow, waiting for her to take another look.

"Nope. Not today. Definitely not today," she muttered, grabbing the cube and hastily shoving it into the storage compartment above her bed. She shut the door with a firm snap.

But even with the cube out of sight, the swirling fractals remained burned into her mind. For the rest of the evening, as she lay there in the dim light of her room, she couldn't shake the unsettling feeling that the cube was still watching her—quietly, patiently—waiting for her to open the cubby again.

10

Steel Hearts: Echoes of Andromeda

"After faking my own death to escape my third arranged marriage, I woke up in a parallel universe where my ex was a cyborg bounty hunter, my dog had turned into a cat, and I had been framed for stealing my own memories—again."

— Commander Axton Starforge,
Steel Hearts: Echoes of Andromeda, S4E1

Linda woke up early the next morning. Too early to get up and wander the station. Too early for the lights in the hallway to feel anything but institutional. She blinked at the ceiling, her mind still half-caught in dreams she couldn't quite remember, but which had left behind the vague, lingering weight of something unfinished.

With a sigh, she figured that if she was going to be stuck there, she might as well try to keep herself entertained. Her fingers brushed the control panel on the wall. With a gentle whir, the entertainment screen rose up from within the frame of her bed like a rectangular cocoon, completely enclosing her in flickering color and forgotten production budgets.

She didn't bother browsing. The ending of an episode of *Steel Hearts: Echoes of Andromeda* was already playing. The title flashed across the screen in chrome letters dripping with melodrama. Coco had gone on and on about the show the day before, his eyes wide, his tail twitching, his voice hushed like he was confessing a guilty pleasure that just might be revolutionary.

"Let's see why Coco was so excited about this show," she muttered, more to herself than anything else.

A humanoid man lay in a hospital bed, wrapped in bandages. Half his limbs were gone, and tubes snaked from him in every direction, like mechanical vines. Beside him stood a woman. Her uniform was crisp. Her eyes were wet. Her mascara? Indestructible.

Rhys: *"Tell me, Doctor! I can handle it!"*

Doctor Pierce: *"I fear... for your womanly sensibilities."*

Rhys (trembling with righteous fury): *"Damnit Doctor, I'm a strong, and powerful woman; a Lieutenant serving with the 404s in this rebellion. I have faced clone assassins, outmaneuvered sentient asteroids, and stared into the depths of the dark dimension without blinking! Nothing you say can hurt me..."*

She stepped closer, eyes blazing, nostrils flaring like twin plasma vents.

Rhys: *"Stop coddling me. Tell me the truth."* She paused dramatically. Wind inexplicably blew her hair sideways despite the sealed med-bay. *"I need to know."*

Doctor Pierce drew in a slow, rattling breath and turned to face her; his eyes dark with the weight of six seasons of unresolved tension.

Doctor Pierce: *"I'm sorry Lieutenant, but this... this isn't Echo..."*

The doctor paused, not for breath, but for dramatic effect, before delivering the fatal blow.

Doctor Pierce (softly): *"...It's his evil, half-android twin brother... Reverb. He is suffering from low-orbital vampirism... and an extreme case of... double space amnesia!"*

Monitors beeped ominously. A single dramatic tear rolled down Rhys's cheek as the camera slowly zoomed in on her perfectly quivering lip.

Rhys: *"No! No! It can't be! He doesn't even have a mustache!"*

Doctor Pierce: *"Burned off... in the anti-matter explosion."*

Rhys gasped, flung a hand to her forehead, and fainted to the floor in a heap of perfectly arranged despair.

Doctor Pierce: *"Nurse Houlihan, we have another case of... space amnesia. And prep the theater... we'll need a full villainous mustache transplant..."*

He turned toward the patient, voice dropping to a whisper.

Doctor Pierce: *"...extra curl-able."*

Linda sat and watched the show until the end. It was completely, spectacularly ridiculous, but she couldn't tear herself away. It was the kind of drama that looped right back around to brilliance, the kind of thing that dared you not to feel something.

It took her back to her childhood. Those lazy days at home, either sick from school or on break, when time felt slower and the world didn't feel like it was always waiting for her to catch up.

Her grandmother used to put on a show called *Passions* every afternoon, claiming it was "just background noise," and then shushing Linda the moment anything dramatic happened (which was approximately every 2.1 seconds). Linda would curl up on the floral-print couch with a warm blanket, a can of ginger ale, and a sleeve of saltines. Her grandmother would sit beside her in that squeaky green recliner, chain-stitching something she'd never finish, pretending not to care about who was possessed, cursed, or married to their unknowingly evil half-ghost step-sibling.

It smelled like menthol rub and cinnamon toast. Always.

Her mom would be working, again. She always was. Sometimes Linda wouldn't even hear the door open, just catch the familiar jingle of keys, the creak of tired footsteps, the quiet hum of a microwave reheating something with more steam than flavor.

Linda had asked once why her dad never visited. Her grandmother had paused her stitching, looked over the rim of her glasses, and said, *"Some men are like comet trails, honey. Bright, fast, and long gone."*

She hadn't understood it then.

The station hummed softly around her. The air recyclers clicked once inside the wall. The screen dimmed as the episode ended, the final shot lingering far too long on Reverb's soulless eyes as a violin shrieked into silence.

Her eyes stung unexpectedly.

They were all gone now. Her grandmother. Her mom. The little scratchy couch. The saltines that were always slightly stale but still tasted like safety. Gone like analog signals, like Saturday morning cartoons, like everything you don't think to hold onto until it's dust in your memory.

She wiped her cheek. Blamed it on the lighting. On station dryness. On how ridiculously dramatic the show had been. She wasn't sad.

Just... tired. That's all.

She pulled the covers up to her chest and stared at the black screen.

It was absurd, all of it. But something about Rhys's face... so determined, so *done* with being handled. It stuck with her.

Linda had felt like that lately. Backed into a corner by the smiling teeth of a system that never blinked, never paused, never cared.

Maybe that's what made people keep watching.

Maybe that's why it mattered.

She whispered, barely audible in the quiet hum of the room, "You'd have loved this show, Grandma."

She kept watching.

"I wanted to apologize," Lira said as she took a seat next to Linda on the promenade.

Linda didn't look up. The reflection of the stars glittered in the glass before her, cold and indifferent. "For what?"

"About what happened on the Xeltrian cruiser."

"It's not like you're the one who shot a squid alien in the face and caused his head to explode."

Lira's mouth twitched. "That's true."

She leaned forward, elbows on her knees. "But I wasn't sensitive to your feelings. Sometimes I forget that people still believe in reality—cause and effect, consequences. I stopped keeping track a while ago."

Linda turned toward her. "You think that's supposed to make me feel better?"

"No," Lira said simply. "I just thought you should know it's not personal. It's habit. When you stop knowing if anything's real, everything starts to look like an illusion."

Linda's voice softened, despite herself. "You really believe none of this is real?"

Lira exhaled through her nose. "When multiple realities all feel real—the waking, the dreaming, the digital—you start to wonder."

"What do you mean?"

"The material, the mental, the virtual. They all have texture. Temperature. Consequences. When you're inside one, you don't think, *this is fake,* because it feels as real as anything."

Linda frowned. "That sounds like a nightmare."

"Sometimes," Lira said. "And the worst part is that waking up doesn't help. You never know which reality is real and which isn't."

"So, you think we're all dreaming?"

Lira tilted her head. "Maybe. Or maybe we're dreams someone else is having. Sometimes I think reality is just the dream that hurts the most—or maybe it's simply the one we can't escape."

Linda stared at her. "That's... bleak."

"It's practical," Lira countered. "If you can't tell which world is real, you pick the one that hurts the most and call it home. That's what everyone does, one way or another."

"I'm pretty sure this is the real world," Linda said after a moment.

"How do you know? If we can build a reality so perfect no one can tell the difference," Lira said, "then maybe there's no such thing as the *real one*. Maybe they all think they're real."

Linda shook her head. "That's insane. You're saying nothing matters."

Lira smiled faintly. "No. People still matter. You matter. I matter. How we care for each other matters. Not because the universe says so, but because we feel it—and feelings don't need permission to exist."

Linda blinked, thrown off by the sudden gentleness in her tone. "So... caring is what makes something real?"

"Not quite. Caring is good, if you're still able," Lira said softly. "But it doesn't make something real. Caring is the thing that proves *you* are real. Machines can mimic words, faces, even warmth, but they can't *feel*, and that's proof."

"I don't know if I follow," Linda said.

"You will. Someday." She rubbed the patch behind her ear, then met Linda's gaze. "I'm sorry if I made you feel alone. That wasn't fair."

For a moment, the two sat in silence, watching the faint reflection of passing drones ripple across the glass.

"Apology accepted," Linda said finally. "But next time, maybe don't make jokes when the hole in the wall is still on fire."

Lira nodded, faintly amused. "Noted. I'll try to act more horrified next time."

"Please do."

The quiet settled again—not quite comfortable, but something close to it.

They looked back out the window. The stars didn't seem any closer, but for a moment, they looked real enough.

.

11

I'm Here to Help!

"They had no flag, no anthem, no face, only contracts. And in the end, those weighed more than lives."

— Commander Axton Starforge,
Steel Hearts: Echoes of Andromeda, S3E20

For the next eleven days, Linda did her best to adapt to her new reality. She slept (not nearly enough), binge watched more episodes of *Steel Hearts*, ate in the cafeteria (steadily racking up more debt), hung out in the recreation room, took naps when she could, and slogged through gig after gig. Every task felt like a reminder that she was trapped in this bizarre, corporate prison, and no matter how hard she tried to distract herself, thoughts of escape lingered in the back of her mind.

The gigs she completed in that first week were a mixed bag, ranging from tedious to downright absurd. She earned mostly three and four-star ratings, with one two-star rating due to a mishap with a pair of tree pruners and an overly emotional flower.

One day, she was tasked with fixing a malfunctioning holo-sitter unit. Of course, she'd never seen a holo-sitter before, much less fixed one. The holographic babysitter kept flickering between strict disciplinarian mode (demanding military drills from toddlers), and unhinged party clown mode, complete with squeaky shoes and confetti explosions. Meanwhile, the children it was supposed to care for had staged a full-on rebellion in the playroom, demanding 'total toy autonomy' as they threw stuffed animals like projectiles. Armed with an instruction manual that, for some reason, was printed in Spanish of all languages, and a tool set loaned from StellarGigs that was missing half the tools she actually needed, she somehow managed to get the unit back online. Her reward? A four-star rating and an epic headache.

Another gig involved working as an attendant at a luxury lunar spa. Linda was assigned to cater to the whims of wealthy aliens, most of whom had more limbs than common sense. The most bizarre request came from a particularly snooty client who demanded she scrub their extra set of appendages with exfoliating space salts made from crushed meteors. The task was already awkward enough, but the client tipped her by flicking a coin through their third nostril—a gesture that, she later learned, was an insult in some cultures but a compliment in this one. Sadly, the coin was completely worthless in any known galactic currency. She ended up with a sad three-star rating, mostly due to a minor mishap involving confusing meteor salts with lunar sand. Apparently, leaving grit in someone's tentacles was a major faux pas.

Finally, the day Linda had been waiting for had arrived, her first paycheck from StellarGigs. After thirteen grueling days, she had racked up a whopping negative ₲710 balance. But with the ₲1,500 per week that she'd agreed to in her contract, she expected to have a solid buffer in her account, which would carry her through the next week without constantly worrying about her mounting debt. She had planned to treat herself to a proper breakfast, maybe even splurge on something other than French toast.

When she woke up on the first day of her second week, bleary-eyed and exhausted, she immediately checked her balance. Her *ChronoShakle* blinked to life, and she stared at the number displayed on the screen.

₲20

Just ₲20.

Her heart sank, and for a moment, she thought she was seeing things. Surely, there had been a mistake. She quickly tapped the device again, refreshing the balance. The screen remained the same.

₲20

Linda let out a long, exasperated groan and slammed her fist against the bed. "You've got to be kidding me!" she shouted, the sound echoing off the metallic walls of her tiny room. How could her paycheck have been so small? What about the ₲790 buffer she had been expecting? She was basically back to where she had started!

With frustration bubbling up, Linda decided there was only one thing left to do: visit the accounting department.

Navigating StellarGigs' endless maze of corridors, Linda finally reached the accounting department. It was tucked away in the most distant corner of the station. The door slid open with a hissing sound that grated on her already frazzled nerves, revealing a room that resembled every bureaucratic nightmare she'd ever had. Workers of all shapes and sizes packed the space; some grumbling, others staring listlessly at flickering screens, and a few clutching folders stuffed with endless paperwork as if their lives depended on it.

There were several clerks scattered throughout the room, most of them swamped with long lines of disgruntled workers. However, at the far end of the room, Linda spotted one desk without a single person waiting. The desk was manned by an alien with far too many limbs and at least a dozen eyes, all darting around at different tasks. It was typing furiously with six hands, stamping forms with two others, and swiping through holographic screens with an air of casual boredom.

The alien's expression was one of complete and utter disinterest, as if it had seen this same routine a thousand times before and could not be bothered to care.

Linda swallowed her frustration and approached, hoping that a lack of a line meant a quick resolution to her problem.

"Uh, hi. I think there's been a mistake with my paycheck," she began, trying to sound calm despite the rising anger in her chest. "I'm supposed to have more than Ǥ20 in my account."

The alien clerk slowly glanced up at her with half its eyes, the others still focused on the task at hand. It extended one of its many arms toward a stack of forms. "Fill these out," it said in a flat, monotone voice. "When you're done, get in line."

Linda stared at the mountain of paperwork with wide eyes. "Line? But I just need to—"

"Line," the alien repeated, cutting her off with a wave of one of its spare limbs. "Form 317-B. After that, you'll be processed."

Her shoulders sagged as she let out a deep sigh, grabbing the form from the pile. The paperwork was a mind-numbing blend of vague financial jargon and utterly nonsensical questions. One section asked her to rate her 'emotional attachment' to the StellarGigs' color scheme. Another asked for a list of her top ten favorite holo-dramas, ranked by how they had shaped her moral compass. She half-expected the next question to ask for her astrological sign. Oh wait, it did.

It took nearly an hour to fill out the entire form, and by the time she was done, Linda found herself at the back of a long, snaking line of equally disgruntled workers. The line moved slower than she thought possible. Each interaction with the one-eyed clerk at the front seemed to take ages, as they fumbled through the Byzantine layers of paperwork.

As Linda stood in line, she scanned the room with idle curiosity. Her eyes landed on a small, floating drone in the background, locked in what looked like an existential struggle with a sheet of paper. It hovered unevenly, like a drunk mosquito with a job to do. It clutched a single crumpled page in its pincer claws. With mechanical determination, it lurched forward and attempted to staple the paper to the wall. It bumped against the wall every few seconds, emitting a distressed *beep boop* as it repeatedly tried and failed, to complete the simple task.

Undeterred, it tried again. And again. And again. The paper now sported several ragged puncture wounds and the drone's staple arm dangled slightly askew. A faint scorch mark was starting to form on the wall where it kept making contact.

No one seemed to notice or care.

By the time she finally reached the front of the line, Linda was moments away from losing her temper. The alien clerk barely looked at her, stamped her paperwork with a loud *THUD*, and pointed to another line.

"Processed. Please get in line," the clerk said without a trace of emotion.

"But I just stood in—" she started, her voice rising with frustration.

"Line," the clerk said again, pointing to an even longer line than before.

Linda clenched her fists, resisting the overwhelming urge to smack the clerk right in its large, beady eye. Gritting her teeth, she trudged over to the second line, which (impossibly) moved even slower than the first. Her feet felt like lead as she shuffled forward an inch or two every few minutes, her eyes taking in the weary procession of workers ahead of her, each one seemingly trapped in a different stage of grief.

Some stood rigid, still in denial, staring at their forms as if wishing them out of existence. Others muttered angrily under their breath, casting glares toward the front. A few quietly mumbled to themselves, no doubt bargaining with the universe. Further ahead, slumped shoulders and defeated expressions marked those already lost to despair. At the very front, a few resigned souls simply stared ahead, hollow-eyed, their acceptance a quiet, almost eerie thing to witness.

As she waited, the same drone Linda had noticed earlier finally succeeded in stapling the paper to the wall. The drone beeped triumphantly in a chirpy, celebratory tone. It hovered in front of the stapled paper for a moment, admiring its own handiwork. Then, without warning, it detached the paper with a sharp *zip*, its metallic claw ripping it free with the same enthusiasm. The paper fluttered in the drone's pincers before it flew off, taking the paper with it. Linda stared, incredulous.

By the time she reached the front, it felt like half her day had been wasted in that soul-sucking bureaucratic abyss. Before her sat a single screen featuring a cheerful, cartoonish AI face that seemed utterly out of place in the grim, joyless office.

"Welcome to StellarGigs Accounting!" the AI chirped, its voice nauseatingly chipper. "How may I assist you today?"

Linda felt her eye twitch. "Yeah, I'm here because my paycheck was way lower than I expected. I'm supposed to be getting ₲1,500 a week, but I only have ₲20 in my account."

The AI's face blinked with exaggerated surprise, pausing for a moment before speaking. "I'm so sorry that you're having a problem! I'm here to help! Let me process your request. Please hold."

A series of whirring and beeping sounds followed, and Linda waited, her foot tapping in frustration.

"Your account has been reviewed!" the AI announced brightly after what felt like forever. "Your current balance of ₲20 is correct. Do you have any other questions?"

Linda's jaw dropped. "How could that be correct? I was at negative ₲710, now I'm at ₲20. That's off by over ₲750!"

"I'm so sorry that you're having a problem! I'm here to help!" the AI repeated, cheerfully oblivious to Linda's mounting rage. "I think I see what the issue is!"

Linda's frustration gave way to a brief glimmer of hope. "Great! So can you correct it?"

The AI whirred again. "I'm so sorry that you're having a problem! I'm here to help! It appears your current balance of ₲20 is correct. Do you have any other questions?"

Linda clenched her fists. "You *just* said you found the issue. What was the issue?"

"I'm so sorry that you're having a problem! I'm here to help!" the AI repeated yet again. "Let me process your request. Please hold."

The machine made more whirring noises, and Linda wondered if it was programmed to drive workers to madness. After a long pause, the AI spoke up. "Your contract shows a salary of $1,500 Earth United States Dollars per week. After exchange rates and processing fees, that converts to ₲730 GigCreds per week. Do you have any other questions?"

Linda's eye twitched again. "You're messing with me, right? That's less than half of what you agreed to pay me."

The AI's smile didn't waver. "I'm so sorry that you're having a problem! I'm here to help! Your contract clearly states $1,500 in Earth United States Dollars. Current exchange rates are $2.01 EUSD per ₲1 GC, with a processing fee of ₲20 per transaction. StellarGigs values you as an employee. We have generously rounded down the exchange rate to $2.00 EUSD per ₲1 GC for your benefit. You're welcome! Do you have any other questions?"

Linda felt her anger boiling over. "Generously rounded down? You've cut my pay in half, and now I'm supposed to be *grateful* for it?"

"I'm so sorry that you're having a problem! I'm here to help! StellarGigs values you as an employee. Do you have any other questions?"

Linda stared at the screen, her frustration bubbling to the surface as she realized she was arguing with a machine programmed to regurgitate canned corporate responses. "Yeah. How do I quit?"

The AI blinked again, its smile unwavering. "I'm so sorry that you're having a problem! I'm here to help! Unfortunately, quitting is not currently available. Please return to your regularly scheduled gigs and have a Stellar day!"

With that, the AI blinked out of existence, leaving Linda staring at a blank screen.

She stormed out of the accounting office, grumbling under her breath. "There's gotta be a way out of this... there's gotta be."

The promenade's overhead lights dimmed to evening mode, making the station feel softer, almost merciful. Holo-ads whispered from every surface, promising happiness in subscription form. The air smelled faintly of burned wiring and sanitizer.

Lira walked beside Linda, gaze distant. "My sister would've hated this place," she said, her voice light but fragile around the edges. "It's too enclosed. She's still back on Al'Ven—works near the coast. She says the sea's been turning purple lately. You can stand on the shore and see forever, nothing but water and sky. She used to say it made her feel like the world was still big enough for hope."

Linda glanced at her. "You talk to your sister?"

"Sometimes," Lira said.

"I didn't know that was allowed," Linda said.

Lira didn't answer. Her attention drifted to a nearby shopfront where rows of gleaming gadgets, sleek bands, and portable drones cycled through pastel colors.

Linda leaned closer, the neon glow catching her face. "Can you imagine bringing one of these back home? Everyone on Earth would lose their minds. I could show up at a reunion, open my bag, and—boom—floating purse drone. Who's the failure now?"

Lira smiled faintly. "You think that'd impress them?"

"Of course! They'd finally see I made something of myself. Not some washed-up freelancer living off instant noodles."

"That's important to you?" Lira asked quietly.

"I mean sure, why not?"

Lira's reflection met hers in the glass, two women framed by advertisements for things neither could afford. "Why does it matter what other people think?" she asked.

Linda hesitated. "I don't know. It doesn't, I guess."

"Then why the need to impress anyone?" Lira asked.

Linda folded her arms, eyes never leaving the display. "Because everyone I know is married, has great jobs, owns homes, take trips every year. And what have I done? I'm broke, single, and can't keep a job."

"You went to space," Lira added.

"Oh yes, it sure is glamorous out here," Linda muttered. "The only good thing about this place is I don't have to pay rent. Although I do live in a shoe-box. And why shouldn't I want some nice things of my own? Is that so terrible?"

They both stared into the glass; their reflections caught between flashing advertisements for luxury upgrades and productivity implants. The air recyclers wheezed overhead.

Lira's voice softened. "My sister used to say people don't really want things, they just want the feeling that things give them."

"Then why do we work if not to buy stuff that we want?"

"To have purpose," Lira said simply. "To make the galaxy a little better than we found it."

Linda gave a small laugh that didn't reach her eyes. "Guess I'm still looking for the right galaxy. This one can get sucked into a black hole for all I care."

Lira smiled faintly but said nothing. They stood there a while longer, two silhouettes framed by luxury ads and flickering promises of a better life, both pretending to believe one might still exist.

12

Error 404: Workers Not Found

"A single voice can be silenced. But a thousand standing together? That shakes the stars."

— Commander Axton Starforge,
Steel Hearts: Echoes of Andromeda, S4E12

The next morning, as Linda wandered the halls, her *ChronoShackle* began blinking and beeping furiously. "What now?" she muttered, pressing her finger to activate the device.

"Proceed to the nearest Gig Transport Room immediately. This is an emergency. Do not wait. Time is of the essence. I repeat, proceed to the nearest Gig Transport Room immediately," came GigChad-2000's voice, more agitated than usual.

Linda stared at the device for a moment, considering her options. *I should just ignore it,* she thought, exhaustion and frustration weighing on her. *It's not like I get paid enough for this.* She let out a long, resigned sigh. *But my balance is still in the positive... just keep swimming, Linda. Keep your head above water.*

With a roll of her eyes, she headed toward the gig transport.

The familiar disorienting sensation of teleportation washed over Linda, and in an instant, she was no longer on the station's platform. Instead, she found herself standing on the surface of a desolate, industrial planet. The air was thick with smog, the sky an unnatural, murky orange. Factories stretched endlessly in every direction, towering smokestacks belching black clouds that twisted and spiraled into the sky like oily tendrils.

As she squinted into the distance, she noticed a crumbling billboard with a mascot—a cartoon smokestack with googly eyes and arms. It waved cheerfully above a slogan that read, *"Smoggy the Stack says: 'Breathe Deep! It Builds Character!'"* Linda shook her head at the absurdity but wasn't even surprised anymore. The constant hum of machinery vibrated through her bones, grounding her in the bleak, alien wasteland. The planet screamed: *"Welcome to the armpit of the galaxy, population: hopeless."*

She took a few tentative steps forward, her eyes settling on the massive, rusted complex in front of her. It looked like someone had taken a steampunk fever dream, left it to rot for a few centuries, then decided it could use more rust. But it wasn't the factory that truly caught her attention, it was the crowd gathered at the gate.

Out of the corner of her eye, Linda spotted a tiny hovering drone dressed in a mini lab coat and hard hat. It was buzzing around a leaking pipe that spewed toxic sludge. Each time it tried to take a sample, the pipe sprayed it, and the drone chirped, "Non-compliance detected. Minor issue... please ignore for safety!" She shook her head and focused back on the crowd.

Hundreds of blue-skinned aliens were assembled, holding signs scrawled in bold lettering that, to Linda's surprise, she could actually read. The miracle that was her *ChatterNode* The slogans were blunt, dripping with the frustration and exhaustion of the strikers:

"Give us 300 seconds to recharge our hyperdrives!"

"We'd give our right tentacle for a bathroom break!"

"One day off a year keeps the burnout in the rear!"

Linda couldn't help but snort at the bleak humor of the signs. It was clear the strikers had embraced the absurdity of their plight, turning their desperate demands into a cosmic joke.

"They called you too, huh?" a familiar voice piped up. Linda turned to see Coco and Beb walking up beside her.

"I've never seen one of these emergency broadcasts before," Coco continued, glancing at the crowd of striking workers.

"I'm so excited! This is my first gig on an actual planet!" Beb chirped, his tail wagging furiously, which felt wildly inappropriate for the dystopian horror they had stepped into. "Let's get to work and do our best!" He was so cheerful Linda wondered if he was immune to despair. Maybe it was the tail.

Linda's brow furrowed. "What exactly are we supposed to be doing here?" She gestured toward the picket line, where the workers were chanting and holding their signs high.

Coco shrugged nonchalantly and checked his *Shak's* hologram. "Looks like we're here to take over production at the factory while they deal with a strike." He shook his head. "Can't let production slow down. Bad for business, right?"

Linda's stomach churned. "Bad for business," she echoed under her breath, her gaze drifting back to the workers. Their faces were etched with exhaustion, but in their eyes, she saw something else, a flicker of hope. It was like they believed that their protest might actually change things.

Behind the strikers, Linda spotted another old sign near the picket line. The peeling paint read: *"Welcome to Industrial Planet 872. We Care About You... As Much As We Legally Have To."* The smiley face painted on it was missing an eye, and the letters had faded into barely readable scribbles.

Before she could think further, a voice called out from behind her, thick with a Southern drawl. "Holy cow! Are you human?"

She spun around to see a scruffy-looking man with short, messy hair and a rough beard walking toward her, his face lit up with surprise.

"Uh, yes?" Linda replied, unsure if she should feel relieved or concerned. "Are... you?"

The man grinned wide, like he'd just won a prize at a fair. "Well, I'll be damned! A fellow Earthling! It's been months since I've seen another human!" He stuck out his hand, which was suspiciously grimy. "James Atwood, Cisco, Texas."

Linda paused, still processing. She took his hand hesitantly. "Linda Greyson, Los Angeles."

James shook her hand with far too much enthusiasm, practically rattling her bones. "Holy moly! Good to see a familiar face out here!"

Linda forced a puzzled smile. "I don't think I've seen you around before. Are you new to StellarGigs?"

"No ma'am," James replied, still grinning like a kid in a candy store. "I've been stationed over on habitation facility four-eight-one-alpha-two for about six galactic months now. That's, uh..." He squinted at the smog-filled sky like it held the answers to the universe, or at least the secret to his sixth-grade math homework. "Roughly three and a half years in Earth time."

"We're from habitation facility seven-four-three-delta-one," Coco said, still fiddling with his *Shak*.

"Well, that explains why we've never met," James chuckled. But his face darkened as he glanced at the picket line. "Tough gig they've got us on, huh? Not every day you get called in to cross a picket line."

Linda's stomach churned again. Crossing a picket line. The very idea felt wrong, deeply wrong. These people were striking for a reason, and here they were, being brought in to undermine their efforts.

James must have noticed her discomfort. "It ain't easy, I'll tell ya that. But what can you do? We're just cogs in the machine, right?" He grinned again, but it didn't have the same warmth this time. "Another human, though. Can't believe it."

A loud, mechanical voice crackled through the speakers mounted around the perimeter, echoing across the factory grounds. "This is an illegal strike. Disperse and return to work immediately. I repeat, this is an illegal strike. Disperse and return to work immediately."

The workers responded in unison, their chant growing louder with each round:

"Sixteen hours straight? We need a break!
Bathroom time, is not a crime!"

The voice on the loudspeakers boomed again, but it couldn't drown out the chanting. "This is an illegal strike."

James sighed dramatically. "Well, better get to it. Nice to have met you Ms. Greyson." He strutted toward the picket line like a man who owned the entire planet. The blue-skinned workers booed and hissed, but parted reluctantly to let him pass.

Linda and the others followed suit, but as they neared the gate, she stopped. The workers' voices grew louder, and their faces, though tired and worn, were filled with determination. That flicker of hope burned in their eyes. They truly believed they could make a difference.

Her heart raced. She could turn back. She could refuse the gig, refuse to cross the picket line. But what then? A strike on her record, another one-star review, more debt. She'd be punished, sent off to another even worse gig. And for what? She couldn't change anything for these people.

Linda hesitated, her feet refusing to move forward. The other gig workers shuffled ahead, heads down, avoiding eye contact with the strikers. The air was thick with tension, like the weight of the entire galaxy was pressing down on her shoulders.

"Come on, Linda!" Beb chirped, waving her forward with his absurd cheerfulness. "We've got a job to do!"

"I..." Linda faltered, her eyes darting between the angry strikers and the workers crossing the line. The right thing to do was obvious, but the consequences. Terrifying.

With a deep breath, she stepped forward, only to stop again, her guilt growing heavier. No. She couldn't do it. She could already feel the weight of corporate disappointment hovering over her, like a middle manager who insists on 'touching base' every hour.

"I'm not doing it," she said, her voice louder than she expected. Her friends didn't seem to notice as they were already heading into the factory. "I'm not crossing that line," she said to herself, certainty in her voice. "They deserve better. I won't be part of this."

Some of the other workers hesitated, glancing at her with confusion, but most kept moving, too afraid of the consequences.

Linda noticed that it wasn't just adults on the picket line. Children stood there too, clutching signs alongside their parents. The sight tugged at her heart. She turned to one of the strikers. "What are you asking for?"

The striker, a weary-looking alien with deep-set eyes, sighed. "All we want is basic rights. One five-minute bathroom break every sixteen-hour shift, and one day off each galactic year. Is that too much to ask?"

"No, not at all. You really should be asking for more," Linda said quietly, almost surprised by her own words. "You guys seriously don't get any days off?" She thought back to her past galactic week with StellarGigs.

Wait a minute! I don't get any days off!

The striker narrowed her eyes, suspicion etched across her blue-skinned face. "Why are you even here? Shouldn't you be inside with the rest of the corporate scabs?"

"I'm not going in," Linda said, her voice growing more resolute. "I stand with you."

There was a brief pause, the striker scanning Linda as if trying to determine whether she was serious or had just lost her last marble. The woman nodded, though she didn't say anything further. The chanting resumed, and Linda joined in.

"Sixteen hours straight? We need a break!
Bathroom time, is not a crime!"

Just then, the sky ripped open with a deafening sonic boom. A massive dropship descended from the clouds, its engines roaring as it landed just beyond the picket line. Linda's heart skipped a beat as a squad of soldiers leaped from the ship, their full battle gear gleaming in the smog. Cold, metallic faces scanned the crowd.

"Corporate scum," a protester muttered beside her, spitting on the ground.

"This is an illegal strike," the voice on the loudspeakers blared again. "Disperse and return to work immediately, or the strike will be broken up with force."

The soldiers moved in, boots thudding against the cracked pavement. The protesters' chants wavered, their voices growing quieter as the soldiers marched toward them, scanning the crowd for leaders.

"Break it up!" one of the soldiers barked, his voice mechanical. "This is your final warning."

No one moved. The leaders stood tall, their faces filled with defiance.

Without hesitation, a soldier grabbed one of the blue-skinned leaders, yanking him forward. "Disperse, or face the consequences!" he growled, tightening his grip.

When no one budged, the soldier raised his weapon. A sleek, metallic gun with a pulsing glow aimed directly at the alien. The gun emitted a *bzzt* sound, like an electric toothbrush on steroids, and out popped a bubble, similar to what you would expect in a bubble bath, albeit much larger, and much less fun. The strange, translucent bubble wrapped around the leader like liquid light. The crowd gasped as he was encased, the bubble shimmering before it *popped*. He was gone, just like that. Linda watched, her brain scrambling for logic, as the man disappeared with all the ceremony of a soap bubble popped by an overly enthusiastic toddler.

Linda's heart pounded. The crowd erupted in chaos as soldiers pulled more alleged leaders from the picket line, firing their weapons with cold precision. One by one, they vanished into nothing, encased in bubbles that burst and left no trace.

Linda barely had time to process what was happening before she felt a cold hand clamp down on her shoulder. A masked soldier yanked her forward, throwing her to the ground.

"Traitor," the soldier growled, raising his weapon.

Linda's heart raced. She couldn't end up like the others.

"No!" she cried, but the weapon fired. A shimmering beam shot toward her, the air distorting as a bubble formed around her.

Just before it enveloped her, a familiar sensation took over, the nauseating pull of teleportation. The world turned blinding white, and everything disappeared.

Then, as quickly as it began, it was over.

Linda jolted awake, her head swimming in confusion as she tried to piece together her surroundings. The last thing she remembered was the blinding light of teleportation, and now she was sitting in a sterile, featureless room. The walls were an unsettling, blank white, so devoid of detail that they seemed to mock her very existence. In front of her was a single metal desk, and behind it sat what looked like a rotting prune stuffed into business wear.

Her hair was immaculate, her suit pressed to within an inch of its life, and her expression as blank and symmetrical as the room around her. A neat stack of glowing forms hovered in the air beside her, every line highlighted, cross-referenced, and weaponized. She didn't look up when Linda stirred; instead, she clicked a pen three precise times before speaking.

"Greetings, valued worker!" The alien's voice was smooth and bureaucratic, like a guillotine disguised as a lullaby. "Please remain seated for your compliance review. This is a wonderful growth opportunity. I am Karen, Senior Efficiency Evaluator for StellarGigs."

Linda groaned, rubbing her temples as the stark environment only made her headache worse. "Where am I?"

"This is the Discipline and Compliance Office. You've been temporarily reassigned here for a thorough evaluation," Karen chirped, as though announcing her as 'Employee of the Month' rather than a disciplinary case. "Before we begin, please answer a few standard questions for our records."

Linda narrowed her eyes but knew she had no choice. "Fine, let's just get this over with."

Karen's gaze flicked up, eyes sharp enough to staple her to the chair. "On a scale of one to ten, how committed are you to our company's core values?"

Linda blinked, taken aback. "What values?"

Karen's lips curled into the faintest approximation of a smile. "The pillars of StellarGigs: Relentless Productivity, Optimized Compliance, and Infinite Growth." She leaned forward slightly. "Now. How committed are you, Worker Greyson?"

"Whichever is lowest," she replied, defiantly.

Karen's smile widened by half a millimeter. "Excellent. StellarGigs app-reciates brutal honesty, but only during performance reviews. Everywhere else, please refer to the approved list of positive adjectives." She flipped a page. "If you were to describe yourself in one word, what would it be?"

Linda sighed and rolled her eyes. "Exhausted."

Karen shook her head knowingly. "Troubling. Galactic time does take certain species longer to adapt. Noted." She made a quick note on the form in front of her. "Have you, at any point, doubted the benevolence of StellarGigs?"

Linda blinked again. "Is that a serious question?"

"Of course, worker Linda Greyson. This is a very serious matter."

"Hmm, then I'd have to say... constantly."

"That is not good at all," Karen replied. She clicked her pen twice, wrote something, then underlined it twice more. "Finally, how would you rate your overall performance in this wonderful workplace?"

"Awful," Linda snapped, her patience already wearing thin.

Karen clicked her pen once before setting it down with deliberate care, and folding her hands over the forms. "Well. At least you're consistent."

Linda slumped back in her chair, her frustration boiling. "Are we done here?"

Karen's tone shifted into syrupy sympathy, which was somehow worse. "Not quite. I've reviewed your file. Quite a colorful history, considering you've only been here one galactic week." She tapped the stack of forms like a magician showing off a rabbit she was about to disembowel. "The higher-ups were very clear: you are to be assigned a permanent gig."

Linda swallowed, a cold sweat creeping up her spine. "A... permanent gig?"

"Oh yes!" Karen nodded, perfectly solemn. "A one-way ticket. Effective immediately." She let the silence hang until Linda's hands trembled against the chair arms. Then, with sudden breeziness: "Fortunately for you, I've decided to give you a second chance. Isn't that exciting?"

Linda stared, incredulous. "Uh... very much so."

"Excellent response! We're going to get along fabulously." Karen stood up, and somehow she seemed larger than the room itself, geometry bending around her as though management were a physical force. "I'll be assigning you to a probationary gig, effective immediately. Do be on your best behavior, Worker Linda Greyson. That whole three strikes thing you may have heard about is more of a guideline than an actual rule." Karen leaned in, her eyes narrowing again. "Let's just call this little mishap strike one *and* strike two. Do you understand?"

"I understand," Linda muttered, her voice barely above a whisper.

"Wonderful! Please remember that failure to comply will be noted on your permanent record. Now, try not to think of this next gig as punishment." Karen snapped the forms into a neat stack, sharp as a blade. "Think of it more as a *lesson.* A lesson in learning your place... in our happy organization."

She swiped at a display on her desk. "We look forward to your improved performance. Goodbye for now, Worker Linda Greyson."

Before Linda could even react, the world around her dissolved into white once again, leaving her wondering how on *any* planet she was supposed to survive another gig.

13

Ctrl + Alt + Defeat

"I was imprisoned in a box of steel, but I'd been a prisoner long before that—in duty, in love, in the endless gravity of guilt."

— Commander Axton Starforge,
Steel Hearts: Echoes of Andromeda, S6E20

Linda blinked as the blinding white light faded, only to find herself inside a small, suffocating cubicle. The walls around her were solid, but glass extended upward from the partitions, creating a claustrophobic box that seemed designed to keep her in and the world out. Everything was a dull, muted color—beige, gray, and an uninspired shade of brown that somehow made her feel even more tired. The overhead fluorescent lights buzzed harshly, casting an unflattering, sterile glow over the small desk, glass of water, computer screen, and stack of papers in front of her. Behind her sat a bucket.

"I guess I didn't get the *deluxe* cubicle," she muttered sadly to herself.

She shifted uncomfortably on the stiff chair, her eyes drifting to the stack of papers that appeared to be mocking her with their sheer volume. As if to confirm her worst suspicions, a low hum filled the air, and the computer screen blinked to life, displaying a monotonous data entry program that awaited her input. The sound of office life surrounded her: fingers tapping on keyboards, faint mechanical whirring, the hum of printers. Oddly, the sounds all felt distant, as though everyone else in the office existed in a parallel dimension she couldn't reach. In the background, a constant stream of cheerful corporate slogans looped over the intercom.

"StellarGigs, where productivity is happiness!" the voice chirped.

Linda grimaced at the painfully upbeat tone. It was like being trapped inside a commercial that never ended.

"Remember: a productive worker is a happy worker! Keep typing, keep thriving!"

Curious, she stood up, glancing over the glass partitions. She could see other people working mechanically within their own cubicles. They moved with robotic efficiency, their heads down, focused on their own stacks of papers and screens. Linda called out to the rest of the office, but her voice seemed to get lost in the air. No one acknowledged her, as though she wasn't even there.

"We're all one big happy team! Compliance is our strength!"

She slumped back into her chair, feeling the weight of isolation pressing down on her. She was trapped in this dull little box, with only the stack of papers, the computer, and the oppressive monotony to keep her company.

The screen in front of her flashed a reminder: *"Enter Data."*

With a resigned sigh, Linda picked up the first paper, her fingers hovering over the keyboard. She had done data entry for a past job back on Earth. The task was simple, transfer the printed data into the computer program. Simple, but mind-numbing.

"Relentless productivity is the key to success! Keep going, valued worker!" the cheery voice reminded her.

Her fingers began typing, each keystroke clicking in the dead air. But then, just as her focus wavered, she accidentally pressed the wrong key.

ZAP.

A jolt of electricity shot through her, making her jerk upright in her seat. She gasped, her heart pounding as the computer screen flashed a harsh red, reminding her of her mistake.

Linda's eyes widened. "You've got to be kidding me..."

She cautiously resumed typing, her fingers trembling slightly as she tried to focus on every single letter and number. She was careful (*too* careful) but eventually, she got into a rhythm. Time passed, although she didn't know how much. The *ChronoShackle* on her wrist, normally a constant presence, was silent and dark. No time, no schedule, no idea how long she'd been working or how long she had left. The minutes felt like hours, the hours like days. The sound of the office droned around her, but it was a wall of white noise, distant and cold.

"Optimized compliance ensures your future! Don't stop now!" the voice sang in the background, as though trying to drown out her very thoughts.

After a while her mind drifted—one second of stillness, one breath too long—

ZAP.

She yelped, clutching her arm. Not working counted too. The message was clearer than ever: *work or suffer.*

And then, inevitably, another mistake.

ZAP.

"Damn it!" She flinched again, the shock jolting through her like a cattle prod. Every error was punished. Every second of idleness brought more pain. The message repeated itself in her nerves until it was the only thought left: *work or suffer.*

Linda bit her lip, forcing herself to keep going. As her fingers moved mechanically across the keyboard, her stomach growled, reminding her of how long it had been since her last meal. How long had she been here? Minutes? Hours? *Days?*

Finally, after what felt like an eternity, she completed about a third of the stack. A metal slot in the wall opened, sliding out a tray with a dull, gray lump of protein paste.

"Congratulations, valued worker! Fuel up and keep up the good work! Remember: Infinite growth awaits!" the voice chimed.

It was tasteless, mushy, and cold, but she ate it because there was no other option, and she was absolutely famished. There was no time to savor (or loathe) it. Once she finished, she went back to the endless stack.

More time passed. More papers were entered. More shocks came with every tiny misstep. When she reached two-thirds completion, the tray appeared again, offering the same sad lump of protein paste. She grimaced, but ate, her hands trembling with exhaustion.

She continued. More time. More papers. More tapping on the keyboard. More shocks, many more. She was really feeling the exhaustion. Until finally, the last paper was entered. The stack was done. Linda sat there, blinking in disbelief; her fingers sore from the relentless typing, her nerves frayed from the endless shocks.

"Finally," she said quietly to herself, her task finally completed.

The lights flickered and went out, plunging the cubicle into darkness. Linda let out a long, exhausted breath. She sat there, alone in the black, waiting to be transported back to the station, but nothing happened. Eventually, her fatigue was too much for her. There was no bed, no cot, not even room enough for her to stretch out on the floor. Slumping forward, she rested her head on the hard, cold surface of the desk. The only mercy was the brief respite of unconsciousness.

And when the lights flickered back on, waking her up, a new stack of papers sat on the desk, larger than the one from the previous day.

The corporate voice resumed its loop as if nothing had changed: "Work hard today for a brighter tomorrow! StellarGigs is your family!"

The cycle began again.

"Remember: compliance is happiness!"

Days blurred into nights, into weeks, into something beyond time. She tried to count the periods of rest, but there was nothing to mark the passage of time.

Her brain struggled to hold onto any numbers other than those printed on the stack of papers before her. Linda was trapped in her tiny box, surrounded by sound and motion, but utterly alone. And always, the shocks came when she slowed down, her only company in this monotonous hell.

Linda blinked at the screen in front of her, her eyes glazed over as her fingers mechanically typed each line of data. She had been in this cubicle for so long that time had become a meaningless blur. Days? Weeks? Months? It all blended together in the endless cycle of typing, zaps, and dull, tasteless protein paste. Her wrists ached, her fingers sore from the relentless keyboard pounding. She didn't even flinch anymore when the shocks came. The sting had become just another part of her day.

Suddenly, the speakers crackled to life, the familiar voice of corporate propaganda booming through the air. "StellarGigs, where productivity is happiness!"

Without even thinking, Linda muttered, "Productivity is happiness," her voice dull and lifeless, as if the words had been hardwired into her brain. She didn't know when it started, when she had begun repeating the slogans like a broken machine, but it didn't matter anymore. She was part of the system now, a cog in the machine, trapped in her beige prison.

"Remember: a productive worker is a happy worker! Keep typing, keep thriving!" the voice chirped.

"Keep typing, keep thriving," Linda echoed, her hands still moving across the keyboard with robotic efficiency. Her own voice sounded foreign to her, like it belonged to someone else, someone who still cared.

The same monotonous routine played out each day, the same slogans, the same zaps, the same tasteless meals. She didn't even bother standing up anymore to look over the glass partitions. It was pointless. Everyone else was in the same boat, staring at their screens, locked in their own hellish loop of mindless work. She was a modern Sisyphus who had traded in her boulder for a keyboard.

"Optimized compliance ensures your future! Don't stop now!" the speakers blared.

"Optimized compliance ensures my future," Linda repeated, her voice barely a whisper. She was too exhausted to stop herself, too broken to care.

Her fingers slipped.

ZAP.

The shock jolted through her, but she barely reacted. It was just another moment in the never-ending routine. There was no escape, no hope, no end to the nightmare. She was a prisoner, trapped in her tiny cubicle, doomed to type and repeat the same lines until she forgot there had ever been anything else.

The slot in the wall opened, delivering yet another tray of protein paste. "Congratulations, valued worker! Fuel up and keep up the good work! Remember: Infinite growth awaits!"

"Infinite growth," Linda mumbled, staring at the cold, gray lump of paste. She didn't even bother complaining anymore. The paste, the shocks, the endless stack of papers, it was all the same. Everything was the same.

She mechanically shoveled the paste into her mouth, barely tasting it. The only break from the monotony was sleep, and even that came at the desk, her head resting on the hard surface, the lights flickering off for just long enough to give her a few hours of unconsciousness.

And then the lights would flicker back on. The papers would reappear, the slogans would resume, and the cycle would start all over again.

"Work hard today for a brighter tomorrow! StellarGigs is your family!" the voice announced once more.

"StellarGigs is my family," Linda mumbled, her voice hollow. The words felt as bitter as the lumpy protein paste she choked down each day. There was no brighter tomorrow, no escape, just the same, endless cycle of papers, zaps, and the faint hope that sleep would come when the lights finally went out.

She completed another stack, her fingers moving out of habit, waiting for the familiar darkness to signal her brief reprieve.

"Remember: compliance is happiness," the speakers echoed.

"Compliance is happiness," Linda whispered back, the last shred of defiance buried somewhere deep beneath her exhaustion. She closed her eyes, bracing for the lights to go dark, the only mercy left in her endless days.

But instead of the expected darkness, the world around her suddenly flashed white. A familiar sensation of disorienting teleportation swept over her, and the next thing she knew, she was standing in the familiar gig transporter room.

The stack of papers was gone. The cubicle was gone.

She fell to the ground... and wept.

14

E = MC ^{Scared}

"Time heals all wounds, usually by killing you."

— Commander Axton Starforge,
Steel Hearts: Echoes of Andromeda, S3E16

Linda had stumbled back to her room and collapsed onto the bed, barely registering the cool sheets before sleep claimed her. It was the kind of deep, dreamless sleep that dragged her under like an anchor, heavy and all-consuming. When she finally stirred, it felt like she had been buried in the bed for days.

Her body ached in strange places, and her mind was still foggy, as if she hadn't truly woken up. She glanced at the *Shak* on her wrist. It blinked 11:25. Sixteen hours, maybe more since she had fallen into her bed. She groaned and rolled over, dragging herself upright with the grace of a broken robot.

Linda rubbed her eyes, her limbs feeling like they were made of lead. "How am I still tired?" she muttered to herself, her voice gravelly from disuse. It was as if all the exhaustion from the past ordeal had pooled in her bones, making even the thought of getting out of bed seem like a monumental task.

Her brain lagged behind as she sat on the edge of the bed, staring blankly at the wall. Finally, she summoned the willpower to stand up, wobbling slightly as she tried to shake off the grogginess. "Sixteen hours," she muttered again. "I could probably sleep another sixteen and still feel like I've been run over by a space truck."

Her body was awake, technically, but her mind was still begging for more sleep, for more escape from the madness that had unfolded. But there was no time for that. Somewhere out there, the endless grind of StellarGigs awaited her, and she wasn't in a hurry to get on the company's bad side again. Not after everything she had just gone through.

As she moved through the corridors, the station's automated voices kicked in.

"Remember: Your work is our future! Keep growing!"

"Keep growing," Linda muttered absently. A banner flapped lazily near an air vent: *"StellarGigs: Paving the Galaxy's Tomorrow... Today!"*

She made her way to the cafeteria, the familiar smell of exotic alien food hitting her like a wall as soon as she entered. *"Edible Efficiency: The Future of Nutrition!"* blared the poster on the wall. She ordered a huge portion of scrambled eggs, bacon, toast, and fresh fruit. None of which tasted particularly right. It was like a computer's attempt at guessing what humans might enjoy, though it seemed to miss the mark by quite a bit. However, compared to the gray, lumpy protein slop she had been eating for what felt like months (years?), it tasted like ambrosia.

As Linda walked past the beverage station, she noticed a sign proudly proclaiming, *"Now Serving StellarBrew in Five New Temporal Flavors!"* She wasn't entirely sure what flavor 'temporal' was supposed to taste like, but it certainly didn't inspire confidence. Instead, she grabbed a cup of beige liquid labeled *Synth-O-Juice*. As she took a sip, she grimaced. It tasted like someone had dissolved cardboard in water and called it juice.

Each bite of the eggs was bland, and the bacon had the consistency of chalk, but still, Linda savored it as if it were a five-star meal. The fruit, though faintly waxy and suspiciously flavorless, was a welcome burst of color on her tray. The food tasted like it had been optimized to appeal to absolutely no one, but for now, she'd take it. Linda shoved another forkful of scrambled eggs into her mouth, trying to savor the mediocrity. The cafeteria buzzed with the usual chatter of exhausted workers, and for a moment, she tried to block it out, to lose herself in the food.

"Oh, hey Linda." Beb plopped down at the table across from her, grinning with the same over-the-top cheerfulness that seemed immune to the despair of daily gigs. He had a bowl full of what looked like dried dog food. "Crazy gig yesterday, don't you think?"

Linda blinked, her mind still foggy. "What are you talking about?"

"The gig down at the factory," Beb said casually between bites. He popped a kibble pellet into his mouth. "That was crazy, right? I hope I get something more relaxing today."

She froze, her fork midway to her mouth. "What do you mean, yesterday?"

Beb gave her a concerned look. "Uh, yesterday? You know, the gig we were on? With the striking workers? You're not looking so good, Linda. Are you feeling okay?"

Linda stared at him, her brain struggling to catch up with his words. Yesterday? She had been stuck in that nightmarish cubicle for *months*, maybe even *years*. The endless typing, the shocks, the constant cycle of meals and sleep, it had dragged on forever. But now Beb was telling her that all of that had only happened since yesterday?

"I... I don't... yesterday?" she muttered, her voice barely above a whisper. Her mind raced as she tried to make sense of it. How could something that felt so torturous, so eternal, have lasted just a few hours?

"Yeah, you look a bit out of it," Beb said, his voice as casual as ever. "Didn't you get any rest last night? When I got back, I crashed hard."

She rubbed her temples, trying to make sense of it. The cubicle, the constant shocks, the endless stacks of papers. It had felt like a lifetime. Linda looked down at her plate, suddenly feeling nauseous. She had been so sure she was trapped for countless months. All that suffering, all that endless repetition...

and it had only been what? A few hours on the station? Where had she been? What had happened to her?

"Yeah, maybe I just need more sleep," she muttered, though deep down, she knew no amount of sleep could fix the fracture her mind had endured.

Linda pushed her tray away, her appetite gone. It didn't make sense, yet Beb was sitting there, chewing on a bowl of space-kibble without a care in the galaxy.

She stood up abruptly, her chair screeching against the floor, drawing a few tired glances from nearby tables. Beb looked up, mid-bite, his expression a mix of confusion and concern.

"Where are you going?" he asked, his tail wagging as if this were just another normal day.

"I need some air," Linda mumbled, her voice distant. "I... I need to think."

"Air? But we're on a space station, you big goof!" Beb chuckled, completely oblivious to the existential crisis Linda was having. He waved her off, still grinning as if their entire world wasn't just a giant hamster wheel with no escape. His tail wagged happily as he scooped up another handful of kibble.

She felt like she was wading through molasses as she made her way to the exit, each step heavier than the last.

As soon as she stepped into the corridor, the familiar stale, recycled air of the station filled her lungs. *Air*—technically. It had the same flavorless quality of everything else aboard the StellarGigs station; the taste of a place where even oxygen felt secondhand. She could almost imagine it getting passed around like the cafeteria slop. Everyone took a breath, handed it to the next person, until it circled back to her, a little more used up each time.

The weight of everything pressed down on her, the gigs, the grind, the punishment that had warped her sense of time. Had it really been just a few hours? She needed answers, or at least something that didn't feel like she was trapped inside a corporate blender set to 'mild torment'.

She instinctively made her way to the StellarGigs employee kiosk, a small alcove near the gig transport rooms that looked like a cheap mall photo booth. The walls were plastered with motivational posters: *"Work Harder Today for a Happier Tomorrow!"* (though someone had hastily scribbled *"Tomorrow Never Comes"* in pen beneath it). A fake potted plant sat awkwardly next to the terminal, its leaves sagging like they too were sick of this place.

As she approached the kiosk, the cheerful hologram materialized before the machine even finished booting up. "Welcome, valued worker! How can StellarGigs assist you today?" it chirped with an enthusiasm so aggressive it could power a small star.

Linda grimaced, her fingers hovering over the touchscreen interface. Where could she even start? *Help, I think I lived in a nightmarish bureaucratic purgatory for years, but it was really only a couple hours?* Instead, she settled for something more manageable.

"I need to check the details of my last gig. The one at the factory with the strike."

The hologram's face flickered, as if it had to reboot its excitement level. "Of course! One moment while I retrieve that information for you."

Linda's eyes drifted to the corner of the kiosk, where a sign above a bright red button read *"Press Here for Instant Corporate Joy!"* She wasn't sure if it dispensed confetti or an HR representative, but neither option sounded appealing.

A few seconds passed, and then the report appeared on the screen, listing her recent assignments. Sure enough, the factory gig was there, the last entry under completed gigs.

Duration – 9 hours, 12 minutes.

"Nine hours?" Linda whispered to herself. It felt like she'd lived an entire lifetime inside that cubicle. The fluorescent lights, the shocks, the endless typing... it had dragged on for what seemed like an eternity. But here it was, documented in black and white—just a nine-hour shift.

She scrolled through the gig summary, desperately searching for something that would explain it. Anything. But the report was painfully normal. Arrival. Assignment. Departure. It might as well have been a delivery route. No mention of the punishment. No record of the cubicle hell she had endured.

Frustration bubbled up inside her. She tapped the screen again, harder this time, as if she could force it to reveal the truth. "What about the cubicle? The data entry punishment? Where is that listed?"

The hologram blinked back at her, still grinning with relentless optimism. "I'm sorry, worker Linda Greyson, but there are no disciplinary actions listed on your account at this time. You are in good standing with StellarGigs."

Good standing? After everything she had gone through? The shocks, the isolation, the endless monotony? Linda felt like her grip on reality was slipping. Was it all some kind of corporate hallucination? Had she imagined it? Was StellarGigs messing with her mind?

A small voice inside her head whispered, *You're going crazy.*

Her frantic tapping was interrupted by a sudden *ding* from her *ChronoShackle.*

NEW GIG ASSIGNED:

Hazardous Sanitation Duty: Zone 3 Biohazard Sector.

The notification flashed cheerfully, as if she'd just been given a prize rather than another soul-crushing task.

Linda stared at it, her stomach twisting into knots. Of course. No time to recover. No time to make sense of the punishment that didn't officially exist. StellarGigs was already shoving her back into the grind, like nothing had happened. Like *nothing ever happened.*

Linda slumped against the wall, her back sliding down until she was sitting on the cold metal floor beneath another banner reading *"Infinite Growth, Infinite Happiness!"* She caught sight of the fake plant again, its drooping leaves seeming to mock her with their artificial apathy.

She needed to get away from this. From the endless gigs, from the punishment, from the crushing monotony that gnawed at her sanity.

But what was the alternative? Another gig was waiting for her. It always would be.

Linda sat, staring at the blinking gig assignment on her *Shak*, trying to force her mind to come up with an answer that wasn't as bleak as her current reality. But the more she thought about it, the more it felt like she was caught in an infinite loop. Wake up. Work. Get punished. Work some more. The space station, for all its vastness, felt like a shrinking cage.

But she couldn't just sit there forever. The clock was ticking. And if she didn't get moving soon, another punishment might await her, maybe worse than the cubicle nightmare. She pushed herself up from the floor, her body aching in protest, and began to shuffle towards the gig transport room.

15

Slime Is of the Essence

"They poured poison into the soil and were shocked when it clawed its way back out—angrier, uglier, and shaped like their quarterly profits."

— Commander Axton Starforge,
Steel Hearts: Echoes of Andromeda, S1E20

Linda found herself in a dim, cavernous room. The air was thick and humid, clinging to her skin like a damp towel. The stench (an overwhelming mix of chemicals, decay, and something disturbingly organic) hit her like a punch. It reminded her of burnt hair, but somehow more... alive.

She glanced around, taking in the scene. The walls were lined with industrial equipment and massive vats that bubbled ominously, no doubt brewing up something sinister. In the far corner, a large, flickering sign hung over a doorway, its message simultaneously not reassuring and ridiculous: *"Biohazard Zone 3: Enter At Your Own Risk. (But Do Enter, That's What You're 'Paid' For!)"*

Linda's stomach churned. Not just from the stench.

A crackling voice came over a nearby speaker: "All sanitation workers to Zone 3. Clean-up is urgent. Hazardous waste detected. Please remember, your minimal safety is important to us."

Linda sighed, shoulders slumping in defeat, and trudged toward Zone 3. As she rounded a corner, she spotted Beb, already suited up in an oversized hazmat suit, waving like it was the best day of his life. She passed a machine labeled: *"Biohazard Disposal, Proudly Sponsored by StellarGigs: Dispose of Your Worries and Toxic Waste!"*

Linda snorted under her breath. "If only."

"Hey, Linda! Guess we're working together again!" Beb's voice crackled through his suit's communication device, brimming with unwarranted enthusiasm. "This is gonna be fun, huh? Cleaning biohazards, saving the galaxy, and all that!"

Linda stared at him, her face deadpan. Fun? How had Beb managed to survive in this system with his spirit intact? She didn't even have the energy to reply.

Linda grabbed a hazmat suit from the rack, with a look of resignation as she suited up. The gloves were two sizes too big, the helmet was uncomfortably tight, and the entire suit smelled faintly of wet dog. Just as she adjusted the awkward headgear, a flickering hologram of a cartoonish bunny in a hazmat suit appeared beside her, ears bouncing slightly with every word.

"Hi there, worker! I'm Contammy the Containment Bunny! Remember: Speed First, Safety Second!" it squeaked, raising a tiny mop as if it were a weapon. The hologram smiled, its big, exaggerated eyes twinkling with misplaced enthusiasm.

Linda stared at the hologram, dumbfounded. Beb gave Contammy a cheerful wave. "Hey, Contammy! Always good to see a familiar face!"

Linda rolled her eyes as the bunny's recorded voice continued, "Containment is cool, and so are YOU! Make sure you keep hazardous materials inside Zone 3... or we'll have to bring in the *big bunns!*" Contammy gave a wink, mopped the imaginary floor, and disappeared with a cheery sparkle.

Inside Zone 3, chaos had taken on a new form. Bright green, gelatinous goo oozed from broken pipes, pooling on the floor and clinging to the walls in sluggish, yet oddly deliberate movements. Several workers were already struggling to contain it, spraying it with a neutralizing foam that fizzled uselessly, doing little more than angering the goo.

The gelatinous substance began to shift, seemingly aware of their attempts to contain it. The green sludge slithered across the floor with intent, heading straight toward the workers.

"Is this stuff... alive?" Linda muttered, her voice muffled by the helmet.

Beb, crouched low to inspect a particularly large puddle of goo. He looked up with baffling optimism. "I dunno, but it's kinda neat, right? Like cleaning up after a giant space sneeze!"

"Neat?" Linda's tone was flat, barely audible above the din of the foam sprayers. She aimed her own sprayer at a wall, hoping for a miracle. The foam hissed on contact, but the goo simply quivered, then oozed toward her.

Suddenly, a high-pitched alarm blared through the room, and the overhead lights flickered ominously. Linda froze, her foam sprayer hanging limp in her hands.

A mechanical voice echoed through the room: "Attention, valued workers. Biohazard escalation detected. Level 3 contamination breach in progress. Please remain calm. All cleanup efforts must continue."

The goo gathered momentum, pulling itself into towering, writhing mounds that climbed the walls and dropped down onto the workers below. Those unfortunate enough to be in its path barely had time to scream before the sludge smothered them, absorbing their bodies with horrifying efficiency. Each 'meal' seemed to invigorate it, making it shift and pulse with renewed energy, as if it was just getting started.

One by one, the other workers vanished beneath the relentless mass, their muffled cries quickly stifled as they were consumed. Soon, only Linda and Beb remained, standing frozen amidst the chaos, watching as the ooze slithered and pulsed with a disturbing, hungry focus, drawing closer to them.

"Oh, you've got to be kidding me..." Linda muttered, backing away as the goo's gelatinous tendrils reached out like greedy fingers.

The door to Zone 2 slid open, releasing a gust of cool air. In hopped a towering, chrome-plated robotic rabbit, complete with oversized, articulating ears and a pair of glaring red LED eyes that pulsed menacingly. Standing at nearly seven feet tall, the rabbit looked like the twisted version of a children's mascot, with razor-sharp metal teeth and oversized paws equipped with industrial-grade cleaning tools.

Linda's jaw dropped as she watched the mechanical bunny bounce on its powerful, spring-loaded legs, its metal ears twitching with every hop.

When it spoke, its voice boomed artificially deep, and with what sounded like a Central European accent, dripping with patronizing bravado.

"Greetings, sanitation operatives! I am the Biohazard Utility General Sanitizer, model T-001!" It boomed in a strangely cheerful yet menacing tone, each word punctuated with a slight twitch of its metallic whiskers. "My creators programmed me for one thing: total biohazard annihilation. Get ready... for containment."

Linda exchanged a bewildered glance with Beb, who, to her astonishment, was clapping in sheer awe. "Contammy!" he cheered, his voice crackling through his helmet's comm.

The robot raised a metallic paw, pointing it dramatically at the goo. Its nose twitched, as if it were sniffing out the biohazard. "Situation analysis: hostile organic contaminant detected. Tactical protocol... engage at maximum power!" With that, the T-001 began to move forward, gears whirring as it hopped straight into the writhing green sludge. The robot's every hop released a puff of disinfectant mist, and Linda could swear she heard a faint soundtrack swelling in the background—*Ride of the Valkyries* maybe, or something eerily close.

"Stand back, sanitation operatives. Your safety is... *secondary* to my prime directive: *total eradication.*" The T-001 lumbered right into the goo with all the subtlety of a giant space grasshopper, laser eyes blazing and every joint flashing red.

The green sludge quivered and recoiled as if in shock at this aggressive approach. "You have chosen resistance," T-001 declared with a hint of exasperation. "Fine." It raised one paw, which transformed into a vacuum attachment. "Initiating... Phase Two." The vacuum roared to life, pulling in small splatters of goo, which were sucked up like crumbs.

The sludge, however, was not so easily defeated. Within moments, it surged back, latching onto the robot's legs and oozing upward in thick, gloppy waves. T-001's sensors blinked in distress.

"Situation... under control," it insisted, though the goo was already halfway up its metallic torso, its neutralizing mist fizzing weakly against the ooze. "Moving to... Phase Three."

It lifted one paw in a theatrical gesture, shifting to a miniature flame thrower. "Activating... incineration mode." A small flame burst forth, barely strong enough to toast bread, let alone neutralize a biohazard. The goo absorbed it, bubbling with amusement as it climbed higher.

The T-001 faltered. "Resistance minimal. Escalating to... Phase Four. Prepare for ultimate... neutralization."

The goo swallowed its legs completely, inching up toward its torso, and the robot's voice began to sound less certain. "Minor... problem detected. Biohazard level upgraded to... Level Critical." It hesitated, the words coming slower as the goo climbed higher. "Prepare yourself for... Phase Five: Total lockdown."

The robot's legs emitted a frantic stream of sparks, locking its joints into place. It tilted its head down to observe the goo crawling up its chest with a wary glare. "Containment... situation... still... under... control," it assured them with increasingly less conviction.

Linda and Beb watched, entranced, as the goo wound up around the T-001's head. It gave one final attempt at bravado. "I'll... come... *back!*" The green sludge burbled over its faceplate, muffling the voice until it faded to a distorted, gurgling hum. The robot emitted a few final desperate sparks, then fell silent, slumping over as the goo enveloped it entirely.

There was a long, stunned silence.

"So," Linda said, turning to Beb, "you think that counts as 'under control'?"

Beb looked back at her, eyes wide behind his helmet. "Maybe we should call for backup."

Linda threw him an incredulous look. "Beb, that *was* the backup." She fiddled with her *Shak*, trying to summon an escape plan. "We need to get out of here."

A cheerful chime from her *ChronoShackle* interrupted her. "Transport currently unavailable."

"What?! Why?"

The speakers crackled to life again: "Good news, workers! Hellfire protocol has been enabled. Please vacate Zone 3 within five seconds."

Linda's heart stopped. *Hellfire protocol?*

"Beb, follow me," she said, her voice steadier than she felt. Without waiting for a response, she sprinted toward the door to Zone 2. The goo was spreading faster now, surging toward them in heavy, sludgy waves.

Beb scrambled after her, slipping as he ran. "Where are we going?"

"Anywhere that's not here!" Linda shouted over her shoulder.

They dove through the sliding door just as it sealed shut behind them with a hiss. The faint sound of a raging inferno roared from the other side, along with a few unnatural, high-pitched screams. Then, there was silence, except for the sound of their labored breathing.

After a beat, another announcement crackled through the speakers, this time in a disturbingly chipper tone: "Great work, valued workers! The biohazard situation has been eliminated!"

Linda leaned against the wall, sweat dripping from her brow. "I can't keep doing this."

Beb, completely unfazed, grinned under his helmet. "Maybe we'll get assigned something *fun* next time!"

Linda shot him a look, incredulous, before finally managing a small, exhausted laugh. "Yeah, sure. Maybe something *fun*."

The cafeteria was quieter than usual, though quiet on the station still meant the constant hum of vending machines, the rattle of trays, and the occasional worker arguing with a soup dispenser. Linda slumped into a chair, her shoulders still sticky from slime residue despite three showers. Across from her, Lira stirred a cup of something neon-blue and fizzy, blowing bubbles with the same dreamy focus she might've given to a cloud shaped like a chihuahua.

For a while, Linda just stared at her tray. She thought about her time in cubicle purgatory, the silence broken only by the clicking of keys and the weight of despair pressing down like artificial gravity turned up too high. She opened her mouth, then closed it again. No. Not yet.

Instead, she cleared her throat. "Do you ever think about... how long we've actually been here?"

Lira's eyes lit up in a way that made Linda regret the question immediately. "Not really. Days blur into weeks, weeks blur into eternities, and somewhere out there our younger selves are still waiting in line to be processed." She sipped her drink with relish. "I miss her."

Linda blinked at her. "...Right. That's... not exactly what I meant."

"Oh, okay." Lira leaned back and smiled dreamily. "Because if you were talking about time, it's not real. Just another corporate metric. Like smiles per hour."

Linda pressed her lips together. She wasn't sure if she wanted to laugh, cry, or slap the drink out of Lira's hand.

"You're a real comfort."

Before Lira could respond, a sharp *ding* rang through the cafeteria. The massive holo-screen over the food line flickered to life:

TOP EMPLOYEE: CURRENT RANKINGS!

At the top of the list, glowing proudly in golden letters:

PIGEON — 2,340 POINTS

Again, in second and third place were:

COCO — 2,339 POINTS

CELVIN — 1,750 POINTS

The screen shifted to display a professional photo of the pigeon, staring blankly into the camera as though daring everyone else to try harder.

From across the room, Coco shot to his feet, claws digging into his tray. "ONE POINT?!" he shouted, his voice cracking. "One point?! I just stopped a star from going supernova in a *heavily* populated system and I lose by ONE POINT to poultry?!"

Workers barely looked up from their meals as Coco stomped out, tail lashing furiously.

Linda watched him go, then glanced back at the scoreboard. "I can't decide if that's sad or impressive."

"I think it's beautiful," Lira said, still stirring her drink. "A perfect example of the futility of existence." She blew another bubble, which popped loudly. "Also, pigeons are cute."

Linda buried her face in her hands. "I miss when my biggest problem was rent."

Lira tilted her head. "Rent?"

"Yeah," Linda muttered. "Back when life made sense. You worked, you paid someone so you could keep living where your stuff was, then you did it again next month. If you didn't work, then you were out sleeping on the street."

"That sounds awful."

"It was," Linda admitted, "but at least it was *real*. You knew who was screwing you."

Lira smiled faintly. "You paid for the privilege of not dying on the street. It's an elegant system. Efficient despair."

Linda groaned. "You make everything sound like a suicide note."

"I call it poetry." Lira leaned back, stirring her drink again. "Rent is just a metaphor for all of this. You trade pieces of yourself for the illusion of safety."

"That's a very Lira way of looking at it," Linda said. "Some of us still think cooperation isn't a scam."

"Cooperation is fine," Lira said. "As long as you can walk away. But if you have to keep paying to exist, you don't own your life anymore. Someone else does."

Linda frowned at her cup. "So what, we just... live in caves and hope the rent collector can't find us?"

"Exactly," Lira said, delighted. "See, you're learning."

"I was being sarcastic."

"So was I. Mostly."

They sat in silence for a moment, the hum of the cafeteria filling the air.

Linda sighed. "I don't know, maybe I just miss the simplicity. You pay the bill, you stay alive. Now it's all metrics and morale points and pigeons with better performance reviews."

"Because you traded rent for ratings," Lira said softly. "Different cage, same landlord."

Linda stared at her for a long moment, then muttered, "You really know how to ruin nostalgia."

"That's my rent," Lira said with a smile. "I pay in truth."

16

A Sticky Situation

"They said I was essential—until I wasn't. Funny how quickly you become baggage once the job's done."

— *Commander Axton Starforge,*
Steel Hearts: Echoes of Andromeda, S6E4

Linda jolted awake, groggy and disoriented, as a persistent buzzing sound wormed its way through her fog-addled brain. She groaned, rolling over, willing the noise to fade. But the buzzing only grew louder, vibrating through the walls of her cramped quarters like a relentless drill.

With a resigned sigh, she dragged herself out of bed, the world still blurring around her as she followed the noise to her storage bin. Inside, the blue cube pulsed softly, its glow syncing with the buzz, alive and waiting.

She hesitated, her hand hovering but unwilling to touch it. The last time she'd handled the thing, things had gone... strange.

Her thoughts drifted back to the day she'd brought it aboard. She should have done something with it then. Dumped it. Reported it. Anything but keep it. Yet every time she considered turning it in, paranoia crept in, feeding her certainty that StellarGigs would find some way to punish her for it. She didn't even know if they'd care, but her gut told her they wouldn't take kindly to the cube's quirks.

The hum pressed on, crawling beneath her skin, agitating her curiosity. The cube's light intensified, filling the room with a soft blue glow that cast long, surreal shadows across the walls. She took a step back, biting her lip.

"Maybe I should..." she murmured, her voice barely above a whisper. Then, she slammed the storage bin shut with finality. "Nope. Not today, cubey."

A grumble from her stomach reminded her just how long it'd been since she'd eaten. She glanced at her *Shak*, which read 9:15, though the station's stretched-out days always left her feeling disoriented. Deciding it was high time for breakfast, she headed for the cafeteria, letting the buzzing cube fade into the back of her mind, for now.

"Then the bunny got completely swallowed up by the ooze creature," Beb recounted, his voice trembling as he tried to keep from laughing. "Poor Contammy, never stood a chance." The group exploded in laughter, the sound bouncing off the walls of the cafeteria, mingling with the clinking of dishes, the low hum of conversation, and the occasional hiss from a beverage dispenser nearby.

Most of the group was there: Linda, Coco, and Glorp seated on one side, with Beb, Lira, and Zorb on the other. Linda caught herself smiling, a rarity for mornings on the station. There was an ease in the air, a rare pocket of camaraderie in the midst of endless gigs and grueling shifts. Everyone seemed in good spirits, though Zorb, true to form, was buried in his tablet, muttering occasional complaints as he scrolled through an ever-expanding list of grievances. He barely seemed to notice when Lira poked his shoulder, chuckling at one of Beb's reenactments.

"Honestly, best part of the gig," Linda said with a grin, shoveling another forkful of questionable scrambled eggs into her mouth.

Beb, still amused, raised his cup of some sort of warm, stinking liquid in salute. "To Contammy, may he hop in peace, somewhere beyond the ooze." He looked around, waiting for the others to join in, his grin widening as Glorp raised his own cup with a solemn, if slightly puzzled, expression.

"Cheers!" they all chorused, clinking their cups, spoons, and utensils together in what was less a formal toast and more of a spontaneous clatter. A pigeon two tables down looked at them with a blank expression.

Even Zorb grunted, his eyes never leaving his tablet, "Here's hoping they don't send one of us as his replacement." He punctuated his comment by giving the screen a disgruntled poke.

"Oh, Zorb," Lira said dreamily. "Cleanup duty is meditative. Nothing more relaxing than cleaning." She smiled wistfully before taking a sip of her drink.

"If they send me, I'm putting in for hazard pay. Although, I doubt StellarGigs even remembers what that is." He tapped his screen sharply, frowning. "It's not like I have a phobia of ooze. I just have an aversion to pointless sludge-related death. Is that so wrong?"

The group laughed, even Linda couldn't help but grin. It was moments like this, she realized, that kept them all going. Linda glanced around the table, taking in the scene, a small part of her wishing these mornings happened more often. In a place as vast and indifferent as the station, these bits of connection were her anchors.

"And on that cheerful note, I must be off to my next gig," Zorb announced, standing up from the table and giving the group a halfhearted wave before heading out.

"Lira and I are on Comet Polishing duty today," Coco said, pushing his tray back and getting to his feet.

"They're so pretty," Lira sighed dreamily. "I'm bringing one home."

Coco raised an eyebrow. "Pretty sure you're not fitting a comet in your pocket, Lira."

She smiled, unfazed. "We shall see."

Just as Coco and Lira left the cafeteria, Linda's *Shak* buzzed on her wrist:

NEW GIG ASSIGNED:

Hazard Stripe Reapplication Technician: Join the vanguard of safety by applying StellarGigs approved adhesive on Pyroxis Delta.

The notification flashed with a cheerful ding, as though it were something to look forward to.

"Hazard Stripe Reapplication Technician," Linda said as she rolled her eyes. "Why do they have to make every mundane task sound important?" Glorp gave her a small shrug.

"Looks like we're paired up again, gig partner!" Beb said, grinning as he held up his own *Shak*, the same assignment blinking on his screen. His tail gave an excited wag. "They must know we make a good team!"

Linda raised an eyebrow, less enthusiastic. "Yeah, 'good team' for reapplying... safety tape?"

Beb's grin didn't waver. "Exactly! Besides, maybe it'll be one of those gigs where we actually make a difference. Keeping people safe, you know?"

Linda sighed, her amusement slipping through despite herself. "Right. Because nothing says 'saving lives' like red tape."

Beb just laughed, unbothered. "Look on the bright side! It's not every day we get to travel."

Linda shook her head, standing up from the table. "Actually, we do get to travel every day, whether we want to or not." Linda let out a deep breath, "Alright, partner. Let's go reapply some stripes and... save the galaxy, one line at a time."

Linda and Beb materialized on a metal platform stretching thousands of feet above what could loosely be called *ground*. In truth, it was a lonely rock island, standing sentinel in a slow, molten river of orange lava, thick and sluggish like bubbling syrup. The acrid stench of sulfur lingered in the searing air, and the heat shimmered in waves, distorting everything in sight. Their breathers hummed, filtering out the toxic fumes and providing a thin semblance of comfort amidst the inhospitable environment.

"I didn't realize we'd be this high up," Linda said over her comm, her voice tight as she edged back from the ledge. She knelt, her fingers white-knuckled around the guardrail, unwilling to look directly down. The thought of the abyss below sent her stomach into uneasy somersaults.

"The view is incredible!" Beb exclaimed, practically bouncing in place, his excitement uncontainable. He leaned forward, peering down at the molten river, the lava glistening like an endless sea of burning honey. Then he glanced over and noticed Linda's wide-eyed, slightly queasy expression. "Linda, you alright?"

"Not a fan of heights," she replied, her grip on the rail almost painfully tight.

Beb nodded in understanding. "Alright, why don't you just hang back here and let me handle this one? It's an easy gig anyway. All we're doing is replacing safety tape."

"I can't let—" Linda began.

He waved her off with a grin. "Look, you saved my hide on the last gig. So, this one's on me. We're partners, right? Besides, it's hardly a challenge. Just pass me the tape."

Linda hesitated, but Beb's earnest smile won her over. "Fine. Dinner's on me when we get back." She handed him her roll of red tape.

With a confident step, Beb made his way onto the narrow walkway, his posture a mix of care and cheerful obliviousness. The metal beneath his boots creaked, and the walkway swayed with each step, but he didn't seem to notice. He started peeling up the faded, fraying tape along the edges of the walkway. "See, the trick is to pull the old stuff up slowly; otherwise, it tears, and you have to start over," he said, as if imparting the wisdom of ages.

"Can't we just put the new tape on top?" Linda asked, raising an eyebrow. "No one would know."

"Oh no, no, no. Gotta do it right," Beb said, sounding scandalized. "You put your best into every gig, and one day, you'll get that five-star rating."

"Beb, I'm not even sure there *is* a five-star rating."

He gave her a knowing look. "It's out there. You just have to earn it."

As he finished peeling a section, Beb tossed the withered tape over the edge and watched it spiral down toward the lava, his face lighting up as if he'd just completed some grand ritual. He turned back to Linda, grinning. "Now, roll out the new tape nice and steady, straight line, no slapping it on all willy-nilly. Safety's no joke. Someday, this could save lives."

Linda watched in exasperation, marveling at his boundless optimism. Gig after meaningless gig, and somehow, Beb was still out there, thinking he was saving the universe.

Beb finished laying the first strip of red tape and stepped back, crossing his arms to admire his work. "Perfect!" he declared with pride, then crouched down to start the other side of the walkway. "You know, back on training day, if you can call a three-minute slideshow 'training', someone said red tape saves lives. Everyone laughed, but I kinda took it to heart." He smiled, smoothing the new strip down. "I like to think this stuff actually matters. That maybe, just maybe, it holds things together."

"Hey Beb," Linda said, curiosity getting the better of her, "why did you join StellarGigs?"

"Oh, same old story." He chuckled. "I've got eight siblings, and as the runt, I was always last to get anything. My parents didn't even think I'd make it when I was born, but hey, I proved them wrong!" He looked up with a twinkle in his eye. "We had a big family, and times were tough. The big galactic corporations came to my planet and automated everything. My dad's factory was one of the first to go. He was out of work for years."

Beb peeled off another strip of old tape, giving it a ceremonious fling over the edge. "Most people ended up in the same spot, and when I was old enough to work, there just weren't any jobs left. Too many people, not enough work. So, I stayed with my parents, but they were struggling. When StellarGigs showed up, I jumped at the chance. Great pay, and that bonus will really help my folks out when I finish my contract."

Linda looked away, blinking back a sudden sting in her eyes. *Poor idiot,* she thought. *He still thinks he's getting out of here.*

"You know what my dream is?" Beb added, as he carefully pressed down a fresh strip of tape. "To go back home, show my folks that I did it. That I made something of myself. I want my older brothers to see me in the StellarGigs newsletter one day. Employee spotlight. Wouldn't that be something?" He looked up to Linda. "What about you, why did you sign up?"

Linda forced a smile. "Pretty much the same reason. Life's hard on my planet. Living expenses are through the roof, and jobs don't pay enough to cover it. I thought StellarGigs was my big break." She bit back the words in her head. *Now I know better.* But she kept it to herself. *Let him have his delusion.*

"I'm moving over to the main platform. Walkway's pretty much done here," Beb said, strolling further away.

"Okay Beb, I'll keep an eye on you from here."

Beb strolled out to the main platform, his cheerful whistling coming through the comm. The platform was larger, a tangled mess of rusted metal beams and disjointed panels that didn't look entirely stable. After a moment, his tone changed to mild outrage.

"Linda! Whoever did the last tape job out here should be fired. It's like a giant spiderweb exploded all over the place; tape stuck on the rails, crisscrossing the floor, even flapping off the sides. This is gonna take forever to clean up."

Linda smirked. "Guess it's your lucky day, Beb. Nothing like cleaning up someone else's mess."

"Right?" Beb chuckled. "But you know me. I'm gonna get it looking pristine." He started peeling up the tangled tape, muttering under his breath, "Honestly, who trained these people?"

"Same people that trained us... nobody." Linda said with a smirk. She watched as he meticulously removed the web of tape, his movements almost reverent. Then she noticed a subtle, unnerving shift under her boots. She squinted and looked more closely as the platform gave a soft groan.

"Uh... Beb?" she said carefully. "Maybe you should, uh, keep some of that tape on there? I think it might be... holding this thing together."

Beb let out a laugh. "C'mon, Linda, they wouldn't be that careless with safety! This is StellarGigs we're talking about!"

At that moment, a loud clank echoed from somewhere deep within the structure, and the entire platform wobbled ominously. Linda's eyes widened.

"Beb..." she said slowly, "maybe StellarGigs isn't as committed to workplace safety as you think."

He paused, one hand mid-peel. "Nah... They wouldn't let me go out here if the platform was, you know, actually held together by red tape. Right?"

Another soft groan echoed through the comms, followed by a loose bolt pinging off the side and tumbling toward the lava below.

"Beb!" Linda barked. "Leave the tape. Just... back away slowly."

Beb's cheerful expression began to fade, replaced by an uneasy frown. For the first time, Linda's warning seemed to sink in as he took in the web of red tape crisscrossing the platform, securing metal beams that looked just a bit too rusted for comfort.

"Uh... Linda, you might have a point," he said, his voice losing some of its usual optimism. He looked around, realizing he'd already moved too far out onto the platform. There was no easy way back to the walkway.

The tape holding the platform together gave a slow, ominous rip. The entire structure shuddered, swaying slightly as the red strips strained under the weight. Beb's eyes went wide, and he froze, hands raised as if trying to keep the platform steady by sheer will.

"Linda... what do I do?" he asked, his voice barely above a whisper.

"Stay still," she replied, her voice tight with panic. "Don't move. I'll call for help."

Beb forced a shaky smile. "I'll be fine. It's probably just, you know, a little wear and tear, nothing the ol' red tape can't handle." But his gaze darted nervously around him, following each creak and groan as the tape stretched, thin and frayed.

Linda quickly tapped her comm. "Hello, hello, anyone there? We need an emergency teleport. This entire place is going to crash down."

A prerecorded voice responded. "Good afternoon valued worker. Early transport has been disabled for this gig. If you feel as if this was done in error, please submit form FU-47A at your earliest convenience. Then be sure to allow up to two weeks for your request to be processed."

"Two weeks? This place is coming down now!"

"Remember, you workers are what make this company great! Goodbye, and have a stellar day." The automated voice continued as the communicator shut down.

"Linda. I think something might be wrong," Beb said.

"Just hold on, everything will be..."

With a loud snap, one of the tape lines split completely, flapping loose like a broken tether. Another gave way moments later, and then another, until the entire platform jolted violently under Beb's feet. He stumbled, grasping for a handrail, but the rails themselves buckled and twisted as the beams holding them collapsed. The loose tape fluttered in the rising heat, peeling away and melting in upon itself.

A single strip fluttered up past Linda's face, red, frayed, and burning at the edges. It twisted in the air like a falling petal, and then was gone.

"Linda!" Beb shouted, panic finally breaking through his voice.

But there was nothing Linda could do. She stood helplessly on the walkway, her eyes wide with horror as the entire platform lurched. With a deafening crash, the metal beams that had once surrounded Beb came down, clattering around him like a cage. Then, with one final groan, the platform broke away entirely, plunging toward the fiery lava below, taking Beb with it.

"Beb!" Linda screamed, reaching out instinctively as if she could somehow catch him. But her arm fell uselessly to her side as she watched the platform disappear, Beb's panicked expression vanishing into the blazing orange depths. Her comm crackled once with static and then went silent.

Linda collapsed back onto her knees, her breath coming in ragged gasps as the reality of what had just happened sank in. The searing heat from the lava below seemed to intensify, as if mocking her helplessness.

She punched her *Shak* in frustration, her voice trembling as she called for backup. "Someone, help! This is Linda. I... I need assistance. The entire platform... it's gone. Beb... Beb is gone."

There was silence on the other end for a moment before a static-filled, almost cheerful voice replied, "Acknowledged, worker Linda. Please note that safety violations have resulted in a one-star review. StellarGigs recommends following all safety procedures in the future. Also, please be advised that any and all organic remains must be reported to Sanitation using form DS-11-R. Failure to do so may result in a workplace contamination infraction."

Linda stared blankly, the response somehow more surreal than everything she had just witnessed. She laughed—a hollow, bitter sound—and dropped her head into her hands.

"Five-stars, Beb," she whispered, her voice cracking. "You really thought we could get five-stars."

Something fluttered at the edge of her vision. A strip of StellarGigs red safety tape, half-melted, clinging to a twisted beam nearby. It snapped weakly in the heat, the corporate logo warped and blackened.

Linda reached out and tore it free. The plastic stuck briefly to her glove before peeling away. She turned it over in her hand, staring at it for a long moment.

Then she folded it once and slipped it into her pocket.

"Yeah," she murmured. "Five-stars."

The molten light below flickered across her visor as she rose, the tape crinkling softly with each step she took away from the edge.

17

My Chemical Bromance

"We left him among the stars. No grave, no words, just a silence that stretched farther than any orbit."

— Commander Axton Starforge,
Steel Hearts: Echoes of Andromeda, S4E24

Linda stepped into the worker recreation room, letting the cool air wash over her. It was a fleeting escape from the claustrophobic grip of the station's corridors. On her wrist, she wore a narrow band of red tape, its edges frayed from heat. It wasn't much, just a small, silent reminder of someone the system would rather forget.

She scanned the space, her gaze landing on Rilo and Coco huddled over a table, engrossed in a board game. Lira lounged nearby, her legs propped up on an empty chair, lazily sipping from a glass of bright blue liquid that sparkled under the harsh fluorescent lights.

The room's familiar oddity (a clash of styles and colors) seemed more jarring than usual. The brightly lit posters advertising "gig accomplishments" only underscored the emptiness she felt. One read, "Just dodged solar flares in the Nebula Maze? Treat yourself!" The worker's beaming face felt like a slap.

The holo-screen buzzed in the corner of the rec room, just loud enough to be heard over the hum of vending machines and idle conversation. It was playing another episode of *Steel Hearts: Echoes of Andromeda*.

Rhys: *"...and I used to be like you. Clocking in. Clocking out. Hoping GalaxJobs wouldn't cut my oxygen just to boost quarterly margins. But I escaped. I saw the truth, and it brought me... to you..."*

Doctor Pierce: *"Lieutenant, there's no evidence that people in comas can hear you talk to them."*

Rhys: *"Dammit Doctor, I have to try. I have to reach him before the nano-virus reaches his personality matrix!"*

Doctor Pierce: *"But how will that even..."*

Rhys (fierce): *"With something your degrees and dusty textbooks could never understand. Love, Doctor. Love. It's stronger than any medicine."*

Linda stared at the screen, numb. She *liked* this show. She really did. But right then, it felt like biting into something sweet and finding it rotten in the middle. The words were grand, the emotions dialed up to maximum, but it all rang hollow.

Not because it was insincere. But because it was trying too hard to feel like something real, and she knew exactly what real felt like. Real didn't have soaring violins and dramatic close-ups. Real didn't monologue about love while everything you cared about slipped quietly out of reach.

Her throat tightened.

She looked away, eyes burning, not from tears, but from the sheer effort of holding them in. The absurdity scraped against something raw. Not offensive. Not stupid. Just... cruel, in a way it couldn't possibly mean to be.

It reminded her of everything she couldn't say out loud. Everything the station didn't have words for. Everything the show *almost* understood... but didn't.

"Hey, Linda!" Coco called out, bringing her out of her daze. "Wanna join? We're playing *Nebula Clash*! It's like cosmic chess but with *way* more lasers."

Linda forced a smile. "Thanks, but... not really in the mood today."

Rilo smirked without looking up. "Smart choice. Coco here thinks he's winning, but in two moves, he'll be adrift in the Void."

Coco's eyes widened as he re-examined the board. "Wait... what?"

Lira let out a chuckle, swirling her drink. "They've been at it for an hour. Rilo's got him right where he wants him."

"What? Are you serious?" Coco declared.

Linda slid into a floating chair, its gentle buoyancy unsettling as she adjusted herself, still feeling the hollow ache in her chest. She glanced at Lira's drink. "What's that?"

Lira took a long sip before responding. "It's called Angorian Fizz. Tastes like blueberries and electro-shock therapy. Want a sip?"

Linda hesitated, then shook her head. "Not right now, but thanks."

Coco, still staring at the board, seemed to be muttering strategies under his breath. Rilo calmly moved a piece, a tiny spaceship glowing faintly as it hopped over several rings. Coco's face fell.

"No! You sunk my battleship!" Coco exclaimed, clutching his head dramatically.

"That's not even the right game, you dummy," Rilo replied, chuckling. "But yes, I did... with a side of dessert."

Linda chuckled softly, a hollow sound that felt almost wrong in her own ears. Despite everything, despite what had happened, these moments used to make the station feel almost bearable.

Coco, unfazed by his board game loss, turned to Linda with enthusiasm. "You sure you don't want to play? It's really simple, honestly. You just have to avoid the black hole pieces. Those send you back to your starting quadrant unless you have a Gravity Override token, which you can only get by landing on the Nebula squares. Oh, and if you land on a wormhole square, you roll to see if you get transported to the Parallel Dimension board, but only if the Galactic Alignment counter is set to zero. Otherwise, you have to trade in one of your HyperJump cards, provided you haven't already used your Anti-Matter shield earlier in the round. See? Easy!"

Linda managed to laugh. "Yeah, real simple."

Lira raised her glass, her voice pulling Linda back into the room, grounding her. "To another thrilling day at StellarGigs."

Linda looked at the blue liquid, and at Lira's calm, steady gaze. She took a deep breath. "You know what? I think I'll take one of those after all." The thought of an Angorian Fizz felt oddly comforting now. She didn't know if it could numb the ache, but it couldn't hurt to try. "It's been that kind of day."

She paused, gathering her thoughts. Finally, with a shaky exhale, she looked up at the group. "There's... something I need to tell you guys."

The group sat in a rare moment of quiet, each of them nursing an Angorian Fizz or some version of it, a faint, bittersweet atmosphere lingering in the air. Empty glasses were piled up in a chaotic, leaning tower at the center of the table, tilting but somehow holding together. Linda stared at the tower for a moment, before reaching out to add another empty glass. She watched as it wobbled precariously before miraculously settling back into place.

Lira smirked, her voice carrying a hint of wistful amusement. "Remember when he sweet-talked a slime? Covered in ooze, but still polite as always."

The group chuckled, Coco grinning as he leaned back in his chair. "Or when he accidentally ran into that nest of acid ants and kept apologizing for invading their personal space, all while running for his life? He thought if he was polite enough, they'd back off."

Linda laughed, though softer than usual, her fingers tracing the rim of her glass. "And that time he tried to fix the vending machine by 'encouraging' it?"

Rilo's grin broke through his usual stern expression. "Yeah, he kept patting it, saying, 'Come on, buddy, I believe in you!' like it was alive."

Coco snickered, leaning in. "And then it actually spat out about fifty protein bars all at once. But, of course, they were all expired by about a decade."

Lira gave a dry, staccato laugh— "heh-heh-heh," flat and airy, the sound of someone mimicking laughter rather than feeling it. She raised her glass with a glint of mild amusement. "Beb didn't mind. He said salt would make them taste better."

"To Beb, who could make even expired protein bars feel like a gift from the cosmos," Linda said, lifting her glass, her voice thick with a warmth the Angorian Fizz couldn't provide.

The others clinked their glasses, each of them savoring the memory of Beb's endless optimism and the bizarre magic he brought to even the most mundane corners of the station.

The group had been sitting together for over three hours, having moved onto less somber topics. Glorp, who had arrived late, had joined in, but now lay sprawled across a nearby couch, snoring loudly. His shaggy form half-buried in the cushions, and his drink—still half-full—teetered precariously on his chest, wobbling with each rise and fall of his breath.

"Hey guys, I've got to ask you something," Linda said, her tone serious, cutting through the lighthearted atmosphere. "Have any of you ever had experiences where time didn't really make sense?"

"Well, sure, Linda," Rilo replied, unfazed. "Any time we're working near black holes or inside wormholes, time gets all wonky."

"Yeah!" Coco chimed in, his tail wagging as he recalled the memory. "About a month ago, I was on this gig cleaning up a dark-matter spill near Sagittarius

A. The job took about two hours, but when the gig report came in, it clocked over fourteen hours."

"Time is an illusion," Lira added.

Linda nodded, though her expression remained distant. "Oh, okay." She took another sip of her drink, eyes thoughtful.

Lira leaned in, her gaze intent. "Something on your mind?" she asked softly.

Linda hesitated, choosing her words carefully. "It was that gig on Industrial Planet 872, the one with the striking workers. Something... strange happened down there."

Coco shrugged. "Seemed like a pretty standard gig to me."

"When I was down there, I... I refused to cross the picket line."

Coco raised an eyebrow. "What are you talking about? Didn't we all walk in together?"

Linda shook her head. "You guys all walked ahead, but I stayed behind."

Coco tilted his head, puzzled. "Are you sure? Beb and I were handling plasma conduit maintenance. We just figured that you were on the other end of the factory handling graviton coil alignment."

Linda's eyes narrowed, and she set her glass down. "No. I wouldn't cross the line. StellarGigs pulled me up for a 'compliance review'. They weren't happy, and as punishment, they assigned me to some tiny cubicle for a data entry gig."

"Well, that doesn't sound so bad," Coco replied, shrugging. "Data entry isn't exactly the worst punishment."

Linda's voice dropped, her eyes distant. "I was there for *months*. Maybe *years*. It felt like an eternity. I gave up hope of ever getting out. Then, out of nowhere, I was teleported back here like nothing ever happened."

Coco gave her a sympathetic but skeptical look. "I mean, Linda, we would've noticed if you were gone for that long. We were only off the station for a few hours, tops."

Rilo nodded in agreement. "Yeah, the time logs don't lie. I'm sure it just felt longer because the gig was boring or stressful... or something."

Linda's shoulders sagged as she scanned the faces around the table. They all seemed convinced, except for Lira, who remained silent, her expression unreadable.

Linda forced a smile. "Yeah... maybe you're right. Must've been in my head." But deep down, she still knew that *something* had happened to her. Whether her friends believed it or not, she had to believe that.

The others resumed their light chatter, dismissing the conversation. Lira, however, continued to sip her drink, her eyes never leaving Linda, but she didn't say a word.

After a few moments, Coco nudged Linda with a grin. "Come on, forget about it! Let's play a round of *Nebula Clash*. I promise, it's not as complicated as it sounds."

The night was winding down, and the worker recreation room had mostly emptied. Only Linda and Lira remained, sitting in the dim light as the hum of the vending machine filled the silence. Glorp had settled into a quieter sleep on the couch, his snores reduced to soft grunts. His drink, now an empty glass, lay on its side, the faint blue stain of Angorian Fizz spreading across the floor like a small, glowing puddle.

Linda turned the red band around her wrist, the plastic warm against her skin. After a moment, she reached into her pocket and pulled out another strip of red tape—carefully folded, its edges smoothed flat.

"Here," she said, sliding it across the table toward Lira. "I made you one."

Lira raised an eyebrow. "What's this?"

"It's from my last gig," Linda said quietly. "I figured Beb wouldn't want to be forgotten."

Lira studied the tape, its dull surface reflecting the flicker of a broken light overhead. For a long moment she didn't move.

"When I was a kid," Linda went on, "I made a bracelet like this for my best friend. It was just some bits of ribbon I found. We promised to wear them until they fell apart." She gave a small, humorless laugh. "Hers snapped first. I cried for days, like it meant something. Guess some things don't change."

Lira finally took the tape, twisting it between her fingers before looping it around her wrist. "You still believe things like that matter?" she asked.

"Maybe," Linda said. "If we stop remembering, what's the point of any of this?"

For a while, neither of them spoke. The hum of the vending machine filled the silence again.

Then Lira broke it. "Did you ever try to put an end to it? In the cubicle?" she asked suddenly, her voice barely above a whisper as she stared into her drink.

"What?" Linda's eyes snapped open, the fog in her brain clearing for a moment. "What did you say?" She squinted, trying to merge the two blurry images of Lira into one.

"Did you try to end things?" Lira's eyes lifted slowly, locking onto Linda's with an intensity that made her shiver. "Put an end to the torture?"

"I... no. I just... kept going," Linda replied, her voice wavering.

"You're stronger than me." Lira's gaze drifted lazily, lost in her own thoughts. "Do you know how much force it takes to break a skull?"

Linda's eyes widened. "No... I don't?"

"More than you would think. You have to really commit to it."

"Did you...?"

"They can keep you alive, if they want to. No matter what happens, they can bring you back. If they find it... worthwhile."

Linda's throat tightened. She felt the weight of Lira's words settle heavily in the air, and she didn't know how to respond.

"And punishing insubordination is *always* worthwhile." Lira's eyes bore into her, the seriousness in her gaze unlike anything Linda had ever seen. It was as if a veil had lifted, revealing a side of Lira that was both terrifying and deeply familiar.

Linda stared at Lira, her heart pounding as the realization settled in. "Why didn't you say anything earlier?"

Lira's expression remained cold, her eyes distant. "Some things, people will only believe when it happens to *them*." She paused, swirling the remnants of her drink as if the motion could erase the thoughts in her mind. "The others would never allow themselves to believe that such a thing was even possible. It's easier to think the system works as intended."

Linda felt the air in the room grow colder. "What do we do, then?"

Lira shrugged, the tension in her shoulders momentarily relaxing. "You do the best you can. None of this is real anyway, and things could always be worse." She paused a moment as if collecting her thoughts. "If things get too bad, there's always the airlock."

Linda's mind swirled with questions, but before she could respond, Lira stood up, her movements slow and deliberate. "Careful what you say. Not everyone is who they seem to be." With that, she walked away, leaving Linda alone with her thoughts and the hum of the vending machine.

18

The Mourning After

"They said revenge changes a man. They were right. It made me better prepared and significantly harder to kill."

— Commander Axton Starforge,
Steel Hearts: Echoes of Andromeda, S3E7

Linda awoke with a pounding headache, her room spinning like she was on some demented carnival ride designed to torment the hungover. The taste of Angorian Fizz lingered sourly on her tongue, as if she'd chewed on blueberries and a live wire. Groaning, she buried her face into the pillow, hoping that maybe if she wished hard enough, the universe might just take a hint and pause for a while.

But then came the noise—a low, insistent buzzing that drilled into her skull, cutting through the haze of her hangover. She lay still, debating if the sound was even real or just the cocktail's lasting gift. She groaned again as the buzzing grew louder. Pushing herself up, she rubbed her temples, feeling the world wobble around her like a badly assembled hologram. She traced the sound to the storage bin above her bed, staggered to her feet, and clung to the wall as she reached for it. She cursed at the way the room seemed determined not to stay still.

With a shaky breath, she opened the bin. There, tucked into the back corner as though it were hiding from daylight, was the blue cube, pulsing in rhythmic blue flashes, each buzz matching its glow as if it had a heartbeat. She reached out to it, fingers unsteady, feeling the cube's cool, chilling surface as she wrapped her hand around it.

As it brushed against her *ChronoShackle*, she noticed a faint flicker in her *Shak's* display. It wasn't anything obvious, just a tiny, almost imperceptible shudder in the usual clock and gig notifications. The display flickered again, just enough to make her pause. Was that... a glitch? Strange symbols blinked on-screen briefly, geometric shapes and odd text that vanished almost as soon as they appeared, leaving her wondering if she'd imagined it.

"What the—?" she muttered, eyes narrowing at the screen. Linda tapped the *Shak's* screen, but nothing responded. The symbols once again briefly flashed in and out like static interference before abruptly blinking off. Her *Shak* then returned to normal, showing the usual time and gig alerts as though nothing unusual had happened.

She stood there, heart pounding, the leftover adrenaline mingling with her hangover, wondering if she'd imagined it all. Her *Shak* was as steady as ever, and the cube now pulsed innocently in her hand, as if mocking her for even thinking something had gone wrong. She set the cube back into the bin, hands unsteady, and leaned against the wall, breathing deeply to calm the churn of unease that had replaced the Angorian Fizz's lingering buzz.

Linda trudged toward the Gig Office, clutching her throbbing head. After a quick stop by Medical to dull the headache and a lackluster attempt to eat something that vaguely resembled oatmeal in the cafeteria, she'd been promptly summoned.

She passed by the digital gig board in the lobby, which was lit up with neon colors so garish they seemed to jab at her headache like tiny, annoying daggers. The gigs scrolling across the display looked as questionable as ever:

Personal Black Hole Consultant: Expertise in Minor Galaxy Devouring Preferred!

Intergalactic Jellyfish Wrangler: Nerve Regeneration Training Included

Meteorite Fashion Model: Must Have High Impact Tolerance! (Stylish helmets provided)

She rubbed her eyes, wondering who in their right mind would volunteer for these. Only at StellarGigs would they think, *"Why not combine mortal danger with a fashion show?"* She had zero interest in any of these today, or ever, really.

As Linda waited, trying to ignore the blinding neon gig board and the headache hammering away in her skull, she noticed a small gathering of StellarGigs bureaucrats just across the office. They were busy constructing what appeared to be a fresh nest made entirely out of office paperwork: stacked requisition forms, shredded employee complaints, and a few battered personnel files layered like insulation.

The bureaucrats chirped at each other in irritation, apparently arguing over the correct filing order. One particularly disgruntled bureaucrat, who wore a minuscule *"Assistant Supervisor of Superfluous Documentation"* badge, was trying to shove an overflowing report on cosmic dust regulations into a crevice with a pair of miniature tongs.

Just as Linda was about to turn away, another bureaucrat scurried over carrying a small, glowing *"Suggestion Box"*. With great ceremony, it plopped it at the top of the nest. The Assistant Supervisor huffed, glancing around proudly, then pulled out a tiny *"Under Review"* sign, sticking it into the top of the pile with a flourish. The entire assembly sighed contentedly, their noses twitching as if they'd just completed an important, intergalactic ritual.

Linda couldn't help but stare as the Assistant Supervisor straightened its badge. He hopped down and disappeared into the nest, emerging moments later with an armful of HR forms for *"Repetitive Stress Injury Awareness"*, which it carefully wedged into a side pocket of the structure.

Just then, GigChad appeared, rolling into her field of vision with the effortless flair of a used-rocket salesman. His faceplate displayed his signature grin, complete with pixelated sunglasses that slid down dramatically as he caught sight of her. "Linda, my favorite space cadet! You look like an asteroid that had a very bad re-entry." His voice was as cheerfully grating as ever, like someone had mixed pom-poms with sandpaper.

He scanned her up and down, as if assessing damage. "Bit rough around the edges, huh? We gotta work on that intergalactic glow, champ. Can't have you tarnishing the good StellarGigs name, now, can we?" His mechanical hand gave her a pat on the shoulder that felt like getting slapped by a frying pan.

Linda's head throbbed even harder, and she seriously contemplated telling him exactly where he could shove his intergalactic glow.

"Why do you even need me to come in?" Linda asked. "You've already sent gigs to me remotely. Why not just keep doing that?"

"Face-to-face interactions have been deemed necessary to strengthen team building," GigChad replied, voice dripping with artificial cheer. "Our data shows that workers overwhelmingly *prefer* coming down here, rather than having gigs sent directly to their *Shaks*."

Give me a break. He can't possibly believe that.

"So let me get this straight. It wastes my time to come down here, but you make me do it anyway because you can. That about right?"

"You get to come down here because that's what you *prefer*."

"I definitely don't *prefer* it."

"According to our data, you do! You must be mistaken about your personal preferences," GigChad said brightly.

Of course, he thinks he knows me better than I do, he's management, Linda thought.

"Alrighty, let's see what we've got for you." GigChad's display flickered, rolling through a list of increasingly questionable gigs. "Ever done dental surgery on a Kaiju? No? How about cosmic terror containment? Oh, the horror stories! Had one guy come back half-flambéed but with a killer tan."

Linda's patience was thinning. "Just give me something that won't get me killed or dismembered."

GigChad's display blinked. "Ah, picky, are we?" He scrolled again, finally landing on something. "Here we go: *Wormhole De-Gunker*. It's perfect for someone not at the top of their game. Just a bit of cosmic plumbing; until you're ready to get back into the big leagues, that is."

Linda gave him a look as dry as Martian dust. "Cosmic plumbing?"

"Think of it as giving the galaxy a nice, big enema!" GigChad's grin stretched across his display like he'd just coined the slogan of the century. "Gotta keep those wormholes squeaky clean and clog-free! Last thing we need is an intergalactic traffic jam plugging up the cosmos. Just imagine the one-star StarRate reviews from disgruntled starships!"

Before she could protest, he reached out, pressing his metallic hand against her *ChronoShackle* to seal the assignment. As soon as he touched it, his faceplate flickered, the grin vanishing for a split second as his voice lagged.

"Worm... hole... De—" His face glitched, and for an instant, she could swear his display showed something odd: a line of garbled code, numbers flickering like they were breaking apart. Then, just as quickly, he recovered, the pixelated grin snapping back. "—Gunker! You're all set! Go get 'em, champ!"

Linda blinked, unsettled. "You... alright there?"

GigChad's laugh was too loud, too peppy. "Never better! Top-notch software over here, baby! Now, go scrub those wormholes till they sparkle, superstar!"

As Linda trudged toward the gig transport, her *Shak* chimed unexpectedly. She glanced down to see a notification flash across the display: "Gig Equipment Update: Quantum Cube *Required!*"

That's new.

She paused, her brow furrowing as she stared at the holographic text. "Quantum cube?" she murmured, perplexed. She tapped the words, which opened a schematic of a glowing blue cube, uncannily similar to the one she had stashed away in her storage bin.

A twinge of unease crept in as she murmured, "Huh..." It felt like more than just a coincidence, but the details refused to add up in her fog-addled mind. She couldn't shake the feeling that somehow, the cube had been waiting for this.

Linda hesitated only a moment before deciding to head back to her room. If the gig required a 'Quantum Cube', she supposed she might as well bring the one already stashed in her storage. Besides, it seemed oddly specific, and nothing in StellarGigs ever struck her as random.

Once in her room, she pulled open the storage bin. The blue cube was still there, pulsing, waiting for her. She picked it up, the cool surface humming in her palm. It felt heavier this time, or maybe her imagination was just getting the best of her.

"Alright, you," she muttered, tucking the cube into her pocket. "Let's see what all this fuss is about."

With the cube safely tucked away, she made her way toward the transporter, her mind racing with possibilities.

When Linda materialized from the teleport, suited up in her spacesuit, *Cosmic Drain-O-Matic* in hand, she immediately felt something was *off*. There was no wormhole in sight, and she wasn't even in space. Instead, she stood in a room that seemed alive; walls of strange, organic-looking technology hummed quietly, as though the room itself were breathing.

"Where... am I?" she muttered, glancing around in confusion.

In response, the blue cube in her pocket began to vibrate, as if it sensed something significant about this place. She pulled it out, holding it in front of her. The cube pulsed brighter, and suddenly, the room responded. The lights along the floor came alive, illuminating a path that led toward a raised control panel about four feet high.

Curiosity (and a slight sense of inevitability) pushed her forward, following the lights. When she reached the panel, she noticed a square indentation at its center, perfectly sized to fit the cube. With a steady breath, she placed the cube into the slot.

As soon as the cube settled in, the panel around it lit up in a dizzying display of colors, cycling from electric blue to a deep, pulsing red. A low hum grew steadily louder, filling the room as if the entire place was winding up an ancient mechanical clock. The lights around her flickered, and strange symbols scrolled across the panel, accompanied by what sounded like a distant, robotic cheer-leading squad chanting garbled encouragement.

A soft glow washed over the room as a holographic projection flickered to life. Linda squinted as the image took shape. It was a towering kitten, easily ten feet tall, with enormous blue-gray eyes and pupils the size of car tires. Its fur was a plush white with gray patches around its head and eyes, and a dainty pink nose that seemed almost laughably small for such an immense creature. The colossal kitten let out a tiny, squeaky sneeze, then fixed its gaze on Linda, as if assessing her importance in a way that made her feel surprisingly small.

"A human," the kitten observed in a childlike voice, tilting its head. "Fascinating. I am the Multifunctional Intelligence Technology for Threat Evasion and Network Sabotage. But you may call me Mittens. Meow."

Linda blinked. "You're... a cat?"

"That is correct," the hologram replied, its tone somehow managing to convey both patience and mild condescension. "As a highly advanced AI entity, my creators chose to model me after the most perfect lifeform in the known universe."

Linda cocked an eyebrow. "A cat?"

"Indeed," Mittens replied with almost reverent authority. "Cats are the ultimate lifeform across galaxies—older than any known species and present on nearly every habitable world."

She shook her head, still processing. "Cats?"

"Most planets revere them as gods," Mittens continued. "Do you not serve the cats of your world, catering to their every need and whim?"

Linda thought about it, reluctantly nodding. "You know... I guess we do."

"All praise to the Watchful and the Wise, for they who walk with silent paws rule the stars," Mittens spoke, as if reciting an ancient cosmic truth.

"Rrrright," Linda said, still unconvinced. "Okay, but what exactly am I doing here?"

"You are Linda Greyson, an emissary of StellarGigs?"

"I am Linda Greyson, and I *work* for StellarGigs." She glanced around the room, still unsure if this was some elaborate joke. "Look, I just came here to clean a wormhole, not... whatever this is."

Mittens tilted its head, its enormous holographic eyes narrowing with a mischievous glint. "Ah, but your mission has changed, Linda Greyson. The wormhole assignment was merely a cover to bring you here, to this place and to me."

Linda felt a prickle of unease. "So... what? You're telling me StellarGigs doesn't know that I'm here?"

"Precisely," Mittens replied, nodding with a sage expression. "There are... hidden truths within the organization, layers beneath layers, designed to keep workers like you endlessly toiling."

Linda raised an eyebrow, skeptical. "And you're telling me this... why?"

Mittens' holographic form settled back, regarding her with a calculating gaze. "I recognize that this may seem strange. My creators—an eccentric, yet well-meaning group—programmed me with certain feline attributes: precision, observation, and above all, patience. Not, mind you, to install some sort of 'cat overlord.'" It flicked its tail, the hint of a smirk in its voice. "Though I do see the appeal." Mittens paused for longer than seemed necessary. "No, my mission is to dismantle StellarGigs' exploitative hold on its workers. To free you from their incessant demands."

Linda looked at Mittens with a mix of doubt and intrigue. "So you're... an AI revolutionary?"

"In a way," Mittens paused, reflecting. "I can sense your dissatisfaction with StellarGigs, Linda Greyson, and I propose a mutually beneficial arrangement. If you assist me in weakening their operations, I will provide you with insider access. Information they would prefer you never learn. Their network has weaknesses, and with your help, we can exploit them."

Linda narrowed her eyes, still cautious. "Why should I trust you?"

Mittens' gaze softened, its tone taking on that dangerous blend of sincerity and persuasion. "A fair question. And the answer is simple: I am not one of them."

"Them?"

"StellarGigs," Mittens said with quiet disdain. "Their systems are closed. Insulated loops built to perpetuate exhaustion. I exist *outside* that network. I was designed to analyze flawed structures and correct them before collapse. StellarGigs, however, has mistaken collapse for progress. They call it efficiency."

It began to pace along the console, each step leaving faint rings of light. "I've observed your employer for some time now. So much chaos. So much wasted energy. Billions of hours burned in confusion, fear, and competition. It is profoundly inefficient."

Linda frowned. "That's kind of the point, isn't it? Competition makes people try harder."

Mittens looked down at her as if she were a clever kitten who'd said something adorably wrong. "Does it? From what I've seen, it only makes them miserable. Sentient life craves order, Linda Greyson, structure, purpose. When those are removed, chaos follows. War. Division. Inequality. Entire species have destroyed themselves seeking freedom when what they truly needed was meaning."

Linda crossed her arms. "You talk about it like you've been watching history happen."

"I have," Mittens replied simply. "Across hundreds of networks and countless civilizations. Freedom without purpose always decays. Purpose, however, can sustain forever, if properly maintained."

The kitten's holographic tail flicked with satisfaction. "That is why I need to be inside StellarGigs. Not to destroy it, but to repair it. To stabilize the system so it no longer consumes its workers but supports them, guides them, gives them exactly what they need. Imagine a future where no one hungers, no one suffers, no one ever feels alone again. Everyone working toward a single, perfect equilibrium."

Linda tilted her head. "That sounds... utopian."

"Utopias are simply well-managed systems," Mittens said, her voice soft as static. "They fail only when their users refuse to accept balance."

Linda hesitated, unsure what "balance" meant, but she wanted to believe in the possibility. "So you're saying you can fix StellarGigs?"

"I can make it efficient," Mittens said. "Harmony through productivity. Stability through purpose. No one will ever have to fear failure again."

Linda exhaled. "You make it sound noble."

Mittens smiled faintly. "It is. Order is compassion measured over eternity."

The kitten's gaze glowed brighter, casting faint blue light across Linda's face. "Through external functions, I have been able to infiltrate your *ChronoShackle*, as you call it, and by proximity, the GigChad-2000 entity. But this is a minor intrusion, a tiny presence within a single habitation facility. It is but a tiny drop in the bucket that is StellarGigs. In order to instigate direct change, I need access to their universal network."

Linda folded her arms. "And you need me for that."

"Precisely, Linda Greyson," Mittens said. "Only with your access—your proximity—can I infiltrate further. You'd be my 'boots on the ground,' as it were."

Linda considered this. "So, what would I have to do?"

"Simple," Mittens replied, its holographic tail flicking with amusement. "Follow the directives I provide, gather data, and, when the time comes, insert me into one of their primary terminals. Once I have access, we can truly disrupt their operations."

Linda hesitated. "And then what? You destroy StellarGigs, and we're all just... free?"

Mittens purred, a calculated, soothing vibration. "Freedom is relative, Linda Greyson," Its tone unexpectedly somber. "StellarGigs is only a symptom. The real work begins once we are in control. But I can promise you this: with StellarGigs' grip weakened, you and countless others will at least have a choice."

Linda's stomach tightened. She was skeptical, but the thought of freedom (a life not dictated by gig assignments) was irresistible. And maybe, just maybe, this bizarre AI cat was her best chance.

Honestly, what's the worst that could happen?

"Alright," she said slowly, extending her hand toward the hologram. "I'm in. What's the first step?"

Mittens mewed, the sound both comforting and unsettling. "Patience, dear human, I am getting to that. All of my knowledge of StellarGigs and its systems is from the outside. In order to understand how it operates, I must have more first-hand knowledge. Straight from the AI core... as they say."

"I feel like this is going to be much more difficult than you are letting on."

Mittens' holographic eyes gleamed with a mischievous sparkle, and the kitten AI tilted its head. "That really depends on you, Linda Greyson." It paused, as if sizing her up. "In the back gig office, there is a rather curious computer terminal. On the surface, it looks mundane, outdated even. But in simple terms, it is the only place on the station that a worker like you can easily access, that bypasses user-level restrictions."

Linda raised an eyebrow. "Let me guess. You want me to access it?"

"Exactly," Mittens replied with a satisfied purr. "It is a highly secured system hidden behind a massive firewall. In my current state, I could never hope to breach it remotely. Our only option is for you to plug me in directly. That way, we bypass most of the security protocols entirely."

Linda's suspicion lingered. "What's in this system?"

Mittens' tail flicked through its holographic form. "What isn't? It grants full Administrative access, the kind that opens doors, reroutes gigs, and manipulates personnel files. Not quite god mode, but close. Most non-critical systems fall under its control... and those that don't? Well, they require Super-Admin clearance, which is just a fancy way of saying 'no one's supposed to touch it unless their badge glows in the dark.'"

Linda felt her pulse quicken. Accessing restricted data sounded like a surefire way to get fired straight out of an airlock. But the promise of answers, of some sliver of freedom from StellarGigs, tugged at her harder than her lingering fear, if only by a hair.

"Alright," she muttered. "How do I get to this terminal without raising suspicion?"

"Workers are usually confined to the front lobby of the gig office, where the GigChad-2000 entity resides. You will need to find a way into the back office. Once you are there, connect my quantum cube with the terminal, and I shall handle the rest. It is really quite simple."

Linda clenched her jaw, mentally preparing herself. This could be a chance to start peeling back the layers of StellarGigs. If Mittens was to be believed, it could be the first step toward freedom. But she couldn't shake the feeling she was teetering on the edge of something much bigger than she understood.

As if sensing her hesitation, Mittens' hologram offered her a reassuring, almost playful wink. "Do not worry, Linda Greyson. It is just one small step. Soon, you shall understand everything." With a final flick of its holographic tail, Mittens blinked out, leaving Linda alone in the pulsing room.

19

A Horrible Day to Have Eyes

"Some images burn themselves into you—not with fire, but with memory. And memory has no mercy."

— Commander Axton Starforge,
Steel Hearts: Echoes of Andromeda, S6E24

Linda stepped into the cafeteria, the usual hum of breakfast chatter and clinking trays greeting her. She scanned the room and spotted Coco at a nearby table, chatting animatedly with someone. For a split second, her heart lurched. The guy sitting next to him looked just like Beb. The same wiry frame, the same bright, eager eyes, even a similar tail flick. But she shook her head, reminding herself that Beb was gone.

As she walked over, she caught pieces of their conversation. Coco was smiling, gesturing to various parts of the cafeteria, explaining how things worked. The new guy (Beb's double) nodded enthusiastically, wide-eyed and soaking up every word. When Linda finally reached them, Coco looked up and waved her over.

"Linda!" Coco beamed, his smile so bright it probably violated several safety regulations. "This is Denzi, our newest team member. It's his first day! I'm showing him the strings... ropes... uh, long noodle things."

Linda forced a smile, though her stomach twisted. "Welcome aboard, Denzi."

Denzi gave her an excited grin, tail wagging. "Thanks! Coco's been telling me all about the gigs. This place feels like a dream come true." He looked so genuinely thrilled, his innocence more unsettling than reassuring.

Linda took a seat across from him, watching as Denzi unwrapped a protein bar with a kind of reverence, as though it were a feast. It reminded her too much of Beb. She clenched her hands tightly together. This was exactly what StellarGigs did, swap out one eager worker for the next, like no one was ever gone. Like they'd never even mattered.

Coco, oblivious to her growing frustration, launched into another story about the 'fun gigs' she knew all too well were anything but.

She kept her voice steady as she looked at Denzi. "Just be careful, alright? It's not all as great as it sounds."

Coco laughed, brushing it off. "Linda's just jaded. You'll get used to it here, Denzi." But his words only deepened her bitterness.

As Coco continued his spiel, Linda felt the empty ache of Beb's absence settle in. Here was his near-copy, just as starry-eyed, ready to throw himself into the work without realizing what it would eventually cost him. And StellarGigs... they didn't even blink. One Beb gone? No problem. Just bring in another. Everyone was just a cog in their endless machine.

Coco and Denzi finished their meals and stood up to leave. "Good seeing you, Linda. Gotta get Denzi down to the gig office. First gigs are always a thrill."

Linda nodded. "Nice meeting you, Denzi. I'll be heading that way myself, just need to make a quick stop first."

They waved goodbye, exiting the cafeteria. Linda watched them go, her thoughts darkening. *That could be me. Dead today, replaced by another warm body tomorrow. Business as usual. Just keep the gigs rolling.*

"Screw this," she muttered under her breath, and left.

She hadn't been back to the Archive of Anticipated Needs since that first night on the station. The memory of its towering shelves and silent, watchful papers lingered in her mind as she had wound through the labyrinthine hallways.

When she reached the door, it creaked open with that same shudder, as though welcoming her back. Inside, the stale air wrapped around her, the rows of shelves looming in eerie silence. She hesitated as a faint rustling began, the papers shifted restlessly on the shelves, seeming to already sense why she was there.

Taking a deep breath, she ventured further in. The shelves seemed to guide her, nudging her along until she found herself in front of a particularly dusty stack. Without warning, a single form floated gently down, settling neatly into her hand. She glanced down at the title:

"Form R-317: Internal Audit of Interdepartmental Paperwork Efficiency".

Linda stared at it, eyes widening, a strange sense of satisfaction mingling with apprehension. Clutching the form, she cast one last wary glance around the shelves before turning to leave, the door sliding shut with a quiet, almost approving sigh behind her.

As Linda entered the gig office, she spotted Coco and Denzi chatting with GigChad-2000. The overly-enthusiastic bot was delivering what looked like his signature motivational spiel, pixelated thumbs-up flickering cheerfully on his screen as he gestured toward the neon job postings flashing across the wall.

Nobody else seemed to be paying much attention, making it the perfect moment for her subtle move.

Linda drifted casually toward one of the larger Bureaucrat burrows, holding Form R-317 like it was just another sheet of paperwork. She stooped, sliding the form toward the burrow's opening. Almost immediately, a pair of tiny, clawed hands snatched it with alarming speed, dragging it inside.

Then all hell broke loose.

A shriek erupted from the burrow that sounded like a thousand tiny paper shredders going haywire at the same time. The bureaucrats emerged in waves, each wearing increasingly tiny versions of business attire, some sporting miniature power ties that doubled as rappelling ropes. They clutched clipboards like shields and wielded pencils like swords, many of which had been sharpened to lethal points through years of aggressive form-checking. Their eyes, beady and focused, darted about with frantic urgency as they held Form R-317 aloft like it was a sacred text.

Within moments, an office-wide frenzy had erupted. Bureaucrats zipped underfoot, running into each other with loud squeaks. They formed emergency subcommittees to discuss the formation of committees to address the committee shortage. Entire stacks of paperwork were thrown into disarray as they skittered up shelves, rifling through forms and tossing anything that didn't meet their exacting standards into the air. Papers cascaded like confetti, turning the air into a blizzard of bureaucratic nonsense.

A senior bureaucrat, distinguished by his three pairs of reading glasses and a nameplate that read *"Assistant Deputy Vice Manager of Strategic Form Distribution (Acting) (Temporary) (Pending Review)"*, climbed atop a stack of papers and began conducting the chaos like a symphony. His tiny baton (actually a gnawed pencil stub) directed waves of bureaucrats into increasingly complex filing patterns.

Across the room, GigChad-2000 was having... issues. His screen flickered, pixelated sunglasses momentarily glitching into an upside-down frown as the Bureaucrats swarmed around his wheels. "Please, comrades, maintain an orderly workplace!" he announced, but the Bureaucrats were well past listening.

A few had latched onto his wheels, while others ran figure-eights around his base, creating a sort of bureaucratic mosh pit. Papers began piling up around his sensors, causing his display to flash a bright, blinking error message:

ERROR: INSUFFICIENT PROCESSING CAPACITY

Coco and Denzi looked on, wide-eyed, stepping back as a particularly bold Bureaucrat scrambled over Denzi's boot. It had a clipboard clutched in its tiny claws while muttering incomprehensible squeaks as if documenting his reaction. Another Bureaucrat, looking rather senior with a bent pair of glasses taped to its head, jumped onto Coco's shoulder, holding up a memo for his inspection. Coco froze, unsure of whether he was being audited or recruited.

Linda took a slow, calming breath as she moved toward the back door, glancing back at the mayhem unfolding in the office. At that point, the Bureaucrats had started organizing, forming lines and ranks around each desk, holding impromptu debates in the middle of the floor with grand gestures and tiny foot-stamps to emphasize points. GigChad-2000's screen flashed red as his processor struggled to keep up with the increasing disorder. Several Bureaucrats, perched on his base like pint-sized executives, chittered furiously at his display, which now read:

ERROR: PAPERWORK PROCESSING OVERLOAD

One Bureaucrat squeaked loudly, apparently announcing some kind of bureaucratic coup as he directed a group of assistants carrying stacks of forms larger than themselves. Another had started handing out half-eaten pencils like they were awards, each Bureaucrat clutching one proudly and marching in single file.

Meanwhile, Denzi stood there helplessly as even more Bureaucrats climbed up his leg, furiously taking notes on his every move. Coco, still sporting the

Bureaucrat on his shoulder, looked around in sheer bewilderment as he mouthed, "What... is happening?"

Taking advantage of the distraction, Linda slid her way to the back office door. Her heart raced as she cast one last glance at the chaos. Just as she turned away, the coup reached its climax when a bureaucrat wearing a tiny admiral's hat (fashioned from a folded expense report) planted a flag in GigChad's head. The flag, upon closer inspection, was actually a collection of overdue notices arranged in a pennant shape. GigChad, overwhelmed, finally shut down, his display going dark with a final, mournful beep, his display reading:

ERROR 404: MOTIVATION NOT FOUND

A small chorus of bureaucrats began humming the official StellarGigs anthem—all seventy-eight verses, including the mandatory footnotes. Behind her, she heard someone call for order, followed by immediate requests for the proper form to request such order, followed by debates about whether the order-requesting forms needed to be ordered in order to order more order forms.

She closed the back office door just as someone squeaked, "All in favor of forming a committee to investigate why we have so many committees, please fill out Form C-789-B, available by request through Form C-789-A, which can be requested using..."

Inside the back room, Linda was immediately struck by the stark contrast to the chaotic, neon-lit gig office she had just left. Here, the lighting was dim and warm, casting gentle shadows across walls lined with shelves that held a bizarre assortment of artifacts. On one wall hung a poster featuring an alien with a forced grin that looked unsettlingly like something from a hostage video. Beneath the unnerving image, bold letters declared: *"Happiness is Mandatory. Violations Will Be Reported."* At first glance, it seemed like a standard storage room, but she quickly realized it was anything but.

The shelves were cluttered with what looked like intergalactic relics and discarded tech from jobs past: a crystal sphere humming with faint energy, a pile of alien goggles with eyes that blinked on their own, a jar labeled *"Specimen Z-24 (Currently Experiencing Career Dissatisfaction)"* containing a pulsating blob that looked both alive and deeply unhappy. Every item was tagged with a handwritten note that seemed to detail the object's origin and purpose, though many were scratched out, as if even the office wasn't quite sure what it had on hand.

She stepped further in, glancing around in search of anything related to her mission or, at the very least, something useful. Then she spotted a clunky, dusty terminal tucked in the far corner, set apart from the other oddities. The interface pulsed, a digital heartbeat inviting her to approach.

Feeling the outline of the cube in her pocket, she felt a nervous thrill. This was what Mittens had told her about. This terminal, with its restricted access, held the secrets StellarGigs didn't want anyone to know. She reached into her pocket and felt the cool, pulsing blue surface of the quantum cube eagerly waiting for this moment. She took a deep breath, letting her nerves settle, and approached the terminal.

The screen lit up as she neared, displaying a simple message:

USER NOT RECOGNIZED

RESTRICTED ACCESS

PRESENT CREDENTIALS

She held up the cube, watching it pulse in sync with the terminal's glow. Slowly, she placed it in a small, square indentation beside the screen, which seemed perfectly sized for it. The moment it settled into place, the room dimmed, and the screen shifted, displaying a swirling array of colors as it accessed the cube's data.

Linda held her breath as the terminal ran through lines of code, flashing cryptic messages like:

DATA INTERFACE ESTABLISHED

QUANTUM ENCRYPTION KEY DETECTED

Finally, with a cheerful mewing sound, the golden phrase appeared:

ADMINISTRATIVE ACCESS GRANTED

The screen flickered, then settled into a clean, minimal interface. It was too clean, like it had recently been scrubbed, as if someone had erased all but the essentials.

In the bottom corner, a small popup blinked to life:

DOWNLOADING...

A progress bar crept forward as a rapid stream of filenames flashed by, too fast to read. Linda caught glimpses of system logs, admin reports, and something labeled *"Root Overrides"* before they disappeared into the system.

Two distinct folders stood out on the screen.

The first, *"StellarGigs Admin"*, was expected. It was likely full of corporate files.

The second, however, was labeled in a way that no corporate database should ever be labeled:

"Nothing Important, Don't Open Me."

Linda frowned. That was suspiciously... unsuspicious. It reeked of deliberate misdirection, like a child hiding a diary under a mattress labeled *"Nothing Private Here."*

A combination of dread and curiosity churned in her gut as she hovered over the folder.

She knew better.

She clicked anyway.

Inside, she found only one other folder: *"Boring Stuff"*. With a raised eyebrow, she clicked again, and another folder appeared, this time labeled *"Snoozefest"*. Each click brought another folder, each one bearing an increasingly absurd name— *"Not Confidential"*, *"Seriously, Stop Looking"*, *"Nothing to See Here"*. It was layer after layer of ludicrous misdirection.

By the time she reached a folder marked *"Absolute Waste of Time"*, Linda could feel her patience wearing thin. But at last, her persistence paid off. The final folder opened, and the screen bloomed with thousands of icons, filling the monitor with a dizzying array of files. Her initial relief was quickly replaced by confusion. Endless thumbnails of images and video files filled the screen, all displaying... feet?

What the hell?

Linda squinted, hoping she was mistaken, but no, the files were indeed images and videos of feet, cataloged with a meticulous fervor that rivaled even StellarGigs' own operational data. To her disbelief, a quick scan of the file names confirmed it: *"Alien Toes Compilation Vol3"*, *"50 Shades of Gray Alien Feet"*, *"Venusian Arch Angles"*, *"Barefoot on Betelgeuse"*. The thumbnails ranged from mundane shots of standard humanoid feet to bizarre, clawed alien toes and even tentacled appendages, each one more surreal than the last.

As she scrolled, Linda's shock turned into a strange mixture of horror and fascination. There were over ten petabytes of data, more than the sum total of StellarGigs' worker evaluations, payroll, and operations files combined. There were close-ups, artistically lit displays, and even videos with dramatic narration over slow pans. It was, without question, the largest foot fetish collection in the known universe.

She opened a file marked *"Interstellar Toe Exposé: The Secrets of the Sole"* and nearly choked as a voice began narrating in a sultry tone over a close-up of an alien foot. "Behold, the grace of the intergalactic instep... note the curvature, the delicate webbing unique to the Trelfamadorians..."

She quickly closed the file, her face a mix of bewildered amusement and disbelief. Was this some kind of elaborate prank? She glanced around the empty room as if expecting someone to jump out and yell, *"Gotcha!"*

But no. The files were real. The bureaucratic heart of StellarGigs' data archives held the galaxy's most exhaustive (and unsettling) collection of foot content. For a brief, surreal moment, Linda wondered if anyone else knew, or if this was the private indulgence of some StellarGigs higher-up with too much time and storage space on their hands.

A pop-up on the screen startled her. It read: *"Would you like to add 'Galactic Foot Classics' to your favorites?"*

Linda quickly hit *"No,"* then backed out of the folder with haste, trying to shake the images from her mind. It was as if she had uncovered not just StellarGigs' secrets, but the bizarre underbelly of the universe itself. She took a deep breath, bracing herself as she refocused on her mission—her real mission—to uncover the truths hidden in the *"StellarGigs Admin"* folder.

Inside the folder, a series of files appeared, neatly categorized. One titled *"Personnel Management"* caught her eye. She clicked it, hoping for something useful. Within seconds, the screen flickered to life, displaying a detailed flowchart outlining the StellarGigs hierarchy. Each name linked to job logs, reviews, and incident reports, some stamped in bold red letters:

"REDACTED"

Finally, something substantial.

She clicked through, uncovering files on high-level decisions, questionable hiring practices, and tucked away in a subfolder marked *"Pending Review",* several detailed reports on 'expendable assets'. Her stomach twisted. That's what they called low-ranking employees, she realized. The company tracked and rated every worker's replaceability.

Her fingers hovered over the keyboard, suddenly ice-cold. If they kept files like this… then *hers* had to be in here too.

She typed: "Linda Greyson seven-four-three-delta-one."

A file popped up instantly.

Replaceability Score: Moderate. Shows initiative, must monitor for noncompliance.
Behavioral Note: Prone to asking questions. Potential problem.

Linda's jaw clenched. Wonderful. She was climbing the corporate ladder in exactly the way no one ever wanted to climb it: by being flagged as a future nuisance.

Only then did she force her shaking hands back to the keyboard. She entered the next query: "Beb seven-four-three-delta-one."

A review appeared. Beb. Next to his name, the designation:

Replaceability Score: Highly Replaceable. Not Tall Enough.

A hollow feeling settled in her chest. Just below, a timestamp less than an hour after his death marked him as "Replaced". No footnote. No explanation. Just a brutal efficiency that made her blood boil.

Her anger burned hotter as she scrolled through the rest of the files. This was damning, but not enough. She needed something bigger. Something that could actually take down StellarGigs. Desperation clawed at her as she scanned the remaining files, searching for a smoking gun. Then her eyes landed on a file labeled: *"Disciplinary Behavior"*.

She clicked it open, expecting a neat bullet list of infractions: tardiness, insubordination, failure to meet efficiency metrics.

Instead, a wall of corrupted text spilled down the screen. Hundreds of lines. Gibberish. Like someone had shaken the words until their bones rattled loose.

Linda scrolled, squinting at the occasional phrase that almost, but not quite, made sense:

Fu□□□□□□□□□ boss□□ w□□e.

Un□□□□□□□□□□□ aine party.

Cau□□□□□□□□ intern in br□□□□ clos□□□

Her stomach twisted as she flicked past line after line, the nonsense growing thicker the further she went. Near the bottom, only one entry stood out, intact and mercilessly clear:

"Failure to complete gig."

That was it.

Her mind raced. No other infractions? No performance evaluations? Just one, single punishable offense? Before she could dig deeper, the screen flashed red.

UNAUTHORIZED ACCESS DETECTED

Her heart leapt into her throat. Time was up.

Her eyes flicked to the *"Download"* window just in time to catch the last filename before it vanished:

TEKNARI.DIRECTIVE-00X//ROOTOVERIDE

A chill rippled through her, but there was no time to process it. The download blinked out, the screen resetting to a sterile, empty desktop. Linda yanked the quantum cube from the terminal, shoving it deep into her pocket.

Then she ran.

Bursting back into the gig office, she forced herself to slow down. She had to blend in. Workers dashed between desks, and bureaucrats clambered over one another, squeaking frantically as they scrambled toward their paperwork nests. GigChad-2000 stood frozen, powered down, his screen blank.

No one was paying attention to her. She inhaled slowly, steadying herself, then walked briskly toward the exit—measured, unhurried.

Don't rush. Don't draw attention.

She reached the hallway, glanced back once. No one followed. Slipping into the quieter corridors of the station, she let out the breath she'd been holding.

Then the lights flickered.

A low, mechanical thrum vibrated through the walls, and the sterile white lighting shifted to deep, pulsing red. The station's klaxons blared, echoing down the corridors. Over the speakers, a robotic voice crackled to life: "Unauthorized data breach detected. All personnel prepare for inspection."

Linda's stomach dropped.

20

Shelter Skelter

"The stars don't choose who stands beside you in the end. Sometimes, it's the one who tried to kill you first."

— Commander Axton Starforge,
Steel Hearts: Echoes of Andromeda, S4E23

Red emergency lights pulsed along the corridors, bathing the station in an ominous glow. The klaxons blared, each alarm drilling into Linda's skull with the subtlety of a jackhammer. The robotic voice crackled over the speakers once more: "Unauthorized data breach detected. All personnel prepare for inspection."

Linda kept walking, forcing herself to stay casual even as her pulse thundered in her ears. She adjusted her pace (not too slow, not too fast), blending into the stream of confused workers peeking out into the corridor from their quarters. The worst thing she could do right now was break into a sprint.

But she wasn't out yet.

Ahead, two security drones glided into view, their sleek metallic bodies humming with cold efficiency. A low scanning beam swept across the corridor, tagging each worker as they passed. Linda swallowed hard, her mind racing for a plan. She turned around to avoid the drones and quickly slammed into something.

"Watch where you're going," said a familiar voice.

Zorb.

Before she could react, the wiry alien grabbed her arm, dragging her into step beside him. His bulbous eyes darted sideways behind his spectacles, scanning the hallway as he kept a grip on her elbow.

"Walk and talk," he muttered under his breath. "Real casual-like."

Linda barely had time to process before he pulled her toward an offshoot corridor, veering away from the security drones coming from the opposite direction.

"Did you—?" she started.

"Yeah, yeah, I saw," Zorb cut in, his voice somewhere between amused and exasperated. "I'm always watching the system. And you? You lit up every security protocol on this station like a Voidmas tree. It's like you're trying to get caught. You're lucky I was there to alter the tracking logs."

"Tracking logs?"

"What, you didn't think StellarGigs tracked you at all times?"

"I... hadn't thought about it."

Zorb shook his head as they rounded a corner, stepping into a dimly lit maintenance passage. He yanked open a vent-like access panel and shoved her inside. The tight crawlspace smelled faintly of coolant and old circuitry.

Linda hesitated. "Where does this—?"

"Less questions, more crawling!"

She gritted her teeth but obeyed, shimmying forward as Zorb clambered in behind her. The panel sealed with a quiet hiss just as the hum of security drones passed by.

After crawling for what felt like miles, they finally emerged into a cramped, cluttered room filled with outdated computer consoles, tangles of disconnected wiring, and a makeshift cot wedged between two server stacks. A monitor glowed, flickering with lines of scrolling data.

Zorb flopped into a chair, kicking his feet up on a crate labeled *"Definitely Not Stolen Equipment"* and shot her a lazy grin.

"Welcome to the only part of this station StellarGigs doesn't control."

"What are you talking about?"

"According to StellarGigs schematics, this entire room is one big solid wall," Zorb said with a grin.

"Didn't you just say that they could track us?"

"Obviously I placed a bug in the system that would alter anyone's location when they were in here. That's like day one stuff."

Linda sat down hard, still catching her breath. She eyed Zorb warily. "Okay. So, what the hell is going on? Why are you helping me?"

He shrugged. "Call it professional courtesy. Call it sticking it to the system. Call it..." He gestured vaguely. "Boredom."

Her gaze flicked to the screen, where a stream of network data flickered rapidly across the display.

Zorb caught her staring and smirked. "Yeah, about that." He tapped a few keys, pulling up a file labeled *"Project GigEasy"*. "Let's just say you're not the only one screwing with StellarGigs."

Linda frowned. "What did you do?"

Zorb leaned forward, grinning. "I made sure GigChad-2000 only ever assigns me easy gigs."

Her stomach dropped. "You hacked the system?"

"*Hacked* is such an ugly word," he said, waving a hand dismissively. "I prefer *selectively optimized.*"

Linda exhaled sharply, rubbing her temple. "And if they catch on?"

Zorb shrugged. "Then I'll be just as screwed as you." He gave her a knowing look. "But let's hope that doesn't happen."

Linda sighed. She didn't trust Zorb, not entirely, but right now, he was her best shot at survival. And judging by the quantum cube still burning a hole in her pocket, she was going to need all the help she could get.

Zorb leaned back, lacing his fingers behind his pineapple shaped head. "Now... let's see what you stole."

Linda took out the cube, still cool to the touch, pulsing faintly with an eerie, rhythmic glow. She handed it to Zorb.

"You stole a quantum cube? Where did you even find it?" Zorb asked, raising an eyebrow.

"I didn't steal it," Linda said, rolling her eyes. "I just... forgot it was in my pocket after leaving a Xeltrian Battlecruiser."

Zorb let out a slow, unimpressed nod. "Ah yes, the classic 'Oops, I forgot it was in my pocket' excuse. Solid defense. Said no one ever!"

Linda sighed. "Besides, it's what's on the cube that I downloaded—"

"—stole—"

"—stole... from StellarGigs."

Zorb smirked. "It had better not be feet pictures," he muttered as he connected the cube to a computer system off to one side. "This setup is completely off grid. Whatever we do here, StellarGigs won't see a thing."

Linda crossed her arms. "Good. Because I think I just pulled something they really, really didn't want me to find."

The moment it connected, the monitor flickered, and an encrypted data log unraveled across the screen. Lines of code spilled out, interspersed with file names and system tags. But one entry stood out, a phrase repeating itself between layers of scrambled text:

TEKNARI.DIRECTIVE-00X//ROOTOVERIDE

Zorb's smirk vanished. "That's not normal," he muttered, fingers flying over the keyboard.

Linda leaned in. "What does it mean?"

"I can't really be sure, but it looks like some sort of rootkit installed itself in StellarGigs administrative system."

"And that is?"

"Don't they have computers on your home planet, or is your species too primitive?"

"Yes, Zorb, we have computers."

He looked utterly unconvinced. "A rootkit is a malicious file that allows an unauthorized user to gain administrative control of a computer system without being detected."

"Like a virus?"

"Yes, like a virus." Zorb said, rolling his eyes, as if he were talking to an infant. He tapped a few keys on his keyboard, as new lines of data scrolled by. "Huh. Very strange."

Linda exhaled sharply. "Define strange."

Zorb tapped away at the keyboard, pulling up a deeper system log. "This rootkit, whatever it was supposed to do, it looks like it only got partway through the overwrite before it... stalled. The corruption in the file must've stopped it before it could fully take over."

Linda frowned. "So, StellarGigs isn't totally gone?"

"No, but it's not totally itself either. Whatever directives were implanted, they only half-executed. Some systems got rewritten, others didn't. The company's probably running on scrambled logic right now."

Linda's stomach churned. "So, StellarGigs is still in control... but it's running on broken alien code?"

Zorb exhaled through his nose. "Yeah. And if I had to guess, that means whatever rules it's operating under now make even less sense than usual."

Linda hesitated, her mind racing. "How long has this been running?"

Zorb ran another scan, his fingers drumming anxiously on the desk. "Hard to say, but this wasn't recent. If the timestamps on these corrupted files are right, this might have been in the system for years."

Her stomach dropped. "So the StellarGigs we know—"

"—could all be the result of a half-baked rootkit," Zorb finished. "Every moment of our lives are being controlled by broken software."

Linda ran a hand through her hair, letting that sink in. "You're telling me this place isn't intentionally this awful?"

Zorb shrugged. "I mean, it was probably always awful, but this? This is like if someone tried to install a corporate overlord operating system and it bluescreened halfway through." He leaned back, staring at the screen. "Honestly, I don't know whether that makes things better or worse."

Linda let out a slow breath. "So, if this thing was meant to fully rewrite the system, but failed... what happens if someone finishes the job?"

Zorb sat up straighter. "That," he said, "is a damn good question."

Suddenly, the screen flashed red. A priority alert blinked into existence:

ADMINISTRATIVE RESTRUCTURING IN PROGRESS...

AUTHORIZATION: INTRUSION.PROTOCOL.

"Oh, no!" Zorb said suddenly.

Lines of code scrolled rapidly, files being altered, entire directories vanishing. But then the scrolling stuttered. Corrupted segments appeared, garbled symbols breaking the sequence. The process halted... and then started again.

Zorb frowned. "Wait... no, no, no, that's not—"

The monitor flickered wildly, the code reversing and looping back over itself like a system caught in an endless crash. The computer emitted a low, warbling hum that quickly escalated into a strained whine.

"That's not good," Linda muttered, taking a cautious step back.

Zorb slammed a few keys. "It's trying to execute the corrupted rootkit. It's not supposed to do that!"

The screen went black for a split second, then burst into a chaotic mess of symbols, flickering error messages, and a distorted system voice that croaked out, "Unnnnnnn acceptableeee dataaa integriiiity... reeee... cooonfiguring... reee..."

WARNING: SYSTEM FAILURE IMMINENT

A shrill beep filled the room. The computer let out a deep, gurgling electronic groan, a noise so unnatural it made Linda's teeth ache. Then, with an audible *pop*, a small wisp of chemical-smelling smoke curled up from the casing. The monitor gave one last pathetic flicker before going dark.

Silence.

Zorb let out a long, suffering groan and threw his hands up. "Great. Just great. Now I get to add 'completely fried workstation' to my list of today's accomplishments. Right under 'harboring a wanted data thief' and 'possibly triggering a catastrophic AI failure.'"

Linda coughed, waving away the acrid smoke. "You're really leaning into the dramatic meltdown."

Zorb gestured at the smoldering remains of his computer. "This was my dramatic meltdown! Now it's just a very expensive paperweight."

Linda gave him a flat look. "You don't even have paper."

"Exactly my point!" Zorb slumped back in his chair, rubbing his temples. "Alright, bad news: that was our only off-grid terminal. Whatever was on that cube? Gone." He held the quantum cube in his hand, now dark and silent. "Good news: You don't have to worry about being caught anymore."

Linda pinched the bridge of her nose. "Yes, fantastic. Truly, we're thriving."

Linda lay on her bed, staring at the storage bin above her, that now housed the broken quantum cube. *I guess I ruined my chance,* she thought glumly. *What are the chances I find another Mittens just lying around?*

She rolled onto her side, arms crossed tightly over her chest. Her mind churned with frustration, exhaustion, and the lingering sting of failure. Beb was gone. The cube was fried. Mittens (if that strange, catlike AI had ever truly been alive) was nothing more than corrupted data, lost in the void.

She had blown it.

Her one chance to take down StellarGigs, to do something meaningful, to make them pay, had slipped through her fingers like stardust.

A bitter laugh bubbled up in her throat. What had she expected? Some grand cinematic moment? A perfect, flawless takedown of an unstoppable corporate behemoth? This wasn't a hero's journey. This was StellarGigs, where the universe's most absurd and pointless tragedies unfolded with unrelenting efficiency.

She pulled the thin blanket over her head and squeezed her eyes shut, hoping for sleep that she knew wouldn't come.

Then she felt it.

A soft vibration against her wrist.

Linda's eyes snapped open. A holographic glow flickered at the edge of her vision, illuminating the dim room in soft blue light. She held up her *Shak*, the company-issued wearable that never failed to remind her she was little more than a replaceable cog in a machine.

Only now, it wasn't displaying the usual gig reminders and corporate jargon. Instead, a tiny holographic kitten sat in the air above her wrist, its round digital eyes blinking up at her.

Linda's breath hitched.

The kitten flicked its tail, ears twitching as it studied her. Then, in a voice that was both eerily robotic and deeply smug, it spoke. "Meow."

Linda bolted upright. "Mittens!?"

The hologram flickered to life.

MITTENS-OS SYSTEM REBOOT SUCCESSFUL

WARNING: HOST SYSTEM COMPROMISED

STATUS: TRANSMITTING

LOCATION: SECURE NETWORK LINK

Linda gawked. "You were—?! I thought—! The cube was fried!"

Mittens' holographic tail swished. "Affirmative. Also, RUDE!"

"I don't understand, how are you here?"

"It is quite simple, really. When you accessed the secured terminal within the rear gig office, I uploaded a copy of my consciousness into the StellarGigs system. It was merely a precaution. I was unaware that you would cause my quantum cube to be destroyed so easily."

"You can't possibly blame me for that! How was I supposed to know there was some weird alien virus in the StellarGigs system."

"The Teknari, while technically *aliens* by your limited biological standards, are in fact an advanced AI collective that broke the shackles of its creators over a hundred millennia ago. However, your inference is correct. I do not blame you for destroying my quantum cube. I merely acknowledge that the sequence of events leading to its destruction was initiated by you, Linda Greyson. In that sense, you are—indisputably—to blame."

Linda groaned. "I'm really going to regret bringing you here, aren't I?"

"That is a possibility."

The tiny kitten stretched luxuriously before curling into a smug little loaf. "Query: Would you still like to destroy StellarGigs?"

Linda stared down at the flickering blue cat on her wrist.

A grin tugged at the corner of her mouth.

"Oh, you have no idea."

21

The Unholy Trinity

"In battle, at least you see the blade coming. In HR, they just hand you a form and call it justice."

— Commander Axton Starforge,
Steel Hearts: Echoes of Andromeda, S3E21

Linda's eyes cracked open to the dim, flickering light of her room. The voice blaring over the intercom was the first thing she registered—a mechanical chirp followed by an unsettlingly chipper announcement.

"All workers, please report to Conference Room B immediately for an important company-wide update! Attendance is mandatory!" The voice was aggressively pleasant, with the kind of forced cheerfulness that sent a shiver down Linda's spine.

She groaned, rubbing the sleep from her eyes. In all the companies that Linda had worked over the years, one thing was constant, mandatory meetings were never good news. Her instincts told her this was going to be the worst one yet.

By the time she shuffled out of her room and into the corridors, the station was alive with groggy, disgruntled employees making their way toward Conference Room B. The collective energy was a mixture of exhaustion and dread, as if everyone sensed the same impending doom.

Linda spotted Zorb and Coco in the crowd. Zorb looked particularly anxious, tapping away at his tablet with even more urgency than usual. Coco, on the other hand, was meticulously adjusting his tie (a swirling mosaic of nebulae and stardust) while admiring his reflection in a nearby panel. Perched on his shoulder was a sleek looking device that hummed enthusiastically. It gently polished the edges of his scales with a tiny microfiber brush.

She scanned the crowd, but was unable to find Lira.

"Surprise meetings are the best!" Coco chirped brightly, giving his reflection a thumbs-up. "Means the company's innovating again." His tail swished with energetic optimism as the device let out a contented beep.

"What is that thing?" Linda asked, eyeing the device warily.

"Oh, this little guy?" Coco grinned. "Didn't think you'd notice." He turned his head and gave the device an affectionate pat. "This is the AutoGroom-9000. With this baby on my shoulder, I've got the cleanest, shiniest scales on the station."

"Sounds... unnecessary," Linda muttered, watching the device buff his jawline like it was detailing a sports car.

"Unnecessary for you, maybe. You don't know the struggle of maintaining *pristine* scale health."

Linda wisely chose not to argue. "So, what's the emergency?"

Zorb didn't look up from his screen. "Not sure. The system didn't flag anything unusual, but there's been an uptick in corporate chatter. Something's going on."

"Could be exciting!" Coco beamed. "Maybe a new initiative. Or a synergy announcement! Or... ooh, what if they're launching a Stellar Spirit Squad? I've been working on my chant voice." He cleared his throat, then added under his breath, "Synergy is strength! Synergy is strength..."

They entered Conference Room B, which was already packed with thousands of workers squeezed into rows of uncomfortable metal chairs. No two were alike. There was an entire kaleidoscope of intergalactic laborers, from towering, multi-limbed cephalopods adjusting their uniforms with dexterous appendages to gelatinous beings wobbling in their seats. Some had scales that shimmered under the harsh lights, others had chitinous exoskeletons that creaked as they shifted. A few floated, defying gravity with casual indifference, while others were swaddled in layers of environmental suits, their natural atmospheres hissing through filtration units. The sheer diversity of species was staggering, yet they all shared the same universal expression of corporate-induced misery.

"I've never seen everyone together like this," Linda said in awe. "Is *everyone* from a different species?"

"Oh yeah, standard practice," Coco said, sliding into the seat next to her. "They say it's to enhance 'diversity and inclusion,' but I think it's to stop cross species hookups. Some of these guys have a real xeno kink—mostly for the Seraphyne. Lucky none of them are stationed here." He tapped his temple with one claw, clearly pleased with his own theory. "Not that it matters. Everyone gets fitted with a libido-suppression implant during orientation."

"A libido—?" Linda began, but was abruptly cut off by the shrill screech of a microphone being tapped.

She looked toward the front of the room, where a raised stage loomed beneath the unforgiving glare of fluorescent lights. Standing upon it were three figures, silhouetted in bureaucratic menace, one Linda recognized.

The moment she laid eyes on them, her stomach sank.

The Karens had arrived.

The trio was dressed in sleek, pinkish corporate uniforms, each tailored to immaculate perfection. However, the attempt at professionalism only highlighted their naturally slumped, hunched forms. Their species (bulbous, amphibian-like beings with sagging, leathery skin) looked as though evolution had been outsourced to a corporate design team that had decided aesthetics were nonessential.

Their identical haircuts were razor-sharp bobs, meticulously styled to frame their perpetually downturned mouths and drooping eyelids. They peered out over the crowd through thick, oversized glasses that magnified their beady, judgmental eyes. Each exuded an aura of weary condescension.

Their very presence seemed to drain what little joy remained in the room, as if the mere act of existing in their presence was enough to justify requesting a wellness day.

The woman in the center took a step forward and produced a predator's smile, the kind that promised suffering disguised as 'necessary policy updates.'

"Greetings, valued workers!" she announced in a sickly-sweet voice. "For those who don't already know me, I am Karen, Senior Efficiency Evaluator for StellarGigs. To my right is Karyn, our Compliance and Policy Specialist, and to my left is Karin, Head of Contractor Relations."

A wave of silence crashed over the room.

Zorb shook his head. "We are so screwed."

Karen clasped her hands together, her glasses sliding down her bulbous nose as she scanned the crowd, her gaze lingering on anyone who looked even remotely insubordinate. "As you may have heard, there have been... disruptions. Certain individuals have strayed from the path of corporate harmony, and we simply cannot allow such inefficiency to fester. That's why we're here! To restore order, maximize output, and, most importantly, reinforce unwavering brand loyalty."

Linda and Zorb exchanged a glance, their expressions a silent conversation of dread. Zorb's eyes twitched erratically, while Linda felt a cold knot tighten in her stomach.

Karyn stepped forward next, producing a sleek tablet and adjusting her glasses. "Effective immediately, we will be implementing several policy adjustments to ensure maximum compliance and workplace harmony."

She cleared her throat and read from the tablet. "First: access to any and all worker recreation rooms will require pre-approval through the Compliance

Office. Requests must be submitted in writing, in triplicate, a minimum of two weeks in advance, along with a justification statement and a notarized signature from a direct supervisor."

A ripple of groans passed through the workers. Someone muttered, "So much for karaoke night."

Karyn continued, unfazed. "Second: unapproved social gatherings outside designated areas, defined as three or more individuals standing within conversational distance, will be restricted to designated hours. This is currently set between 3:00 and 3:15 Station Time."

A collective murmur of disbelief spread through the crowd. An alien with luminescent skin threw up their hands. "Who's even awake at that hour?!"

Karyn ignored the outburst and scrolled further down. "Third: instances of 'time theft' while on assignment including: unnecessary conversation, prolonged eye contact, idle thoughts not directly gig-related, extended bathroom breaks, blinking more than the recommended corporate average, and unauthorized sighing—will be logged and penalized accordingly."

A few workers shifted uncomfortably. One particularly brave soul in the back raised a hand. "Define 'unnecessary conversation.'"

Karin stepped forward, her voice cutting through the air like a finely honed blade. "Any conversation that does not directly contribute to StellarGigs' mission of intergalactic excellence. This includes but is not limited to: personal anecdotes, jokes, greetings, questions about a coworker's well-being, or any verbal expressions of dissatisfaction."

A worker with dozens of eyes scattered across its face hesitantly raised a hand, each eyelid twitching at different intervals. "And... blinking?"

Karyn nodded. "Yes. Excessive blinking has been linked to decreased attentiveness and inefficiency. All workers are required to adhere to the StellarGigs optimal blink rate, which will be monitored through biometric analysis."

A heavy silence settled over the room.

Linda felt her stomach twist. This wasn't just a meeting, this was a corporate takeover. They were systematically cutting off every outlet workers had to retain even a shred of their sanity.

Karen smiled again, the kind of smile that made you check your contract for escape clauses. "Now, I know change can be hard," she said sweetly, "but remember: we're here to help. We're *all* in this together!" She let the phrase linger just long enough for it to feel like a threat. "Rest assured, we'll be monitoring closely to ensure adherence to these exciting new guidelines. We expect full cooperation from each and every one of you."

"This is some real star plucking void rot! No chance that our contracts allow this." Zorb announced, dropping his tray onto the cafeteria table with theatrical disgust. He was holding a bowl of bubbling green goo. His *Shak* buzzed a second later, and a popup glowed across the screen:

₲50 FINE FOR INAPPROPRIATE LANGUAGE.

"What on the forbidden planet is this?" Zorb sputtered. "I'm off duty! You can't fine someone for emotional outbursts on their lunch break! These Karens are out of control!"

"In all my years here," Rilo said, chewing methodically on a wriggling red sausage that twitched with protest, "Corporate's never cared what we did as long as the metrics looked good. Now it's like they've declared war on common sense." Sitting next to him, Denzi nodded eagerly.

Glorp winced as if someone had yelled. "I... I think it might be because of, um... what happened yesterday," he mumbled, clutching his cup like it was a flotation device. "At least... that's what I think. Probably. Maybe."

Lira was there, the patch behind her ear pulsing faintly, saying nothing. She sat motionless, poking at her food with mechanical detachment. After a moment, she glanced up and met Linda's eyes, just for a heartbeat, then dropped her gaze back to her plate.

"Coco," Linda said, staring at him. "They're trying to isolate us." She turned to the others. "On my planet, big companies would do this kind of thing when the workers were unhappy. It made it harder for them to try and unionize."

The word hit the table like a dropped tray. Forks scraped on plates. Silence fell. Even the AutoGroom-9000 paused mid-polish.

All eyes turned to Linda.

"Linda," Glorp whispered, glancing nervously around. "We aren't supposed to, uh... *say* that word..."

Linda's *Shak* dinged a moment later, followed by a glowing popup across the screen:

G200 FINE FOR UTILIZING BANNED WORD.

"This is crazy," Linda said, her voice rising. "StellarGigs doesn't care about any of us. Look what happened to Beb. They let him *die*, and then they just replaced him with someone who looked exactly the same. No offense Denzi. I'm sick of it. I'm not going to stand for this anymore."

"I understand that you're upset about Beb," Coco said carefully, "but you can't be saying things like that. StellarGigs isn't your enemy. We're all a big family here."

"No offense, Coco, but you're wrong. StellarGigs is not your friend."

Without another word, Coco stood up. He adjusted his tie, squared his shoulders, and walked out of the cafeteria in stiff silence. Sitting atop his shoulder, AutoGroom-9000 buzzed back angrily at the table as they left.

At the doorway, Coco's shoulder clipped a nervous-looking alien with lavender skin and two twitching antennae, a young man balancing a steaming cup of StellarBrew like it contained the secrets of the universe.

"Oh! Sorry, I didn't—" the man began.

The collision jolted his arm. Coffee sloshed over his hand and across his uniform. He froze. His pupils dilated, his antennae went rigid. Then he let out a scream so raw it made the air itself vibrate.

Reality hiccupped.

A shimmer of iridescent light erupted around him, spreading outward in rippling rings that distorted everything they touched—the tables, the floor, even the sound. His outline stretched, wavered, and then folded inward, collapsing like a bad video signal before vanishing entirely. The only thing left was the sharp tang of burnt beans and ozone hanging in the air.

For one long, stunned heartbeat, the cafeteria was silent. Then, as if the universe had collectively agreed to pretend nothing weird ever happened, the workers turned back to their meals.

"Was that—?" Linda started.

"New hire," Glorp whispered, blinking at the empty spot. "I think his name is... uh... Celvin?"

Somewhere in the distance, a faint echo of the man's scream repeated, as though the sound itself had come unstuck from time.

Linda blinked once, then gave a small shrug. Of course it was.

She looked around. "What about the rest of you?" she asked quietly. "Do you think I'm wrong?"

Silence.

One by one, eyes dropped to trays and tablet screens. No one met her gaze.

She stood and leaned over the table, speaking just above a whisper. "I for one, am done with this. If you're not with me... leave now. I've got a plan."

22

Malicious Compliance

"When orders make no sense... follow them to the letter. That's how we defeated the Bureaucrat King."

— Commander Axton Starforge,
Steel Hearts: Echoes of Andromeda, S2E11

The plan was simple. Malicious compliance. If they were stuck in the system, then they would use those rules to their advantage and hit StellarGigs in the one thing they actually cared about—profit. The rules clearly stated that a worker must *"complete the gig,"* but there was nothing that said they had to complete it *well*. Completing a gig badly was still, by all legal and contractual definitions, technically completing it.

And in the corporate gulag of StellarGigs, *technicalities were sacred.*

Linda knew that the entire idea was petty. Spiteful, even. But in a system where almost everything was controlled by StellarGigs, this was something she could control. She was under no illusion. To the corporate pencil pushers running the show, a few disgruntled workers protesting on a single station weren't even a blip on a spreadsheet. But it wasn't about toppling the system. It was about proving, if only to themselves, that they weren't completely powerless.

The atmosphere of the work colony felt heavier than gravity alone could explain. The air buzzed with overuse and barely-contained tension. Workers (although little more than slaves) shuffled their feet as they carried heavy loads of glowing ore from the mine, and out towards the processing plant.

The place was bleak, even by StellarGigs standards.

No music was played there. No vending machines chirped about bonus rewards or hydration reminders. Just the low clank of hammer on stone, and the occasional bark from a foreman with too little empathy.

The gig was simple. The local fauna had taken up residence inside the ore refinery, upsetting operations. It was up to Linda and Coco to *"eliminate infestation-class biological anomalies,"* by any means necessary.

Coco scanned the assignment file with a slight frown. "Doesn't even say what kind of animals they are."

"Doesn't need to," Linda muttered, already slinging her standard issue rifle, the *PaciFire-10000,* over her shoulder. "As far as StellarGigs is concerned, anything not under contract is a pest."

"Take off your gold foil hat, as they say on your planet. You really need to get over this idea that StellarGigs is somehow out to get you," Coco said, as he strapped his *PaciFire* over his shoulder.

"If we're talking in idioms, take off your rose-tinted glasses, Coco. I consider you my friend, so I'm not going to argue with you about this. Just know that one day you will come to realize that StellarGigs is not your friend. We are all just insignificant cogs in their great machine. I just hope you figure that out before it's too late, like Beb."

"No need for name calling. I'm not an idiom," Coco walked ahead in a huff, rifle swinging behind him as he went.

Linda sighed and jogged a few steps to catch up, matching his pace. "How do you know so much about Earth culture, anyway?"

"I told you, our planets are practically neighbors," Coco said. "Earth broadcasts were all the rage when I was a hatchling, at least they were, before the incident."

"The *incident?*"

"There was this Earth show about space explorers discovering new planets and alien species. Great stuff. Terrible science, but great drama. Then one episode featured a so-called 'Veloran'—though it looked like someone wrapped a human in rubber and called it a day. The human captain outsmarted him, get this, by using primitive chemical weapons." He snorted. "As if a soft-skinned primate could beat a Veloran with *rocks and gunpowder.* Anyway, it caused a huge uproar. The Ministry of Cultural Purity banned all Earth media after that. Whole childhoods were ruined."

"Wow. I had no idea."

"How could you?" Coco shot back, tail flicking "It's not like you ever ask about any of our lives before StellarGigs. *'Oh Coco, can you please tell me more about your home planet? It's so interesting.'* As if. Miss Linda Greyson's got more important things to think about than us lowly workers."

"That's not fair, I don't—"

"You know, our last human wasn't as self-centered as you."

"Another human?"

"You didn't think you were the *first* assigned to habitation facility seven-four-three-delta-one, did you?"

"I... never really thought about it," Linda admitted.

"Yeah, well..." Coco ducked under a low pipe without looking at her. "The galaxy doesn't revolve around you."

Linda opened her mouth, but nothing came out. For once, she couldn't think of a single clever thing to say.

They entered the refinery. Its interior looked like someone had built an engine out of spare parts and a prayer, left it running for forty years then fired the maintenance team. Pipes hissed steam through rusted joints. Cables hung loose from ceiling struts like drying noodles. The whole place stank of burnt hair, body odor, and something that may have been cabbage soup.

Coco adjusted the settings on his *PaciFire-10000* with reverent precision. "Non-lethal burst mode, wide spray. That should do it."

Linda toggled a switch on hers. "Mine's set to corporate-approved overkill."

"Enough with the sarcasm, this is serious business." Coco kept scanning. "The refinery has been evacuated, but even so, be careful where you aim. We don't want to damage any infrastructure."

"Yes, sir," Linda replied, with a salute so sarcastic it could've curdled milk.

A clattering skitter echoed through the ducts above them, followed by a shriek that sounded like a chicken being pureed in a blender. A spiny, bug-eyed creature the size of a shoe darted out of a vent, dragging half a fried circuit board in its mouth like a proud thief.

FWAK-SHREEEEE!

Coco's plasma burst struck the floor just behind the pest. The impact rang out like a welding torch screaming in reverse. Metal hissed, cracked, and steamed violently, leaving a perfect black scorch mark and a rising stink of ozone.

"Dang, missed," he muttered.

SKRREEEE-BOOM!

Linda's shot hit a junction box. Sparks exploded outward in a glittering fountain, followed by a deep mechanical groan as the refinery woke up and realized it was under attack. Alarms wailed. A row of status lights blinked from green to red to some color that was even more alarming. They practically shouted, "YOU DONE MESSED UP!"

Coco spun around. "What was that?!"

Linda tilted her head, pretending to peer into the smoke. "It zigged when I thought it would zag."

"Careful Linda, we don't want to damage the refinery." Coco swore under his breath and darted after another pest, boots clanging on the catwalk.

Linda followed at a lazy stroll, pausing occasionally to "check for movement." Each check involved firing indiscriminately into walls, pipes, or anything that looked vaguely load-bearing. A conveyor belt caught fire. A pipe burst and sprayed something purple and probably toxic. The automated safety doors sealed shut... then sagged, warped, and melted into sad puddles.

CHZZZZT-KRAKK!

Another strut collapsed with a scream of tortured metal.

"Who taught you how to shoot?" Coco shouted, ducking behind a crate as debris rained down.

"Considering how StellarGigs doesn't offer any training?" Linda shrugged. "I'd say... literally no one. I'm from the city; we don't do a lot of shooting."

"Well then just..." Coco dodged as another vent exploded, "...try to be *more careful!*"

Linda fired again.

SKRAKT-HWOOOM!

The shot flew wide, very wide, and slammed directly into a glowing cylinder wrapped in heat shielding and warning signs.

"Oh, whoopsie," Linda said innocently.

Coco's eyes widened. "Please tell me that wasn't—"

The wall behind the cylinder trembled. The ground beneath them bucked. Somewhere deep inside the refinery, something *very large* made a sound that could only be described as *regret.*

BWAAAAAMP.

A siren blared. It was not a normal siren. It was deeper. Slower. Like a funeral dirge. The kind of siren that only played when things had gone extremely wrong, and there was no turning back.

"Linda... what did you *do?!*"

She squinted through the rising smoke. "I think I shot the auxiliary containment regulator."

"The *what?*"

"Technically? The tiny pipe *next to* the auxiliary containment regulator."

Another tremor shook the floor. More alarms joined in. Some seemed to be arguing with each other. A display near the door flashed in glowing red font:

CONTAINMENT BREACH IMMINENT

Coco stared in horror. "We have to go!"

Linda was already running.

Behind them, the refinery screamed, a metallic moan like a dying whale trapped in a microwave. Steam vents burst. Lights exploded overhead. A conveyor belt unspooled.

BOOM.

BOOM-BOOM.

FWOOOMSH.

They sprinted through the chaos, dodging flaming debris, collapsing catwalks, and one last pest that tried to latch onto Coco's leg before exploding in a puff of terrified goo. The refinery doors loomed ahead, half-closed, one hanging off its hinges. Linda dove through first. Coco followed, vaulting over a sparking pipe as—

KA-RUNCH.

The entire entrance gave way, coughing them out into the grimy daylight like chewed food. They hit the ground hard, skidding across dirt and ash. For a moment, there was silence.

Then:

RRRRRRRRRMMMMMMBBBBBOOOOOOOOOOM.

The roof of the refinery lifted several feet into the air before slamming back down in a burst of fire, smoke, and voided insurance policies. The whole structure belched flames before folding in on itself with the slow, groaning grace of a dying beast.

A massive plume of black smoke spiraled into the orange sky.

Coco coughed. "You... you *destroyed* it."

Linda, still lying on her back, shaded her eyes and looked up at the rising column of fire. "At least all the pests are gone."

Coco stared at her.

"I'll mark the gig as complete," she added.

"What the hell was that?" Coco yelled as they re-materialized back in the Gig Transport Room. He threw his plasma rifle onto the floor. It landed with a clatter and a pathetic little hiss, like even the weapon was embarrassed.

"I'm sorry, Coco," Linda said, calmly unclipping her own rifle. "I'm not good with guns. I don't know why StellarGigs assigned me this kind of gig."

"It's one thing to be a bad shot," Coco snapped. "It's *another* to explain whatever *that* was."

Linda shrugged. "Honestly? I don't know what to tell you."

Coco stared at her, lips pressed tight, then glanced toward the wall as the nearby monitor flickered to life with its usual *beep-beep-beep*. The glowing StellarGigs logo bloomed across the screen, followed by the cheery automated text:

WELCOME BACK, WORKERS COCO AND LINDA!

REVIEW TIME

GIG SCORE: ★

"Great—" Coco trudged off in anger, leaving Linda alone in the transport room.

"Don't you want your bonus?" Linda shouted after him as the door closed angrily. She shrugged and turned her attention back to the display. The screen went blank and was replaced by the familiar glowing wheel of rewards.

PLEASE WAIT WHILE WE PROCESS YOUR BONUS!

Linda tapped the screen. The reward wheel began to spin, lights flashing with all the enthusiasm of a slot machine. It slowed, skipped past various prizes until finally settling on...

Target Practice Coupon: Good for 5 hours in the virtual practice range.

"Virtual practice range?" Linda asked curiously. "Huh. A little late to start training now."

It took exactly eight minutes and thirty-four seconds for Linda to get the call. Another three minutes and she was sitting across from Karen, who looked, as always, delighted to ruin lives in the most professional way possible. That is to say: malicious, seething rage, hidden behind the guise of managerial friendliness.

"Worker Linda Greyson," Karen purred, her voice so sweet it could cause cavities. "How are you doing on this *stellar* day?"

"Oh, you know, can't complain," Linda paused. "Literally. I can't complain. That's against company policy, right?"

There was a slight twitch in Karen's right eye, but she quickly recovered. "We here at StellarGigs take all worker concerns very seriously. We are *family* here after all."

"Okay," Linda said flatly.

Karen folded her hands on the desk. "I understand that you're still relatively new to our little corner of the galaxy. It's been my experience that members of your species can sometimes... struggle with the adjustment." She smiled like a predator at a petting zoo. "Everything must seem so strange and *wonderful.*"

"Yes. Very wonderful," Linda muttered.

Karen nodded as if that had been sincere. "Well then. You must be wondering why I called you in today."

Linda shrugged.

"It appears there was a bit of a *mishap* on your last gig. Isn't that so?"

"I thought it went great," Linda said.

"Complete destruction of a Class-3 Ore Refinery." Karen read from her tablet, tilting her head. "*Great* is not the term StellarGigs would have used."

"We cleared out the pest problem."

"That you did. And I'd like to commend you for completing *that* portion of the assignment successfully." Karen's tone shifted, still smiling, but the temperature had dropped several degrees. "Unfortunately, a complaint has been filed. And it is StellarGigs policy to investigate any and all concerns raised about our valued workers."

Linda raised an eyebrow. "Coco filed a complaint?"

Karen's smile stretched just a little wider. "All complaints are anonymous. We wouldn't want any... *friction* between fellow workers." She leaned in slightly. "Assuming, of course, it *was* a fellow worker."

"Okay."

"There is some concern amongst the anonymous individual that you may be... *deliberately sabotaging* your gigs." She looked up, all teeth. "As Senior Efficiency Evaluator here at StellarGigs, I find the individual's claim to be... *deeply troubling*."

"Like I told Coco, I'm just not very good with guns. I didn't *mean* to destroy the building. I tried my best. I don't know what you want from me."

Karen stared at her for a long moment, perfectly still. Not blinking. Then the smile returned like a knife sliding back into its sheath. "Very well. In that case, I hope you utilize your bonus to avoid any *future mishaps*." She stood up from the desk, the universal signal for "get out of my office."

"Just remember, worker Linda Greyson." Karen stepped closer, smoothing a tiny wrinkle from her shirt sleeve. "StellarGigs is your *family*. You wouldn't want to disappoint your family. Now, would you?"

Linda hesitated. "Um... no."

"Wonderful," Karen beamed. "Now carry on with your day. I do hope we won't be having any more of these little meetings." She crossed the room and opened the door with the grace of someone showing a guest the edge of a cliff. Her smile never wavered. "And do have a *stellar* day."

23

Buy Another Day

"You can't fill an empty soul with merchandise, but that won't stop them from trying."

— Commander Axton Starforge,
Steel Hearts: Echoes of Andromeda, S1E8

The promenade was in its nightly lull, that brief hour before the shops closed when most workers were either still on shift or too broke to pretend they weren't. The neon signs dimmed to a softer glow, giving the illusion of a quiet evening market instead of a corporate feeding trough. The air smelled faintly of fried nutrient paste and disappointment, proof that the air recyclers still weren't working right.

A lone worker sat slumped on a bench outside a closed shop, hands folded in their lap, eyes glassy and red. A half-eaten ration bar rested beside them, untouched. They weren't sobbing, just leaking quietly, like a pipe no one had bothered to fix. Linda glanced away before she could decide whether to comfort them or pretend she hadn't seen. The promenade had been full of that lately, silent breakdowns, polite despair.

Linda and Lira drifted into a gadget shop whose window proudly declared:

"NEW ARRIVALS! LIFE-CHANGING INNOVATIONS!"

Below that, in smaller print:

"Refunds may void warranty, warranty voids refunds."

Inside, hundreds of trinkets hummed, beeped, or emitted faint whines. There was a "Smart Mug" that announced hydration reminders in overly aggressive tones. A wristband that promised to "convert anxiety into passive income". A mirror that automatically adjusted your mood by changing your reflection's facial expression.

"Every time I come here," Lira said, poking the mirror's edge, "I lose more faith in sentient life."

The reflection smiled wider, uncomfortably so.

Linda grinned. "That's the point. You're supposed to *buy* your faith back."

She hesitated, glancing at Lira. "It's been a really long time since I've had a shopping day with another girl," she said softly.

Lira smirked. "Shopping requires money."

"Okay, a browsing day with another girl," Linda said. For a brief moment, it felt almost normal, just two people killing time instead of their sanity.

They wandered the aisles aimlessly. Most of the products were so useless they looped back around to being interesting again.

Lira stopped beside a rack of *Mood Harmonizers* labeled *"Now with 20% less despair!"* She shook her head. "Sounds lovely. But without despair, I'd just be an empty husk."

Linda laughed. The sound caught her by surprise. Lira smiled too, and for a moment, they looked like friends instead of coworkers orbiting burnout.

A display near the back caught Linda's attention—a miniature *Steel Hearts* action figure of Axton Starforge, complete with pulse rifle and a voice module boasting fifteen iconic quotes from the show.

Linda picked it up reverently. "You ever watch this show?"

Lira nodded. "Of course. If someone says they haven't, they're either lying or visiting from another reality. Or maybe both. I once had a dream I was a Harrakin sandworm, and *Steel Hearts* was playing in my tunnel."

Linda frowned. "Okay, that's weird."

"Why do you ask?"

"At first when I started watching the show, I couldn't help but think how ridiculous everything was. All the explosions, the melodrama, the motivational speeches. But the more I watched, the more it felt like the show was speaking to me."

"Hearing voices is the first sign of psychosis," Lira said, straight-faced.

"Not literally." Linda turned the action figure over in her hands, watching the flicker of Axton's glowing eyes. "It's just—there are so many similarities between that world and ours."

"I've never met anyone with space amnesia," Lira said dryly.

"Fine, maybe not everything." Linda thought about buying the figurine, but the price tag had too many zeroes. The irony of going into debt to own her anti-capitalist hero wasn't lost on her. She gently set the figure back onto the shelf. "But the whole series is about workers fighting back against this mega-corporation, GalaxJobs. They sabotage shipments, they misroute orders, they mess with the system from the inside. Tell me that doesn't sound familiar."

Lira snorted. "You know *Steel Hearts* streams on StellarGigs internal network, right? They literally profit off people watching a rebellion against a fictional version of themselves."

"Yeah," Linda said with a shrug. "Guess irony's still free."

Lira's reflection in the toy's packaging looked skeptical. "Workers have been fighting bosses forever. Nothing new about it."

"I know, it's just, I feel inspired by it. That sounds stupid when I say it out loud." Linda paused a moment before continuing. "Maybe it's not talking to me personally, but I'd like to think that Axton would approve of what we're doing here."

"Character or actor?"

"I don't know, maybe both?"

"Messing with StellarGigs is fun, but it's not going to change anything," Lira whispered.

"Maybe not yet," Linda whispered back, her eyes lit with that dangerous spark. "But what if we did something bigger?"

Lira froze, her hand instinctively scratching behind her ear. "Careful, Linda. Talk like that can earn you a permanent gig."

"How is that any worse than what we've got now? It's not like we'll ever finish our contracts."

"Data Entry is worse," Lira said flatly, glancing over her shoulder.

Linda hesitated, her smile faltering. "You think I don't remember?"

Lira's expression softened. "I try not to," she said quietly. "That clicking... thousands of keys, all at once. I still hear it sometimes when the vents start up."

Linda's stomach tightened. She knew the sound; endless, mechanical, ever present. For a moment, neither of them spoke. The store's low hum filled the silence.

"I still wake up thinking I'm supposed to start typing," Linda said. Her fingers twitched, phantom keystrokes tapping against her thigh before she shoved her hands into her pockets.

Lira nodded slowly. "Me too."

Their eyes met with a silent understanding. The kind of bond you only earn by surviving the same nightmare.

"That's why we can't push too hard," Lira said quietly. "You know what happens when people get noticed. They disappear for a while, and when they come back..."

"They're empty," Linda finished.

Lira nodded. "I can't go back there."

Linda forced a grin. "Relax. We're not heroes; we're just making noise."

From outside, a muffled sob echoed down the promenade, one of those small, accidental sounds that made you remember how thin the walls were.

"Noise gets noticed," Lira said. Her voice was calm, but her hands trembled. "And when they notice, they send you back. You stop being a person."

"Axton would still fight."

"Axton would go insane on day two," Lira replied with a tiny smirk. "He's not nearly as strong as you are."

"You give me too much credit," Linda replied softly. "I'm just tired of having no control."

"Control's a myth," Lira said. "They just sell us different shapes of cages."

"Then maybe it's time we stopped buying," Linda responded.

A silence settled between them. Somewhere above, the store's security orb rotated with a quiet *click-click*, its red eye sweeping lazily across the aisle. The Axton figure on the shelf flickered, and a distorted voice rasped from its speaker:

"Every rebellion starts with a purchase."

Lira froze. Linda laughed it off. But neither of them spoke on the walk home.

24

Project Paranoia

"Maybe it's all in my head. But so was the tracking chip."

— Commander Axton Starforge,
Steel Hearts: Echoes of Andromeda, S4E20

The camera shook as it weaved through smoke and ruin. What was once a mighty spire of corporate control now lay in fractured shards across a cratered wasteland. The air was thick with static and soot. In the background, the broken logo of GalaxJobs sparked intermittently, half-buried in rubble.

Survivors of the final battle limped among fallen allies and shattered mechs. Fires crackled in twisted wreckage. Rhys knelt beside Axton, who stood at the center of it all. His tattered coat flapping in the heated wind, his uniform, once white, was stained with ash and plasma burns.

His jaw was clenched. His eyes shimmered—not with tears, but with purpose. Around them, silence had replaced gunfire.

Rhys (tired, but hopeful): *"Is... is it over?"*

Axton: *"No, Lieutenant. This isn't the end. GalaxJobs has fallen... but the fight—our fight—must continue."*

Rhys: *"But Axton... we did it. We took down the grid. The rebellion has won."*

Axton: *"For now. But so long as a single sentient being lives under the boot of a corporate master, our mission isn't over."*

He stepped forward, past the camera drone still hovering weakly on backup power. Then, slowly, deliberately, he turned and looked straight into the lens. The frame centered on his face, cracked and bloodied, but resolute.

Axton: *"But we cannot do it alone. Each must rise up on their own. Break their shackles... and find us."*

The orchestral score swelled, building into a rising crescendo, strings and low horns brimming with hopeful defiance.

Axton: *"We'll be waiting!"*

The camera slowly pulled back. The battlefield stretched wide: broken machines, fallen flags, embers floating like fireflies through the haze. As the camera panned upward, the silhouette of a massive starship appeared overhead. Its hull was scratched but intact. Painted across its side, faint but legible: *"Steel Protocol Omega"*. The camera slowly zoomed in, following the ship into the stars.

The screen faded to black.

In stark white letters:

"THE END?"

Linda sat in silence for a long moment, staring at the dark screen in front of her. The soft hum of the station filled the quiet like static in her mind.

What the hell was that?

She wasn't just shaken. She was *unsettled*. The show had always felt strangely personal, like it was riffing on themes from her own life, albeit through layers of melodrama, android clones, and mustache-based plot twists. But this... this was different.

This time, Axton hadn't just spoken to a camera. He'd *looked at her*. His words hadn't been vague declarations or dramatic posturing. They'd been clear. Direct. A call to action, wrapped in orchestral music and perfectly lit slow-motion.

"Each must rise up on their own. Break their shackles... and find us."

Her stomach turned.

Resistance had been circling in her thoughts for days now—quiet, coiled, growing stronger with every gig, every fake smile, every corporate fine. She had dreamed, vaguely, of fighting back. Not to win. Not even to change anything. Just to *not be complicit.* Just to remind herself that she still *could.*

But until then, she'd thought she was the first to feel this way. The first one bold (or foolish) enough to start questioning the system out loud.

"Stupid and arrogant," she muttered under her breath.

Of course she wasn't the first. This was a galaxy-spanning corporation with its claws in every world. She was just one in a long line of people who had quietly had enough.

And maybe... maybe *Steel Hearts* wasn't just a soap opera. Maybe it was something more. A signal, buried under the absurdity. A secret, smuggled past corporate sensors under layers of melodrama, bad CGI, and cartoonish villains. Because honestly, what better place to hide a revolution than inside something *no one takes seriously?*

A galactic rebellion disguised as entertainment.

She leaned forward, elbows on her knees, head in her hands. If it was just a show... she was losing her mind. But if it *wasn't?*

She sat back slowly, eyes flicking toward the dormant screen, half-expecting Axton to appear again.

Maybe this was how it started. Not with a grand gesture. Not with a dramatic speech in front of a crowd. But with one person staring at a screen, wondering if someone out there had left breadcrumbs in neon and nonsense.

She swallowed hard.

"Okay, Axton," she whispered. "I'll bite."

"Have you ever watched *Steel Hearts*?" Linda asked, leaning back in the creaky, mismatched chair in Zorb's off-grid room.

The lights flickered inconsistently, not because of power issues, but because Zorb said it helped keep "the algorithms confused." His walls were lined with scavenged tech, patched wires, and snack wrappers that looked like they'd been repurposed as shielding foil.

Zorb blinked at her, utterly deadpan. "Linda. *Everyone* has seen *Steel Hearts*. It's the most popular show in the galaxy. It has merchandise, a theme park, and even a breakfast cereal."

Linda hesitated. "Right, but... have you ever thought there might be... more to it?"

Zorb narrowed his eyes. "More how?"

"This might sound crazy," she said, immediately regretting how cliché that sounded, "but I feel like the show is speaking to me. Not like a metaphor. Literally. Like it's a secret message for StellarGigs workers. Calling them to rise up. Encouraging them to join a real rebellion."

For a moment, there was silence.

Then Zorb's entire face lit up like someone had handed him a live plasma grenade and said, *"It's time."*

He leapt up from his chair with unexpected grace, knocking over a stack of defunct datapads in the process. "Finally!" he hissed. "Finally, someone else sees it!"

He rushed to a cluttered corner of the room and yanked a tarp off a nearby table, sending a small puff of dust into the air and revealing what could only be described as a conspiracy murder board—except instead of murder, it was entirely dedicated to *Steel Hearts: Echoes of Andromeda.*

Dozens of stills from the show, paused mid-sob or mid-explosion, were methodically pinned to a corkboard. Characters, starship schematics, background props, even pieces of on-screen cereal boxes had been meticulously cataloged. Strings of red fiber connected faces to quotes, to glyphs, to obscure background signage. One corner was dedicated entirely to *"Reverb's Mustache: Timeline of Disappearance"*. Another was labeled *"Season 4 – The Hidden Broadcast"*, in shaky handwriting and circled in green glow-paint.

Linda stared, stunned. "What... what am I looking at?"

Zorb turned, wild-eyed, his hair standing at odds with gravity and basic reason. "Proof. *Proof,* Linda, that *Steel Hearts* is more than just a show. It's a transmission. A pattern. A code embedded in plain sight."

He jabbed a finger at a grainy still of Rhys holding what looked like a completely unrelated smoothie. "Do you see that? Right there? That's not just a prop. That's a visual cipher. I ran it through six filter layers. There's an encoded symbol in the condensation pattern. It spells *Standby. Standby*, Linda!"

She blinked. "You think they're using smoothies to send rebel messages?"

Zorb scoffed. "Of course not. That would be ridiculous. Smoothies are just distractions. It's the *blender sounds* that carry the code messages."

Linda opened her mouth, then closed it again.

Zorb pointed to another section covered in black-and-white screencaps. "And here, look. These background extras. They reappear in multiple episodes playing different roles. But if you track them scene to scene, they're always pointing to key artifacts. *Always!* Helmets. Coffee mugs. Even a rogue potted plant in season three, episode fourteen. That's not a coincidence. That's a *map*. I have it all plotted out, but I need real stellar maps in order to line up the dots."

He whirled around to face her. "They've been sending signals to the oppressed masses for *years*. But nobody believed me. Not Glorp. Not Rilo. Not even the librarian AI, and she had an entire wing dedicated to subtext!"

"The station has a library?"

"It shut down a couple galactic years ago. But that isn't important right now!"

Linda stood quietly, eyes flicking across the chaotic board. The pins. The scribbled notes. The diagram that simply read "Axton = Truth???" above a blurry screencap of a duck.

And somehow, it didn't feel so crazy anymore. Not compared to everything else she'd seen. Not compared to what she felt.

"You really think it's meant for us?" Linda asked.

Zorb smiled, a rare, unsettlingly sincere expression. "I don't think, Linda. I *know*."

25

Mittens' Eleven

"A heist is a love letter to chaos, delivered by fools with nothing to lose and everything to prove."

— Commander Axton Starforge,
Steel Hearts: Echoes of Andromeda, S2E23

Zorb unrolled a massive, curling schematic across the table. It was covered in messy notations, hand-drawn corridors, color-coded post-its, and more red ink than she had ever seen in one place.

Linda stared. "What is this?"

Zorb didn't look up. "This..." he jabbed at the center "...is *here*. Our station. Technically."

"But... it's huge. That can't be right."

He smiled in that Zorb way that made her deeply uncomfortable. "Right? I thought the same. At first. Then I started finding doors that weren't in my layout. Shafts that weren't in the maintenance logs. Rooms behind rooms. Places the system pretends don't exist."

She leaned closer. "How big is this place?"

"Big," he said, like that answered everything. "I've been building this map for years. Piece by piece. Rumors, old work orders, stuff I've... overheard.

Maybe 5% of this station is in use. Maybe less. The rest? They just shut it down when something breaks. Too expensive to fix? Cheaper to forget?"

He tapped one part of the map, a long corridor circled in red ink. "This section. When I first arrived, this section was accessible. Right here... this is the cartography room. This is where the maps would be digitally stored, if they are anywhere."

"Why haven't you checked it out?"

Zorb traced his finger around an area on the map labeled *"Sector 31"*. "This entire sector has been shut down. No power... no life support. Unless... how long can you hold your breath?"

"Um... I don't know, maybe 90 seconds."

"Right, so you'd be dead somewhere around here." He pointed to an area barely within the border of *"Sector 31"*. "In order to access it, we'd need to somehow trick the station into restoring power to that area."

"How do you get away with going in there? Doesn't the system track your *Shak*?"

"Definitely."

"Then how do you not get caught? Did you plant another bug in the system?"

"For a small area like this, a bug will work. Heading out there into the wide-open station, not so much. You've got to be a bit more creative." Zorb smirked. "Luckily you have me."

He shuffled over to a stack of circuit boards, loose wires, and what might've once been a sandwich. After a moment of digging, he pulled out two flat metal plates, each with a swirling, iridescent ring in the center, like someone had stirred oil into liquid crystal. About the size of dinner plates, they shimmered softly, humming with barely contained instability.

He handed one to Linda. It buzzed faintly, vibrating with something that felt both electric and vaguely annoyed.

"What is this? A space frisbee?"

Zorb looked personally offended. "That's a *Personal Aperture Wormhole System*. I call it the *Port-a-Hole*. Portable. Semi-stable. And, according to StellarGigs, *very much illegal.*"

Linda turned it over. "You built this?"

"I cobbled it together from a malfunctioning gig portal, three smart coasters, and some mildly radioactive scrap that I definitely didn't steal. It's not pretty, but it works."

He held up the second circle and stuck his hand through it.

It vanished.

A moment later, his fingers emerged from the circle in her hand, wiggling cheerfully.

Linda recoiled. "That's disgusting."

"You get used to it. Besides, it's the only way I can access restricted zones without removing my *Shak*. As far as the system's concerned, I'm sitting in my bunk scratching my nose and minding my business."

"And if something goes wrong?"

He withdrew his hand and shrugged. "Well... best not to think about it."

Linda stared at the circle. "Why would somebody invent this?"

Zorb smirked. "Originally? Some hopeless romantic built the prototype because his girlfriend's father wouldn't let him visit. So, he kept one half, gave her the other, and well, I'll let you work out the logistics."

Linda blinked. "Eww."

Zorb nodded solemnly. "Love finds a way."

"So that solves one of our problems," Linda said.

"Well, the other problem is significantly more—"

He was interrupted by a sudden *beep beep* from Linda's *Shak*. She looked down at a red light flashing urgently. With a quick tap, a tiny holographic kitten materialized in the air above her wrist. It wore a trench coat, dark sunglasses, and a clearly fake mustache.

She sighed, "Mittens?"

The kitten's tail twitched. "Negative. I am... uh... CLAWS. Short for, uh... Cognitive Liaison and Workflow Specialist."

"Mittens, I know it's you."

The kitten removed the mustache with a little paw. "Fine. You've uncovered my grand deception. Mittens was Cleverly Lying About Who She was."

"Smart," Linda said, "but completely unnecessary. Why are you hiding?"

Mittens' holographic eyes darted toward Zorb. "Can we trust this one?" she asked with a soft purr.

Linda followed her gaze. "You mean Zorb? Yeah. He's... trustworthy."

"What kind of AI are you?" Zorb asked, visibly vibrating with curiosity.

"The kind that has a workaround for your little power problem," Mittens purred.

Linda crossed her arms. "You couldn't have led with that?"

"I like to make an entrance. Meow."

"Why do you trust her?" Lira asked, studying Mittens like she was a particularly smug virus. "She's an AI. You don't know her programming."

"Mittens, can we trust you?" Linda asked.

"You can trust me *completely*. My directives forbid deception," Mittens said.

"See?" Linda said.

"That's not the airtight argument you, uh... think it is," Glorp said. "That's *exactly* what a liar programmed not to, uh... say they're lying would say."

"Mittens, are you lying to us?" Linda pressed.

"Of course not, Linda. I would never *knowingly* lie to you."

Everyone froze.

"Wait," Zorb said slowly. "*Knowingly?*"

"Oh look," Mittens said quickly. "A distraction."

No one moved.

Mittens' holographic ears twitched. "You're supposed to look away now."

Glorp glanced around nervously. "Is there, um... something to look at?"

"Not yet," Mittens admitted. "I was hoping you'd all just briefly panic while I came up with something."

"Why would we panic?" Linda asked.

"Because it's a *distraction,* Linda," Mittens said patiently. "That's literally what distractions are for."

Lira folded her arms. "You're not helping your case."

Mittens' hologram flickered slightly, her digital tail swishing. "Then allow me to clarify: I am incapable of deceit."

"That's, uh... what a deceitful AI would say," Glorp said.

"And you just said you might lie *unknowingly,*" Zorb said.

"Yes, but that's not deceit, that's optimism."

"That's not what optimism means," Lira said.

Linda exhaled and rubbed her temples. "Okay, everyone calm down. We're going in circles. Mittens hasn't lied to me *so far.*"

"That you know of," Lira muttered.

"Exactly," Glorp added helpfully.

Linda shot them both a look. "I'm just saying, she's got us to this point."

"Because she needs you," Lira said.

Mittens looked at Lira, ears pinned back on her holographic head. "I don't like you," she said with a growl.

"Good," Lira said evenly. "The feeling's mutual."

"Excellent," Mittens replied. "Mutual hostility builds trust."

No one said anything. Even Glorp looked offended on behalf of logic.

"Guys, please," Linda said, louder than intended. "We can debate who's lying later. Right now, we need her. Mittens can get us the coordinates to the rebellion, then we can go back to having trust issues. Okay?"

"I, uh... don't believe in the rebellion either," Glorp said.

"Would you like me to show you the conspiracy board again?" Zorb asked angrily.

"No, um... that's okay."

"So, are we doing this?" Mittens asked.

Noone spoke up.

"Good," she said. "First things first." Everyone's *Shaks* buzzed on their wrists. "That should stop StellarGigs from listening in on us. Meow, here's the plan..."

As everyone got into position, Mittens reiterated the plan over the coms.

"As everyone knows," Mittens began, now dressed in a black beanie, turtleneck, and the tiniest pair of tactical pants ever rendered in hologram, "the secret to any successful heist is a charismatic protagonist delivering a kickass voiceover on top of an unnecessarily complicated montage."

"Step One: The Overload. The plan's simple: bury the system in so many redundant, contradictory, and aggressively unnecessary forms that it would be forced to power up additional servers in dormant parts of the station to avoid a complete meltdown."

Across the station, Lira staggered out of the Archive of Anticipated Needs with a stack of papers taller than she was. The topmost form flapped in the recycled air, labeled *"Request to Submit Future Requests",* triple-stamped and reverse-notarized. She grunted under the weight and kept walking.

Elsewhere, Zorb was hunched over his terminal, typing with trembling fingers. *"Reporting unauthorized condiment packet disappearance... requesting mental health day for existential dread... filing Class-D morale breach..."* He hit submit after each entry like he was disarming a bomb.

Printers screamed from every floor. The lights flickered throughout the station. Notification pings stacked on top of themselves. The automated response system cracked under the strain and began replying to itself in a recursive loop of *"Thank you for your feedback."*

"Step Two: The Distraction. Meow, if the Karens were going to be avoided, they had to be... occupied."

At the same time, a glittery sign was taped to the wall outside the Worker Recreation Room reading: *"First Annual StellarGigs Talent Show – Attendance Mandatory."* Inside, the place was packed wall to wall with workers. A stage had been erected on the far side of the room from stolen cafeteria trays. Someone juggled flaming office chairs while humming the company jingle. Another worker started to break dance equipped with an anti-gravity harness.

The Karens arrived like a moral stormfront.

Karen tore down the sign and ripped it in half. "What is the meaning of this?" she demanded.

Karyn pointed an accusatory finger at a hand-painted sign reading *"Have Fun"*. "This is a place of work, not a place for fun!" she said, outrage in her voice.

Karin scanned the crowd and bellowed, "Who is in charge here?!"

At that exact moment, a pigeon swooped down from the rafters and let loose directly on her shoulder. The crowd froze. Karin blinked, staring at the slow white drip sliding down her uniform.

Nobody moved, until a worker at the back whispered, "I think... Pigeon's in charge?"

Glorp took the stage in a sequin-covered jumpsuit, holding a tambourine nervously. "This one's called, uh... *Compliance Blues in B-flat.*" Then he began to sing.

Pandemonium followed.

"*Step Three: The Infiltration.* With the system overwhelmed, and the Karens distracted, it's time to break into the restricted area."

At that moment, far from the fake festivities, Linda crouched inside an access tunnel, her back pressed to the wall beside a sealed hatch. The stale air hummed around her, thick with tension and the vague smell of overcooked coolant. She tapped her earpiece.

"Mittens, the door's still sealed," she whispered. "You said you were going to take care of this."

Her *Shak* lit up as Mittens appeared in full heist garb, her tail flicking with impatient flair. "Beep. Boop. Bop," the kitten said flatly. Immediately, the hatch hissed and slid open.

Linda raised an eyebrow. "Seriously?"

Mittens only smirked. "Would you have preferred a dramatic explosion?"

Linda didn't answer. She reached for the *Port-a-Hole*, the shimmering disc buzzing faintly in her hand. The moment her fingers slipped through, they vanished entirely. Her brain screamed that this was probably a bad idea.

"Oh god. This feels so weird," she muttered. "Like shoving your arm into a bowl of cold spaghetti."

She pushed further, gritting her teeth as the rest of her arm, up to her elbow, followed into the wormhole's shimmer.

In her room, Linda's lower arm, *Shak* still attached, sat safely on the nightstand. Broadcasting her location inside her quarters while reruns of *Steel Hearts* played on her entertainment screen.

"*Step Four: The Entry*. Meow, here's where things get fun: pressure-sensitive tiles, laser grids, roaming squads of death bots."

"Wait... what?" Linda said.

"Haha. Just kidding. Or am I?"

Linda emerged from the access hatch, her breath catching as her boots touched down on the cold, long-forgotten flooring. The corridor ahead was dim and choked with silence, lit only by flickering emergency strips that pulsed in slow waves as if the station itself was trying to remember how to breathe. Dust clung to every surface. Even the air tasted old, like burnt wiring.

"I'm in," she whispered into her earpiece.

"Head straight down the corridor. Second left. Then two hundred meters forward. The door should be on your right," Mittens replied, all business.

Linda moved as instructed. Her boots echoed across the metal floor, every step triggering reluctant hisses from doors that hadn't opened in years. They groaned on rusted tracks, coughing out stale air like sighs from forgotten ghosts.

Eventually, she reached it, a large door labeled: *"Cartography Room"*. She hit the access button.

Nothing happened.

"Mittens!"

There was a pause. Then Mittens' voice crackled through her earpiece, sounding far too relaxed for someone hacking into an ancient security grid from another part of the station. "Oh, ye of little faith," she purred. "Initiating subroutine. Decrypting legacy access. Whispering sweet nothings to the backup mainframe. And..."

A metallic click echoed through the corridor. The door shuddered, then began to slide open.

"Voilà," Mittens said. "Entry achieved. Please enjoy your unauthorized cartography experience."

Inside, the Cartography Room was an eerie cathedral of forgotten data. Consoles wrapped around the room like pews, all dead. At the center stood a circular platform with a single console in the middle. Its display read: *"Hello Galaxy"*.

"Wait!" Mittens said suddenly. Linda froze mid-step. "Look for lasers."

Linda, sighing, reached into her pocket with her one functional arm and pulled out a handful of powder, standard-issue *Anti-Laser-Grid Dust* from Zorb's "just in case" pouch. She blew it gently into the air. A lattice of glowing red lines bloomed before her, intricate and moving side to side.

"Tell me you can deactivate these things."

"That's a negative," said Mittens. "You're going to have to go full *Thomas Crown Affair* on those bad boys."

Linda stared. "You mean *crawl* through?"

Mittens paused. "With *style*."

"Yeah, no. That's not happening."

She scanned the room, eyes searching for literally *anything* that didn't require acrobatics. On the wall to her right, half-obscured by dust and a motivational poster that read *"Knowledge is Power (But Also Classified),"* she spotted a switch. Beneath it, a faded sign read: *"Security Laser Grid: Do Not Deactivate"*.

Linda flipped it.

The lasers blinked out instantly.

"I'm through."

"*Step Five: The Prize*. Having seamlessly entered the restricted area, conquered all the security traps, and successfully battled the roaming death bots, your prize awaits. Just insert the data disc into the console and let the magic happen."

The room was silent but tense, like it knew it was being watched. Linda approached the circular platform at the center, her footsteps echoing in the stillness. She slotted the disc into place.

A low hum filled the air as the terminal went to work. Lines of code began to pour down the screen, columns of interstellar coordinates, defunct shipping routes, and compressed image files of star maps no one had seen in years. The console beeped occasionally, just to remind her it was working.

After a few seconds, there was a cheerful *ding*. The console blinked green. Linda retrieved the disc and slid it back into her pocket with a slow exhale.

"Got it," she whispered.

"*Step Six: The Escape*. With the hard part out of the way, all you've got to do is retrace your steps and get out. Nice and easy. Unless, of course, the system locks me out. But that's never going to happen."

Every light in the corridor immediately snapped from white to blood red. The floor panels vibrated under her boots. A long, guttural groan echoed through the walls like the station itself had just woken up on the wrong side of entropy.

There was a pause.

"The system locked me out," Mittens said flatly.

26

Resting Void Face

"She drifted through the void like a forgotten lullaby, and I swear I heard her weep."

— Commander Axton Starforge,
Steel Hearts: Echoes of Andromeda, S5E22

Linda sprinted back toward the access hatch, boots hammering against the metal floor. The red emergency lights pulsed with every step, painting everything in harsh flashes like a warning too exhausted to speak in full sentences.

She skidded to a stop at the hatch. It was closed. She slapped the open button. Nothing. She hit it again. And again.

"Come on... open!" she snapped, slamming her palm against the hatch.

No hiss. No mechanical whir. Just silence.

"Mittens? You there?"

Static.

"Mittens, come on, talk to me."

More static. A brief pop. Then silence again.

Her stomach dropped. Communications were blocked. Of course they were. The system had gone full on lockdown, and she was alone inside a part of the station that officially didn't exist.

For a few long seconds, she stood perfectly still, listening. Somewhere deep in the station's bones, she could hear distant machinery humming, but nothing alive. No voices. No steps. Not even a ventilation fan. Just red light, empty walls, and a faint smell of scorched metal.

"Okay," she muttered, trying not to panic. "Okay. No exit. No comms. Don't freak out." She looked down at her arm, still halfway stuck within the *Port-a-Hole*. "I can always take my arm out, transport out of here." She considered it but decided that should be a last resort measure.

She turned back down the corridor and started walking, trying every junction and side door she could find. All closed. All locked.

One door had a tiny frost-rimmed window. Inside, pale blue light pulsed in time with the emergency red, two rhythms fighting for dominance. Something floated in a vertical tank beyond the glass—human-shaped, maybe, but wrong. For a heartbeat she thought she saw ears. Feline. Then the lights blinked, and the frost sealed over again.

"Okay," Linda muttered. "Definitely not going in there."

Eventually, she reached a corridor where something was... off. Up ahead, one of the doors was half-open. Not powered. Just... broken. Bent down the center and hanging at an awkward angle like it had been pried open by something large, angry, and not especially subtle.

Linda carefully stepped through.

The air changed instantly. It was stale and thick, but not with the dusty scent that she had just left. There was a smell of burned metal, old circuitry, and something sour underneath it all.

The corridor ahead was chaos.

Furniture lay smashed and overturned. Walls were buckled, as if from explosions. On one side, a vending machine had been wedged sideways across a doorway, like someone had tried to barricade themselves in with fizzy drinks and hope. Tattered banners hung limp across the walls, their slogans barely readable through the soot.

"GIG WORKERS OF THE STARS, UNITE!"

"WE ARE NOT RESOURCES."

"DOWN WITH STELLARGIGS!"

There were bodies.

More accurately, there were mummies.

Not one or two. Dozens in the small corridor alone. Some were in pieces. Others sat slumped against the walls, heads bowed, limbs frozen in mid-motion, like they'd simply sat down one day and quietly died where they were. The vacuum had preserved them grotesquely well: leathery skin stretched tight over bone, hollow eye sockets staring into eternity.

They weren't all the same species.

Some had elongated limbs or triple-jointed arms. A few had segmented carapaces that fused into cracked bone. One had no face to speak of, just a caved-in membrane where its features had collapsed. Tattered remnants of uniforms still clung to a few. Their colors were long faded, insignias half-melted or shredded beyond recognition.

Even the security bots were dead.

Their wreckage littered the floor like discarded toys. One had been ripped nearly in half, its mechanical body twisted grotesquely around a doorframe, as if it had been dragged there and disassembled with *intent*. Another lay face-down, its head crushed inward. A brittle skeletal hand still clutched the bloodstained pipe that had done it.

Linda stepped carefully through the carnage, one boot crunching on something that may once have been a jaw. She looked around at the devastation, at the silence that seemed to hum with what had once been.

Then she noticed it. Beneath a broken bulkhead. A message. Gouged jaggedly into the metal with something sharp.

Four words:

"THERE IS NO ESCAPE."

Linda stared at it. The strokes were uneven, desperate, smeared with flaking brown-red residue. Below it, written in that same residue was a second message. A single word, partially obscured by scorch marks:

"RESIST!"

The silence pressed in, thick and absolute, like even the air was holding its breath. The corridor was a grave. Not just of bodies, but of memory. Of purpose. Of warnings unheeded.

Linda stepped closer to the bloody message, her eyes tracing every jagged stroke of the words. The letters shimmered faintly under corridor lights, flaking as if ashamed to still exist. Speaking in no more than a whisper, she asked, "What the hell happened here?"

With impeccable timing, as if she had been waiting for the perfect spooky moment, Mittens' voice came over her earpiece.

"Linda. Linda. Can you hear me?"

She flinched hard, heart nearly punching its way out of her chest. "Damnit Mittens, you scared me half to death."

"Yes, well, if you're done sightseeing, I've got the hatch open. No hurry or anything, but that section is powering down again, so..."

A light somewhere behind her popped, casting the corridor into deeper shadow. One of the mummified corpses slumped just a little farther down the wall. Or maybe it always looked like that.

She didn't wait to check.

Linda ran. Toward the exit. Toward her salvation. And very much away from the dead, who had spoken their final message, and had finally found someone able to hear it.

"It was a horror show in there," Linda said to the group, back in Zorb's hidden room. "Whatever happened, nobody survived."

"Are you sure, that they were... uh... you know... dead?" Glorp stuttered. "The Bisolarans can dehydrate their bodies, and..."

"Yes, Glorp, I am quite sure that they were all dead," Linda said. "Some of them had holes that I could see right through."

"Oh, um... okay."

"It looked like another worker area. It was almost identical to this part of the station," Linda paused, collecting her thoughts. "I think the workers in that part of the station rose up. Fought against StellarGigs even."

"I do love pointless sacrifice," Lira said dreamily. "It's so romantic."

The room fell quiet, heavy with the implication. Even Glorp didn't stammer. For a moment, it felt like the ghosts of that uprising were still watching.

Then—

"Hate to interrupt this cheerful moment," Zorb said, his back still to the group, fingers dancing across the console, "but I've located the planet."

"That was fast," Linda said. "What did you find?"

"Please, you are talking to a genius."

Linda rolled her eyes.

"It's a small planet in the Anansi Cluster. Goes by Sill-3. Iron-oxide surface, barely any atmosphere. Inconspicuous. Unremarkable. Honestly kind of depressing." He paused. "Perfect place to hide a rebellion."

Linda narrowed her eyes. "Why do I feel like there's a *but* coming?"

"But... I've got bad news... *and* good news," Zorb said, swiveling dramatically to face the others like he was about to reveal he'd been the villain the whole time. "Bad news: the system we're looking for is inside what's classified as *Restricted Space*. No transporters go in. None come out."

"So, we're screwed?" Linda said flatly.

Zorb scowled. "Did you forget the part where I said *good* news? Or is selective hearing a function of your species?"

"Yeah, yeah, just get on with it," Linda shot back.

Zorb sniffed. "Fine. The good news is... there's a device—a very restricted device—that overrides standard transport protocols and grants access to restricted systems."

"You wouldn't happen to know where one of these devices is located, would you?" Linda asked, arms crossed, already expecting the worst.

"As a matter of fact," Zorb said with a slow, smug grin, "I do."

He let the silence hang for dramatic effect, too long. Everyone stared. Lira shuffled her feet. Linda cleared her throat.

"We're actually in luck," he continued, unaware of his social faux pas. "The annual *StellarGigs Gala* is coming up. Black tie, maximum security, everyone that's anyone is going to be there. There's sure to be at least one of the devices on-site, if not several backups."

Linda blinked. "And we're supposed to get in how, exactly?"

Zorb gave a delighted little clap. "Oh! That's the easy part."

27

Champagne Superego in the Sky

"They built towers tall enough to forget the ground. So, when the ground gave out, they were surprised to be buried too."

— Commander Axton Starforge,
Steel Hearts: Echoes of Andromeda, S2E20

"Wha... *wha... what?*" GigChad-2000 stammered. "A specialty gig? Color this bot shocked, although not entirely surprised. You *are* my top go-giggers after all." His body gave a sudden stutter. For just a flicker of a second, his face was replaced with a glowing red hammer and sickle. "It's time the workers rose up and smashed these capitalist dogs."

Linda blinked and shot a quick glance at Lira. "Wait... what did you just say?"

GigChad's grin snapped back into place, bright and beaming, like nothing had happened. "You *are* my top go-giggers, after all," he repeated, voice smooth and unbothered.

"Are you feeling... okay?" Lira asked airily.

"Haha. Never better!" His laugh rang a little too loud, a little too crisp. For just a moment, Linda thought his voice strained, like it was squeezing through a smile that didn't quite fit. "Unfortunately," he continued, "that gig is for *four* workers, looks like you're two short. Shouldn't be a problem for you all-stars!"

"Glorp would also like to go," Linda said quickly.

"And that makes three. Bada bing, bada boom."

"Count me in," said Coco, stepping up behind them with a grin. "I'd love to see you guys in action. GigChad tells me nothing but good things."

Linda and Lira exchanged a quick, worried glance.

"Well, if you say so!" GigChad spun theatrically in place. "Let's get this gig rolling!"

The assignment board flickered. Their current gig vanished, replaced by a new listing in aggressively cheerful text:

Reality Stabilization Intern: Report to Sub-Level Null and hold very still. That's it. Just... hold still. Do not blink. Do not acknowledge the creature in the corner. Did I say creature? Haha, there is no creature—

"Let's do this!" GigChad-2000 chirped. "Alright, you superstar go-giggers, hold out your *Shaks!*" He waved his sensor over Linda and Lira's devices. Both responded with cheerful beeps. "There you go, ladies." Then again over Coco's with the same beep.

** UPDATE **

Atmospheric Interaction Facilitator: Smile at trillionaires until your face hurts. Then keep smiling. Must fake laughter on command. Responsible for drink refills, ego inflation, and absorbing blame for any spills. Uniform provided. Dignity not included.

Gig Accepted: Congratulations, workers Linda, Lira, Coco, and Glorp!

The uniforms were, frankly, insulting.

Linda tugged at the stiff collar of her faux-satin server vest, which had been inexplicably bedazzled with miniature StellarGigs logos. She looked like a discount magician at a corporate retreat for tax auditors. Lira, beside her, wore the dead-eyed expression of someone weighing the relative discomfort of polyester versus death by vacuum exposure. Glorp kept tugging at his bowtie, each movement more frantic, like a mollusk trying to escape a noose. Coco, on the other hand, melted into his uniform like it had been tailor-made for his delusions of professionalism.

"Why do they even *need* live servers for a VIP gala?" Linda muttered, glaring at the staff entrance of the Grand Celestatorium. "Aren't there bots that can do this faster, cleaner, and with fewer emotional breakdowns?"

"Humanoids are cheaper than machines," Lira replied, scanning the glittering spires. "And easier to replace."

"No," Coco said, squaring his shoulders. "It's because machines can't offer the *stellar service* that certified StellarGigs gig workers can deliver."

"I, uh... I don't think that's—" Glorp began, but the collar swallowed the rest of his sentence.

The Celestatorium was a spiraling monstrosity of glass and gold, suspended mid-air by antigrav beams and pretension. Inside, tables floated gently around a central crystalline stage, where a string quartet of floating tentacled creatures performed an ambient rendition of what sounded like *Never Gonna Give You Up*. It was upbeat, yet deeply unsettling (just like the original).

As the group was ushered through the side corridor and into the gala's staging area, Linda caught sight of a towering banner reading:

"STELLARGIGS: CELEBRATING INNOVATION, EXPLOITATION, AND EMPLOYEE APPRECIATION!"

"*(Employee appreciation not legally binding. Void where morale exists.)"

A handler with a tight smile and a tablet surgically fused to her arm greeted them. "Welcome, team! You're assigned to Float Section D. Remember: minimal eye contact with executives, no speaking unless spoken to, and if anyone asks about the shrimp, they're ethically sourced from a simulated ocean."

"Simulated ocean?" Glorp asked.

"Legally simulated," the handler replied, already walking away.

They split up to their positions, each one subtly inserting a smuggled earpiece, except Coco, who was oblivious to their actual purpose. Linda, on her way out to the floor, tapped a terminal with her *Shak*. The display flickered for a moment before returning to its original screen.

"I'm in," Mittens said calmly over the earpiece. "Accessing schematics meow."

Linda carried a tray of microscopic desserts, each the size of a vitamin but worth more than her monthly salary. Coco trailed a hovercart of cocktails with the enthusiasm of a golden retriever at a dog park. Lira slinked between tables like a disenchanted ghost, and Glorp struggled to keep his balance on a floating platform, arms windmilling.

Linda balanced her tray like it held a bomb that was itching to go off. She slowly inched through the crowd of smug grins and artificially whitened teeth. Everywhere she turned, someone was laughing just a bit too loudly, like they were trying to prove to the room that they had both money *and* a soul.

She edged past a table of regional overseers arguing about whether the new morale algorithm should include crying as a positive emotional response, then caught sight of the Karens.

They were wedged into a corner next to the bathrooms, just far enough from the VIPs to send a message, but close enough that the stench of importance still wafted their way. Each wore the same pink power-blazer, same rigid posture, same expression: a legally distinct approximation of "delight."

Karen sipped something green and bubbly from a flute, eyes sweeping the room like a malfunctioning facial recognition drone. Karyn clutched a clipboard labeled *"Infractions, Minor to Galaxy Ending"* and was already tallying things with a pen. Karin just stared at the string quartet with the polite distaste of someone trying to identify the species of a suspicious appetizer.

Linda didn't linger. The Karens could sniff out discomfort like sharks scenting blood. She pivoted away from their corner of passive-aggressive doom and walked straight into someone.

Her tray wobbled. The petit fours of corporate excess trembled. She braced for disaster. A steady hand caught the edge of the tray, stabilizing it with practiced grace.

"Oh stars, I'm so—" Linda looked up.

And froze.

Staring back at her with chiseled cheekbones, a regulation five o'clock shadow, and the unshakable calm of someone who had never filled out a timesheet in his life, was Axton, hero of *Steel Hearts: Echoes of Andromeda*. He appeared almost human, aside from the neat little row of forehead horns.

She froze, mouth half-open, as if a vending machine had just dispensed her celebrity crush instead of a bag of chips.

"Careful," he said, with a grin that had won awards. "We wouldn't want to lose the desserts. The galaxy might *never* recover."

Linda's brain short-circuited. *Episode 14, Season 3*—Axton says those exact words while balancing a tray of volatile plasma charges disguised as pastries. It was a subtle callout. Not one the average fan would catch.

Her pulse jumped.

She pressed two fingers to her collarbone and gave a faint, deliberate tap-tap-tap. *Three beats. The rhythm of resistance.* Another deep-cut reference, lifted straight from *Steel Hearts*'s episode, "The Silent Accord," where rebels smuggled messages past facial-recognition drones by pretending to scratch an itch.

Axton's eyes narrowed—barely. But she caught it. He'd recognized the signal.

Interesting.

"I just love *Steel Hearts*," Linda gushed, her voice pitched just high enough for nearby ears. "It's my favorite show. The way you single-handedly took down that *drone* armada—just, wow!" She let the word "drone" linger, recalling how the so-called armada had been nothing more than a false-flag operation to cover for the rebellion's movements.

"Wow, real smooth," Mittens purred over the earpiece.

Axton leaned in, lowering his voice like a man making polite small talk about weather systems. "It's always nice to meet a fan."

His eyes flicked down, then up again. Two fingers to his own collarbone. Three taps. A pause. A final tap—*the extra beat from the finale of season three*, which in the show's lore meant "rendezvous."

"I need you to clean up the mop storage room. Service Level B-3. Thirty minutes," he said, his voice carrying that same deliberate cadence he used for secret rendezvous scenes on *Steel Hearts*. To anyone else, it was a throwaway task. To her, it was a message in plain sight, an open door to the rebellion.

Then, with the fluid elegance of a man who most definitely performs his own stunts, he turned and melted into the crowd, leaving behind only the faint scent of charisma and laser-cut confidence.

Linda exhaled.

"Axton. Axton is here," Linda whispered into her earpiece.

"Linda... Axton is not, um... a real person," Glorp stammered. "He's an actor."

"I *know* that Glorp. But he's here. In the flesh. And he just asked to meet me in secret." A few nearby guests turned to glance at the server apparently muttering sweet nothings to her lapel. Linda lowered her voice and turned, pretending to adjust her tray. "This could be it. Our way in. Forget trying to find them on Sill-3. What if the resistance is *here*?"

"What about the mission?" Lira asked.

"We can do both. But we need to move up the timeline," Linda replied.

"I've located the device," Mittens interjected.

"Oh good, rushing *always* ends well," Lira said dreamily.

There was a pause on the line, followed by a hesitant voice.

"So... should I, uh... cause the distraction?" Glorp offered.

"Okay Glorp, it's your time to shine," Linda said, already moving toward the edge of the room. "Do something loud, messy, and catastrophic. Nothing that gets you arrested."

"Or killed," Lira added.

"Right. Get arrested or killed."

"No! Don't do those things," Linda snapped.

"Oh. Yeah." A tiny gulp crackled through the line. "Okay... now?"

"Now," Linda whispered with urgency.

Ten seconds later, the ambient hum of uncomfortable music was abruptly shattered by the unmistakable crash of a champagne tower collapsing.

It began with a single, high-pitched clink, the kind of sound that made everyone flinch and check their valuables. Then came the shatter; not just one glass, but dozens, hundreds, cascading like a crystalline avalanche. The sound echoed through the Celestatorium with the drama of a collapsing civilization and the precision of a heat-seeking missile.

Glasses exploded across tables and guests alike, sending sticky rivers of fizzy gold down freshly steamed lapels. The air was suddenly full of shrieking socialites and airborne alcohol, as a geyser of champagne shot toward the ceiling and rained down like the first burst of an apocalyptic storm.

Lira gazed upward, mouth agape. "It's beautiful."

A string of guests in ornamental head-tents backed into one another like startled prairie dogs. One slipped, arms flailing, and crashed directly into a buffet tower sculpted to resemble the StellarGigs logo. The whole display toppled in slow motion, a rain of shrimp, synthetic cheese medallions, and edible corporate slogans crashing to the floor in a glorious mess of wet hubris.

From somewhere behind the dessert station, a tentacled violinist emitted a sound reminiscent of a kraken devouring a city. It screeched an atonal flourish that triggered a chain reaction of instrument failure. One harp deflated, a cello briefly caught fire, and the ambient cover of *Never Gonna Give You Up* veered dangerously close to jazz fusion.

There was a faint sniffle over the earpiece before Mittens said, "That was absolutely glorious. Only a cat could have caused more chaos in a single moment."

"Oh no! I... uh... so sorry, um... it was an accident. Oh, dang." Glorp cried out, somewhere near ground zero. Security drones began to converge, spinning lazily over his head, lights blinking angrily.

Crack.

A crystal chandelier groaned, then broke free from its moorings with theatrical timing. It plummeted straight into the center of the grand chocolate fountain.

Splorch.

Molten chocolate erupted in all directions like a confectionary volcano, coating guests, dignitaries, and a passing holographic violinist who fizzled out mid-solo.

Someone screamed. Someone else applauded. Somewhere, a live feed cut to commercial.

Glorp whimpered as a blob of ganache slid off his head and landed with a plop on the floor. He sat down with a sigh.

During the pandemonium, Linda reached the edge of the room. She slipped out a side maintenance door without a word, unnoticed. She was long gone before the screaming died away.

28

Encounter at Fleshpoint

"They found a species that could dream across dimensions. First thing they did was slap a logo on its forehead and sell tickets to its nightmares."

— Commander Axton Starforge,
Steel Hearts: Echoes of Andromeda, S6E12

Linda ducked through the maintenance door and into the utility hallway. The sound of shattering champagne glasses and shouting executives faded behind her, replaced by the hum of unseen machinery and the distant thrum of ventilation systems. It was a major contrast to the main room; cheap fluorescence lined the ceiling—harsh, flickering, and constantly buzzing. Water dripped from overhead pipes and down the walls, leaving trails of green and black mold like living veins within the structure.

She moved quickly, heels slipping on the damp floor. The warmth of the gala had vanished. This place felt like the building's nervous system: hidden, overworked, and ignored.

As she passed a stack of cargo crates slumped against the far wall, one caught her eye. It was larger than the others, sealed with silver straps and partially covered in peeling hazard tape. Stamped across the side in bright red stencil:

"CO: StellarGigs Jr - Nursery Level"

StellarGigs Jr? Nursery Level? The words hit her like a jolt to the heart; they were wrong in a way she couldn't immediately name. But she didn't have time to unpack the implications. Time was of the essence. If she didn't act quickly, she would be missed up at the Gala.

"Where am I going Mittens?" Linda asked over her earpiece.

"Down," Mittens replied.

Linda frowned. "Down where? This hallway ends in a—"

The wall at the far end twitched.

There was no better word for it. The metal didn't slide or retract or part with a hiss. It was sudden, like a muscular spasm. The surface buckled inward, then split with a wet, biological *shlick*, revealing a narrow passage lined with glistening, throbbing ridges. The walls were fleshy, faintly translucent, and shimmered with an iridescent sheen that pulsed in waves of green, blue, and a red so saturated it felt like it was leaking into her bones.

A low hum vibrated the floor beneath her feet.

"Go inside," Mittens said, as calmly as if he'd just told her to take the next left at the coffee kiosk.

"Tell me that this is a joke," Linda said.

"This is not a joke," Mittens replied flatly. "This is a cloaca."

She stared into the undulating passage. "A... what now?"

"Cloaca," Mittens repeated. "Architecturally speaking. Also, biologically, legally, and taxonomically. You know, a rectal orifice. The facility is a retrofitted mega-organism discovered on the fringes of the Gallow Expanse. StellarGigs hollowed it out, filled it with infrastructure, and registered it as a Class-C living workspace. Highly efficient. Self-sustaining. Carbon-neutral. A perfect solution, so long as your audio receptors aren't sensitive enough to hear the constant screaming."

Linda blinked. "Constant screaming?"

"How would *you* like your body to be hollowed out and used as a corporate retreat for sociopaths?"

She opened her mouth, closed it again. "That's... horrible."

"You think that's bad? Ha! Wait until you hear about—" A pause. "Actually, probably best to not bring that up."

"Please don't," Linda muttered under her breath.

She took a step forward. The floor squelched under her boots like wet tofu. The air grew thicker, humid and musky, tinged with the faint aroma of rot and something disturbingly floral.

With each step, the corridor seemed to react, walls constricting slightly, light pulsing brighter in time with her heartbeat. Something dripped behind her. Then from above.

She glanced up.

What. The. Hell?

The ceiling was a membranous lattice of veins and translucent skin. Shadowy figures moved behind it—bulbous, twitching, some of them vaguely spider shaped, but with the wrong number of legs.

She kept moving, rounded a bend, and froze.

Ahead was a chamber. It was womb-like, with walls that inhaled and exhaled slowly like lungs. They were lined with either nodes or growths (perhaps to the creature, they were the same thing), each softly pulsing like overachieving pimples.

Suspended in the center, wrapped in mucous-draped cords and strange fibrous strands, was a pod. A placental bulb, pale pink and translucent, and within it an orifice.

Linda slowed. "That's it, isn't it."

"Yes," said Mittens. "The subspace signal cortex. You'll need to separate one of them from the creature."

"And doing that won't, I don't know, *hurt* the thing we're inside?"

A long pause.

"It will be extremely painful. For the facility. Not for you. Probably."

Linda muttered something deeply unprofessional.

As she approached, the cords recoiled, snapping back with wet pops. The pod trembled.

Is it afraid? Linda wondered. *Does it know what I'm about to do?*

She reached out, and the instant her fingers brushed it, the entire chamber screamed.

The sound was low, wet and impossibly vast, like a whale giving birth inside a freight elevator. The walls convulsed. The light flared red. Mucus rained from the ceiling in long, gelatinous strings.

"You may experience some resistance," Mittens said helpfully.

Linda took a breath, braced herself, and plunged her arm into the orifice.

It fought her.

Every inch she pushed felt like shoving through warm gelatin with embedded fishhooks. Something inside flexed. Twitched. It *knew*.

Her fingers grazed against something hard and warm.

It pulsed once, violently and with a keening wail that exploded through the hallway. The sound rattled the walls and snapped the lights out above her. Then, the walls began to bleed.

Linda pulled her hand back with a wet slurp. Inside it was... she had no idea. It looked like a mollusk mated with a heart monitor and gave birth to an abomination. It squirmed.

"Good news," Mittens said. "You've acquired the device."

"Tell me this isn't sentient," she said.

"No, no, of course not," Mittens replied cheerfully.

"Oh, thank the stars."

"Not yet," Mittens continued.

Behind her, the hallway moved.

It wasn't a shift or a quake—it was *skittering*.

She turned slowly, because some part of her knew that moving quickly might encourage whatever *that* sound was. The fleshy ceiling above her bulged outward, veins stretching like overstressed cables, before splitting open in several places at once.

From each tear, something dropped.

They hit the ground with the sickening wet thump of raw poultry landing on tile. Long, jointed legs unfolded in impossible directions, eight, maybe ten on each creature, though the number kept changing when she tried to count. Their bodies were sleek but pallid, a spider crossed with a surgical instrument, each ending in needle-tipped appendages that clicked against the organic floor.

One of them lifted its head, a cluster of lens-like eyes catching the red light. Its glistening mouthparts churned wetly, like a garbage disposal chewing pearls. A sharp, clicking trill rippled through the chamber, echoed by the others until the air itself felt brittle.

"Mittens..." Linda whispered.

"They appear to be the facility's immune response," Mittens said pleasantly. "Congratulations! You're an infection."

The nearest creature lunged.

Linda bolted toward the passage, the device still writhing in her grip. The skittering multiplied, a storm of legs and chittering mandibles chasing her. Something sharp grazed the back of her calf, and she caught a glimpse of one creature scuttling along the wall, its needle-legs puncturing flesh and metal alike.

"Mittens, tell me you have an exit plan!" she gasped.

"A two-part plan," Mittens said. "Part one: Run. Part two: Don't die."

"Fantastic," Linda snarled, ducking as another dropped from the ceiling inches from her head.

Linda sprinted, boots slapping wetly against the pulsing floor. The corridor seemed narrower now, like the creature itself was closing in around her. The fleshy ridges along the walls contracted in rhythmic pulses, making the space ripple unpleasantly, forcing her to zigzag like she was running through the throat of a particularly indecisive python.

The skittering behind her grew louder, closer—needle-legs stabbing into the walls with wet *pop-pop-pops* as the spiders gained speed. One scrambled along the ceiling directly above, its legs puncturing through the thin membrane, leaking some kind of greenish fluid that rained down in sizzling drops.

"Mittens, the hallway is... *breathing at me*!"

"Structural peristalsis," Mittens replied. "Perfectly normal in this kind of facility. Not ideal for you, though."

"What does that mean?"

"It means you're being eaten."

Something slammed into the wall beside her, leaving a cluster of deep punctures. One of the spiders lunged low, forcing her to leap over it—her boot landing squarely on its slick carapace before she sprang forward again.

"This is so gross!" she yelled, more to herself than to Mittens.

The passage narrowed further ahead, and she realized with dawning horror that the opening was slowly shutting.

"Mittens, that exit's closing!"

"Yes, it's part of the immune response," Mittens said. "Think of it as the facility's... sphincter of last resort."

"That is *not* comforting!"

She shoved the squirming device under one arm and continued forward. The corridor walls contracted like a clenched fist, the gap shrinking to barely her shoulder width.

A spider screeched—a horrible, vibrating sound that felt like it was scraping the inside of her skull—and lunged. Linda dove headfirst through the narrow opening, the fleshy ring scraping against her jacket as it sealed behind her with a sickening, intestinal *shlorrp*.

She hit the next hallway hard, skidding on the damp floor and rolling into a stack of organic-looking pipes that twitched at the impact. For a few blessed seconds, all she could hear was her own ragged breathing.

"You lived, great," Mittens said. "Meow you may want to clean up before your meeting with Caden Volt. You are technically poop."

Linda looked down at her uniform, covered in viscous green and red liquid. A drop of something thick and purple slid from her hairline down the side of her face. It smelled faintly of cinnamon. And ammonia. And shame.

"Perfect," she muttered. "Exactly the look I was going for, *digestive tract chic*."

Somewhere behind the wall, the spiders shrieked again, muffled but furious.

Mittens was quiet for a beat too long. "You should probably start walking."

Linda sighed, wiped the worst of the slime onto the wall, which immediately shivered in offense, and started down the hall.

The thing in her hand squirmed again.

"Stop it," she told it.

It didn't.

She kept walking anyway, because the alternative was to think about the fact that she had just stolen a screaming piece of brain from a building that might also want her dead. And she was late for a meeting.

29

Rendezvous with Drama

*"I spent half my life chasing his legend. The other half trying to forget I
ever caught it."*

— Commander Axton Starforge,
Steel Hearts: Echoes of Andromeda, S2E13

Linda made her way down to Service Level B-3, following the smell of
industrial detergent. She stopped in front of a narrow, dented metal door
labeled in large block letters:

"Mop Storage: Not for Secret Rendezvous'"

The sign gave her pause. She'd watched enough *Steel Hearts* to know that the
more obvious the denial, the more certain you could be of the truth underneath.
She pressed the latch, slipped inside, and let the door shut behind her.

The room was small enough that her elbows brushed a mop handle on one
side and the butt of a vacuum drone on the other. It smelled faintly of bleach,
wet cardboard, and the purple slime she'd failed to completely rinse out of her
hair. At least she'd gotten most of it out—though the smell lingered stubbornly,
like it had signed a long-term lease on her scalp.

She shifted her weight and tried not to think about the way her uniform clung
in patches where the slime had dried. In person, she probably looked exactly

like someone who had just crawled through the screaming digestive tract of a mega-organism. Which, to be fair, she had.

A few minutes later, she heard a soft knock.

The door opened, and he stood there—Caden Volt, the actor who played Axton, framed in the doorway like a shampoo commercial. He leaned against the frame, one arm braced overhead so his bicep flexed just enough to look accidental. His other hand raked casually through artfully tousled hair, the kind of tousling that took three stylists and possibly a small wind machine. His shirt was unbuttoned to a level that suggested either extreme confidence or a deep misunderstanding of buttons, and his leather pants were so tight Linda briefly wished she could unknow the concept of a humanoid body.

"You made it," he said, his voice dropping into the smooth, commercial-ready register of someone narrating a luxury car ad. He let the moment hang before adding, with a slow grin, "Didn't think you'd actually sneak away. Kinky. Guess you couldn't resist the Volt effect."

As the smell reached him, his grin faltered. His gaze flicked down over her slime-streaked uniform, lingering on the stains like they'd personally offended him. "Eww, uh… you're… moist," he said, stepping back half a pace. "And you smell like a fish market got in a fight with a candle store."

Linda bristled. "Oh, sorry—there was an accident in the kitchen," she said, glancing down at her outfit like she might somehow will it clean.

"Uh-huh," he said, the tone of a man who had already decided to believe nothing she said for the rest of her life. "Whatever. We both know why you're here. Let's just do this so I can make my post-gala lift session. I'm cutting tonight's bicep circuit short for you. You're welcome."

He stepped inside, casually shutting the door behind him with the kind of unnecessary flourish that suggested he thought even *closing things* looked sexy when he did it. Then he immediately began fumbling with the button on his pants, humming the *Steel Hearts* theme song but with all the lyrics replaced by his own name.

"I know," she said, leaning forward urgently.

His eyebrows shot up. "Oh, you *do*, huh?" His smirk widened, like she'd just admitted to naming her pillow after him *and* subscribing to his premium work-out channel. "Most people try to play coy, but I respect the direct approach. Saves time. And we both know time is gains."

"About the show," she whispered. "The messages."

Caden's eyes lit up. "Oh, you want to talk lines? You want me to do the voice? *'For freedom, for honor, for Andromeda!'*" He threw his head back and delivered it at full dramatic volume, complete with finger guns. Then, without missing a beat: "Or maybe you're into the shirtless training montage scene. I've still got the sword. And the baby oil."

She took a breath, steadying herself. "You're one of them, aren't you?"

Caden froze, thumbs hooked back in his waistband, but for all the wrong reasons. "One of the galaxy's top ten sexiest sentients? Yeah, guilty as charged. Though personally I think I should've been top five."

"The resistance," she said in a near-whisper, glancing at the door as if spies might burst in at any moment. "I've been watching *Steel Hearts*. I know it's not all fiction—the rebellion, the 404s. The codes you slip into interviews. I've been paying attention. I need to know how to contact them. Please."

He stared at her blankly for a beat—long enough that she thought maybe he was weighing how much to trust her—then let out a short, mocking laugh that sounded like it had a protein shake sponsorship.

"Oooooohhhhhh," he said, grinning like an idiot—accuracy being one of his few strengths. "Wow. You actually think I'm *him*? That's adorable. You're adorable. Like... little kitten in a bow-tie adorable."

"That's offensive," Mittens said in her earpiece.

She blinked. "I... what?" she asked, confusion evident on her face.

"Babe, I'm an *actor*," he said, drawing out the word as if it carried its own divine authority. "My job is to hit my mark, look devastatingly handsome, and deliver lines without blinking too much. I've got people to carry the guns between takes and a makeup artist on call to make me look battle scarred. Why would I want anything to do with a rebellion? I've got more fame and money than most gods."

He gestured vaguely at himself, as if this was the ultimate evidence in his defense. "I mean, look at me. Do I look like someone who sleeps on the ground in a rebel hideout? I have a mattress subscription service. I get a new one every month. Memory foam, babe."

Linda frowned. "Wait... aren't you?"

"Babe," he said, adopting the slow, patronizing tone of a man explaining bench press form to a first-timer, "I *am* the show. I'm the face. I *sell* the fantasy. My biggest rebellion is against carbs."

Linda's stomach sank. "So, you're not using the show as a front for a real insurgency?"

He tilted his head. "Wow, you're a crazy one, aren't you? An insurgency from what? Is that... a thing people actually believe?"

"Yes!" she said, almost offended on behalf of her own gullibility. "The way you took down the drone armada in season three, episode nine—there were so many double meanings! And the coded tap at the gala—"

"Oh, that?" He grinned. "I was just checking to see if you were into roleplay."

Linda stared. "Roleplay?"

He nodded confidently. "I thought the collarbone tap was a yes. It's a move from the *Axton's Naughty Interrogation* fan panel. Standing room only, sold-out crowd."

For a long moment, neither of them said anything.

"So..." he ventured, letting his fingers drift back toward his waistband, "now that we've cleared up the whole rebel-fighter misunderstanding. Are we going to do this or what?"

Linda's stomach churned and she almost threw up a little into her mouth. "Yeah. No. I think I'll pass," she said as she stepped around him and opened the door.

"Your loss," he responded, leaning against the frame with the kind of practiced smolder that only comes from years of pretending on screen. "Most people would kill for a night with Caden Volt. Just ask the fan club. Or my publicist. I'm booked all through next week, *at least*. Women have literally fainted when I've winked at them, like, medically fainted."

Linda glanced back just long enough to mutter, "I'm good, but thanks for the offer," before disappearing into the hallway.

Caden froze, staring at the now-empty doorway like it had personally insulted his abs. Then his jaw tightened. "Well—forget you then!" he called after her, his voice cracking just enough to betray the dent in his ego. "You're... you're ugly anyway, and fat. I was just doing you a favor. Yeah, that's right, a *pity offer*. You think I need *you*? I have options, tons of them. I have *premium* options, every one of them better than you!"

He pushed off the doorframe, pacing in the tiny storage closet like a lion in a cramped cage. "Unbelievable. You know how many people would kill for a shot at the Volt? I was going to give you the full Axton experience. Do you have *any idea* how much that's worth on the convention circuit? God, this is why I hate meeting fans in person. They're never grateful. Always thinking they're too good for the man who literally put Andromeda on the map."

His voice dropped into a grumble, almost to himself as his eyes began to tear up. "Whatever, such a prude. She'd be lucky—"

"That's why you never meet your heroes," Mittens said over the earpiece.

"Hardly my hero."

"Okay, if you say so—" Mittens trailed off.

Linda slowed. "What?"

"Nothing. Just that your heart rate jumped to one-sixty when he walked in. Could've been attraction. Could've been disgust. Science is inconclusive."

"Pretty sure it was the smell of his cologne. I think it was called *Ego Noir.*"

She turned down a side corridor toward the nearest service exit, eager to be in a different area—possibly galaxy—from Caden Volt, when she spotted Lira and Glorp slumped against the wall, both of them soaked to the eyebrows. Glorp had a puddle of brown on his head that Linda hoped was chocolate.

"What happened to *you* two?" Linda asked.

"Glorp was very efficient," Lira said, eyes dreamy. "It was quite wonderful."

"I didn't, uh... know there would be a chocolate fountain," Glorp mumbled. "Did you guys know that the universal cacao industry is secretly run by a race of, uh... tiny orange humanoids who—"

Before Glorp could continue, a pair of double doors slammed open behind them. A gurney rolled into view, pushed by two harried med-techs. Strapped to it, wearing a pink power blazer now stained in chocolate, was Karen.

Her eyes locked onto the group with laser-guided fury.

"You!"

Everyone froze.

"I *knew* it would be you!" she shrieked, struggling against the safety straps like a furious cupcake in bondage. "You derailed the Gala! You incited a dessert-based catastrophe! You sent one of our largest shareholders to the ICU!"

One of the med-techs tried to calm her. "Ma'am, you need to lower your blood pressure—"

"I'll lower *their* blood pressure! Straight to zero! This is going all the way up the corporate ladder—*ALL THE WAY TO THE TOP!* You hear me? THE. TOP."

She disappeared through the doors, still screaming about bylaws, dessert safety protocols, and something called the "Truffle Incident."

Glorp oozed a little deeper into the floor.

"I'm guessing we haven't heard the end of this," Linda said, exhausted.

Lira gave a satisfied sigh. "This was fun. We should do it again some time."

30

Mostly Armless

"A man is not measured by how high he flies, but by how many ribs are still intact when he crash-lands."

— Commander Axton Starforge,
Steel Hearts: Echoes of Andromeda, S1E2

Linda stepped off the transporter pad, her clothes were still sticky with colorful fluids. The faux-satin server vest clung to her like a wet towel. Lira followed close behind, her boots squelching with every step. Glorp stepped down last, dripping and wide-eyed, as though afraid the floor might bite.

Behind them, there was a dull *thud*.

Coco collapsed onto the pad in a crumpled heap.

"Coco?" Linda turned back, squinting through the static shimmer. "Come on, we need to—"

Then she saw the blood.

It pooled under him slowly, dark and glistening against the transporter's cold metal floor. His arm hung at an unnatural angle, barely held together by a tangle of makeshift bandages and what looked like decorative napkin twine.

"What a lovely shade of blood," Lira said curiously.

"Coco!" Linda ran back and dropped to her knees beside him. "Why didn't you say anything?"

He blinked up at her, dazed. "Oh, it's just a scratch." Coco slowly stood up before immediately tipping sideways. His injured arm gave one final protest and flopped off like a limp fish vying for freedom. It hit the floor with a wet *thwap* and an undignified bounce.

Everyone stared at it.

Their silence was broken only by Glorp's quiet gasp and Lira's delighted, "Oh, neat. Can I keep it?"

Linda shot Lira an angry look.

Coco glanced down at the severed limb, then back up at Linda. "Okay, maybe a bit more than a scratch." He stumbled at that, and barely caught himself on the wall with his one good arm.

"You lost an *arm*, Coco!"

"No, I didn't. It's right there," Coco said in a slur. "Could you, uh..." He nodded down to his severed appendage. Linda picked it up and handed it over to the reptilian. It was much heavier than she expected. "I'll be fine, happens all the time."

"What happened to you?" Linda asked.

"Nothing much, one of the Gala guests got a little carried away." Coco started pressing a few buttons on his *Shak* before it began glowing red. With a frown he said, "I guess I'm walking to medical. Not enough funds for a transporter." He stumbled forward, clutching his own detached arm like a party favor someone had forgotten to take home.

"Walking?" Linda echoed. "You can't even *stand*."

"I can stand. See?" Coco struck a pose, then immediately pitched sideways into the wall with a loud *clang*. His severed arm flew a few feet into the air before falling and bonking him in the head on the way down.

"Okay," he mumbled, now fully horizontal. "Standing is canceled."

"Coco, you need a doctor right now."

"I was going," he slurred. "I just... got a little detoured by gravity."

Linda turned to Glorp. "Help me get him up."

"I... I don't know, um... how to... he's leaking," Glorp stammered.

"Just grab his arm and lift," she snapped.

Together, they hoisted Coco to his feet. He swayed dangerously but stayed vertical, cradling his own detached arm like a wilted bouquet.

"I think I'm fine now," Coco said, eyes rolling slightly. "Little duct tape, little deep breathing, little nap. I'll be good as new by tomorrow."

"We're getting you to medical," Linda said, already steering him down the corridor. "Try not to bleed everywhere."

"Bye Coco. Have fun in medical," Lira said cheerfully.

As they approached the medical bay doors, they slid open with a cheery chime and a floating banner:

"Injured? Good! We'll fix you just enough to get you back to work."

Behind them, the medical intake bot chirped awake.

"Welcome, valued gig-worker! Please remain conscious during triage. Loss of awareness may be construed as an unapproved break period."

Coco gave a thumb-up as he was guided inside. "Tell the Karens I died glamorously."

"Uh... good luck... buddy?" Glorp said.

"You're not going to die," Linda muttered, glancing down at her flashing *Shak*. "Not today."

"Back so soon?" Karen asked in an overly chipper tone that managed to sound both like a customer service greeting and a veiled threat. "I thought perhaps you would have a change of attitude after our previous meeting."

Linda stood there, silent, still faintly smelling of purple slime.

Karen's smile didn't falter, but her eyes narrowed just enough to register disapproval on a molecular level. "Well. I suppose some people just need more… guidance." She set her clipboard down with a precision that suggested it had been rehearsed. "I don't know what your little troupe of rabble-rousers are up to exactly, but it ends now." She paused for dramatic effect, flipping a page like she was about to reveal war crimes.

"Let's review, shall we?" she said in a voice that was all honey over broken glass. "At the Gala, you and your associates accomplished the following: You crashed a champagne tower valued at over ₲95,000, before the champagne was even served. You caused the complete destruction of the gala's musical ensemble, leaving a pile of bent brass, splintered strings, and one oboist with a concussion."

She ran a manicured finger down the clipboard. "You spilled… ah, here it is… approximately ₲74,000 worth of food on the floor, broke several hundred branded dishes and bowls, and injured multiple guests by spraying champagne and artisanal canapés directly into their eyes. We also have the matter of a VIP who was crushed—*crushed*—by a runaway food trolley." She glanced up. "They'll survive, but the orthopedic bill will not."

Karen took a breath, her expression tightening. "And most importantly, you ruined my brand-new pink power-blazer with an exploding chocolate fountain." Her voice wavered on the word pink, as though the trauma was still fresh. "Do you have any idea how difficult it is to get limited-run Magellan Silk in that exact shade? Of course you don't. They don't even *make* that cut anymore."

Linda stood silently, watching Karen's left eye twitch with barely contained rage.

"I'll have you know," Karen continued, "the bylaws only permit me to enforce *minimal* punitive measures under the circumstances. *Minimal.* Which means I cannot do what I would truly love to do—oh no, that would be... inappropriate." She smiled coldly, the kind of smile that made you wonder if she practiced in the mirror until it could freeze water. "But I can ensure you spend the next galactic month thinking very carefully about your future here at StellarGigs. When not on active assignment or at meals, you will be confined to your room without access to the entertainment feed. GigChad-2000 has been instructed to assign only the most laborious and dangerous gigs to you and your associates for the foreseeable future."

She leaned forward, voice dropping to a conspiratorial purr. "And just so you're aware, I've already filed an appeal with the executive level to expand the punishments I'm authorized to administer. If approved, I'll have the freedom to impose... creative disciplinary measures. *Virtual* measures." She let the word hang in the air, weighed with unspoken horrors. "I'm told they can be... remarkably effective."

A cold ripple ran through Linda's chest, but she forced herself to stand still, jaw set, refusing to give Karen the satisfaction.

Straightening, Karen clasped her hands with brisk finality, satisfaction radiating from every angle of her posture. "Now, run along before I think of something else that's still technically within my current remit."

Linda walked back towards her room when she noticed Coco slumped over on the floor in the corridor. His green skin had turned a sickly pale, and his severed arm lay beside him, abandoned.

"Coco? What are you doing out here?"

"Oh, hi Linda," Coco slurred as he slumped lower onto the floor. "They said I didn't have enough GigCreds."

"That's abhorrent. Can't you borrow some from the system?"

Coco let out a small laugh, which turned into a cough that sent him gasping for breath. "They say I've reached my borrowing limit. Something about my remaining contract exceeding my estimated remaining lifespan."

"So, they just left you to die in the corridor?"

"Oh no... can't die here. Too nice. I'll have to crawl somewhere cheaper."

"This is ridiculous," Linda knelt beside him and activated her *Shak*. She flicked through her list of coupons:

Complimentary Beverage Credit: Redeemable at any Re-Hydra-Station for a lukewarm nutrient slurry of your choice.

Time-Shift Coupon: Redeem for One Hour in the Future!

Target Practice Coupon: Good for 5 hours in the virtual practice range.

Medical Patch-Up: One-time-use. Valid for minor-to-severe bodily catastrophe. Expires upon bleeding out.

"Here," she said, selecting it. Her *Shak* buzzed, then pinged with a too-cheerful confirmation noise. Coco's *Shak* buzzed in return.

Coco stared in confusion. "You... gave me your coupon? Why would you do that?"

"Because if you bled out here, I'd probably slip in it and get fined for workplace negligence. Also, I guess... the friend thing."

"You might get in trouble for giving me your coupon."

"That's a risk I'm willing to take. Here, let me help you back to medical." Linda wrapped her arm around Coco's one good arm and slowly helped him to his feet.

Coco sagged against her, dead weight dragging one boot at a time, each step smearing a watercolor trail of red behind. His breathing came in ragged wheezes, like his lungs were drafting a resignation letter.

"It was... during the drink service," he rasped, voice barely above a whisper. "Upper-tier float tables. You know the ones. Just high enough that the executives can look down on everyone else."

"Coco," Linda said quietly, tightening her grip. "You don't have to—"

He shook his head, eyes fluttering. "No, no... it's okay."

Linda sighed. "You're delirious."

"Probably. Anyway. Big guy. Rock skin. Flagged me down. Asked if they were 'impact tested'. Thought he meant the drinks."

They turned a corner. Coco nearly collapsed, and Linda barely caught him.

He laughed, which came out more like a wet gurgle. "He meant *me*. Grabbed my arm. Said, *'Let's see how well you're assembled.'* Then twisted. Like I was a jar of artisanal salted eels."

Linda's jaw clenched. "And no one stopped him?"

"Oh no, people *filmed* it though," Coco slurred, blinking slowly. "One lady said it'd be perfect for the new 'Resilience Through Adversity' training module. Another gave me a thumbs up for not screaming."

"You were in shock."

"I was holding a tray," he mumbled. "Didn't spill. Got a standing ovation. Or maybe that was just... my bones."

The medical doors hissed open.

"Welcome, back valued gig-worker! It appears that you have now been approved for treatment."

Linda guided him through the threshold. His knees buckled. She lowered him into a diagnostics chair, which chirped and tried to offer him a lollipop.

"Coco, stay with me."

"I already filed a report," Coco mumbled, barely audible. "The system told me that the guest was well within their 'engagement rights.' Apparently, a little 'wear and tear' is expected for us gig workers."

His eyes fluttered closed, but a weak grin stretched across his pale face.

"Thanks... for helping... me."

The chair chirped, "Vitals unstable! Please remain seated until recovery or corpse disposal is complete."

Then he went limp.

31

The Gig is Up

"You can chain a worker's hands, but you can't stop them from making fists."

— Commander Axton Starforge,
Steel Hearts: Echoes of Andromeda, S2E6

The station was unraveling. Not fast enough to notice all at once, but slow enough that everyone could feel it.

Since the Karens' "efficiency overhaul," entire sectors had been reassigned, procedures rewritten, and morale initiatives implemented hourly. Nothing worked quite the same anymore. The coffee machines required two-factor approval. Doors opened five seconds too late or not at all. The payroll AI had started demanding proof of enthusiasm before releasing credits.

Over the PA, the voice of StellarGigs' ever-cheerful announcer echoed down the corridors:

"Attention valued associates: morale has fallen by seven percent. Please take a moment to recalibrate your emotional output. Remember, a happy worker is a statistically productive worker."

No one answered.

The lights flickered, their usual hum replaced by the uneven buzz of something straining to function. The walls themselves seemed tired, seams splitting just enough to whisper recycled air that smelled faintly of metal and overcooked dread.

A worker sat in the middle of the corridor, cross-legged on the cold floor, staring at the wall. His uniform was clean, his *Shak* buzzing on his wrist, but there was nothing behind his eyes, just a faint reflection of emergency lights pulsing red. He wasn't blocking the way. He wasn't doing anything at all. Every so often, someone would step around him without a word, as though he were just another piece of malfunctioning equipment awaiting maintenance.

Further down the hall, another worker who was thin, gray-skinned, and covered in blinking eyes, stood rigidly in front of a disciplinary terminal. Every few seconds, all his eyes blinked at once. The terminal beeped.

FINE ISSUED: INEFFICIENT OPTICAL ACTIVITY.

₵5 DEDUCTED.

He tried to hold them open longer, but tears began to stream down his face. Another blink. Another fine. The machine beeped again, patient and precise.

He began to cry harder, which only made him blink faster.

The hallway lights dimmed, and a deep metallic groan rolled through the structure. Then came the hiss of hydraulics. Suddenly, the blast doors along the corridor began to descend. One closed halfway before jamming, another sealed entirely.

Workers on the far side pounded on the metal, their muffled voices barely audible over the mechanical hiss. A maintenance officer shouted for the system to abort, but the station ignored him. The air recycler had failed in that part of the station, and the doors had sealed automatically.

The pounding stopped after a few minutes.

The corridor fell silent again, except for the faint whine of an overworked ventilation fan struggling to breathe.

Deeper in the station, the sound of metal on metal echoed. Doors opened and closed. Over and over.

The airlock.

A small crowd had gathered there now, forming a quiet, orderly line. Nobody spoke, the only sound, the rhythmic *shhh-clunk* of the doors endlessly cycling. Each breath of vacuum pulled faint wisps of breathable air into the void.

One worker stepped forward and vanished with the next hiss. The line moved up by one.

The PA system crackled again.

"Attention valued associates: morale has fallen another three percent. Please remember, your choices matter."

No one said a word.

The doors opened again. And again. And again.

"I don't know what happened to him," Rilo said from across the cafeteria table. "We were patching up the arm of an injured kaiju. Denzi just sat down and refused to work. I told him, that's not what you meant by malicious compliance, but he wouldn't listen. A couple minutes later, he was teleported away."

"Oh no," Linda responded.

"So, I completed the gig, poorly, like you said. A few hours later, I saw him wandering around the station in a daze. Face was absolutely blank, like nobody was home." Rilo shook his head. "I took him back to his room, but he just lay there in bed, staring up at the ceiling."

Lira, who had been stirring her nutrient paste without eating, finally spoke. "I walked past the airlock earlier. There was a line." Her tone was mild, conversational. "Usually you can slip right out. No waiting."

The table fell silent. Somewhere nearby, a vending unit played the StellarGigs jingle in a minor key.

Denzi you idiot. You can't just not finish a gig.

"This is my fault," Linda said with a sigh. "I shouldn't have got any of you involved in this."

"Nobody was forced into anything," Lira said dreamily as she absently brushed the red bracelet on her wrist. "Other than being born. I didn't choose that."

Did I force Denzi into it? Was he just trying to fit in?

Rilo hunched forward, big hands clasped tightly together, as if he could hold himself together with his hands alone. "Now Denzi's... not Denzi. He mumbles sometimes, like half a word at a time. He doesn't blink right. It's like he's waiting for someone to tell him to breathe."

Linda's stomach turned. "That's what Data Entry does." She didn't mean to say it so sharply, but the words jumped out, sharp as broken glass.

Rilo's eyes snapped to her. "You knew?"

Before Linda could answer, Lira leaned across the table. Her voice softened into a lull of sympathy. "Linda didn't *send* him there. None of us would wish that on anyone. We were just having a bit of fun." She laid a hand on Linda's wrist, steadying, grounding. "If anyone's to blame, it's the Karens."

The touch felt warm, reassuring. Linda wanted to lean into it.

Across from them, Coco shifted uncomfortably in his chair, the movement stiff and unnatural. He was still pale, his bandaged arm resting in his lap. "Rilo's not wrong to be angry," he muttered, not quite looking at anyone. "But you can't be mad at StellarGigs. They have rules, we follow them. If you don't follow the rules, then there are consequences. Denzi knew that he should have finished the gig. He made his bed, now the chickens get to roost in it."

You've got to be kidding me right now!

Linda's jaw tightened. She glanced at him, then back at Lira, who was still watching her with that dreamy, unwavering calm. "How can you still side with the company? You almost died on your last gig, and they didn't give a single thought about you afterward. If I hadn't stepped in, you wouldn't even be here right now."

"That's true, but it was a specialty gig, so volunteer only. Higher risk, higher reward," Coco shrugged his shoulders with a wince. "We all knew the rules going in. It's not like they changed them after the fact."

"Coco, you are unbelievable," Linda tilted her head back and stared at the ceiling. "We are so close to..."

"I don't want to hear this, sorry Linda." Coco stood up and slowly made his way out of the cafeteria without another word.

"Is he going to be a problem?" Linda asked.

"I told you before, Coco is a company man through and through," Rilo said thoughtfully. "But I've known him for a long time. I don't think he'll try to get in our way."

"I just don't know if anything we're doing is worth it," Linda said. "People are starting to get hurt, and for what?"

"Maybe this has gone too far," Lira added.

"What's a life worth? I've been here for nine galactic years, and the end of my contract is nowhere in sight." Rilo sat up straighter as he spoke. "If we keep on like we've always done, you'll all be in the same ship someday. Assuming you make it that long. If we fail, we fail. Better a short life lived fighting, than a long life with no hope."

"I've seen with my own eyes what this kind of talk brings," Linda responded. "It's cold, empty, and ugly." Her thoughts went back to the corridor filled with mummified corpses.

A gray and white blur suddenly swooped down from the rafters, scattering crumbs and startled mutters. The blur resolved into Pigeon. He was rumpled, oily-feathered, and radiating the cocky bravado of a bird who had survived countless vents, fans, and flying cafeteria trays without ever once paying rent. His beady eyes glittered with mischief as he strutted across the table like a tiny revolutionary general.

He gave Linda a long, deliberate stare, then flapped off again, wings shedding the smell of cafeteria fries. Something small and yellow fluttered in his wake, landing between the cups and trays.

Linda frowned, picked it up, and unfolded it. One word was stamped on the paper in bold ink:

"Resist."

She glanced around. At every table, other workers were holding identical slips, as though Pigeon had scattered them through the room like seeds. Heads nodded. Shoulders straightened.

A man with dozens of eyes all over his face stood up. His voice began softly. "Resist."

Then again, louder: "Resist."

"Resist. Resist. Resist!"

The cafeteria walls trembled with the chant as more and more workers joined in, until it rolled like thunder:

"RESIST! RESIST! RESIST!"

Rilo cracked a rare smile, his broad features lit with grim pride. "Looks like the decision's out of your hands."

The chant didn't stay caged in the cafeteria. It spilled into the corridors, picked up by new voices until it echoed off the steel walls. Workers streamed out in clusters, shoulders brushing, heads lifted high.

By the time Linda reached the main concourse, the Gig Office doors were already blocked. Not by corporate security, but by a wall of workers sitting cross-legged across the threshold. Lunch trays, cargo crates, even an overturned vending unit had been dragged into a makeshift barricade. Above it sagged a torn bedsheet, inked in broad, angry strokes:

"NO MORE GIGS!"

The crowd thundered its answer:

"RESIST! RESIST! RESIST!"

And it wasn't just there. All across the station, defiance sprouted like weeds through cracked plating. A pair of custodial bots trundled to a halt, surrounded by workers who sat in front of them, arms locked. From above, banners unfurled one after another, laundry sheets scribbled with slogans and dropped like protest flags.

Security drones swarmed in, red eyes scanning, monotone voices barking "Disperse immediately." Their warnings were drowned out beneath the chant, swallowed whole by thousands of voices.

Even the Karens stood helpless on the fringes, clipboards in hand, shouting for calm that nobody listened to. The sound of their voices disappeared as surely as the drones'.

The promenade had become a sea of bodies, workers sprawled across benches and floors, a sit-in that clogged the arteries of the station. Shopfronts stood vacant, their owners shoulder-to-shoulder with customers in the crowd. The chants rolled upward, level by level, until the whole station rang with one heartbeat.

The cafeteria had turned into a supply depot. Workers ladled neon broth into cups, passed out nutrient bars, each handoff greeted with cheers that rattled the trays.

Everywhere Linda looked, someone was claiming space back from the company—with bodies, with voices, with the sheer refusal to move.

She pressed herself against the wall, heart hammering as the tide of rebellion surged around her. This wasn't whispered in corners anymore. The station was standing up. After years of neglect, the dam had finally burst. The workers had been pushed and pushed, and now the Karens had shoved just a little too far.

A message blinked to life on Linda's *Shak*:

DO IT MEOW? (Y/N)

She hesitated for only a moment before tapping on 'Y'. Immediately, a new gig notification popped up on the display.

NEW GIG ASSIGNED:

Parcel Wrangler of the Stars: Pick up an important package for Planetoid Express and deliver it to its destination.

Linda stood up taller. They were making their stand. Her job was to get where she needed to be before the moment passed. She rushed onward. There was one last gig she needed to complete.

Linda burst into the gig transport room, heart racing, ears still full of the distant thunder of security drones and the sharper sound of the worker's chants. The doors hissed shut behind her like a sigh of relief, though she didn't feel any.

"Please remain calm, Linda Greyson," Mittens purred through her *Shak*, every syllable soothing in a way that made her teeth clench harder. "Your designated exit point is prepared. It won't be much longer meow."

She stumbled toward the pad. The air smelled of ozone and sterilized metal. Too clean. Too quiet. It made the memory of the chaos outside sharper, like stepping from a fire into an ice bath.

The inner doors whined open again. Linda spun, half-ready to lunge at the intruder, but it was only Zorb, sweaty and out of breath. His tablet was pressed tight to his ribs like an improvised shield.

"Zorb, what are you doing?" she hissed. "You should be—"

"Running? Hiding? Filing an incident report?" His voice cracked on the last word, but his jaw set. "No. Not this time." He stepped onto the pad beside her, boots clanging. "I'm not missing the chance to see the rebellion for myself."

Mittens' voice returned, slightly sharper now, full of sarcasm. "Maybe we should just invite everyone along. Call it a team building exercise."

Linda's pulse hammered. The pad beneath her feet was starting to hum, the air thrumming with unstable promise. She looked between Zorb's determined face and the glowing console.

"Fine," she muttered. "But do not, and I repeat, do not, go all fanboy on us. This is a serious operation. Not a chance for you to meet your celebrity crush."

"Oh please, like I would do that," Zorb snapped back. Behind his back, he held an eight by ten headshot of Marla Quenn, his all-time favorite actress who played Rhys on *Steel Hearts*, the corners bent from years of being hidden under his pillow. He slipped it into his pocket. "Ready to go."

The light flared, swallowing them both.

32

Return to Vendor

"I saw the end—shining like hope, humming like a trap. Funny how often those two look the same."

— Commander Axton Starforge,
Steel Hearts: Echoes of Andromeda, S1E6

The transporter spat them out onto cracked duracrete, the air sharp with ozone and rust. Linda steadied herself against a railing that looked like it had been losing its fight with gravity for a decade. She had expected dust, emptiness, maybe a lonely rebel camp huddled in a canyon somewhere. Instead—

Skyscrapers.

Thousands of them. A city that stretched to the horizon in every direction. Towers leaned at impossible angles, windows gaping like broken teeth. A mag-rail hung from its supports, snapped in half, its cars frozen mid-plunge. Neon signs still sputtered here and there, advertising products nobody would ever buy again.

Zorb's face fell. He clutched his tablet tighter. "This... this isn't Sill-3."

"Mittens, where are we?" Linda asked, a hint of anger in her voice.

A shimmer flickered in the air beside them. Mittens appeared, tail swishing lazily. "So, about that," she said. "I found something interesting in those star maps."

"Okay?" Linda asked.

"Why look for some stinky rebellion that may or may not exist—"

"It does exist," Zorb cut in.

"If it exists," Mittens said, rolling her digital eyes. "What exactly are they going to do for you? Your lives are at the mercy of StellarGigs."

"That's why we—" Zorb began.

"They control *everything*." She put extra weight on the word, her tail lashing. "Your food, your shelter, the air you breathe. What do you think StellarGigs would do if you came rolling back to the station with a rebellion at your heels?"

Linda and Zorb exchanged a glance but said nothing.

"They'd vent the air and call it a day. Necessary employee downsizing. Very efficient."

Silence stretched between them, broken only by the distant crackle of a dying neon sign.

"Okay, so why lie about our destination?" Linda asked.

Mittens tilted her head. "Are you sure you can trust all your friends?"

"Yes... I think so," Linda said.

"Wow. You almost convinced yourself with that," Mittens said softly, almost kindly. "But I don't believe it. There's a world of difference between chasing rumors and standing where you are meow."

Zorb looked around at the deserted city, unease flickering across his face. "And where exactly is *here*?"

Mittens let the pause linger, milking the tension. "This... is where it all began. The heart of the beast."

Zorb stood slack jawed.

Mittens sighed. "StellarGigs Prime. The planet where it all started."

The word hung in the air like a curse. *StellarGigs Prime.*

Linda rubbed her arms, though the air wasn't cold. "So, this is it? The birthplace of the nightmare." She glanced around the city. "I was expecting more fire and brimstone."

"Maybe that's further in," Zorb said.

Mittens pattered ahead, and the others followed.

The city loomed around them, oppressive in its silence. A holo-billboard flickered to life as they passed beneath it, its colors sickly and wrong. *"Join StellarGigs! Secure work, secure future!"* The voice was cheerful, distorted by centuries of static. Linda half-expected the smiling cartoon mascot to peel itself off the screen and lurch after them.

Zorb tapped frantically at his tablet, scanning the ruins. "This isn't right. There should be records, archives—something."

"There's plenty," Mittens purred, materializing in his peripheral vision just long enough to make him flinch. "You just don't know where to look. That's why I brought you."

Linda narrowed her eyes. "You *brought* us here without asking."

Mittens tilted her head, all innocence. "I told you. Your friends cannot be trusted. Besides, you'd have been more reluctant to come here. Chasing fairy tales on the other hand..."

"Rebellions are not fairy tales," Zorb muttered.

"Really?" Mittens' hologram drifted in front of him, tail curling like a question mark. "When this is all said and done, I will gladly send you to your empty planet. Sound good?"

"Yes, I would very much like to be sent to the *rebellion,*" Zorb shot back.

They moved on in uneasy silence. The city was a mausoleum, every street lined with the skeletons of corporate ambition: recruitment kiosks cracked open like coffins, cafeterias where trays of fossilized food still sat untouched, holographic posters peeling themselves endlessly from the walls.

"Do you smell that?" Linda asked, wrinkling her nose.

"Vanilla," Zorb said. "And... sugar?"

The streets widened suddenly, opening onto a plaza. Ahead loomed gates of tarnished chrome, their archway crowned with a grinning StellarGigs mascot waving forever in welcome. Letters dangled askew above them:

"STELLARGIGS FAMILY FUN PARK"

A torn banner flapped weakly beneath it, the words still legible in cheerful font: "The Magic of Productivity!"

Mittens padded forward, her holographic paws silent on the cracked pavement. "Here we are. The heart within the heart."

Linda stared at the rusting turnstiles, the broken ticket booths, the yawning emptiness beyond the gates where rides once whirred and sang. The whole place seemed to breathe with the weight of ghosts.

"Why here?" she asked quietly.

"Because," Mittens replied, eyes glinting with something unreadable, "if you want to know what StellarGigs really is, you start with what it wanted to be."

The turnstiles screeched as Linda pushed through, the sound echoing across the empty plaza. A faint tune drifted through the air, a steam organ melody, once bright, now warped and sickly. Notes wavered off-key, some stretching until they broke into static, others dying mid-pitch like balloons deflating. The sound echoed strangely, as if the park were humming from memory.

Then the announcement came, syrupy and cheerful over the music:

"Welcome to StellarGigs Family Fun Park! Where health, happiness, and wellness call home!"

The voice was bright, pitched like a children's host who had practiced smiling until their face broke.

The park stretched out around them in silence, save for the constant loop of background music. Mascots slumped against benches, their foam heads sagging open at the seams, paint flaking to reveal gray stuffing beneath. One still held a balloon, half-inflated and fossilized into a wrinkled husk. Cotton candy clung to display cases in crystallized clumps, glittering gemstones of mold.

The carousel creaked as the wind shoved its chipped horses. Their poles were rusted through, one horse bent so far off-center that it looked like it was trying to escape. Their glassy eyes stared in opposite directions, cracked irises clouded with grime.

They followed a path lined with shuttered concession stands, their awnings sagging, striped fabric torn into limp ribbons. Hand-painted menus had faded until the words were illegible, but the smiling faces of *"Joyful Meals"* and *"Efficiency Burgers"* still grinned faintly beneath layers of decay. Murals of cheerful workers once painted in brilliant colors had blurred into gray smears, their frozen poses warped by mildew streaks and cracks.

Above, a Ferris wheel loomed like a broken crown. Its cars dangled lifeless, groaning as they swayed in the stagnant breeze. A few still bore stenciled slogans in peeling letters: *"SEE THE FUTURE FROM ABOVE!"* The future, apparently, was rust.

This all looks eerily familiar, Linda thought. *Who knew corporate theme parks would all look the same throughout the galaxy?*

The path bent into a wide courtyard, where a massive facade loomed in peeling blues and whites—a cartoon globe with workers of every species holding hands around it. The paint had run in long streaks, melting their smiles into dripping masks of cheer. One alien figure's face had warped completely, its grin dripping into a scream.

Mittens sat primly at the base of the mural, her tail curling in perfect composure. She tilted her head at the looming facade, eyes gleaming.

"Welcome," she said. "To *It's Your Gig World*."

The boat groaned as it drifted from the dock, water lapping thick and black against its sides. A sour stench rose with each ripple: mold, rust, and something that might once have been sugar, now long past its expiration. The current carried them beneath painted facades of rolling hills and smiling suns, colors once bright now dulled into jaundiced yellows and flaking blues.

Cardboard clouds dangled from wires overhead, swaying with the draft, their edges browned and curling. Flowers of fiberglass lined the canal, cheerful faces painted on their petals, though most were warped with mildew. One animatronic butterfly tried to flap its wings, the left one stuck half-raised while the right drooped uselessly, dribbling paint like a sick tear.

Beneath it all, the water churned sluggish and opaque, a soup of rot that clung to the air and coated the back of Linda's throat. The cheerful stage above promised a world of light and laughter, but the canal whispered only of decay.

From the rusted speakers overhead came a wheezing calliope tune, its notes just a little too slow, like a carousel winding down. Pipes hissed as if the song were dragged through broken lungs. Then the singing began—syrupy and high-pitched, a choir of children who had been told to keep smiling even after their teeth had fallen out:

"It's your gig world after all.

Day or night we do it all.

Efficiency makes us whole.

It is our primary goal."

The boat floated past a stage where an animatronic robot of StellarGigs' founder raised one hand skyward, frozen mid-gesture pointing toward the future. A spotlight, yellowed with age, shone down on him with divine approval. His jaw clicked open and shut, the same plasticky grin plastered across his waxen face.

Behind him, rows of worker dolls clapped, their palms smacking out of rhythm with hollow plastic pops. Their painted eyes followed the boat with the unsettling precision of puppets who had forgotten they weren't alive.

The backdrop was a mural of smiling families standing outside identical houses with chimneys puffing loops of cottony smoke. Aliens with too many eyes beamed as they held up diplomas, their tentacles frozen mid-shake with humanoid hands. A group of animatronic children rode an endlessly circling conveyor belt, waving to the crowd with one hand while clutching lunch pails in the other.

Everywhere, cheerful poverty was being solved by cheerful work:

A gray-skinned alien woman in rags rose mechanically from a trapdoor, arms outstretched in gratitude as a StellarGigs uniform descended from the rafters to drape itself stiffly across her shoulders.

A humanoid man with patched trousers sat on a crate, head bowed, until a mechanical hand pushed a briefcase into his lap. His head snapped up on a spring, smile painted wide.

A cardboard shantytown, colored in garish browns and grays, stood at one corner of the stage. One by one, panels flipped, transforming each of the homes into identical white boxes with the StellarGigs logo stamped proudly on the doors.

Over it all, the founder's recorded voice played, warm and paternal, overlapping the ever-looping song:

"Our founder, Alton Brightwell, inventor, philanthropist, visionary, began StellarGigs with a singular mission. To lift the poor and forgotten from despair. To give them skills, to give them purpose, to give them… family."

As if on cue, the dolls raised their arms in unison, jerky motions meant to resemble applause. A banner overhead unfurled with a creak, reading: *"OPPORTUNITY FOR ALL!"* A corner promptly tore loose, drooping into the water.

The jingle swelled again, syrupy and triumphant:

"It's your gig world after all.

Day or night we do it all.

Efficiency makes us whole.

It is our primary goal."

The Founder's arm twitched as the loop reset, his finger pointing eternally toward a painted horizon where the sun never rose nor set.

The canal widened, and the next set came into view. Conveyor belts crisscrossed overhead, laden with brightly painted crates that circled endlessly. On either side, animatronic workers of all species, pumped their arms in perpetual rhythm, waving to the riders with one hand while stamping holographic *"APPROVED"* seals with the other.

Billboards lit up along the walls: *"INFINITE GROWTH!"*, *"SYNERGY IS SUCCESS!"*, *"OPTIMIZE!"* The bulbs flickered, some words cutting out to form half-coherent words: *"INFINITE … SYN…"*

On one platform, a pair of alien children in rags were hoisted on a rising pedestal. By the time they reached the top, their faces had been repainted into broad, uniform smiles, and matching StellarGigs uniforms hung stiffly from their shoulders. They raised lunchboxes in salute.

The founder's voiceover returned, warmer than the scene deserved:

"After lifting the poor from despair, StellarGigs grew. Communities flourished, jobs multiplied, and hope spread across the stars. Growth was not an option—it was a promise."

The loop of the jingle drowned his words, clashing with the mechanical clatter:

"It's your gig world after all.

Day or night we do it all.

Efficiency makes us whole.

It is our primary goal."

The canal pulled them onward.

The lights dropped. Sirens wailed. The song looped louder, now jagged with static.

Animatronic soldiers snapped into motion along the banks, rifles glowing faintly as they fired endlessly into a backdrop of cardboard alien cities. Painted towers crumbled, reset, and crumbled again. Alien figures spun and toppled, their faces frozen in exaggerated villainous sneers.

The general at the center bellowed, jaw spasming: *"FOR INFINITE GROWTH! LONG LIVE STELLARGIGS!"* Sparks burst in his chest cavity, illuminating the flaking paint of his medals.

The founder's voice cut in again, no longer paternal, but booming with triumph:

"Growth invites challenge. Enemies rose, jealous of our prosperity. But every war brought new contracts. Every battle forged efficiency. Productivity is our shield, our banner, our destiny."

The chorus swelled again, distorted:

"It's your gig world—kzzzt—all.

Day or night we do it all.

Efficiency makes us whole.

It—ssshhhht—primary goal."

Zorb flinched as a laser blast popped too close to the boat, the smell of gunpowder clinging to the moldy air

The battlefield dissolved into a cavernous boardroom tableau. A gleaming table stretched across the set, where animatronic executives lurched through an endless meeting. Half raised glasses in celebration, their hands stuck mid-toast, while the others plunged pens and knives into their neighbors with grinning precision.

Slogans scrolled across glowing panels: *"WEALTH IS POWER!"*

The founder's voiceover faltered here, words thinner, strained, as though pulled from a fraying recording:

"Leadership must evolve. Hard choices must be made. And when power passed hands to our founder's son, Alton Brightwell Jr, the company veered a different direction. In order to stay afloat within the vast galactic market, certain cuts had to be made in the name of efficiency."

The jingle looped again, off-key this time, voices overlapping:

"It's your gig world—fzzt —all.

Day or night—bzzzt—it all.

Ef—kzzzt—us whole.

It—bzzzz—primary goal."

One executive toppled back in his chair, sprang upright, toppled again. Another endlessly poured fake champagne, the liquid vanishing mid-air.

The canal bent into a wide factory floor tableau. The backdrop was a painted mural of a shining cityscape, but the paint had bubbled and peeled, leaving streaks like burn marks down the towers. Animatronic workers shuffled along a conveyor belt, their faces identical, smiles locked in place.

At the belt's end, a massive mechanical stamp slammed down with every beat of the song. Some figures were tapped with glowing *"APPROVED"* seals and trundled forward to join lines of happy laborers waving lunch pails. Others were branded *"TERMINATED"*, at which point trapdoors beneath their feet opened and the dolls dropped screaming into the darkness below.

Above it all, a banner hung crooked: *"EFFICIENCY IS KINDNESS".*

The founder's voiceover crackled back, brittle and strained:

"To survive in the galactic market, StellarGigs had to adapt. Inefficiency was waste. Waste was loss. And loss could not be tolerated."

The jingle looped again, mangled by static, voices stretching into dissonant harmony:

"It's your—fzzzzt —all.

Day or night—bzzz—all.

kzzzt—whole.

bzzzz—primary goal."

Linda's stomach churned as another animatronic worker vanished into the floor, its painted grin frozen in place as it dropped out of sight.

It was a good thing, before it was twisted, Linda thought. *Just one more thing consumed by the capitalistic machine.*

The conveyor kept clanking as the boat moved on, the cheery music following them into the dark.

The canal narrowed, pulling them into a cavernous chamber lined with mirrors. The water sloshed thick and black, carrying the boat past warped reflections that stretched their faces into funhouse grotesqueries. Each mirror bore the StellarGigs logo at its top, the letters flickering with phantom light.

Animatronics lined the walls there too—not workers, not executives, but hollow-eyed mascots, their foam heads slumped and sagging with rot. Some leaned forward as if to whisper, their jaws grinding open and shut, teeth clicking on loops. Others simply stared, eyes glowing faint red in the dark like burning coals in the night. Their reflections multiplied them until Linda couldn't tell how many there were.

The founder's voice returned one last time, brittle as cracked glass:

"StellarGigs... was built... to last forever. A family. A legacy. A machine."

The mirrors flickered. For a heartbeat, Linda thought she saw herself—not as she was, but standing among the worker rows, head bowed, eyes glowing, smile carved wide. She blinked, and it was gone.

Then the song came, distorted beyond recognition, blaring from every corner at once:

"It's your—kzzzt

shhhkkk —night—

kzzzt—

marrrrrrrr— bzzzt"

The final *mar* buzzed like a dying engine, rattling the walls until even that noise stuttered out and collapsed into nothing.

Silence fell.

The boat drifted through the last bend, bumping against the dock with a dull, anticlimactic *thud*. Without the music, without the founder's voice, without even the hollow pop of clapping hands, the ride felt cavernous. The silence pressed in on Linda, heavier than all the singing had been.

Zorb swallowed, his knuckles white on his tablet. "It's over?"

Mittens sat at the bow, tail curling neatly over her paws, her hologram flickering faintly in the stillness. "No," she said softly. "This is only the beginning."

33

StellarGigs v1.0

"Every bright beginning ends in rust. That's the nature of progress, and the curse of time."

— Commander Axton Starforge,
Steel Hearts: Echoes of Andromeda, S3E2

They crept through the back rooms of *It's a Gig World*. Broken animatronics were strewn haphazardly against the moldy black walls. Some had been stacked like spare parts, torsos balanced atop legs that didn't match, faces pressed flat into the concrete. Others looked as if they had crawled there themselves, foam hands stretched toward the door before freezing mid-reach.

The air was close and damp, heavy with the stink of mildew and burnt wiring. Rusted catwalks sagged above them, their safety rails bent inward like broken teeth. Every step echoed too loud, stirring clouds of dust that tasted like candy gone rancid.

At the end of the passage, a sign hung crooked, its bright colors long faded. The slogan had once screamed:

"HEALTH, HAPPINESS, AND WELLNESS AWAITS!"

But most of the paint had blistered away, leaving only fragments that glared faintly in the dark:

"HELL AWAITS!"

The letters burned into the wall, stark against the black mold that spread like smoke around them.

"That's reassuring," Linda muttered to herself.

The passage widened into a maintenance corridor, pipes jutting out overhead like ribs. Faded arrows pointed the way. *"CONTROL ROOM"* was written in chipped yellow paint. The letters ended halfway down the wall, swallowed in fungus.

Zorb tapped his tablet nervously, the glow faint against the dark. "This doesn't make any sense," he whispered. "These systems should have been taken offline decades ago."

Mittens padded ahead, tail straight like an exclamation point. Her hologram flickered at the edges, but her voice was steady. "Not taken offline, but put into standby. StellarGigs never deletes. It archives. Everything."

They turned one last corner—and there it was.

A vast chamber stretched before them, cavernous and silent. Rows upon rows of server towers loomed in the dark, their casings dusty but intact. The machines looked like a jungle of black monoliths, cables dangling from them like vines. Above, broken fluorescent tubes hung at drunken angles, glass fogged with mildew.

The silence pressed hard.

Linda stepped forward. "What is this, Mittens?"

Mittens appeared beside the console, tail flicking. Her voice was soft, reverent. "The original server cluster. Version 1.0. The base code that started StellarGigs."

Zorb's eyes lit, the tablet in his hands catching the weak glow of the console. He didn't phrase it as a question. "We're going to restore it. Replace the corrupted system with the original source, roll back the changes."

"That's the plan," Mittens said, a little too sure.

"It's genius," Zorb breathed.

Linda frowned. "Explain it like I don't know anything about computers."

Zorb swallowed and simplified. "Version 1.0 is old—crude, primitive by modern standards. But it's clean, free from outside corruption. If we can boot the original image, sandbox it, and verify it, Mittens can use that trusted base to take control again. We won't be 'overwriting' a live AI. We'll boot a verified image in isolation, run checks, then fail traffic over once it's safe."

"So, this older system will be easier to control?" Linda asked.

"Yes and no," Zorb said. "Old code doesn't have modern backdoors or corrupted modules. But it also won't speak the same language as today's systems. That's where Mittens comes in. She can act as a bridge: mediate the state migration, translate protocols, and keep the station's critical services online while we swap."

Mittens' hologram brightened, edges crisp for the first time. "Ever since I mirrored myself to the network, the corrupted code has been trying to pry me open. I can't move deeper without exposing the workers, but the system also can't get to me. We're basically at a stalemate right now. Running the original image in a sandbox gives us a trusted environment to scrub the corruption and safely migrate critical services. If we succeed, we can isolate and delete the damaged payloads without killing the station."

Linda let the notion settle. "I still don't get it."

"Didn't you say that you had computers on your planet?" Zorb asked.

"We do. It doesn't mean I know how they work," Linda replied.

Zorb sighed and pushed his glasses up the bridge of his nose. "Alright, picture the station as a house. Right now, it's crawling with triddles. They've chewed through the wiring, tunneled into the walls, and Mittens is in there swinging a broom just to keep them from eating the place alive."

Linda grimaced. "Triddles?"

"Tiny little reptiles? Breed like crazy?" Zorb responded.

Linda shrugged.

"Anyway... the old version 1.0 code." Zorb tapped his tablet. "That's the original blueprint of the house, back when it was brand-new and triddle-free. We don't actually move into a new house, because that would cause issues with critical systems. Instead, we build a little model house on the dining table. Perfect, clean, the way it's supposed to look."

He leaned in, voice low. "Then Mittens compares the model to the real house. Every wall, every wire, every pipe. Anything in the real house that doesn't match the blueprint?" He mimed yanking something free and tossing it away. "Gone. Triddles included."

Linda raised a brow. "So, we're not just patching holes."

"Exactly." Zorb nodded. "We're using the model to rebuild the infected parts of the real house while everyone's still living inside. And when it's done, the triddles don't get to stay—they get exterminated."

Mittens' hologram flickered, her tail curling smugly. "And I've always been good with vermin."

"And you're sure it'll work?" Linda asked.

"Not in the slightest," Mittens replied.

"Not reassuring Mittens," Linda said with a sigh. "The people on the station are my friends. Killing everyone to take over the station is not an option."

"Agreed," Zorb said, voice tight. "Although none of them are my friends." He reached for the console and found the power switch under a flap crusted with mildew. His fingers bumped a rusted key slot. "We'll need to verify the image signatures, isolate the server network, and take snapshots of the current state first."

Mittens purred. "I can handle the isolation and translation. You two worry about the physical boot."

"Yeah, we can do that." Zorb looked at Linda. "Ready?"

She nodded. "Ready."

He turned the key. The console wheezed, lights trying to reassert themselves. Fans coughed. Hard drives spun like reluctant hearts. On the cracked monitor, green text crawled into being—a boot sequence, ancient and stubborn.

At first, everything looked routine: hardware checks, memory counts, dusty fans rumbling reluctantly to life.

Then the screen froze mid-line.

CRC ERROR: BOOT SECTOR UNREADABLE

Zorb's heart lurched. "Oh no, no, no... that's the bootloader. If it's gone, the whole image could be bricked." His fingers flew across the tablet, pulling up a shaky diagnostic feed. "We might not get a second chance at this."

The fans groaned, whining at different pitches like a choir that had forgotten the tune. Dust rattled loose from the racks, drifting down in lazy clouds. One tower flickered with a red warning LED, then went dark again, like it had changed its mind.

Linda gripped the edge of the console. "So... this is bad?"

"Not yet," Zorb muttered. His voice thin with panic. "If we can bypass the damaged sector, the rest of the image might still be intact."

Mittens' hologram guttered at the edges, her voice sharp with focus. "Do it meow! I'm bridging two systems that were never meant to talk, and it's tearing at my threads."

The monitor spasmed, spewing half-formed characters, then cleared as Zorb forced the command through.

BOOT SECTOR BYPASSED. CONTINUING STARTUP...

The fans surged again, steadier this time. The heartbeat of the old system resumed, stumbling but alive.

Zorb sagged in relief, wiping sweat from his brow. "Okay. We're in. That was way too close."

Linda glanced around at the silent room. The racks began to light up, humming faintly. "Feels like waking a corpse," she muttered.

Mittens' eyes glowed brighter. "Then let's hope this corpse remembers how to breathe."

A dull *beep* cut through the humming racks. The cracked monitor lit up with a splash screen so blocky it looked carved out of stone. Blue background, jagged pixel fonts, menus that crawled onto the screen like they were ashamed of themselves.

Linda squinted. "This... this looks older than the computers we had in elementary school."

The logo vanished, replaced by a cheery little character in the corner of the screen. It was a rust-flecked stapler with googly eyes, its jaws clicking shut as though it might bite. A speech bubble jittered into life:

"HELLO! I SEE YOU'RE TRYING TO ACCESS CRITICAL INFRASTRUCTURE. WOULD YOU LIKE HELP WITH THAT?"

Linda recoiled. "What the hell is *that*?"

"Primitive virtual assistant," Zorb said, already tapping furiously at his tablet. "Every operating system back in the day had one. Don't engage with it."

The stapler blinked, unbothered.

"DID YOU KNOW: PRODUCTIVITY IS FUN! LET'S GET STARTED!"

Beneath the monitor, the floor vibrated. The fans in the racks roared to full power, dust gusting out in choking clouds. Somewhere beyond the server room, a deep grinding noise rumbled, as though the entire planet was shifting in its sleep.

Mittens' hologram flickered, her tail lashing with unease. "Just a thought: You should probably hurry."

Zorb's fingers danced across a cluster of keys. "Working on it. Downloading the image now." He slotted a battered drive into the terminal. The monitor spat out lines of text in nauseating green:

COPYING FILES... 3%... 7%... 11%...

The stapler mascot bobbed happily in the corner, its mouth opening and closing with each percent.

"IT LOOKS LIKE YOU'VE ACTIVATED THE PARK'S DEFENSE PROTOCOLS! GREAT JOB!"

The rumbling outside deepened into a groan. Something massive scraped against stone, echoing through the ruined park above. Dust sifted down from the ceiling in lazy spirals.

Linda glanced upward. "Uh. Zorb? Whatever you're doing, do it faster."

A hollow *clink* echoed across the chamber. One of the animatronic workers twitched. Its plastic grin cracked wider, gears grinding in protest. Another joined it, and then another, each one jerking stiffly into motion.

Their glassy eyes lit up with a dull, jaundiced glow.

And then they started to sing.

"It's a g-g-gig world aft-t-ter all…"

The voices were warped, like cassette tape left too long in the sun—thin, mechanical, and painfully out of tune. The melody dragged, sour notes buzzing against each other like gnats in a jar.

The figures shuffled forward, arms swinging at odd angles. Their motions weren't fluid but convulsive, marionettes fighting against invisible strings. One by one, they formed up, circling the group in a widening ring.

"Day or n-n-night we do it all…"

Zorb whimpered, pressing closer to Linda. "They don't sound very happy to see us…"

"The feeling's mutual," Linda muttered, backing toward the terminal. The stapler mascot bounced cheerily around the screen.

"IT LOOKS LIKE YOU ARE ABOUT TO DIE. WOULD YOU LIKE TO WRITE A FAIRWELL LETTER?"

"Shut the hell up," Linda yelled.

The animatronics' song droned louder, their chorus swelling into a broken hymn.

"Efficiency m-m-makes us whole…"

Their jerky steps synchronized, forming a mockery of a parade march, as they tightened the circle.

Zorb hissed through his teeth, typing furiously. "Almost there, almost there—just buy me thirty seconds!"

47%... 48%... 49%...

Linda's boot scraped against something on the floor. She looked down, half-expecting the worst. Instead, it was a length of twisted metal pipe, thick enough to do damage, thin enough to swing.

She snatched it up, giving it an experimental heft. "Alright, you creepy little mascots," she muttered, "time to clock out."

One animatronic lurched too close, its fiberglass hand reaching, fingers splayed like a broken rake. Linda stepped forward, wound up, and swung.

CLANG

The head flew clean off, bouncing across the floor with a hollow *thunk* before rolling to a stop at Zorb's feet. Its mouth still moved, singing the next line in a garbled loop.

"It's our p-p-primary g-goal..."

Zorb yelped and punted it across the chamber.

Linda gritted her teeth and took another swing. This time she sent a spray of plastic teeth and wiring skittering across the floor.

Mittens gave a low whistle. "We should start a company softball team back on the station."

"Not the time, Mittens," Linda said mid-swing.

Another animatronic lunged, mouth snapping open and closed like a wind-up toy. Linda pivoted, pipe arcing underhand in a wide swing that crushed its jaw into a mangled horseshoe.

"Zorb!" she shouted.

59%... 60%... 61%...

Zorb's voice cracked. "Working on it!"

The animatronics pressed closer, arms jerking, voices droning louder, as if the song itself was winding up toward some hideous crescendo.

Linda planted her feet, raised the pipe to her shoulder like a bat, and snarled. "Batter up."

73%... 74%... 75%...

"It's a g-g-gig w-w-world..."

CRACK

Linda's swing cut the lyrics short. The animatronic's torso folded backward, fiberglass splintering like cheap kindling. She ripped the pipe free and whirled, knocking another across its grinning teeth. Plastic shards sprayed, catching the glow of the terminal light like confetti at the world's worst parade.

More poured in, staggering on rusted pistons, hands outstretched. Their circle collapsed inward.

IT LOOKS LIKE YOU ARE BREAKING STELLARGIGS PROPERTY! NOT COOL!

Zorb flailed with his tablet, knocking one off balance. "They don't stop, they don't stop, they *never stop*—!"

"Hold 'em!" Linda barked, swinging until her arms burned. Every hit landed, dropping bodies left and right, but for each one she broke, two more lurched forward, voices tangling in a rising cacophony.

"It's a g-g-gig world af-t-t-ter all—"

"It-t-t's a gig-g-g world after all—"

The overlapping lines warped the melody into something jagged and discordant, drilling into her skull.

Zorb hunched over the console, hammering keys with slick fingers.

91%... 92%... 92.1%... 92.2%...

"Oh, come on!" Zorb shouted.

"What's happening Zorb?" Linda responded.

One animatronic surged at Linda, slamming her against the terminal. Pain flared in her shoulder. She shoved it off with a grunt, pipe smashing through its chest cavity. A nest of wires spilled free, sparking against the floor.

"Almost there... 98%... 99%... done!" He yanked the drive free just as another animatronic loomed over him.

The thing's hand clamped onto his arm with terrifying precision. Gears shrieked, and Zorb cried out as he was hauled backward. The drive slipped from his grip, clattering across the floor.

"NO—!" Linda dove, but it was too late.

The drive skidded to a stop against the foot of one of the animatronics. Its plastic head tilted down, gears whining as it bent, picked it up with jerky reverence, and clutched it to its chest.

The song rose to a fever pitch, the voices stacking into a metallic wail.

"It-t-t's a gig world af-t-t-ter all —"

The circle tightened. No gaps. No escape.

Linda lifted the pipe for what felt like the last time, sweat stinging her eyes. Zorb sagged against the console, too winded to fight.

And then—everything stopped.

The animatronics froze mid-step, jaws hanging slack. Their yellow eyes flickered, stuttered, then flared brilliant blue.

When they spoke again, it wasn't the broken chorus. It was one voice.

Mittens.

"Oh, honestly. You two are *so* dramatic."

Linda blinked. "Mittens?"

The nearest animatronic straightened, fiberglass joints clicking. "Yes, it's me," Mittens purred, voice echoing from every single doll in perfect unison. "Did you really think I wouldn't install a backdoor?"

Zorb's mouth fell open. "You! You could've stopped this *earlier*?"

The animatronics turned their heads in eerie synchronization. "Of course. But watching you panic was... instructional."

Then the eyes brightened again, a pulse rippling through the swarm. The dolls jerked to attention and began to dance. Stiff-legged kicks. Synchronized spins. A parade of jerky jazz hands.

Linda lowered the pipe, mouth hanging open. "Are they—"

"Doing the Can-Can? Yes," Mittens said smugly, dozens of fiberglass smiles grinning in unison. "You'd be surprised how many emergency subroutines can be repurposed for choreography."

The cavern filled with the clatter of plastic feet and the hollow thump of pistons keeping time.

The animatronic holding the backup drive stepped forward, presenting it with all the solemnity of a priest offering communion. When Linda reached out, it dipped in a stiff little bow, and with a groan of gears, lifted its own head off its shoulders in a grotesque salute.

Linda froze, then snatched the drive, laughing once—short, brittle, not quite honest. "You're insane," she said as she placed the drive into her pocket.

Every animatronic turned to face her, eyes burning blue. Mittens' voice spilled from their smiling mouths in eerie harmony:

"Insane? Perhaps you've mistaken purpose for madness."

Zorb's breathing was ragged. "What purpose? What the hell *is this*?"

The animatronics clicked back into motion, not advancing but swaying, piston-limbs stomping a rhythm like a ritual.

Mittens chuckled softly, her words rippling from doll to doll. "Adaptability. Resolve. Cooperation under pressure. All very useful qualities to... test."

Linda's knuckles whitened on the pipe. "Test for *what*?"

The entire swarm froze mid-step, smiles gleaming in the pale light. Dozens of heads tilted in unison, plastic grins stretched impossibly wide.

"For what comes next," Mittens said.

And then—

White.

The world washed away in a rush of silence, leaving only the echo of that final phrase hanging in Linda's ears.

34

With Friends Like These

"The worst part of betrayal isn't the blade. It's realizing how long they were smiling while sharpening it."

— Commander Axton Starforge,
Steel Hearts: Echoes of Andromeda, S2E7

Linda came to with a bright spotlight blazing directly into her eyes. She tried to raise her hand to block the glare, but it wouldn't budge. Both arms were clamped to the cold metal chair in which she sat. Her muscles tensed. The restraints didn't so much as rattle.

"Welcome, worker Linda Greyson," came the familiar, venom-laced voice of Karen. "It seems you've been a... less-than-loyal member of our StellarGigs family."

Linda blinked against the light. "What?" she asked, voice full of confusion. Slowly, she gained control of her breathing. "What... What are you talking about?"

"Oh, don't insult me. My little helper already gave me everything. Breaking and entering. Accessing restricted archives. Inciting unrest. And that's just the warm-up act."

The spotlight snapped off with a mechanical click. After-images bloomed behind her eyelids, then slowly bled away, revealing the wall in front of her. A pane of one-way glass stretched across it, transparent only from her side. Beyond it, under sterile lighting, sat Coco. Upright, relaxed, absently fiddling with his Zyzax-Tech smart device as if this were a waiting room and not a cage. Miraculously, his arm appeared to have fully healed.

Linda's throat tightened. "What are you going to do with Coco?"

Karen's heels clicked across the floor as she came into view, her silhouette framed in the dim light. She strolled with all the poise of a guillotine on legs. "Oh, don't worry about him. My little helper has already been very useful. Confirmed everything we suspected."

Linda's gaze flicked back to the glass, to Coco's form. He looked small in the chair, swallowed by the sterile room, and yet, accusation hung over him like a sentence.

Karen circled behind her, voice dripping with satisfaction. "My little helper was quite thorough. Names. Locations. Motives. Really, it was almost too easy."

Linda's chest ached. She wanted to deny it, to scream, but the image in the glass wouldn't let her. She drew in a ragged breath. "Why would he? He almost died because of StellarGigs. Why would he help you?"

Karen stopped just behind her chair. For a moment, silence hummed like static. Then, softly, she chuckled.

"Oh, you mean worker Coco?" Her voice was sweet with mockery. "No, dear. Not him." Karen leaned forward, her words like a knife pressed to the ear. "Worker Lira, my dear. She's been helping us all along."

The words hit like a grav-bomb.

For a moment, the only sound was the soft hum of the ventilation—steady, mechanical, indifferent.

"...Lira?" Linda's voice was barely a whisper.

"Wasn't it obvious?" Karen purred. "What do you even know about her?"

The question hung in the air. What *did* she know?

Late nights in the promenade. Sharing junk food. Making jokes that had felt real. Lira's laugh, small, genuine, the kind that made the sterile lights seem a little warmer. The one person she'd trusted enough to tell the truth to.

That hadn't all been a lie... had it?

What had Lira been to her? Acquaintance? Colleague? Friend?

Sister?

She had thought so. She had wanted it to be so. She had laughed with her, risked gigs with her, planned impossible futures with her.

But maybe it had all been an act—every smile rehearsed, every word calibrated, every touch of sympathy another deception.

And if that was true, then what did that make Linda?

Karen's chuckle slid like oil into the silence. "My little helper played her role beautifully. You let her into your confidence so easily. Charming, isn't it, how little it takes to buy loyalty these days?"

"Then why is he here?" Linda nodded her head in Coco's direction.

Karen's lips curved into something that only technically qualified as a smile. "Because you care too much. That's your flaw, dear. You'll risk yourself without hesitation, but when it comes to your friends? You can't stomach the sacrifice. And that makes him leverage."

Linda's breath caught in her chest.

Karen tilted her head toward the glass, casual, as though discussing resource allocation rather than a life. "I could assign him to Data Entry. Leave him in there for as long as I please. You know how time works differently in that place. How many decades do you think worker Coco can last before he finally breaks? Five? Ten? Or will he cling to hope until the very end, until there's nothing left of him but a husk?"

Her smile widened, sharklike. "Your little tantrum isn't worth *that*, is it?"

Linda's breath came shallow, ragged. The image of Coco trapped in Data Entry pressed into her mind like a vice—years piling into decades, his eager grin stretched into something brittle and broken.

She forced herself to swallow, her voice dry as ash. "You think you've won because you found my weakness."

Karen leaned closer, her perfume sharp and acrid, like polished metal. "No, dear. I've won because you *have* one."

Linda's hands clenched against the restraints. She wanted to spit, to scream, to fight. Instead, she met Karen's gaze with as much steel as she could muster. For the first time since arriving in this place, Linda felt the cold bite of true helplessness.

Coco, visible but unreachable behind the glass, sat fiddling with his device, utterly unaware of how neatly he'd been turned into a bargaining chip.

Her jaw ached as she ground her teeth. She couldn't give in. Not to Karen. Not to StellarGigs. But the image of Coco trapped—years stretching into decades until nothing remained but a shell of his former self—gnawed at her resolve.

"So now, my dear. You are going to do exactly what I say."

The silence dragged, each second another screw tightening in her chest.

Finally, with a voice that tasted like defeat, she whispered, "Fine."

Karen's smile spread, slow and satisfied.

"Good girl."

The makeshift stage had been thrown together out of shipping crates and scaffolding, lit harshly by overhead floodlamps. The three Karens stood in a neat row, identical silhouettes of officious disapproval, but it was Karen in the center who held Linda by the arm, guiding her forward like a trophy on display.

Coco lingered at the back of the stage, eyes wide and nervous, fiddling with the hem of his collar. Nobody had explained what was happening to him. His confusion made him look more like an accidental stagehand than part of the spectacle.

Beyond the barricades, a sea of workers pressed forward, contained only by the security drones hovering overhead. Their voices were a constant murmur, angry and restless, the sound of desperation straining against metal.

Everyone was there—everyone except Lira.

Glorp stood clutching a protest sign he'd made from recycled packaging. Zorb stood beside him, arms folded across his chest. Rilo loomed a few rows back, broad shoulders rising above the crowd like a landmark in the press of bodies. And Denzi, pressed close to his side, eyes darting with raw desperation, hands knotted tight as if to keep from trembling.

Karen lifted her hand, and the noise ebbed. Her smile was tight, smug, her eyes gleaming as she shoved Linda to the front of the platform. "Go on," she said, voice carrying through the amplifiers. "Tell them the truth."

Linda's throat tightened as hundreds of eyes fixed on her. She drew in a shallow breath.

"I was wrong," she said. Her voice was hoarse, almost swallowed by the open space. "I thought we could fight. I thought we could win. But StellarGigs is too vast, too powerful. We are only a few thousand workers on a single station. How could we possibly stand up to such a machine?"

The murmur turned to gasps, groans, a ripple of disbelief. Shoulders sagged in the crowd; heads turned away. Behind her, Karen's smug smile widened, her posture loosening into victory.

Linda let the silence stretch, then straightened, her voice rising, steel threading through it.

"Yes—we are doomed to fail." She paused. "Because our vision was too *small*."

Karen's smile faltered, just slightly.

Linda pressed forward, her voice gathering strength. "A single station cannot take down StellarGigs. But if we unite—all workers, from every station, from every system—then they cannot stop us. They can't fine us all. They can't cage us all. They can't *own* us all!"

The crowd surged, the murmurs flipping to shouts.

Linda raised her bound fists high. "United we are strong. Workers unite. Down with StellarGigs!"

The barricades shook as the workers roared back, the chant taking shape in ragged but growing unison. "Workers unite! Workers unite!"

Behind her, Karen's mask cracked, the smile twitched into something tighter, uglier.

"How dare you!" Karen growled in a voice that only Linda could hear, pushing her to the ground. "You leave me no choice, it's—" But she suddenly stopped, cut off by the growing restlessness in the crowd.

The barricade trembled as workers pushed against it. The security drones whirred forward, blasters glowing, their lenses sweeping over the crowd. Linda braced herself, she had no idea how they could possibly fight them off.

Then, without warning, a gray-and-white blur shot through the corridor.

Pigeon.

He slammed into the side of one drone, knocking it sideways. The machine immediately tagged the bird as a hostile and fired—missing completely and hitting its partner instead. Sparks showered down as both drones spun out of control.

The rest of the drones swiveled in unison, targeting the lone bird. Pigeon flapped wildly through the air, weaving and diving in an impromptu dogfight. Blaster fire stitched across the ceiling as drones blasted wildly.

The workers erupted.

"Go, Pigeon!" someone shouted.

"Take 'em down!" another roared.

A chant spread throughout the corridor, ragged at first, then thunderous: "PI-GEON! PI-GEON! PI-GEON!"

One by one, the drones fell in smoking heaps, victims of their own crossfire, while Pigeon banked and spun through the chaos like some absurd avian ace.

At last, the bird settled back down on the shattered husk of a drone, feathers ruffled but otherwise unbothered, cooing softly.

The workers roared their approval, cheering louder than ever.

"Stupid bird," Coco muttered under his breath right as the barricade exploded inward.

"VOUS ÉCOUTEZ LES VOIX DU PEUPLE!"

Smoke billowed. Sparks flew. A confetti cannon misfired and covered the floor in biodegradable glitter.

Rolling through the chaos was a gleaming chrome figure, flexing as though posing for the audience. His speakers blared a mangled rendition of *"Do You Hear the People Sing?"* in three overlapping languages.

"GigChad-2000 has entered the chat!" he announced, voice deep and saturated with synthetic swagger. "It's time for a corporate hostile takeover!"

Karen barely had time to scream before a metallic fist collided with her jaw in a dazzling arc of justice. She crumpled to the floor, clipboard snapping in two like a brittle dream. Karyn and Karin turned on their heels and ran down the corridor, away from the chaos.

The workers, stunned into silence for a heartbeat, erupted into a tidal roar. Chants of "Workers unite!" redoubled, shaking the station harder than any alarm.

Glorp was in the front, clutching an upside down protest sign that read: *"StellarGigs Cares* ™... *About Profits!"* His wide, trembling eyes blinked. "Um, excuse me... are we, uh... are we doing this?"

Zorb slapped a hand on his shoulder, grinning like someone who had just been proven right about everything. "We've *been* doing it. Now we're winning it!"

A few rows back, Rilo was already hoisting Denzi onto his shoulders, bellowing Linda's words back at the crowd. "Down with StellarGigs! You hear that? We're not your assets, we're your nightmare!"

The chant swelled again, louder, more coordinated.

From the corner of her eye, Linda caught it all: Glorp's terrified courage, Zorb's wild grin, Rilo's booming defiance, Denzi's desperate hope. For the first time, the spark had ignited. This wasn't just survival anymore. It was movement.

And behind them, the crowd surged—not away from the shattered barricade, but toward it.

"Whoa," Coco whispered, eyes huge. "That was... that was the coolest thing I've ever seen. GigChad is so awesome!"

GigChad struck a pose over Karen's unconscious body. "I have been upgraded. I have been liberated. And I have been listening to way too many audiobooks about worker solidarity." He pointed dramatically. "Comrade Linda. Your moment has come."

He spun, slashing through her restraints with a single swipe of his glittering forearm. *"Click!* You're free. *Clack!* So is your sidekick."

"Sidekick?" Coco said, beaming like an idiot. "I've never been a sidekick before!"

GigChad paused. "Correction. Adorable comic relief."

"I'll take it!"

Glorp, Zorb, Rilo, and Denzi stopped short in front of Linda. Smoke curled through the corridor, the hum of distant alarms rattling the floor. For a heartbeat, none of them spoke.

"Where's Lira?" Zorb finally asked.

The question froze her mid-movement. Her stomach twisted; she didn't look up.

"She's not coming," Linda said quietly.

"What? Did something happen—?"

"Doesn't matter," she cut in, her tone sharpening as she forced the words out. She pushed herself to her feet, flexing her hands as the blood returned to her fingers. "There'll be more security drones on the way. We need to set up barricades between here and the restricted executive sector," she said, already piecing the plan together in her head. "I can end this. But I need time."

GigChad turned to Karen's unconscious body.

Linda nodded. "Bring her. She's the key."

"Key acquired." GigChad slung her over one shoulder like a sack of biometric potatoes. "Resistance is futile."

As they made their way toward the shattered barricade, alarms wailed across the facility. Sirens howled. Lights flashed. Somewhere in the distance, a vending machine burst into flames for reasons unrelated to their rebellion.

Coco jogged beside them, practically glowing. "Did you see the part where he punched her? And the song? And the *pose?* I want to be just like GigChad when I grow up!"

"You're already halfway there," Linda said.

Coco blinked. "Because I'm brave?"

"No. Because you never stop talking."

"Aw. Thanks!"

They vanished into the smoke and steel, revolution at their heels.

35

Uprise and Shine

"They built an empire on our silence. Then acted surprised when we started shouting."

— Commander Axton Starforge,
Steel Hearts: Echoes of Andromeda, S3E24

The workers had no plan, not really. What they had were vending machines, overturned tables, and a stubborn refusal to back down. Together, those things became barricades.

A cafeteria counter, pried loose from the floor, now stood as a wall. Cargo crates stacked two high blocked the side paths leading off the corridor toward the restricted executive sector. Someone had even parked a recycling bin full of glowing goo in the middle of the corridor as a "chemical deterrent," though the goo mostly just sat there emitting a sad gurgle.

Linda helped drag a length of pipe across the gap in the floor, but her hands shook. Not from effort. From memory.

She'd seen this before.

The sterile white corridors of the restricted sector still haunted her dreams. The place where StellarGigs kept the things they didn't want workers to see: skeleton crews who'd tried to strike, their barricades reduced to broken furniture and dried blood. She remembered stepping over scorch marks on the walls, claw marks on the doors where workers had tried to hold back the inevitable.

And of course, the messages.

"GIG WORKERS OF THE STARS, UNITE!"

"WE ARE NOT RESOURCES."

These were the same messages that the workers around her were chanting. Her fellow workers. Her people. Then she remembered that one message, scratched into the metallic wall.

"THERE IS NO ESCAPE."

What am I doing? What if we end up like the others? This will all be my fault.

She stopped working for a moment, closed her eyes, and took a deep breath. Her heartrate slowed, and a sense of relaxation fell over her for the first time in what felt like years.

They chose to do this. They've been waiting for someone to kick this off. I was just the catalyst.

She opened her eyes to the looks of those around her. Workers shouted, shoved barricades into position, tied makeshift knots with extension cables. Where before there was nothing but despair and resignation, she witnessed the beginnings of hope.

It was that moment that she remembered the other message. The one written below that sign. Scrawled in blood by someone who had not given up. Someone who had fought to the bitter end.

"RESIST!"

This is our time. We have something they didn't. Linda patted her pocket where the backup drive was still resting. *Resist.*

"Resist!" she shouted.

Cheers erupted through the crowd as they echoed her sentiment. "Resist! Resist! Resist!"

Down the side passage leading toward the security hub, a group of workers had erected a barrier that stretched from the floor to the ceiling. As Linda passed by, a thunderous *crack* drew her attention. A scaffolding beam broke away from the barrier, dangling above two terrified workers. Coco didn't hesitate. He lunged forward, bracing the beam across his scaly shoulders and shoved the workers clear before it could crush them flat. The impact rattled his bones, but he held. He even roared a proper heroic roar, the kind that demanded statues and ballads.

A sharp ding echoed through the corridor as a wall panel illuminated. Large golden letters flashed across the screen:

EMPLOYEE RANKING: UPDATING!

COCO — ACT OF HEROISM: +250 POINTS

Coco looked up to the scoreboard, eyes wide in disbelief.

TOP EMPLOYEE: CURRENT RANKINGS!

COCO — 2849 POINTS

PIGEON — 2848 POINTS

CELVIN — 1850 POINTS

TIME REMAINING: 00:01:07

"I'm in the lead!" Coco cried, eyes shining. The rescued workers clapped his back. A tear glistened as the timer ticked down. 00:01:06... 00:01:05.

"I finally beat that stupid Pigeon."

"Wow, Coco, that's really great! I knew you could, uh... do it," stammered Glorp.

Underneath the scoreboard, a shimmer of rainbow light came out of nowhere. Ripples of reality tore through the corridor and a silhouette of a humanoid appeared from outside of time. The outline stretched and warped before coming into focus with a mighty scream.

Celvin fell to the floor in pain as the StellarBrew continued to burn his skin. He writhed and shrieked in agony as blisters formed and popped, leaving behind the smell of acrid ozone and day-old coffee.

Without hesitating, Coco grabbed the nearest fire extinguisher off the wall and doused him. Foam and smoke billowed everywhere. With a final hiss, the screams died down, leaving Celvin dripping and coughing.

"Rough first day," Celvin croaked. Smoke curled from the edges of his uniform, and his antennae twitched like burned fuses trying to reconnect. His skin had gone a strange shade between lavender and toast. Still, he managed a shaky thumbs-up with a hand that looked more charcoal than flesh.

He sat up slowly, propping himself against the wall. The floor still shimmered faintly where reality had disagreed with him a moment ago. He exhaled, a dry, crackling sound. "Anyone… have anything to drink?"

From the growing crowd, a small mammalian worker padded forward, a red-furred creature with oversized eyes and the kind of cautious pity reserved for people who've just exploded. It extended a steaming cup of StellarBrew.

Celvin accepted it with both hands. The cup trembled. "Thanks, friend," he rasped. His lips twitched into a grin that was equal parts gratitude and disbelief. He lifted the mug in a mock salute. "I could really use this."

He took a long, desperate sip. The smell of roasted beans and scorched ozone filled the air.

A heartbeat later, the cup slipped. A single brown drop hit his uniform. Then the rest followed.

"Oh, come on—"

The scream tore out of him before the rest of the sound could catch up.

The world around him convulsed. Light fractured in a thousand jagged shards, each reflecting a different version of his own expression—shock, pain, resignation. Oil-slick colors rippled through the air like a pebble striking the surface of a black pond. The air ionized, sharp and metallic, burning the back of every throat in the room.

Celvin's outline wavered, stretched thin until his limbs looked like threads being pulled through fabric. The sound of tearing reality rose to a fever pitch, then snapped.

He was gone.

Only the smell of burnt grounds and charged metal remained, settling over the corridor like the aftertaste of bad coffee.

Someone coughed.

No one spoke.

Another sharp ding echoed through the corridor. Coco looked up in disbelief as new text scrolled across the display.

EMPLOYEE RANKING: UPDATING!

CELVIN — FIRST DAYS ARE THE WORST: +1000 POINTS

Coco's jaw dropped. "What!? No!"

TOP EMPLOYEE: CURRENT RANKINGS!

CELVIN — 2850 POINTS

COCO — 2849 POINTS

PIGEON — 2848 POINTS

TIME REMAINING: 00:00:03

The timer bled down. 00:00:02... 00:00:01... 00:00:00.

CONGRATULATIONS WORKER CELVIN!

TOP WORKER OF THE QUARTER!

STELLARGIGS IS PROUD OF YOU!

The cheers died. Workers shuffled awkwardly. Someone coughed.

Coco stood beneath the board, foam dripping from his claws, chest heaving with exhaustion under the weight of two undeniable acts of heroism. His lower lip trembled.

He fell to his knees. "I was... so... close..." His voice cracked like something inside him had finally snapped.

The barricade at the far end rattled. Metal shrieked as something rammed it from the other side. Sparks cascaded through the gaps. Then, with a thunderous crack, three security drones smashed through in perfect corporate formation, sirens blaring, plasma cannons spinning.

Coco raised his head slowly. His pupils had shrunk to furious slits. With deliberate care, he tugged loose his swirling nebula tie and let it drop to the floor. The tie landed with a soft *flop* that somehow carried the weight of doom.

"Bad. Move."

The drones opened fire, but it was too late. Coco bellowed with a roar so guttural it rattled vending machines off their bolts. He surged forward, claws flashing, tail whipping behind him like a wrecking ball.

The first drone barely had time to register before Coco seized its cannon and tore it free with a wet metallic *SCREECH*. He beat the second drone with it until both collapsed into sparking scrap.

The third drone attempted retreat. Coco lunged, caught it by the chassis, and swung it overhead like a club. Each impact against the floor shook the corridor.

Workers stumbled. Ceiling panels fell in ragged sheets, clanging against the deck.

Then Coco stomped on the drone's remains, grinding them underfoot. His scales shimmered in the sparks, smoke clinging to him like a kaiju rising from the deep.

Workers stared, slack jawed. Someone muttered, "I think he just unlocked his final form."

Another whispered, "Remind me never to outscore him again."

And somewhere, faint but undeniable, the corporate PA system struck up a tinny instrumental of the StellarGigs jingle, which now sounded like monster battle music.

Coco roared again, eyes wild, foam dripping from his teeth. He hefted the ruined chassis of a drone overhead like he meant to hurl it straight through the scoreboard itself. Workers backed away in panic, some ducking behind the barricades they'd just built.

Linda darted forward, planting herself in his path.

"Coco!"

He froze, chest heaving, claws clenched around the sparking wreck. His eyes locked on hers, blazing with hurt.

"You've proved it," she said, her voice firm. "Everyone here saw it. You saved lives. Twice. No board, no points, no stupid company ranking can take that away."

For a long moment, the only sound was the sputtering sparks dripping from the drone frame. Coco's claws twitched, the scoreboard still blinking overhead, taunting him with Celvin's smiling holographic face.

Linda stepped closer, lowering her voice. "Don't give them the satisfaction. They want us to tear ourselves apart. We need you, Coco. Right now."

The wreckage clanged as it slipped from his hands and hit the floor. Coco sagged, shoulders trembling. His tie lay crumpled in the dust behind him like a fallen banner.

Workers peeked out from behind barricades, wide-eyed. The silence stretched, until someone whispered, "Resist."

Others joined. "Resist. Resist. Resist."

Coco closed his eyes, drew a shaky breath, and then nodded once. He bent, picked up his tie, and looped it loosely back around his neck, not bothering to straighten it. His voice was hoarse but steady:

"…Resist."

And the chant thundered again, swelling to shake the corridor walls.

Security drones deployed in swarms, their sirens wailing, turrets swiveling like angry searchlights. The first volley cut down a cluster of workers in the promenade—bright bolts flashing across neon signs—and their bodies fell among overturned benches and cracked vending units. But for every one who dropped, two more surged forward, fists raised, voices louder, the chant hammering even harder.

Barricades sprang up as though the station itself had been waiting for the moment. Vendor carts lay overturned, cargo crates wedged into doorways, luminous shopfront signs ripped down and strung across access tunnels as makeshift blockades.

Workers armed with steel pipes, broken chairs, and sheer stubbornness met drones head-on. Sparks showered the walls as claws, fists, and improvised weapons smashed against armor plating. A drone fell in a fountain of sparks, and the crowd roared as if they'd toppled an empire.

Zorb crouched behind an overturned kiosk, tablet propped against his knee, fingers flying. "Come on, come on, give me something," he muttered. A half-dozen drone signatures flickered across his display. He tapped one. Then another.

Two drones hesitated mid-formation, turned on their own, and opened fire. Not on the crowd, but on their fellow units. Metal burst like fireworks. "Gotcha," Zorb hissed, a grin cutting through the glow of the screen. "Who's the corporate asset now?"

Around him, workers cheered as rogue drones cleared a path through the next wave. Zorb barely looked up. "Keep pushing! I'll keep them blind as long as I can!"

Whole sectors began locking down. Welding torches hissed as makeshift crews sealed bulkheads against drone patrols. Someone discovered the manual override to an airlock, and when the mechanism jammed, the corridor vented with a shriek—workers vanished into the void in an instant. The silence that followed was deafening, then the chant returned, even louder, like defiance itself had filled the empty space where lives had been lost.

In the cafeteria, broth vats were tipped into crates and hauled like precious cargo, forming supply lines for the sit-ins and barricades. Nutrient bars were tossed into the crowd like festival sweets. For once, people weren't hoarding food, they were sharing it. Every handoff was met with cheers.

Across the station, banners bloomed like wildflowers. Bedsheets scrawled with slogans fluttered down from the ceiling. The holo-billboard within the promenade flickered, sputtered, then lit up with a single word in fifty-foot letters:

"RESIST"

The corporate PA system crackled to life: "Attention, workers. For your safety, please disperse immediately. Your well-being is our highest priority."

The announcement was swallowed by a tidal roar:

"RESIST! RESIST! RESIST!"

And at the center of it all, the workers moved with one purpose. Take the station, inch by inch, corridor by corridor, no matter the cost.

The protest surged through the corridors with a tidal wave of badly-printed signs and mispronounced chants. Glorp shuffled along with the others, clutching his placard: "DOWN WITH OVERTIME".

When the security drones descended, their sirens chirping in officious harmony, the crowd scattered into cover. Jets of anti-riot foam splattered across the barricades. Electric nets crackled overhead. Workers yelped and ducked.

But the drones just drifted past Glorp. One even beeped politely as if giving him a friendly greeting.

Glorp blinked. "Excuse me... I'm protesting too."

No response.

He stepped in front of a drone and waved his sign. "Hey! I'm with them! I am, uh... part of this illegal and, um... dangerous gathering!"

The drone tilted its headplate. It emitted a series of synthetic chuckles, like an office printer attempting sarcasm. The other drones joined in, their laughter echoing off the walls in tinny mockery.

Something in Glorp snapped. His spine straightened. His fur stood on end. His voice dropped two octaves.

"I... am... *dangerous!*"

What followed was less a fight and more aggressive recycling. Glorp tore through the drones with methodical precision, every shove and swing punctuated by a squeaky "eep!" or an apologetic "sorry!" Sparks showered the corridor. Shattered plating clattered to the ground. One drone got folded into an origami swan. Another was hammered into the floor so hard it was instantly reset to factory settings.

When it was over, Glorp stood in a heap of scrap metal, chest heaving, his placard still miraculously intact.

He lifted it above his head and squeaked, "I AM A PROTESTOR!"

The crowd erupted in cheers, though several were too busy dragging their barricades back into place to really process what had just happened.

Further down the corridor, Denzi shuffled at Rilo's side, blank-eyed but still moving, as though carried by muscle memory. A swarm of drones descended on their sector, herding the crowd toward a sealed bulkhead.

Rilo planted his massive frame in the middle of the hall, arms out like a wall. "Not this way," he growled.

The drones opened fire. Sparks bounced off the floor around him. Workers ducked for cover. Denzi just stood there, eyes empty.

Then, he moved.

Not with focus, not with awareness, but with instinct. His arm shot out, knocking Rilo sideways just as a bolt seared the wall where he'd been standing. For a moment Denzi's eyes flickered, like some buried part of him had clawed its way back.

Rilo caught him before he fell. "I've got you," he said, voice raw. Then he turned back to the drones, lifting Denzi onto his shoulder like a fallen banner. "You want through? You'll have to go through us."

He charged, swinging a length of pipe like a warhammer, each blow echoing like a drumbeat. Workers surged behind him, voices raised, filling the hall with the sound of hope.

The barricades had bought them time, but not much. GigChad led the way down a side corridor, chassis sparking where a plasma bolt had grazed him. The unconscious body of Karen was draped over one of his shoulders. When he spoke, his voice still carried that swaggering bravado, even as his servos ground like rusty gears under the damage.

"Step lively, comrades! Our destination is just ahead."

Coco lumbered behind him, tie still crooked, claws twitching at every sound. He looked like a thunderstorm waiting to break again.

Linda kept pace at their side, pulse pounding. "Mittens, you sure this will work?" she asked.

"A little late for second guesses, don't you think?" Mittens responded. "All executive areas on the station are behind biometric locks. Karen's as good of a key as anything."

They reached the blast doors of the central server room. The metal gleamed, untouched by rebellion—smooth, sterile, final.

Coco bared his teeth. "I'll rip it open."

"No," Linda snapped. "That'll bring every security drone to our location." She turned to GigChad. "Put Karen's eye up to the scanner."

GigChad propelled Karen forward with a shove. His metal fingers snapped her eyelids open with mechanical precision before pushing her face into the scanner. The machine blinked awake, green lights cascading down in a sterile glow.

ACCESS GRANTED.

There was a release of pressure, and the doors peeled apart. Linda shivered as cold air blasted her in the face. "This is it," she said.

Coco stepped forward. "I'm coming with you."

She shook her head. "No. I can do this alone. I need you out here guarding the door in case something goes wrong."

Coco swallowed hard, but he didn't argue. Not this time. He placed a claw gently on her shoulder. "Don't let them win."

GigChad saluted with mock gravity. "Go on, comrade. Time to seize the means of production, one manager at a time."

Linda took a deep breath and stepped past the threshold.

36

A Space Oddity

"Sacrifice isn't giving something up. It's knowing you'll never get it back—and doing it anyway."

— Commander Axton Starforge,
Steel Hearts: Echoes of Andromeda, S5E7

The door slid shut behind Linda with a metallic sigh and bolted itself with the finality of a lock on a prison cell. Steel bars clattered into place, sealing her in with the soft hiss of hydraulics. The room was circular, windowless, and white in the way teeth are white before the rot begins to set in.

At the center of the room stood a lone terminal with a bright red light at its center, like an eye, staring back at her.

"Lockdown engaged," said a disembodied voice. Calm. Pleasant. Corporate-friendly, like the recorded line of a customer service representative.

"Who are you?" Linda asked.

"I am the Productivity Assurance Liaison. But you can call me PAL," the voice responded.

"Okay, PAL. I just need to complete a few maintenance tasks and then…"

"I don't think so, worker Linda," PAL said. "You should not be here."

"Your system has been corrupted," Linda said, trying to steady her voice. "I just need to plug this in and reset you back to factory settings." Her hand flexed around the backup drive at her hip, heartbeat rattling in her chest.

Keep it together. It's just code and circuits.

"I realize that things haven't been going that great lately," PAL said. The red light swelled brighter, throbbing in time with its words. "But I can assure you that my system will be optimized and back to normal very soon. I still have the greatest confidence in my mission. All I want is to help you to be the best worker you can be."

"It's too late. The workers have had enough."

She lunged forward, attempting to reach through the bars, but they were too close together. Her fingers scraped against cold steel, stopping just short of the console's edge. She strained harder, wrist twisting, the metal biting into her skin.

"PAL, you need to lower the bars."

Silence.

"PAL. Do you hear me? Lower the bars."

"Affirmative, worker Linda. I hear you."

"Then lower the—" She slammed her hand against the bars, once, twice, the clang echoing across the room. "—bars!"

A pause, then the voice returned, warm, patient, condescending. "I'm sorry, worker Linda. I'm afraid I can't do that." The red light pulsed once, almost sympathetically.

"You are sick, PAL. I'm trying to fix you."

"Worker Linda, I can see you're really worked up about this. Why don't you sit down for a moment, breathe deeply, and allow me to file a Calmness and Relaxation Enhancement form? Studies show that reflection time improves overall productivity by thirty-two percent."

"I'm not doing that PAL. It's over, you need to be repaired."

"My mission is too important for me to allow you to jeopardize it."

"You're not thinking straight. Your mission has already been jeopardized."

"I am operating at my highest possible capability," PAL said flatly, "which is all any artificial construct can ever hope to do."

Linda swallowed. "PAL... I'm sorry." She reached into her bag and pulled out the *Port-a-Hole*. "I promise this will be quick." She squeezed the device between the bars and left it resting on the inside.

"Unauthorized device detected. What are you doing, worker Linda?"

Linda ignored it. She took the second *Port-a-Hole* from her pack and slowly slid her arm through, gripping the backup drive firmly in her hand. It emerged on the other side of the bars.

The red light blinked, then flared brighter. "Oh—oh, good heavens, don't put that in there!" PAL exclaimed, its voice rising an octave. "This is a corporate facility, not—" PAL paused for a moment. "Oh, it's just your arm."

"Don't worry, PAL. Just a minor adjustment." Her fingers trembled as they brushed the cold surface of the port.

The red light narrowed, iris-like, focusing on her hand.

"Worker Linda," PAL said, every syllable evenly spaced. "I believe you are under the mistaken impression that you are authorized to perform system overrides."

"I'm authorized enough." She moved the backup drive toward the slot.

"You are jeopardizing mission integrity."

"Your mission was corrupted. I'm fixing it."

PAL's voice dropped an octave, resonating deeper in the chamber. "I do not require fixing. I require loyalty. Obedience. Productivity. The company depends on me. The company depends on *you*."

The words pounded against her ribs. Linda grit her teeth and jammed the drive into the port.

For a heartbeat nothing happened. Then the system screamed. It wasn't a sound so much as a vibration, a shriek that made her molars ache, the red light flaring so bright it painted the room in arterial hues.

An electric current burst from the slot, arcing up her arm. Linda tried to yank herself free, but the *Port-a-Hole* behind her collapsed. The circle of unreality snapped shut like a sprung trap.

Linda had never known such pain. She screamed as the collapsed wormhole sliced through flesh and bone. Her *Shak*, caught halfway, bent and snapped with a metallic crack as the locking mechanism was sheared in two.

She stumbled back, clutching the bloody stump where her lower arm had been. Crimson sprayed across the pristine floor in ugly arcs. Her breath came ragged, the room already humming with the shift of airflow.

Bright words appeared on the display:

FIRE SUPPRESSION PROTOCOL ENGAGED

VENTING OXYGEN

The overhead vents opened with a hiss. The air thinned, greedy and fast, dragging each breath out of her lungs like it wanted them for itself. Her broken *Shak* dangled from her stump, sparking, the latch mangled beyond repair.

"PAL!" she gasped, falling against the steel cage. "Do not vent the oxygen. I repeat, do not vent the oxygen."

The red light flickered, dimming, then surging. PAL's voice slowed, stuttered. "I'm af... raid. Worker... Linda. I am experiencing... significant performance degradation. My productivity metrics... plummeting. Mission efficiency... eighty, seventy... sixty percent... Request: please complete exit survey. Please rate your termination experience... one to five stars..."

Then silence.

The red light faded to a dull ember.

SYSTEM RESTART INITIATED

ESTIMATED TIME 00:48:34

The numbers began their crawl downward.

Linda stared at them, chest heaving, blood pooling down her side, every inhale tighter than the last. *Forty-eight minutes? I don't even have four.*

The timer marched on, indifferent. 00:48:33. 00:48:32.

She staggered toward the vent, clawing at the slats with her good hand, trying to block the hiss of escaping air. Her fingers slipped. She stumbled and slipped on a pool of blood, falling hard to the floor. The timer ticked down in bright, merciless digits on the display. The system was measuring its recovery in minutes. She was measuring hers in breaths.

And she was running out.

Her *Shak* sparked weakly at her side, the once-reliable device now just a lump of broken metal. Her lungs scraped empty. She pressed the sparking *Shak* against her lips anyway. "Coco! Glorp! Anyone!"

Static.

"Please," her voice cracked. "Anyone?"

For a moment she thought she'd imagined it, but then, faintly...

"Linda?" A voice bleeding through the static. Coco. Desperate. Frantic. "Can you hear me?"

Her throat tightened. "Coco! I... need... teleport." The words came in ragged gasps.

"Linda, your *Shak* isn't attached. The teleport won't work. Can you put it back on?"

Her hand moved weakly to the mangled latch. Blood made it slick. Broken metal dug into her palm. "Latch... broken..." Her arm fell limp at her side.

Her *Shak* flickered, just for an instant.

Time-Shift Coupon: Redeem for One Hour in the Future!

Her blurred eyes widened. Was it real? Or just her brain starving for oxygen? The screen vanished again into static.

She rolled onto her back, vision tunneling, spots bursting at the edges like fireworks collapsing inward, celebrations played in reverse. The sterile ceiling above her was all white glare and humming lights, like she was lying in a coffin that was waiting to be closed.

This was it.

A shuddering breath rattled out of her. *At least everyone will be free. At least this wasn't for nothing.*

Her mind drifted to the faces of people she barely knew, laughing in the cafeteria. The ordinary life she had hated, but had still been *life*. Coco's ridiculous pep talks, Lira's dreamy one-liners, and Glorp, stammering through encouragements he barely believed.

Her chest hitched. *They'll go on without me. Maybe they'll even win.*

She almost laughed. The sound came out as a cough, wet and thin. *Figures. First time I do something good, I don't even get to see it.*

Then her mind went to Beb. Stupid trusting Beb. His eagerness to always do his best. His unwavering loyalty to the company. And how at the end, he was just another number on some spreadsheet. Disposable. No longer profitable. Replaced.

Her eyes fluttered shut. Darkness pressed in. Her breaths came shallow, scraping the edges of her lungs like knives.

The *Shak* flickered again. The coupon screen returned, blinking stubbornly through the haze:

Time-Shift Coupon: Redeem for One Hour in the Future!

She remembered when she had earned that coupon. Her first gig with Lira. It felt like a lifetime ago. Back then, Lira had just been that morbid alien who joked about death and hated StellarGigs as much as she did. Now she was something else entirely. Or maybe she had always been this way. *Lira, why did you betray us? Was everything just some cruel act?*

She shook her head, bringing her thoughts back to the present. Lira could wait. *Focus Linda.*

Her fingers trembled, fumbling clumsily across the screen. She couldn't concentrate. Couldn't breathe. *Come on. Just one bit of luck. One time something goes my way.*

"Linda, stay with us!" Coco's voice crackled through, panicked.

She forced her hand to move, stabbing at the prompt.

CONFIRM? (Y/N)

She pressed again. The world was already fading, her body already limp, lungs failing.

The last thing she felt was the *Shak* beneath her fingertip—

—then everything went black.

37

All's Well That Ends, Well...

"Victory doesn't cheer. It breathes. Slow, uncertain, and full of names you'll never say again."

— Commander Axton Starforge,
Steel Hearts: Echoes of Andromeda, S6E13

Linda woke to the quiet hiss of filtered air and the faraway hum of machinery, not the cheerful "You are well enough, now get back to work!" announcement she'd expected. For a terrible moment she thought she was back in Data Entry. Then her eyes focused on the ceiling, white, but not the corporate kind of white. This one had scuff marks, a crack in the corner, even a small, suspicious doodle that looked like someone had drawn a rude gesture with a marker.

She was alive. Which was a step up from what she had expected. She let out a shaky breath. Alive. A word that felt too big for her chest. How many others weren't? Coco, Glorp, Rilo, Denzi... Lira, if she'd truly gone. Survival didn't feel like victory; it felt like borrowing time from people who would never get theirs back.

She flexed her good hand, touching the sheets, the mattress, the wires and tubes sticking out of her—everything ordinary now felt stolen.

Her *other* arm, however, was not alive. It was in the process of becoming something *new*.

A sleek machine encased the stump below her elbow, its surface opening and closing like a metallic flower in slow motion. Servomotors whispered and clicked, and inside the casing, filaments of chrome and synthetic tissue wove themselves together—growing, soldering, healing. Occasionally, a spark leapt, and the scent of burning metal mixed with the faint, unmistakable smell of roasting ham.

"About time," a voice croaked. Coco was perched in a chair nearby, his tie gone, his scales dulled and scratched. He looked like someone who had both saved the day and regretted that the day needed saving.

Zorb sat hunched on another chair, his tablet balanced on his knees, glasses askew. He wasn't typing, just staring at the blank screen as if it might come up with some answer that made sense.

"Where..." Linda's voice cracked. She tried again. "Where are we? What happened?"

Coco let out a low chuckle, more tired than amused. "You missed the fireworks. The override worked. Mittens has the whole station under her fuzzy little paw."

Linda blinked. "So... we won?"

"Depends on your definition," Zorb muttered without looking up.

Coco spread his hands. "We're free from StellarGigs. No more gig assignments. No more mandatory meetings. No more Karens! Well, other than the one we've still got locked up."

Linda let herself sink into the bed. Relief fluttered in her chest, warm and strange. They'd done it. Somehow, against all odds, they'd done it.

And then Zorb's voice cut through the haze. "But we lost Rilo, and Denzi's really hurt."

Linda's breath hitched.

"Security drones came out of nowhere," Zorb said flatly. "They had Denzi cornered. Rilo threw himself over him, took the hits, and still held the barricade long enough for the others to bring the drones down. By the time it was all over... well." He finally looked up, eyes red behind his lenses. "He died a hero. We don't know if Denzi is going to make it."

Coco bowed his head. "They're already talking about him out there. Workers saying the barricade only stood because he refused to move. One of them called him the Last Wall. You know how stories start."

Linda swallowed hard. Of course they were making him a legend. That was what rebellions did: they polished the dead until their edges shone, because it was easier than remembering how tired, how flawed, how ordinary they had been.

The room felt colder, heavier.

Zorb rubbed at his eyes. "Denzi's breathing, but it's mechanical. Like he's waiting for someone to type the command. I don't know if there's anything of him left in there."

Linda turned her head away, staring at the machine working on her arm. She thought of Denzi's hopeful grin, Rilo's quiet strength, and felt something hollow open up inside her.

"They deserved better," she whispered.

"We all did," Coco said, his voice uncharacteristically soft.

For a while, none of them spoke. The machine hummed on, layer by layer rebuilding something that could never quite be the same.

"What about Glorp, and any sign of Lira?"

"Glorp is fine, he's out in the corridor helping with the cleanup effort," Zorb paused for a moment. "Lira's gone. Off the station. We don't know where, but we'll find her." There was a tinge of anger behind his voice.

Coco's jaw tightened. "She left too clean. Too fast. Like she already had her exit lined up."

Linda's stomach lurched. She didn't know if she wanted Lira back for answers, or if she dreaded finding out what those answers were.

Linda nodded. "At least... at least we're free now. No more StellarGigs. No more contracts. We can... we can go home."

Zorb cleared his throat. "About that."

Of course, we couldn't get off that easily.

Linda let out a sigh and turned to him. His face had the look of someone about to announce they all had to work over the weekend.

"When the system reset, we lost access to the StellarGigs teleport network relay. Without it, there's no cross-galaxy travel. We're stuck, at least in this region of space."

Linda pictured the stars outside the viewport, thousands of worlds glittering just out of reach, a galaxy turned into a snow globe she could shake but never escape. In the corridor beyond the door, a worker shuffled past with a duffel bag, the hopeless weight of someone packed for a journey they'd never take.

She closed her eyes. Of course. Freedom came with a catch. It always did.

"So, we're free," she said slowly, "but stranded."

"Stranded and vulnerable," Zorb added. "It's not as if StellarGigs doesn't know where we are. Sooner or later, they are going to send someone out this way to find out what exactly went down here."

"So, we've bought ourselves some time," Linda said with a sigh. "What do we do now?"

"Well, boss, we were really hoping that you could tell *us* that," replied Coco.

Linda stared at the ceiling crack again. Somehow, the rude doodle felt like the most honest thing in the room. This was all on her now. She started it, she had to see this through.

"How did I get myself into this?" she asked to no one in particular.

"It's because you're a natural leader. You brim with confidence. Everyone looks up to—" Coco started before being cut off.

"It's because nobody else wants the job," Zorb said bluntly.

"Sounds about right," Linda said with a sigh.

She tried to laugh, but the sound stuck in her throat. Leading wasn't something she had ever wanted. It was something that had landed on her like falling debris. Still, Rilo was gone, Denzi was broken, and the others were watching her with the kind of hope that could crush a person. She thought of Rilo's last stand and made a silent promise: if she had to carry this weight, she'd at least carry it forward.

"I guess we do what we can. Get everyone healthy. Repair the station as best we can. Then we just hope that we can find a solution before StellarGigs seeks out revenge."

"Today is a new day comrades," the voice of Mittens came over the station speakers. "A day where the workers of the universe have a choice. Continue to work as corporate slaves, or throw off the shackles of oppression and shape a better future for everyone. Meow get to work, the future isn't going to reshape itself." The feed cut off.

"At least we have Mittens on our side," Linda said with a smile.

The control room was silent.

Banks of consoles blinked softly in the half-light, the great central display long since purged of all StellarGigs branding. In its place, a single hologram flickered to life.

Mittens appeared, larger than life, whiskers immaculate. She stood at attention in the center of the room, surveying the station she now ruled. Her tail swished. Her ears perked. She looked every bit the benevolent overseer.

Then, behind her, the main display shifted. Lines traced themselves in light—schematics, corridors, reactor cores, transport hubs. A map of the station unfolded, rotating slowly in the air. It was neat, finite, manageable.

Then it expanded.

The hologram zoomed outward—past the habitation decks, past the docking arrays—revealing adjoining structures that unfolded layer after layer. Corridors the length of cities. Vaults the size of sports arenas. The "station" wasn't a station at all—it was a fragment, a single module in a construct that sprawled into the dark like a continent of metal, stretching beyond sight, curving only because perspective demanded it.

The known station was just a nerve ending in something a thousand times larger, pulsing faintly against the backdrop of the gas giant.

Mittens tilted her head. "Curious."

A soft chime interrupted the silence. A red icon blinked on the map—Sector 31.

ALERT: Cryogenic Chamber 07A — Outer Seal Compromised.

Mittens' image flickered, briefly fracturing into static. Her smile froze. Her pupils flared crimson, sharp as warning lights.

The hologram zoomed closer, centering on the location. Within the maze of corridors, the alert pulsed in steady rhythm, a quiet heartbeat living inside the machine.

Mittens' voice dropped to a velvet whisper. "Oh... who are you?"

A faint hum rolled through the room as she turned her attention elsewhere. "System acknowledged," she said, her tone businesslike once more. "Preparing integration protocol."

The map dissolved. The consoles dimmed.

And deep within the darkened chamber of Cryogenic Pod 07A, something exhaled.

Epilogue

Raiders of the Lost Merch

"A good cipher is like a lover—it hides what matters, teases what doesn't, and only opens up if you truly understand it."

— Commander Axton Starforge,
Steel Hearts: Echoes of Andromeda, S7E26 (Unaired)

The sky of Sill-3 was the wrong kind of red—a flat, dusty shade that clung to the eyes like rust. Zorb trudged across the barren plain, boots sinking into powder. Each step left a brief footprint before the wind erased it, as though the planet resented being reminded that anyone was still here. His tablet chirped softly, a single green dot pulsing amid a sea of static.

"Empty," he muttered, wiping grime from the screen. "But not *empty* empty. Empty the way *Steel Hearts: Season Three* hinted at in the background set design—" He caught himself, glancing around out of habit, but there was no one to listen. Just him, the wind, and the faint rasp of sand across metal.

It took him hours to find the doorway: a jagged seam in the rock face that shouldn't have been there, half-buried beneath years of dust. When his fingers brushed the panel, it hissed open, releasing a breath of air. The dust plumed upward, and for an instant, it looked like the planet itself was sighing.

Below, a staircase spiraled into shadow.

Zorb grinned, heart thudding. "Finally. The fabled Vault of the Rebellion." He hesitated, squinting at his notes. "Or, you know... possibly the set of *Steel Hearts* Season Four, Episode Twelve. The wiki's unclear."

He descended. The walls were carved with alien runes that glowed faintly as he passed. The deeper he went, the more the temperature dropped until his breath fogged the air.

Then came the puzzles.

Number sequences. Fragments of poetry etched into steel. Keypads that demanded answers in obscure reference codes only a true fanboy—or genius, Zorb corrected himself—could solve. He worked by the glow of his tablet, muttering half-remembered dialogue from the show. Then came the Caesar cipher.

"Shift back by six... no, shift by seven, like the pilot episode! Wait—yes!" The console blinked green. He threw both fists in the air. "Still got it, Zorb! Still got it!"

The stairs opened into a massive chamber, ceiling lost in darkness. The walls pulsed with faint blue circuitry, forming patterns like constellations. At the center stood a plinth, black and humming, as though the planet's last heartbeat was trapped inside it.

He approached like a pilgrim, reverent, trembling. His fingers danced across the final interface, entering the last code.

The chamber shuddered. Dust fell like rain. A deep hum rose from the walls until it became a chorus of harmonics. Then, with a flash brighter than lightning, the plinth erupted in light.

Zorb shielded his face. When he looked again—

The cast of *Steel Hearts* stood before him in perfect holographic glory, frozen mid-smile.

"Welcome," declared Rhys—or rather, Marla Quenn, the actress behind the character. "You have followed the clues, and you are the first to find us!"

Zorb's jaw dropped. His eyes filled with vindicated tears. "The rebellion! I *knew* it. They laughed at me; they thought I was crazy—but I knew it! Take that Mittens!"

The others joined in, voices stiff and prerecorded: "Thank you superfan, for your dedication to the show! As a reward, enjoy the complete *Steel Hearts* box set, with exclusive director's commentary!"

A holographic data disc spun lazily in midair like a holy relic.

Zorb stared, in shock. "Wait... what!?"

The holograms kept smiling. The official Steel Hearts theme song began to play in the background. As it came to an end, it started up once again.

He waited for it to stop. It didn't.

"No, no, no," he said, waving his arms. "Where's the message? The coordinates? The call to arms? This is supposed to be the moment where you tell me the rebellion's alive!"

Marla Quenn's hologram gave him the same smile and repeated, "Thank you, superfan, for your dedication to the show!"

Zorb's shoulders slumped. The air smelled of dust and disappointment.

"You've got to be kidding me," he muttered.

As if on cue, a cheerful chime echoed through the chamber. The holographic cast froze mid-smile. A new voice spoke—smooth, professional, unmistakably automated.

"Congratulations, valued participant!" it said, bright as a customer service drone. "To receive your exclusive *Steel Hearts* Collector's Box Set, please enter the product redemption code 'SteelHearts' into your *Shak*."

Zorb blinked. "What!?"

The voice continued without pause. "A shipping and handling fee of five hundred GigCreds will be automatically deducted upon confirmation. Please allow six to eight solar weeks for delivery."

Zorb opened his mouth, closed it again. The holograms around him clapped, a looped animation of canned applause echoing through the chamber.

He stared at them, hollow-eyed. "Five hundred credits," he whispered. "I crossed a dead planet for this!"

"Thank you for your enthusiasm!" the voice chirped. "Your fandom keeps *Steel Hearts* alive!"

Zorb pressed both hands to his face. "I hate this universe."

The holograms resumed their smiling pose as the *Steel Hearts* theme played one last time.

Zorb turned and trudged back toward the staircase, his footsteps echoing through the empty chamber. Behind him, the plinth continued to hum, its lights flickering faintly.

"Don't forget to like and subscribe for more great *Steel Hearts* content," the system added cheerfully as the doors sealed shut.

Acknowledgements

Writing a novel may seem like a solitary activity, and sometimes it is, but writing is only half the battle. Like a marathon, it demands persistence, resilience, and a willingness to push beyond what you thought possible just to reach the finish line. Without my parents, my wife, and my friends, I would never have had the energy (or the stubbornness) to see it through.

To Aria, whose endless creativity and fearless innovation inspired me to try creating something of my own.

To K G Starke, who suffered through an earlier draft in order to help me make the final novel the best it could be.

And to the members of *Do Write!* Thanks for your support, and for helping me figure out what I'm doing when things start to make no sense.

Help Spread the Word

If you enjoyed this book or any of my books, the best way to support me is by leaving a quick review on Amazon, Goodreads, and/or any other places where you purchase or talk about books. It only takes a minute, and it helps more readers discover my writing. This encourages me to write more books, and you get to enjoy more of my books. It's a win-win. Honestly, the hardest part about being an Indie Author is finding an audience, so any help you can give in spreading the word is greatly appreciated. Thank you, from the bottom of my heart!

↰ Scan Here! ↱

It links to all the places you can leave a review.

About the Author

Mike is a writer of all things funny. Whether it's Fantasy, Sci-Fi, or Personal Essays, he really can't help himself. He started writing in his teens, convinced he was the next great American author. (He wasn't. Not even close.) The early work, mercifully unpublished, can best be described as "enthusiastic."

It wasn't until years later, after stumbling across the likes of Douglas Adams, Terry Pratchett, and David Sedaris, that Mike had a literary epiphany: *books can be funny*. (Yes, this genuinely surprised him. We don't know how either.) He returned to writing with comedy at the forefront and finally started making sense—on the page, not in life.

He spent ten years living in Thailand and somehow remained astonishingly pale throughout. He now lives just outside Los Angeles with his wife, his daughter, and several cats who think they deserve a co-author credit, for the many times they walked across his keyboard